MONSTERLAND

ABOVE

(BOOK IV)

MICHAEL OKON

ISBN: 978-1-950080-16-8

"...is like to that which is above."

- The Emerald Tablet of Hermes Trismegistus

For Mom

*You are the only one who knows what my
heart sounds like from the inside.*

ABOVE

AS ABOVE

"ARE YOU SURE?" Dreg faced the porthole and watched the stars speed by.

Vincent didn't answer him, forcing Dreg to repeat the question. "Vincent, did you see him? I think I saw Nate when we were transported out of the room."

"It's your imagination trying to fool you. I told you several times already, he was killed in Washington the day we opened Monsterland." Vincent softened the harshness of his voice. "Now we both know what it's like to lose—"

"I know what I saw! It was my son, and he was hurt!" The words burst from Dreg's mouth.

"I promise you, it wasn't him. The man you saw was half-covered in blood. It was your

mind playing tricks on you."

Pacing the room, Dreg shook his head. "I don't know. Besides, it's not the same. Rosemary isn't dead. She merely escaped!" Dreg watched Vincent's brows lower with fury. "Quite honestly, Vincent, I think you let her. You had the means to stop her."

Vincent's jaw hardened. "Baseless accusations. Tread carefully, Dreg. I don't like your tone."

Dreg continued, oblivious to the anger in Vincent's voice. "You say Nate is gone." Dreg felt emotions clog his throat. "I just don't know."

Vincent walked awkwardly in his direction, his prosthetic legs stiff and unyielding. "I wish I could tell you differently. It's impossible. His helicopter went down. Taken out by the military. All our plans are ruined." He fisted both of his artificial hands and banged them against his legs, making a hollow sound.

"How do you know it was the military?" Dreg demanded. "I find it hard to believe that with all your careful strategies, something like that happened. You thought of everything. All those plans and backup plans—"

"Nothing went as it should have, as you well know!" Vincent exploded.

Dreg frowned. It was true; Nate wasn't the new president. Monsterland and their home base, *Shark Park*, were in enemy hands, and they found themselves exiled to orbit the Earth on an alien ship.

"You know me, Dreg. I always have a backup. Now that I'm fully awake, I'm thinking clearly again." A calmer Vincent was studying his reflection in a mirror that hung on the wall of their quarters aboard the Thalen ship. It was a human affectation their hosts had installed. A memory surfaced in Dreg's mind of a mirror he hung in his parakeet's cage. He enjoyed observing the bird watching his reflection and wondered briefly if the aliens were getting the same charge from their behavior.

For as long as Dreg knew Vincent, deep thoughts were going on beneath the surface. If only he could get a bead on where Vincent's mind was going. Vincent sounded reasonable again, but instead of reassuring Dreg, it made him more anxious.

Vincent could be all affable and charming one minute, but within the blink of an eye, his mood changed. Dreg sighed with exhaustion when he heard Vincent's fisted palm slam the mirror.

"This is what it's come to?" Vincent muttered through clenched teeth. He was staring at multiple images of his face on the spider-webbed surface of the glass.

Dreg stuffed his own feelings down deep to attend to Vincent's temper. "You've broken it! It was a gift. Please calm down. Your old body was riddled with bullets. It was the best our good hosts could do—"

Vincent spun so fast that Dreg didn't have time to react. His face twisted, letting Dreg know that this was going to be unpleasant.

One never knew which Vincent would respond. Dreg watched Vincent march toward him. His long, gloved fingers gripped Dreg's neck and squeezed his windpipe until he could no longer drag in air. Dreg struggled against him, his voice a mere croak.

"I. Am. The. Most. Powerful. Person. In. The. Universe." *Never a good thing when someone uses punctuation when they speak.* Dreg flailed his arms, but Vincent refused to let go.

Vincent Konrad lifted him almost to the ceiling in the room. Dreg gurgled a bit, his eyes going wide, his vision became a field of jiggling dots. He heard Vincent make a disgusted sound and felt himself lowered. His feet brushed the floor before Vincent casually tossed him onto the built-in couch against the wall.

Dreg landed with a huff of expelled air and scrambled to his feet again, clutching Vincent by the coattails, effectively halting him.

Vincent teetered on stiff legs, spinning awkwardly until he tipped over and landed on the slab that served as his bed for the last few weeks.

Breathlessly, Vincent pushed himself onto his elbows and blew stringy strands of hair covering purple-tinted eyes that burned with fury.

Dreg studied the disaster that was Vincent's face, wondering if the pale magenta was a sign of anger or the last of the alien fuel that kept him alive. The substance has settled into the lines and crevices of Vincent's skin, making him look as though his face were a road-map of sorts. It was, Dreg reasoned. Each scar, every wound, was a reminder of the journey that brought them to this point.

Scuttling over like a crab, Dreg sat next to him. When he spoke, he maintained a well-modulated and intimate tone. This strategy worked best when Vincent was in one of his moods. He had to get him regulated before their hosts arrived.

He feared that with Vincent's latest bouts of ingratitude, they were wearing out their welcome on the spaceship. "They had a woman's body, but I told them it wouldn't do. This mannequin was the only male specimen that didn't reject your head."

"A moot point. My head is fine now."

"Thanks to the Thalens and the handy, dandy battery they installed."

"It's much more than a battery, you idiot. As I understand, it's powered by a quantum lattice. I am constantly being renewed, but, and it's a big but, it's a movie prop!" Vincent cried. "Nobody will take me seriously."

"I don't agree." Dreg worried his bottom lip. "Think of it, Vincent. This host body is not alive; we don't have to keep it soaked in alien fuel. It's made with heavy-duty material." Dreg tapped the chest. "High-Density Polyethylene."

"It's the same stuff they use to make milk containers!" Vincent grumbled.

"Think of the durability. That material lasts for years in the landfills."

"They could have used an android like the medical one they gave me back home. It was working so well until Rosemary shorted him out." Vincent paused and then laughed, thinking of his feisty daughter's destruction of her jailers and escape. "She's a wily one."

Dreg went on, ignoring the comment about Vincent's daughter, "They had a perfect Xenomorph body ready to go, but they were afraid you'd scare the sh—."

"Enough," Vincent ordered.

Dreg could tell there was no more fight left in his boss and went on reasonably, "But it was missing parts, and we are quarantined right now. They seem scared of other aliens flying about. Patrols have made movement difficult." He paused to allow that information to sink in, then added with a touch of tenderness, "Don't you remember I told you that?"

Vincent threw his head back onto a pillow and rested one wrist over his eyes, his mood now morose. Dreg lifted Vincent's heavy legs onto the divan, then sat down next to him. He watched Vincent struggle with despair.

"Truth is, I'm not sure exactly what I remember." Vincent's voice was barely audible. "Maybe we should—"

"Don't!" Dreg interrupted him. "We've come too far, Vincent."

"Damn that Wyatt Baldwin. I should have crushed him when I had the chance."

"He's just a kid," Dreg said.

"He's a man. A seasoned warrior," Vincent said between clenched teeth. "I hate him."

"Don't think about Wyatt, or any of his friends, think about all the good you did for the world. Think about how close we were to Plan B."

"I have to." Vincent's eyes turned feverish. "He destroyed everything. He thwarts my every move." He jumped up and paced the room. "It's like he knows my thought process."

"Don't be ridiculous. It's dumb luck."

Vincent shook his head, and Dreg could hear Vincent's new

teeth gnashing. They were made of an unknown metal, and their bright gleam gave Vincent's mouth a jack-o-lantern quality.

Dreg moved over and patted the seat. "Patience, Vincent."

Vincent brooded, his face a deeper shade of purple.

They sat in silence, lost in their own thoughts.

They had been routed by that pesky Wyatt Baldwin and his equally annoying friends, who now included what was left of the United States armed forces. Vincent had been soundly defeated by the military and transported aboard Spekator's ship in a molecular tractor repositionable ray.

After a minute, Vincent shook his head. "Maybe you're right."

"Of course, I'm right." Dreg was emboldened. "I would agree with you that the vacuum cleaner was not an especially good idea, but Spekator said—"

"Spekator *said*, Spekator *said*." Vincent sat up abruptly, his face mottled again. "Don't tell me what *Spekator* said."

"They had to attach your head temporarily to the vacuum cleaner. It was only until they could find a suitable host body."

"Spekator has a fondness for small human appliances and Hollywood memorabilia. That's why they chose this… this… *manne-quin*. I feel like a movie prop."

"A movie prop? Vincent!" Dreg rose to his feet. "I'll have you know this was the very suit they used for the Sleepy Hollow remake, you know, the film that they made before everything shut down."

Vincent glared at him from across the room.

"Spekator and his crew lifted it along with some of the sets from a warehouse in New Mexico. You should see what they have in their storage space below deck."

"A regular film studio. Spekator does have a flair for the dra-matic." Vincent laughed bitterly. He raised his head and looked down at the black pants, frilled shirt, and the midnight cape that wrapped around his sturdy new limbs.

"At least they attached your head." Dreg's eyes twinkled devilishly. "And, you have that added feature."

Vincent swiveled and, with a quick spin of his neck, twisted his head to hold it under his arm, his mouth gaping in a macabre grin. Vincent looked around the room, his eyes gleaming. "I will admit, it does have its charms."

"Oh, you're a fright, alright, Vincent. Think of the optics!" Dreg clapped his hands.

"How can I be the Headless Horseman without a horse?" Vincent whined petulantly.

"A minor inconvenience, Doctor," a high-pitched voice said from the doorway with a chuckle. Spekator floated in. "However, one that is easily remedied."

"If only those nasty teens could be so easily handled. I must find a way to eliminate them and get my plan back on track. It's time for me to return home."

"To Prendick Island?" Dreg asked.

"No, you moron. To Monsterland. It began in Monsterland, and it will finish in Monsterland."

CHAPTER 1

THE GANG IS BACK IN TOWN

Army Base 1
California Coastline across from Prendick Rock

"WHAT ARE WE going to do about them?" Wyatt sat on the shore's sand opposite Prendick Rock. "It's hard to believe what is going to come out of those eggs."

"It would be inhumane to smash them," Howard Drucker said softly, his eyes on the rolling waves.

"*Inhumane!* They're not human! If you saw what that beast did to Jade, you would have no compunction in wiping those eggs and the monsters that are due to hatch from the face of the earth." Melvin's face was mulish. He threw small pebbles at the shoreline with a little too much force. They made epic splashes on the water's surface.

The three friends sat on the beach watching the armed forces corral the surviving zombies into pens where they couldn't continue to dine on the public. Each one of the teens sported a bandage where they had suffered injuries from the last battle. Today was the first day Howard's mother allowed him out of bed.

Howard turned to Melvin and said, "You never told us what you did with her body."

Melvin swallowed hard and shrugged. "Jade? She's gone."

"We know she's gone, but we'd all like to go and put flowers on her grave. You did bury her, Mel?"

Melvin was silent, his Adam's apple bobbing. He kept his gaze on the horizon. "No, I didn't. I couldn't find her in the lagoon. She was missing."

"How could she be missing?" Wyatt scratched his head.

"Did you look—-" Howard started.

Melvin jumped up, his face as red as his hair. "Of course I did. I searched every part of that lagoon until I couldn't breathe. She's not there. I can't explain it, just like you can't explain what happened to Vincent and Dreg. Maybe it ate her," he added more to himself.

Wyatt nodded. He knew all three of them were thinking back almost three weeks ago when they finally found Vincent Konrad in his underwater lair, only to have him vanish into thin air right before their eyes.

"Perhaps he found a way to beam himself somewhere," Howard offered.

"I don't think so. That stuff only happens on television. No, Konrad had help." Melvin paced the dune where they sat.

"Had to be aliens." Wyatt nodded. "There's no other explanation."

Howard turned to him, his glasses crooked. "What makes you say that? There's a million possibilities."

"Here we go," Wyatt mumbled.

"A rip in the space-time continuum, they might have hijacked technology on invisibility from the army, a time warp, mass hypnosis, a special cloak, quantum realm, time travel… magic."

Wyatt looked upward, his eyebrows raised. "It wasn't magic. What about the blue lights we saw?"

Howard turned his stare to the sky. "Oh, right. The lights, I forgot about them."

"Lights? How could you forget about something like that?" Melvin asked, his jaw dropped.

"Mel, there's been so much going on. I was kind of out of it for a while." Howard rested his chin on his knees.

"Still—" Mel began.

"My dad debriefed us. I guess the blue lights slipped our minds." Wyatt nodded in agreement.

"Besides, I never said it couldn't be aliens. Tocho said it was similar to abductions he'd heard about on the reservation," Howard finished.

"What are you guys talking about?" Melvin was more impatient than ever.

"We saw these strange lights." Wyatt pointed to where the clouds scudded across a crystal-clear sky. "Up that way." He gestured vaguely at a mountain range.

Melvin considered the jagged peaks, the grayish color still smoking in places where fires raged out of control. "It might have been some rogue air force planes. There are bases all over California. Someone could be flying an aircraft of sorts." Melvin shrugged. "I highly doubt it was aliens." He kicked at an anthill with his bare foot, then smoothed over the hole with his big toe. "Like that's all we need now, an alien invasion."

"Cut it out. You're like an alien invader to those poor ants!" Howard shoved Melvin's foot out of the way and tried to recreate the anthill.

"These crafts moved like nothing I've ever seen," Wyatt persisted.

"Not to mention, they were fast. They maneuvered in tandem and then—" Howard snapped his fingers. "They disappeared, just like that!"

"Just like Vincent and Dreg." Wyatt shredded a single strand of tall grass. "It would explain a lot."

Howard stood up, shaking the sand from the back of his pants. "Wyatt's right. They moved in ways no Earth ship could. How could I forget about that?"

Wyatt looked at his wristwatch, which Carter had given to him. It hung loosely on his forearm, and when he moved, the metal band clanked heavily. His cell phone used to be his tool for telling time, but that was no longer working. "A lot was going on. It's not easy keeping track of everything. Between finding out giants exist, fighting the killer clowns of LA, and navigating your rocky love life, it's no wonder. Don't you have to meet Keisha, like two minutes ago?"

Howard shook his head. "In a bit. She's taking a class on shape-shifting with John Raven. Hey, are either of you two interested in trying…" Howard's voice trailed off when he saw Melvin's smirk.

"Been there, done that. Nope, I imagine I could teach John Raven's students a thing or two about shapeshifting," Melvin said with a laugh.

Howard studied Melvin and replied, "There is a difference, bro. They are selective and morph by choice."

Melvin puffed out his considerably built-up chest. "I'm selective, *bro*, and I've figured out how to change into a werewolf at will. I'll stick with my species of choice, the master of the monster domain—"

"Spare me. I will admit the werewolves reign supreme when it comes to loyalty and bravery, even strength, but nothing beats a vamp in cunning."

"Please!" Wyatt threw up his hands. "I will never measure monster against monster. Monsters are created by man, not by nature. Do you think that giant friggin' octopus out there is a monster or an accident of nature?" He pointed to the horizon where the ocean curled and rippled with whitecaps. "Vincent Konrad is the only monster I know, and he makes all others pale in comparison."

The three teens turned to look at the crashing waves, each lost in their thoughts, reliving the frightening moments that had stripped away their boyhood and propelled them on a journey into a world that no longer resembled the one in which they had grown up.

"It's not fun anymore," Howard said glumly.

"It's not funny either," Melvin agreed.

"No, everything has changed, and there is no way we can put that genie back into the bottle. I'll never look at a monster the same again." Wyatt sniffed, thinking of his late father, a zombie who sacrificed his own life to save Carter and himself when Vincent tried to kill them. He looked at Howard's stricken face. "Can you call my father or Keisha a monster?" he paused and glanced at Melvin, "Can you call Jade and Melvin monsters?"

"What about Grillos or Danai?" Melvin said after clearing his throat.

Howard sighed. "I think there's probably a bit of a monster in everyone."

"Maybe we have to redefine the word." Melvin stalked away.

Howard moved closer to Wyatt. "He's probably right."

Wyatt nodded, his face solemn. "Maybe by labeling them it creates the perception of their being a monster."

"Wow, that's profound, Wy." Howard grabbed Wyatt's wrist and glanced at the watch.

"Hey, get your own." Wyatt yanked his arm away.

"I would, but all the watch stores have closed."

They stared at each other, acknowledging the enormity of what had happened to their world.

"I used to love apocalyptic books. Reading about how people learn to adapt." Howard's eyes were wistful.

Wyatt blew out a puff of air. "It's nothing like that."

Howard nodded grimly. "I can't believe this happened."

Wyatt swallowed hard, remembering the loss of all his friends and family. "I keep thinking this is a nightmare and when I wake up—"

They stood together silently, allowing nature to surround them with the fresh smell of the ocean and the reassuring cries of the seagulls overhead.

"Look at the positive side, no worrying about a date for prom—" Howard reasoned.

"I'd give anything to go back and be able to talk to my mom." Wyatt sighed. "I just don't know…"

"What?" Howard asked.

"How is all this going to turn out?" Wyatt's voice was forlorn. "I am—"

"Afraid?" Howard paused. "I think we all are. There's no formula, no precedent. We have no idea what will happen. If Vincent is with aliens, we're toast."

"How will we win against something like that?" Wyatt was thoughtful. "Superior technology, who knows what they're capable of."

"Maybe they captured him, and they are looking to communicate with us," Melvin called from another dune where he was examining the remains of a dead fish. "Can you imagine if they think we're all like him?"

"*Whoa*, that would be bad," Wyatt said.

"Impossible, they have to have been studying us for years. Think of all the abductions. They must realize we come in all different varieties," Melvin said.

All three looked at each other, stricken.

"I'm just saying." Melvin shrugged without making eye contact.

Wyatt cleared his throat and said softly, "It's not looking good."

Howard placed a hand on Wyatt's shoulder. "You might be right, but we can't let it paralyze us."

Wyatt shivered. "It's been one thing after another. I don't know if I have anything left. Put a fork in me, I'm done."

"We just have to push forward, Wy. Be present. We have to learn not to dwell on the past. You can't worry about the future. It hasn't happened yet." Howard looked him full in the face. "I think the best advice I can give is just live for today."

Wyatt's throat clogged with emotion, and he couldn't say anything even if he wanted to.

"You okay?" Howard asked.

Wyatt nodded.

"I might as well get a head start on fixing Konrad's phone. Keisha should be there soon." Howard dashed off, sand flying in his wake.

Wyatt watched him go, then turned to see Melvin walking some distance away, a lone figure, his shoulders slumped. He looked back at the ocean, then at the mountains on the other side, the proximity of both closing in on him. Melvin moved along the ridge of the dunes, his hands in the pockets of his bright yellow surfer shorts, his auburn head downcast.

Howard was correct; there was no going back to the past. It was over and done with. While the thought of the future gave him chills, it was still unknown. Wyatt decided to plant himself in the present. He put a foot down, watching it disappear into the soft sand. He was sinking and sinking fast. His heart beat a little faster. He pushed forward and took another step, staggering a bit. Panicked, he looked for his friend. "Mel," he shouted, finding his voice. "Mel. Wait up!"

Wyatt jogged to catch up with Melvin. He sprinted over the beach and stopped when he reached him. "Mel. Wait. Nate, I mean, President Owens wanted to talk to me. Wanna come?" He looked at Melvin hopefully.

"Why?" Melvin asked.

Wyatt shrugged. "I dunno. Got something better to do?"

Melvin looked out at the ocean. He didn't answer.

Wyatt took a big breath. "I wasn't happy in Copper Valley. I missed my old life, but even with that, I knew I was going to Barston Community. I had some idea of my future. Now—" his voice tailed off.

Melvin was quiet for a minute, then shuddered as if trying to shake off a bad mood. "I guess. Got nothing better to do, either."

"I never thought this would ever happen." Wyatt's voice was so low that it almost disappeared in the wind.

"What?" Melvin stopped walking.

"An apocalypse. That only happened in video games or movies, you know?"

Melvin sorted a mirthless laugh. "Yeah, we're not in Kansas anymore, Dorothy."

Wyatt raised his brows. "Uh-huh. Reality sure is different."

"I'll say. But I don't even know where I fit in anymore." Melvin sighed, his gaze falling on a cluster of sand dollars half-buried in the sand, his breath catching in his throat.

Wyatt looked down. "They're pretty."

"Yeah. Jade would have loved them." Melvin's voice ended in a shudder. "I don't want to go back to the lagoon without her being there." He looked Wyatt in the eyes. "Might as well spend a few minutes with the leader of the free world, or whatever is left of it. Okay, come on."

Wyatt watched Melvin walk toward the command tent, feeling small and insignificant against the expanse of beach and pounding waves. He felt tears sting his eyes. Dashing them away, he took a deep breath and thought, Howard and Keisha were brilliant, Melvin was strong; he had no idea where he fit in this new world. He kicked the sand and jogged after Melvin.

CHAPTER 2

YOU'LL BE BACK TO YOURSELF IN NO TIME

Smokey Springs, Nevada
20 miles west of Las Vegas

AT FIRST, THERE was light. It hurt to open her eyes, so she didn't. She listened. It was quiet but for the beeps and trills of machinery. In truth, she didn't care enough to investigate. She felt heavy, and without trying, she knew nothing was working, so she slept. She slept and slept and slept until she could no longer distinguish between wakefulness and her sleep state.

Time passed in that hazy way that made it hard to determine day or night. Jade wasn't sure if she was really slumbering or in some kind of altered state of consciousness. Sometimes, she heard everything but remembered nothing of what she saw.

It was as if her brain couldn't identify familiar images, and while on some level she knew this should frighten her, it didn't. She floated in a sea of apathy, ignoring all stimuli and blissful in her state of indifference. It was only the cold swab of alcohol and the intrusive steel of needles in her good arm that heightened her awareness for a second before she plunged back into nothingness.

These moments of lucidity might have lasted for days or even a month. It could have been a year, for all she knew. Time seemed as weightless as she felt, and while occasionally a rare sense of urgency assailed her, she couldn't pin it down. It fluttered like a butterfly, teasing with importance, yet when she attempted to capture it, it dissolved into a rainbow of sprinkles, leaving nothing but a vague memory.

Sounds made no sense, as if her primal memory had been wiped clean and everything had to be relearned. The only thing she was sure of was that she was tied to her bed, loose enough that it didn't hurt, but definitely a captive. Each time she came to awareness, it was with the understanding that there was one set of hands taking care of her, and they were not familiar to her.

By the time she finally managed to crack one eyelid open, she recognized her captor/caretaker by his rapid footsteps and his slightly off-key voice as he hummed to himself. Everything was blurry, making it hard to focus. Her field of vision was off, as if one of her eyes wasn't working.

He spoke often, not to her, so much as to an invisible audience in a low, raspy voice. Jade identified him by scent, and not only did that still work, but it felt heightened as well. It was as if she could taste things by their fragrance. Her caretaker had a slightly yeasty odor, like baked bread, and his breath was sweet, as if he had drunk Whisp all the time. She caught sight of blurred snatches of him, the top of his hairy hand, a rumpled white lab coat, his hunched shoulders.

The man worked steadily, and she was tempted to open her eyes fully to check her surroundings. It felt impossible. One eye opened easily. The other felt blocked. She studied him while he flitted around the room like a demented hummingbird, his arms always in motion. From what she caught of him, he was short; his wire-rimmed glasses could be found alternatingly resting atop his balding head or askew on his potato-shaped nose.

She noticed there were no street sounds. The absence of noise made it feel like they were in the sound booth at the high school, and dampness permeated the room, giving it a dull, heavy feeling.

When she was sure she was alone, she opened the working eye and explored the room from under lowered lashes. The lack of sunlight was replaced by strange blue light. No windows interrupted the concrete walls. Columns of computer terminals surrounded her, and she lay in a nest of tubes and wires. Wrapped in blankets, she wasn't sure if she was hot or cold; she just knew she was uncomfortable. The hard table underneath her bore into her hips and backside until she felt numb.

Classical music played in the background all the time, day or night, until she wanted to scream from it. She learned that one side of her body moved easily enough; she was able to stretch the fingers on the left, the other side felt—*gone*, for lack of a better word. The idea of this made her heart flutter, and she could hear the machinery clang in response.

"I know you're up." A firm finger lifted her eyelid, revealing an ugly face close to hers, the dark hairs that sprang from its nostrils magnified.

Firming her lips, she resolved not to speak. She couldn't anyway; half her face didn't respond to her commands.

As if he could read her mind, she felt a gentle palm pat her cheek and a sympathetic voice say, "No worries, kiddo. You'll be back to yourself in no time."

Jade jerked in her spot. She recognized that voice. It was Mr. Otto Enoch, her tenth-grade science teacher. The school board fired him from Copper Valley High for his wild conspiracy theories and the agendas he preached to his students. The board of education replaced him with Wyatt's mom.

"You are one lucky girl!"

"Where am I?" Jade strained against the leather straps holding her down. She raised her heavy head, causing lights to flash behind her eyes and pain to explode on the right side of her skull. Jade moaned from the force of it.

"Easy, Jade. You'll ruin all my handiwork." The sharp smell of alcohol, and jab of a needle worked quickly and efficiently, bringing darkness and eliminating the agony. Her last thought was of Copper Valley and her cheerleading squad.

CHAPTER 3

FINDING THE INNER VOICE

"NO, KEISHA. STOP your thoughts from going there," John Raven admonished gently.

Keisha blinked rapidly, trying to stop a tear from escaping her eye. She had been thinking of Jade. Jade made everything more fun. Everything was simpler a year ago when all she had to worry about was life at Copper Valley High. It was uncomplicated, then. Now Jade was gone and murdered by a shell creature who dragged her to who knew where.

Life after Monsterland was no match for what was important back in the past. Things like grabbing a meal at Instaburger, the chess club, or running late to cheerleading practice took center stage. All she thought about was trying to pull Howard Drucker's nose from his books to notice her, even if she had to discuss quantum travel to do it. She took a deep breath in an attempt to bring her wandering mind to John Raven's morphing lesson.

John Raven hit a metal bowl with a red felt-covered gong, and a clear bell-like sound filled the meadow, chasing old memories from her head.

"I thought those were Tibetan," Keisha commented, one eye open and directed to the curved black basin decorated with brass inlay. She wanted to appear interested.

John reached over and tapped her forehead. He didn't fool easily. She slid her eyes shut.

"Better." She heard him say. "They are, and what makes you think I don't appreciate other cultures?" John asked.

Keisha's voice droned on, her intellect kicking in. It was her refuge when she felt insecure. "The sound of the gong hitting the singing bowls produces harmonization that allows—"

"Enough, Keisha. Let the vibrations relax both sides of your brain. It's going to stimulate stress relief and, in the process, wash the toxins from your body. Sound therapy calms the mind—"

"We all know Keisha needs a calmer mind," Tocho said through gritted teeth, his jaw trembling with suppressed rage. He was sitting behind her in the flower-strewn grass. "She's usually all over the place."

Lily, her best friend, and Wyatt's girlfriend threw Tocho a dirty look.

John Raven sighed, "She's made her choice, Tocho. You have to accept that she prefers Howard Drucker to you. Now concentrate!" John hit the brass bowl harder, the resulting gong and the vibration that followed drowning out all sound and stopping any further conversation.

Keisha managed a swift glance at Tocho, his tightly clenched mouth, coupled with his ramrod-straight back, letting her know he was still angry. The stern lines of her face melted with sympathy. She was sorry she had hurt him, but she couldn't ignore her true feelings.

John Raven walked behind her and lightly tapped her head with the felt-covered gong stick. "Concentrate," he said in the maddingly calm voice. He hit the bowl again, and the clear-sounding music of the metal surrounded them.

Keisha tried to center herself, letting the vibration wash through her, but her brain struggled knowing she had bruised Tocho's feelings. She didn't mean to break his heart, but he became an unwitting casualty when she reconnected and finally remembered her friends. Tocho's ache radiated from his body into hers, and she winced from the pain of it. It wasn't that she didn't like him; she actually did. They had a lot in common, and his kindness had served as a lifeline when she felt alone in her amnesia. Once she came back to herself, she remembered that she wanted to be with Howard Drucker, and that was the right place for her.

In her mind's eye, she compared the two men. Tocho was all coiled strength; his agile body was wired to feel everything around him. Howard was preoccupied with the universe and the plethora of information streaming through it. She remembered Tocho's corded muscles and smooth skin, her body pinging into awareness of him, but couldn't explain the thrill when Howard drew near. Her mind quickened to his brilliant thought process. It was as though one of them stimulated her body, while the other stimulated her brain.

Keisha's spine collapsed, making her curve inward. John Raven pushed his knee against her back, preventing her from slumping in defeat.

The firm pressure of John Raven's leg reminded her to sit up, galvanizing her resolve. Her thoughts spun back to the few blissful days when she didn't remember her former life, or Howard. It was easier not to feel bad about him when she didn't recall his place in her heart.

Once her memory flooded back, she knew it was Howard she belonged with, but the recollections of Tocho didn't evaporate this time, making her feel his pain of the loss of their relationship. She should have spoken to him and broken it to him more gently. Perhaps, even waited a bit longer. Thoughts, like a swarm of butterflies, took off in her head, combined with all the *shoulds* she could have done. Her life was filled with hundreds of *shoulds*.

Tocho ground his teeth again, making Keisha wince from the sound of it. She heard John Raven's low voice speaking behind her, but couldn't comprehend everything he was saying. It was in his native language. While she hadn't mastered it yet, Keisha did catch a word or two and understood John's soothing comments. She jumped when she felt John's whispered words next to her own ear and the switch to English.

"The intention of today's meditation is for you to let go of all the *shoulds* and relax in the notion that you are following your instincts." It was as if he read her mind, she thought with astonishment.

"There is nothing you need to do…" His voice trailed off and moved further down the line of students. Keisha took a deep breath in through her nose, her body filling with oxygen. She blew it out through her lips and knew what John was going to say before she heard the words.

"Easy, Keisha. Don't force it." His voice floated across the meadow.

Keisha took another breath, slowing the exhale, allowing the air to visit all parts of her body. She felt lifted. Her body felt lighter.

"Great job," John said, rewarding her efforts. He was closer again, his voice filling her head. "Find that breath, bring it inward and nourish all of your body, slowly, carefully, then exhale, *no…* no stop rushing. Let it seep out. Do another, let it massage your organs, revitalize and feed them with all the sustenance they need. Inhale…. *Exhale…* that's right. Let go. Let yourselves be soothed by the rhythms of life."

He kept repeating the words like a mantra until all Keisha felt was the oxygen bubbling through her bloodstream, filling every cell of her body. Sound receded, and she stopped feeling the heat of the sun on her back. Sweat trickled from her hairline, and while Keisha knew it was there, she felt detached from her body.

John Raven's low voice was the only thing she heard. "Feel the blood coursing in your veins, reaching the furthest ends of your existence. Inhale… *exhale…* expand as it comes in and contracts as it leaves. *Expand…* and contract."

Her body inflated with air like a balloon, and for a minute she felt airborne. She jerked her eyes open and saw the serene faces of her friends. A look of warning from John Raven caused her to close them, and she fell right back into the meditative state with ease, as though she had been doing it her entire life.

"Yes, yes, this is the rhythm. You all can do it. Slowly, Lily." His voice trailed off as he addressed his great-niece. "Don't rush, my little bird."

Time slowed, tension melting away like ice in the sun. Keisha felt her shoulders relax. All that existed was John's hypnotic voice. She listened to him, taking note of each of his comments. It made sense. He was telling her to leave the world behind. Her problems shrunk as he spoke, becoming so small they could fit on the head of a pin. Feeling safe for the first time since opening day at Monsterland, she gravitated toward that sensation. Flashing images distracted her. Her parents, who died in each other's arms in Copper Valley, Howard's face when she didn't remember them, Tocho's hurt and anger hurtled through her consciousness, and no matter how hard she tried to block them, they continued to intrude. She worried about the world, about her friend's feelings, and their perception of her. She bit her lip, scared of anger or resentment forcing her to become the monster Medusa again. That was one morphing creature she wanted to avoid.

There was silence in the clearing, John's commentary droned on like a hum, as if she were in the middle of a hive. It filled her head. On some level, Keisha knew he was speaking to each of them individually, but she didn't care.

Focus, she urged herself. All she wanted was to stay in the comforting bubble away from choices and hurt feelings, but every so often, reality reared its ugly head, tearing her heart anew.

"Do you hear it?" John whispered behind her ear, his breath

ruffling her hair. "The noise in your head? *Did I do the right thing? Make the right choice?* It won't stop. It persists in questioning your judgment."

Keisha forced her brain back to the cadence of John's mesmerizing voice, casting out every thought from her head.

Her scalp tightened, goosebumps traveled up and down her skin as if struck by a bolt of electricity. She was plugged in, becoming a vast cell of energy. It vibrated within her, every organ, all of her joints, her bones rattled from the growing force of it. She could feel herself shaking, her teeth clicking in her skull like a demented skeleton.

"Let it go, Keisha. It will resolve itself," John Raven crooned. "Trust in the universe. That voice in your head makes you anxious and judgmental about yourself. It's the voice of guilt. But you have nothing to be sorry about. Remorse follows you like a lovesick puppy, but you did nothing wrong. You are too hard on yourself."

A tear slid down Keisha's cheek. She felt John's gentle hand wipe it away.

"You think you always have to be perfect, but we live in a flawed world, and unreal expectations are not only impossible, but we all discover that perfection is an illusion." John was next to her now, on his knees. "You know this. You know this because your inner voice has told you to think this many times. You understand the concept for others, but you hold yourself to a higher standard. I ask you? Who are you to be your own judge?"

Keisha quieted the turmoil by retaking a deep breath. The tremors slowed. Straining, she listened for an internal noise, begging her soul to speak to her.

"You know the truth! Search for your inner voice, the one connected to your higher self. Find that truth—the essence of you. Don't forget to breathe, that's right, take a deep breath. Let it speak and more importantly, listen to it."

In her mind's eye, everything vanished. Clouds cleared as

clarity took hold. The earth rotated, and Keisha felt the world adjust around her.

John's voice was all she heard, and she knew he was speaking only to her. "And when the understanding comes, know that this inner voice will guide you with kindness… not stress or guilt in a hurricane of *shoulds*."

Electricity crackled, the hairs standing up all over her body. The air turned warm and static, and her skin glowed as if bathed in a shower of sparks. It didn't burn, she realized with a start; it was a gentle spray surrounding her in a force field of light.

John's voice sounded louder. His words developed into powerful punches. The letters rained down, her skin absorbing them as if parched. "Breathe in the light, breathe out the toxins. Breathe in love, breathe out guilt. Breathe in acceptance, breathe out perfection." He paused. "Trust yourself."

A drum nearby began beating a steady rhythm. Keisha embraced it, her body taut as a bowstring, pulsing with each thump.

"Imagine the animal. Free it from its hiding place," John said softly.

It was different this time, so different she couldn't wrap her mind around it. She didn't think about Medusa or snakes. They were not part of her lexicon. She bent forward eagerly, waiting to join, knowing this was right.

Everything changed subtly; she wasn't sure if she imagined it. Keisha held her breath, letting the sparkle caress her body, enter through her skin, bubble through her veins until she was lighter than air.

Her body arched, slowly and deliberately. Keisha shifted, feeling the ground fall away. She was rising, a breeze rushing around her. The ground fell away, and Keisha squeezed her eyes shut.

She was morphing, but in a new way, carrying her to a curious new reality. It was quicker, more defined, her body neat and efficient.

There was a novel strangeness, a slow burn. Something bigger was happening than anything Keisha could have imagined. The urge to open her arms wide forced her to spread them like a giant wingspan. She pictured them unfurling beside her, the breeze lifting her above the earth.

Keisha gasped from the unexpectedness. She was airborne. It had a familiar quality to it. She'd morphed into a kestrel before. Something had changed. While she wanted to examine the difference, Keisha was afraid to lose her concentration.

Heat engulfed her. Gasping, she dropped, falling in a rapid descent, halting suddenly as if held up by invisible strings before her body could hit the ground. John's voice came from far away, ordering her to breathe through it, holding onto the changes occurring.

Slowing her breath, she inhaled deeply, allowing the air to circulate throughout her bloodstream, sending it roaring like a charging river to every nook and cranny of her form. She rose again, buoyant and unrestrained, her arms snapping and spreading like a giant sailboat, or a superyacht. She kept her movements slow, deliberate, savoring the power, each motion moving her upward. She knew instinctively that she was no small bird.

Wings flapped. Keisha tightened her eyelids, afraid to look, scared that she'd plummet to the ground or be disappointed that her imagination created a distorted reality. Holding her breath, she evaluated the sound of air *whooshing* past her. Her scientific mind could not rest. She listened hard.

These were not the small wings of a kestrel; they were large and leathery. Lifting higher, Keisha rose like a phoenix, her body filled with fire, her bones hollow and delicate.

She spun in a circle, her long neck stretched out, uncurling as if it had been a coiled snake. Opening her eyes, she twisted and saw a reptilian tail lash out. Keisha peered down through the clouds, watching in awe as they parted. She let the brisk air cleanse her, a small smile tugging at her lips, or maybe it was her beak. Worries and fears, the perception that she was not enough, dissolved into showery sparks. She arced in triumph, her wings spread out twenty feet wide on either side, their scalloped edges allowing for greater speed. Opening her mouth, her shout of triumph died when fire raced from her throat, lighting up the airspace around her. She soared, bouncing from one end of the sky above the meadow to the end of the valley.

She allowed the wind to carry her higher, tears glistening in her eyes. John Raven waved below her, his face filled with longing and pride. The sun felt good on her skin, and she closed her eyes, savoring its warmth. With each turn, each powerful thrust of her wings, she examined and dissected what she felt.

Her first experience shapeshifting was as Medusa. It scared her. She was all anger and venom. She studied with Lily and her uncle, learning how to morph into a kestrel. While she loved the freedom of flight, it was limiting, leaving her small and powerless.

All this time, she was wrong. She allowed the limitations she placed on herself to curb her true intentions. She twirled in awe, watching as all the other students made room for her. They gaped from the sidelines at her boundless energy, the wisdom of the ages coursing through her veins. She banked, flying over a small reservoir, marveling at the bright red reflection of her scaly image.

Keisha knew that this was what she was supposed to be, not the Western concept of a dragon as a monster, but the Eastern truth that dragons were the source of good luck and strength.

The Earth's gravity subtly pulled her back. Keisha's spine curled inward with fatigue. Her racing heart slowed, and her body felt the weight of lethargy tug at her. She refused to let it slow her down. It was glorious. Never could she have imagined anything like this. She didn't want it to end. What if she failed the next time she tried? What if she could never repeat what she accomplished here today? *What would Howard think?* She paused, a chill running down her long spine. Would he see her as a giant science experiment? *Should I even share what happened today? Dragons scare people. What if Howard considers me a monster?*

She didn't have time to ponder it. Opening her eyes, she saw John's elated gaze. "You finally listened to her, your inner voice."

Keisha nodded, her eyes glazed, a worried look on her face. She was coming down, gravity deflating her elation. Reality chained her back to earth. Freedom evaporated. All she could think about was Howard's reaction.

"This is just the start of your story," John told her, pressing the frown lines on her forehead. "It is going to be great."

Yeah, great, she thought. *What the heck was she going to do with a dragon?* She wanted power, strength, not a thing of nightmares. *Is this who I really am?* Again, her mind raced. *What would Howard think?*

Keisha made eye contact with Lily, who beamed back at her.

"You did it. Oh, Keisha, you were magnificent. I have to admit, I'm not surprised. You always outdo everyone else!"

Yeah, Keisha thought glumly, a fake smile pasted on her lips. Wait until Howard sees it. She cupped her forehead with her hand. *Oh, my goodness, what have I done?*

Lily clapped her hands rapidly, looking like an excited cheerleader, while Keisha's heart contracted with grief. She liked Lily. She really did, but she doesn't understand.

Keisha wanted to talk to Jade. Jade would understand what she felt, what she was afraid of. Her uncomplicated old life was fading fast. She missed home.

CHAPTER 4

LILY OF THE VALLEY

"WYATT, STOP!"

Wyatt and Melvin stopped their trek up the dunes toward the command tent. Wyatt saw Lily waving one arm and calling his name. He caught Melvin looking at him with a lopsided grin. "You go on, I'll catch up," Wyatt told him.

Melvin gave him a saucy salute and left.

Lily was breathless by the time they met up. "Didn't you hear me? I've been calling your name for a while." Her eyes locked on the feather poking out of his shirt pocket. It was her feather. Wyatt carried it with him since he picked it up at the Battle of Monsterland.

Wyatt shook his head.

"Deep thoughts?" she asked, her brown eyes were sympathetic.

Wyatt looked away guiltily. "You give me too much credit."

"Is something wrong?" Lily asked. "It's like you've been avoiding me since the battle."

Wyatt shook his head. "Everything's fine. Well." He amended, "as fine as it can be."

They began walking slowly, their feet leaving footprints in the sand. Wyatt's hands were in his pockets, and while their shoulders bumped, they both appeared to be slightly uncomfortable.

"How did your training go?" Wyatt changed the subject.

"Amazing. Keisha morph—" Lily halted her word mid-sentence.

"Yeah?" Wyatt looked at her.

"Keisha's coming along splendidly," Lily said a bit too fast. "My uncle wanted you and Howard to try to take a class. Hopefully, at home, in the valley?"

"Maybe in a few months." Wyatt watched her smile fade.

"You're not coming back with us."

Wyatt didn't answer. Lily stopped walking, and they paused together, the breeze caressing them. Lily's long, dark hair whipped around her face. Wyatt reached up, and the tendrils wrapped themselves around his wrist. It used to comfort him, but instead, he felt trapped, as if it was locking onto him. He tried to disengage the strands, but the breeze prevented him.

Lily's bottom lip trembled. She pushed his hand down, breaking the contact between them. "You wanted to find yourself. Well, did you?"

"That wasn't—"

"Don't lie to yourself, Wyatt. There's nothing here for you. Unless you count killer clowns and stupid, indestructible sea creatures."

Wyatt opened his mouth, but Lily went on, "I thought you had to get it out of your system."

"Get what out of my system?" Wyatt answered hotly. "It's all so easy for you. You have your uncle, the reservation. You have a place where you belong."

"You're not the only person who lost somebody. My father is gone, too." Lily sobbed.

Wyatt reached to pull her close, but she yanked herself away.

"Lily, we don't even know what's going to happen when those things hatch."

Lily spun to the left, "'There is no fear where there is faith.'"

"I don't understand."

"It's a Kiowa proverb. Where is your faith, Wyatt? We'll defeat those things like we've overcome everything else."

Wyatt thought back to their crazy car ride to Stocktonville. Lily sat beside him in Carter's cruiser. Never once did she shy away from danger. She was braver than probably anyone else he'd ever met.

"I..I.." he stuttered.

"Poor Wyatt Baldwin, never getting what he wants. You know, maybe you should realize that sometimes none of us get what we want."

She stalked off, her face held high.

"Lily!" he called her. "Lily! It's not about getting what I want," he finished lamely. He stood

in the silence, the wind whistling on the lonely beach. He glanced to the right and saw the endless sand, and toward the left, the troops massing for action. Taking a deep breath, he said to himself, "It's about finding a place where you mean something."

CHAPTER 5

WHO KNEW GIANTS WERE SENTIMENTAL?

Army Base 1
California Coastline across from Prendick Rock

"I MISS HOME," GRILLOS said with a sigh.

Rosemary looked his massive body up and down. "I didn't know giants could be such big babies."

"I'm tired of being poked and prodded," he complained. "I've been here long enough."

"I thought you were dead." Rosemary sat on a stool next to Grillos, the giant, tenderly touching the bruise on his cheek. He was flat on his back, fifteen overfilled black trash bags serving as pillows. He was partly under a makeshift awning of the hospital tent, his large feet sticking out and resting on a trio of bushes. Stretching, she brushed his hair back from his temple. She felt a strange connection to this super-sized man.

"*Pshaw.*" He waved a huge hand, and it caused the air to swirl and eddy near her face. "Winded, but not dead. That wall knocked me down. By the time I came to, Vincent Konrad had made his escape, once again."

"It took fifteen people to carry you back from the battle." She gave him a stern look. "I swear, I could hear your bones rattling in your chest."

Grillos's face reddened to the roots of his hair. "It was a big wall," he said sheepishly.

"You saved my life." Rosemary rubbed the bandage under her shirt where a bullet had grazed her. "If you hadn't blocked the wall when it fell, it would have killed most of us."

Grillos started to sweat. Rosemary climbed up his chest to dab his skin.

"That's what friends are for." Grillos groaned as he tried to move into a comfortable spot.

"So we're all friends now?" Rosemary teased him, a smile gracing her wide lips. She patted the gauze on his forehead carefully, where she knew a twenty-four-inch gash was healing. "I still don't know how he did it."

"Who? Your fath… I mean, Vincent. The man has more tricks up his sleeve than a magician. He certainly disappeared like one."

Rosemary looked at him, her eyes wide. "That wasn't a magic trick. More like some special force field that transported him somewhere else."

"I just want to get out of this place." Grillos shrugged his massive shoulders.

"Not until the doctors release you, Uncle." His niece, Danai, came by with a plastic trash can filled with a bubbling liquid. "The army medic wants you to drink this."

Grillos grimaced.

"All of it, Uncle." Danai pouted prettily.

Grillos squinted up at her. "You're growing by the hour, Danai. You're sure about staying with these…" He glanced around the full hospital tent. "… minkins. Don't you want to come home with us to your mama?"

Danai sighed. "No, I like it here, crazy clown-like creatures and all." She was so tall that her head grazed the top of the tent. Crouching a bit, she cleared a space beside him and settled down. "I will admit they're strange, but there's an element of fun to their anxiety. I can see why our ancestors left them and moved underground."

"Really?" Rosemary asked. "How so?"

"You humans live a life of constant tension, whether it's about your position in society, your looks, or who has more… junk. You place importance on the oddest objects."

Rosemary looked puzzled.

"You know, possessions, all that nonsense. Minkins worry about the stupidest things. They only find happiness when they feel everybody is doing worse than them."

"Surely you don't feel that way about Wyatt and his friends?" Rosemary leaned closer to watch Danai's face.

Danai laughed. "Howard and Wyatt are sweet. They are the main reason I want to stay here."

"If you find the rest of our population unstable, why choose to live with us?" Rosemary kneeled on Grillos's chest and gently blotted his sweaty forehead with a bath towel. "Sounds like an awful lot of maintenance."

Danai shrugged. "It would seem so, but aside from finding them entertaining, we have a lot to learn from minkins."

Grillos spat out some medicine and laughed so hard his eyes teared. "Like what?" He choked a bit.

"I don't know yet, Uncle. I… I think… Look, giants were miserable living underground. All we wanted was to be allowed to come above. We don't want riches or other things these minkins fight for. We just wanted our place on the surface of the planet."

Grillos nodded. "True."

"Minki… *erm*, humanity." Danai opened her arms wide and waved them, gesturing to the people surrounding them. "They have it all, and yet they exist like they're unhappy. All they do is fight with each other. There has to be a middle ground. And maybe we are the ones to teach it to them."

"You don't fight over property?" Rosemary stopped what she was doing to look at the giants. She slid off Grillos's chest.

"Not underground and not between our clans. Only idiots fight over dirt. Between our people, we never kill; nobody goes hungry. There is no envy or greed. Other than my cousin Henny, that unhappy rascal, Jötnar, and Danai, no giant has ever complained." His brows lowered in consternation.

"I wasn't unhappy at home precisely, Uncle. I just didn't want to be forced to marry and breed. But for my smaller size, it wouldn't have been an issue. Otherwise, I was perfectly content with my life."

"Sounds like a wonderful place. I don't know why anyone would want to live in this jungle," Rosemary muttered.

Danai lifted the tent flap and looked outside. "I don't see a jungle."

"It's an expression. Meaning our society is a jungle and we all are animals ripping each other to shreds."

"It's funny," Danai laughed.

"What?" Rosemary was puzzled.

"You minkins don't appreciate your limited lifespans. You waste precious time over nonsense."

Rosemary looked from Grillos to Danai's innocent faces and asked, "What do you expect to accomplish here?"

"Maybe we can help, then." Danai smiled. She tipped the garbage can toward her uncle's mouth. "Drink it up, Uncle."

Grillos peered down at the liquid, took a swig, and belched

loudly. The tent flaps billowed out, and the army medic threw him a dirty look.

"I feel better already!" he declared. Grillos rolled up into a sitting position. "Tell your other uncles and father we are heading out soon."

Danai nodded. "Tomorrow?" She took the empty trash can from him.

"No, later today. I miss home, and we must make haste if we are to travel through the mountains."

Rosemary held onto his shoulder, as if to push him back down. "Are you sure you're well enough? Your ribs were broken!"

"Enough of this coddling. We heal fast. It's something in our blood."

Danai's eyes flashed with alarm. "Uncle, you must travel back the way you came. You can't go through the mountains!"

He shook his head. "Not if we want to move quickly—"

"I insist," she interrupted, her face pale.

"What's this about?' Rosemary paused what she was doing. She looked from Grillos to Danai, but their mouths remained stubbornly quiet. "Grillos?"

"She has a right to know," Danai said. "Especially if she is to travel with you."

"There are dangers in the mountains that we do not have in the desert."

Rosemary patted her hip, where a Colt was tucked into her waistband. "Don't worry. I'm prepared."

Grillos grunted in agreement. "So am I." He turned to his niece and glanced around at the industrious group of doctors and nurses. He smiled, changing his demeanor, his teeth as large as seat cushions. "I can see you like it here. You always enjoyed a challenge. We don't have enough of them where we come from."

"Except for the giant slugs," Danai said grimly.

"What… sl…slugs," Rosemary stuttered. "Who said anything about giant slugs?"

"Don't worry about anything." Grillos waved his hand, dismissing the subject.

"Is that what you were talking about before?" Rosemary asked, her face taut.

"See, you're making her nervous," he admonished Danai, while not answering the question. His huge hand engulfed Rosemary's smaller one. "Human, you have so much to learn about our world." Grillos stretched. He nodded to his niece. "You're a good nurse, Danai. I am almost healed."

"I'm going to be a better doctor," Danai said and stood and rushed off, snatching his

rumpled bedding as she dashed away.

Grillos gently lifted Rosemary and placed her on his shoulder. "I think I missed you when

You weren't sitting here."

Rosemary laughed. "Who knew giants were sentimental?" She tugged his ear playfully.

"Whichever of your nieces decides to stay, they'll be an asset to the community."

"They are all staying. They've decided they want to remain together in your world." Grillos cleared his throat. "I'm happy they will have each other."

"Hold on." The giant slid out from the tent, rising to his full height of thirty feet.

Grillos wiggled his back until he heard a loud crack. With a satisfied groan, he began

walking toward the encampment.

"You know, you should have asked me first," Rosemary said, but there was enough humor in her voice to understand she didn't mind.

"Wot?"

"You can't keep plucking me off the floor and putting me on your shoulder as if I don't have a say in the matter."

Grillos looked at her, horrified. "I would never!" he sputtered.

He shook his head. "First, Danai, and now you! Speak up, woman! If you don't like something, let me know."

"Seems fair enough," Rosemary said. "And don't call me, woman."

"Why not?"

"It's not respectful."

"I see." Grillos shook his head. "I have a lot to learn about your ways."

"Yes, you do." She was impressed with his easy acceptance. "Is it like that with your kind?"

"Sometimes," Grillos replied, his voice faraway.

Rosemary was wondering what life would be like if all you had to say was, 'I don't like something,' and people respected each other enough to stop. She looked down at her belly and the baby sleeping in her womb. It seemed much bigger than she thought it should be. She had limited experience with these things, and she was only a few weeks along. *Should her stomach be popping like this?* Her belly strained against the buttons of her shirt.

Something fluttered inside. Rosemary's breath caught. Resting a palm over the tiny movement, she felt her heart contract with love. It was a new experience, and it humbled her. She held her hand, hoping it would happen again, just to prove she didn't imagine it. This was her child, a living soul dependent on her for everything. The baby kicked again, and Rosemary gasped with delight. *You are real and mine, to love and keep safe.* So, this is how her mother must have felt. She remembered her as a lioness, protecting Rosemary with a fierceness she had finally come to understand.

"You okay, up there?" Grillos's voice was concerned.

"Fine," Rosemary answered with a slight hesitation. She turned inward, reflecting on her pregnancy. She knew she would shelter her baby from Vincent, even though it had been implanted there without her permission. She wondered who Vincent had picked for the father. Taking a breath, she decided she didn't care. This was her baby, and hers alone.

Grillos looked up at her, his face full of concern. It was as though he could sense her feelings. "Rosemary?"

Rosemary nodded, "Yes, Grillos. I'm perfect."

Grillos shook his head. "Are you having second thoughts about making this trip?"

Rosemary didn't answer. Her brain had shifted to wondering about their differences. She looked at the vast expanse of sea before her and sighed. She missed it already. She squirmed, feeling uncomfortable in her clothing, which now seemed too tight. She pulled the ends of her shirt closer as if to shield her baby. She never shied away from an adventure, but she looked down at her expanding girth. Now she had to worry about someone else? She bit her lip, her forehead wrinkling. Was she being irresponsible, starting a journey like this?

Grillos looked over his shoulder. "Whatever it is, Rosemary, that curdles your thoughts, understand you have control over it."

Rosemary raised her eyebrows. *If only, Grillos*, she thought. *If only I had control. I've never had control of anything in my life, except when I was out at sea and captain of a ship.*

She patted her stomach. *Too many deep thoughts, little one. I don't have to worry about you for some time.* She sat back to enjoy the sway and roll of Grillos's steps. She was moving as if on a three-masted schooner, the ground racing past her as Grillos picked up speed. Taking a deep breath, she realized she felt the same lightness she experienced on the waves and wondered if it was all about the movement or a state of mind. It felt right being with Grillos. He gave her a comforting sense of belonging.

They walked a distance until they came to the command tent. Grillos lifted the top, sending the guards into spasms. He held out his arm for Rosemary to slide down the side of his body, landing with a slight jump.

"Relax, stand down!" President Nate Owens ordered. "Glad to see you up and about, Grillos." He turned to Rosemary. "You're well?"

"Aye, Mr. President. Ready to fulfill my new role."

Grillos nodded in agreement. "We'll be setting off soon."

"Are you sure you don't want to stay with us?" Wyatt called out.

Grillos shook his head. "We have to return to our community and start our plan to build homes on the land at the base of the mountain."

President Owens said, "Of course, as we agreed."

"We will take the ruins of Monsterland and create our new settlement. After all, we had built most of it."

Wyatt stared at the giant. "I still can't believe you constructed the theme park right under our noses."

"Dr. Konrad picked sleepy little Copper Valley just for that reason. We've been living underneath your town for eons. How else do you think he accomplished the project in so short a time?"

"I thought he was really organized," Wyatt said, his voice low.

Carter, Wyatt's stepfather, made a derisive sound. "Looks like he pulled the wool over everyone's eyes from the beginning." Something passed between Wyatt and his stepfather.

Carter placed a reassuring hand on his stepson's shoulder and told him, "He fooled everyone, Wy."

"Not you." Wyatt's face was bright red with embarrassment.

The mood of the room became reflective with everyone considering their culpability.

Melvin cleared his throat, breaking the silence. "I would ask that you leave the lagoon area the way you found it, Grillos. I claim it as mine."

Grillos looked at him for a long while and agreed. "We will live next to you."

"Rosemary, you can take my hut and use it until I get back," Melvin told her. "Just don't change anything."

"Thanks, of course. That's very kind of you." She smiled at him. She looked around the tent. Who'd have believed a werewolf and a giant would be negotiating living space? She glanced down at the pensive teen named Wyatt. There was a connection between them; she felt it. She knew somehow that conduit was her father. "What are you going to do about Vincent?" she asked.

"Nothing," Wyatt said, his jaw tense. "Once he rears his ugly head, we will…" His eyes opened wide, and he apologized. "Oh, sorry."

"No, don't worry. I think my father is ugly too," she assured him. "There's a difference between ugly on the inside and ugly on the outside." Rosemary gazed up at the giant, her eyes misty with tears.

Grillos smiled back.

"Until he makes his presence known, we have no idea where he is or what his plans are." Wyatt paced the room.

"He might be dead," Melvin said.

Rosemary shook her head. "Nope. I'd know. I didn't know him for long." She shivered. "But it was enough for him to get under my skin." She held up her arm, showing a scar where Jötnar had removed a transmitting device. "Whatever. At least he'll never be able to find me." *Or my child*, she finished the thought silently.

Grillos swiveled his large head and gently patted her hair. "We'll keep you from harm's way, Rosemary. After all, you are our ambassador to the human world."

"You don't mind that I am Vincent Konrad's daughter?"

Grillos laughed. "You didn't pick him as a father, and you have more than proved you are not of the same ilk. No, I don't mind, and I'm sure neither will the others."

"I just wish I knew where that old bastard was," Rosemary said under her breath.

She wasn't the only one who thought that.

CHAPTER 6

FOOL'S MATE

VINCENT STEPPED INTO the command center before Dreg and watched the Thalens clear a space at a larger counter in the middle of the room.

"Your planet is composed of an odd assortment of creatures, Doctor. I'm not quite sure what you could want from *any* one of them." Spekator's voice had an irritating quality that grated on Vincent's nerves. The alien had no observable mouth, so the disembodied sounds had a surreal effect.

It made Vincent question the voices he heard in his head; were they his thoughts or Spekator's? He had to be very careful about what he was thinking.

Spekator went on. "I've never seen such a useless group of entities, except for your marine life. The oceans are home to a vast array of fascinating creatures. Perfect living organisms, in an ideally organized world."

"Precisely why I created my Great White Shark Park. Our sealife does not disappoint, unlike the rest of the inhabitants of my planet," Vincent grumbled.

"Our thinking as well." Spekator studied the doctor and then added, "It all started with Artificial Intelligence. Humans stopped using their brains."

"Which you thoughtfully provided." Vincent smiled, his new teeth gleaming. "And they were so proud of their accomplishments."

Spekator inclined his head, his eyes twinkling. "We provided the blueprint. We simply wanted to see if humanity would take the bait."

"A humorous metaphor," Konrad smirked.

"What? Dreg was confused.

"We were talking about marine life, and Spekator made the observation about humanity taking the bait… get it? Marine life, as in fish taking the—. Oh, forget it, Dreg. You were saying, Spekator?"

"Yes, well, my point exactly. Your population has become too reliant on Artificial Intelligence. Lazy. They've forgotten critical thinking and problem-solving. This will make them much easier targets."

"They won't know what hit them," Vincent agreed.

"Even President McAdams couldn't decide without consulting his computer. Your entire civilization is useless," Spekator scoffed. "They've lost all their abilities, skills." The oversized head dipped. "It is a shame. Visiting this planet used to be an exciting experience. Watching humans through the ages work out their issues, create, or learn used to be fun. They are dull as dishwater."

Dreg raised his eyebrow. "Dishwater?"

"Yes, Dreg, dishwater. You know, it's opaque, flat—"

"Gray?" Dreg supplied.

Vincent gave a pointed stare at the gray body of the Thalen and shook his head.

Dreg swallowed. "What I meant to say is that gray is… exciting."

Vincent quickly changed the subject; he needed Spekator to

facilitate his return to Earth. Once again, the smooth salesman, he placated the alien. "That's why I used the monsters, to cull and winnow out the unproductive members of our society. See." Vincent pointed to the image of the Earth revolving on the screen. "They do not need all the services they used to think were necessary: movies, nail salons, fancy purses, cars, many materialistic things. Manufacturing and trade have stopped. Nobody is creating goods anymore. They don't remember how to be functional. We don't need all those people cluttering up the planet using necessary resources."

Vincent and Spekator strolled away from Dreg, their two heads bowed together.

"Indeed. Those commodities will soon be replaced with more important ones. They will learn that all they should have to consider is survival. The population will work for the true essentials of life: food and shelter. Only the strongest will survive." Spekator clapped his spindly hands.

"Yes, they will be ready and eager when you splice your genes with theirs. A new planet, filled with hybrids, Thalen, and human DNA mixed in harmony to produce a superior being." Vincent paused. "I don't like being away this long. Monsters are running rampant. Humans are regrouping. I must return."

"Patience, Doctor. Rosemary is not ready to deliver."

"You're not listening to me. I must go back. We're not comfortable here, on your ship. It's unnatural." Vincent shuddered.

Spekator took a long look at Vincent's artificial body and let out a laugh. His sloped shoulders jiggled with mirth. Vincent suppressed the anger that bubbled inside of him and sighed with impatience. He stalked to one of the seven portholes lining the wall of the ship.

Staring out the window, he tapped his foot impatiently. He was tired of being confined to the craft. It didn't help that no one was listening to him. They passed the moon, its pocked, grayish countenance matched Vincent's ravaged face.

In the background, the trills and bells of the spacecraft filled the silence. Vincent recognized the single long blast as a signal for incoming messages from the mothership. Several bleats of a sheep-like horn were from engineering. The strum of strings, similar to a harp, was a signal to report to your station.

When Vincent first awoke from his twilight sleep after surgery, he marveled at the alien efficiency. They were organized, frugal with movement and conversation. Except for Dreg, he enjoyed the silence and absence of human contact. Lately, though, something had changed. The quiet bothered him. It was as if he almost missed the messy and unpredictable side of humanity.

The aliens drifted from station to station on the ship, communicating telepathically; their giant, oval-shaped heads seemed to breathe as they spoke. Spekator, he'd learned, had been assigned to them, as the alien could communicate through thought brain wave transference with them.

Vincent challenged Spekator by claiming loftily that, with his superior intelligence, he didn't need to speak telepathically. He could understand Spekator perfectly.

Spekator shook his gray, oversized head sympathetically and explained he had almost blown out Vincent and Dreg's brains when he attempted communication the first time.

Vincent responded with a rude noise to show his displeasure. Dreg nudged him, and when he looked at him, Dreg whispered, "Don't be disrespectful, Vincent."

A warning siren went off, and Spekator floated to one of the stations.

The alarm steadily became more strident, and the Thalens' eight-fingered hands glided over the instruments urgently.

"What's going on?" Vincent demanded. The crew all glanced toward one of the rear portholes. A cigar-shaped craft hovered in the distance.

"Another ship. Is it one of yours?" Vincent stared out the oval window.

"No, Scalis." Spekator hissed the name. "They're keeping their distance for now, waiting, just waiting," Spekator added. He glided quietly next to Vincent.

"I've heard of them. What kind of species are they?" Vincent leaned closer to get a better look.

"Reptiles." Spekator's expression didn't change, although Vincent noticed his voice was strained.

"Ah, reptiles. Dr. Frasier indicated that many of the governments on Earth had made contact with them."

"Frasier?" Spekator inquired.

"The scientist I worked with on Earth. He was the one who contacted you."

"Of course. Did he contact the Scalis, too?" Spekator peered closely at his face.

"Dr. Frasier only had access to your ship. While your crew members had died in the crash on impact, he reported that several of the reptiles, I mean, Scalis had survived and were kept under top secret lock and key by our government." Vincent shrugged and continued. "I asked President McAdams about it before he was killed, but he couldn't validate anything."

Spekator appeared to let out a deep breath. "So, you haven't negotiated with them?"

"What's your connection to the Scalis?" Vincent asked.

"We have been enemies for eons."

Vincent observed the enemy ship from the porthole. "Surely you have the power to overcome them?"

The oversized head dipped. "Of course. However, the fact that they are here before they were supposed to is alarming the First Minister. Our coordinates have been leaked."

"Seems like you must have a spy lurking about." Vincent's voice was soft. This pleased him. The overconfidence of the Thalens was beginning to wear on his nerves. He was used to being the most powerful person in a room, and somehow, the aliens made him feel inconsequential.

"He's having a conference with Ambassador Plinth as we speak."

"As I recall, *you* weren't supposed to be here either," Vincent scoffed. "I was to prepare Earth for your arrival and eventual colonization. Start the scrubbing of humanity, eliminate the monsters, and choose the appropriate survivors for our new race."

Spekator's eyes became heated. "And yet, here you are, with nothing accomplished."

Vincent stiffened. "Nothing accomplished! I created an apocalypse. The world is ripe for you. Once Rosemary has her child, they will see that the fittest species will have a better chance of surviving and not going extinct. I believe I gave you the upper hand."

"The upper hand belongs to us and us alone." Spekator's moved closer, causing Vincent to back away.

"You need me."

Spekator didn't respond.

Vincent moved around him. "It's chaos down there. You don't know or understand them.

They will knuckle under any of my...*our* demands." Vincent's eyes gleamed with triumph. Vincent peered closely at Spekator. The alien didn't seem impressed. He kept glancing at a monitor Vincent couldn't read. "There's something else bothering you."

Spekator paused as if weighing whether to share more information.

"What is it?" Vincent urged.

"We've located a Va'Rok ship. They are stationed in that quadrant." Spekator pointed

a spindly finger to an empty area of space.

"I don't see anything." Vincent looked out the porthole. "Va'Rok, you say. I wonder. What exactly do the Va'Rok look like? I've never seen an image."

"No one knows. Very secretive. The Va'Rok deploy invisibility devices, such as the cloaking shield they're using on their ship now. See, we can detect them on our instruments." He gestured to the console.

"*Humph*, but you have no idea what they look like. Maybe you aren't the superior species I thought you were."

Spekator's skin turned a mottled red, and Vincent continued oblivious to the tension.

"It was my understanding that you *all* obey the Intergalactic Treaties. Yet, it seems everyone is breaking the rules." Vincent narrowed his eyes. "Remember, no matter what, this is my planet and you will yield to my supreme command."

Spekator appeared distracted; he glanced at the rear porthole with narrowed eyes.

"Why do I feel that you're not telling me everything? Allies are supposed to share," Vincent said through gritted teeth.

"Are we truly allies, or are you just using us to get the resources you need?" Spekator's voice was oily.

Vincent turned his steely gaze back to Spekator. "You doubt my loyalty? How can we be allies if you don't trust me?"

Spekator looked him up and down. "Trust builds solid relationships."

"Exactly. You trust me and I'll trust you," Vincent told him. "Now, I demand to speak to Ambassador Plinth as soon as he's finished his meeting with the Minister. Where is he?"

"As you say." Spekator was meek again. "I'll contact him." He lowered his bulbous head as though he was listening to something Vincent couldn't hear. He moved a bit away, turning his face from Vincent.

His mood swings were making Vincent feel dizzy. Negotiating with aliens was not like anything he'd ever done. He couldn't get a bead on their true motivations, if they had any. It was impossible to read a situation when your opponents showed no emotion.

Vincent paced the room, considering the significant nuances in speech patterns and microfacial movements, including expressions of disappointment, worry, happiness, and fear. Vincent had trouble reading their faces. Doubt replaced any feelings of loyalty Vincent had. He wanted to get off the ship and Spekator out of his head.

Spekator wafted back, his almond-shaped eyes heavy, and sighed, "The Ambassador is..."

"Yes?"

One of the Thalen crew drew their attention to the large monitor in the front of the bridge. The frozen body of the Thalen ambassador drifted past them.

"Clearly a disappointment to the First Minister. Too bad. I liked him." Spekator sounded droll.

Vincent couldn't tell if Spekator was genuine or sarcastic. He was beginning to dislike his hosts immensely.

The bridge went silent.

Spekator looked at him sideways. "There are hundreds of planets filled with lifeforms, but this part of the galaxy now belongs to the Scalis, Va'Rok, and Thalens."

"What do you mean by that?" Vincent had the strange sensation that he was outplayed.

"We outbid the others."

"What others?" Vincent demanded.

"Intergalactic beings from all over the galaxy."

"You've divided our planet?" Vincent was incredulous and started to pace the room.

"Not just your planet, this quadrant of space. Each section is being parceled into groups of three, and those willing to pay the largest amount of Ursars will maintain the habitable planets in their area. We have the responsibility to prevent the inhabitants from destroying their resources and home. You earthlings simply can't coexist with each other, so your planet is being protected to keep it from ruin. It must be kept viable for future colonization."

"And you all respect the boundaries with each other?" Vincent was deep in thought.

Spekator dipped his head. "Once dominance has been settled."

Vincent quietly digested this information, and Spekator dropped another bombshell. "It's not the first time this end of the galaxy will be colonized. Only this time, it will be led by me."

"What? Has this happened before?"

"It was before our planet had interstellar capabilities. It was a blind colonization, and there are no records of who won the occupation."

Vincent stopped pacing. "That's incredible." He stroked his chin thoughtfully. "Strange you don't know the prior winner."

"It was thousands of years ago. The records were destroyed in the Jupiter Wars."

"And here we are again. Parceling up the planet, I mean. You know, in 1493, Pope Alexander VI thought to divide the known world between Spain and Portugal."

Spekator drifted over, his large head cocked to one side. "Was it successful?"

Vincent observed the alien, feeling that his answer held great importance. "At first, it was. Then it led to major disputes and even warfare. Sometimes, the locals ignored the treaties and dealt with whom they wanted. Maybe that was the cause of your Jupiter Wars."

"*Hmmmm.* Not likely. That conflict was a trade war. Tell me more about your Pope Alexander."

"Not much more to tell, but eventually Spain and Portugal's dominance was challenged by other powers who didn't feel bound by treaties not made by them." Vincent paused and studied the spacecraft on the monitor. "You know I didn't agree to this. I only negotiated with you. What if the Scalis or the Va'Rok are chosen?"

"They won't be," Spekator said smugly. "We are the superior candidate. Don't forget, we responded quickly when you reached out to us."

"Dr. Frasier engaged the communication system on one of the

crafts that crashed in Nevada years ago. It's not as if we had a choice of whom to contact."

"You used our fuel to power your body and annihilate the humans in your world. I believe, Doctor, that you owe *us* a debt."

"It wasn't your fuel once it was abandoned on our planet," Vincent shot back.

Spekator waved his hand dismissively. "Well, then, let's say the planet's aligned." Spekator snuffled in an interpretation of a laugh. "Consider yourself lucky that it was our ship you found. The Scalis think they can bully their way in, and no one knows what's in a Va'Rok's mind. We need your planet."

"Yes, my planet. My population. The species I choose to survive. I want to remind you that the combination of our DNA was to build a new race of hybrids that would follow my lead and protect my world." With each sentence, Vincent's voice became more shrill.

"We have much at stake, Doctor. My planet is dying." Spekator's tone was conciliatory.

"As is mine."

"But not because of *our* abuse. Our sun is due to expire. You've squandered this magnificent resource." Spekator turned to the monitor where the planet rotated in blue and green glory. "None of you deserve it."

"I beg to differ," Vincent said absently, his eyes glued to the revolving planet on the monitor. "I have loved my planet, used it gently, tried to nurse it back to health." Vincent felt a profound longing he'd never experienced before. He missed...*home*. In all the years he moved around, he never considered the concept of a permanent residence he could call his own. North America circled into view, and his eyes locked onto the Mojave Desert, locating Copper Valley. He could taste the dry air, see the brightness of a new day, and feel the sun beating down on him.

"Are you alright, Vincent?" Dreg touched his arm, pulling him from his reverie.

"Quite all right, Dreg. Quite." Vincent realized that Copper Valley was his place, and he needed to return there.

He glanced up at Spekator and understood the alien was using him, not the other way around. He was at Spekator's mercy and needed to connect with *terra firma*. He understood with stunning clarity that this alliance was not what he thought it would be. He created the chaos of Monsterland to overthrow governments and rise to power.

He stared at Spekator and then down at the plastic body they had provided. They never had any intention for him to rule the planet. They will get rid of him as soon as he achieves their goals. If they had, they would have spliced their DNA with his and wouldn't have stuck his head on a useless mannequin. The realization came with stunning clarity as his thoughts crystallized. Vincent had to fight from his element, not theirs.

Vincent Konrad stalked to the exit to leave the room. "Do you play chess, Spekator?"

"No, it's a silly human game."

"Have you ever heard of the term Fool's Mate, Commander?"

Spekator cocked his head like a dog.

Vincent laughed for the first time since he woke up from surgery.

Dreg followed Vincent off the bridge. "What was that all about, Vincent?"

They paused in a windowed hallway. Vincent spoke in a whisper. "Fool's Mate. Two moves to win."

"I don't understand."

"We need to go home. We can't do anything from here."

"What are you planning, Vincent?"

"Yes, yes. I need a plan." Vincent paced the small hallway, his tall head grazing the ceiling. "First, make contact with the Sasquatch, then find Rosemary. The game will be ours." Vincent explained.

"Sasquatch? You mean Bigfoot? How will you meet with them? They're just legends."

"No, not a myth or legend. Living, breathing beings, and they're going to help us get out of this mess."

"I still don't get it."

Vincent sighed in exasperation. "The Thalens have shown their hand. It's a stalemate between the Scalis, Va'Rok, and our hosts."

"Okay. I don't get how that is a problem."

"We may have backed the wrong horse, so to speak. All these aliens plan to do is divide the planet and deplete our resources. They are fighting over sovereignty. And I think that once they've won, they won't need us anymore."

"Sort of what you did to the vamps, zombies, and werewolves?" *Not to mention the*

humans and my boy, Dreg added silently.

"Shut up, Dreg. You don't understand politics."

"Vincent. It makes no sense. We are completely in their debt. That is no way to treat them. They put you back together."

"I know only one thing, Dreg. We must return to Monsterland and employ everything we have to defeat them, because once they win, we'll be disposable."

CHAPTER 7

TWO FRONT WAR

"WE'LL BE PULLING out tomorrow," President Nate Owens announced. "We'll split our forces-"

"We are totally screwed." Melvin shook his head.

"What, Saunders?" Colonel Drucker asked.

"We can't leave, sir!" Melvin's raspy voice filled the tent. He gestured toward the ocean beyond the walls of their army-issued canvas. "You haven't seen what those creatures have done. There are going to be hundreds of them once they hatch."

Owens ran a hand through his salt-and-pepper hair. "I understand, but we can't just sit here waiting. I'm leaving the bulk of Colonel Drucker's troops to deal with them." He paced in front of a makeshift table, a crude hand-drawn map of the coastline draped over it like a tablecloth.

"Those monsters will destroy your troops!" Melvin shouted,

his face red. "I've fought that thing. Your soldiers will be no match for them."

Wyatt sat quietly in the corner, his face set, until he saw Melvin's frustration and anger. Getting up, he moved closer, fearing his friend might morph into a werewolf again. "Mel!" he implored.

The president must have felt the same way, because he rested his hand on Melvin's shoulder and nodded with understanding.

"That shell monster was indestructible. I thought it was dead." Melvin turned to face the others in the tent. "I smashed it into dust, and it still came back to kill Jade." His voice hitched when he said her name.

"Maybe there was another one?" Wyatt said. "And you didn't know. How could you?"

Melvin sat down on an overturned paint bucket, his face draining of color. "I never thought of that."

"I don't even have Navy Seals, let alone a battleship to get those things," Owens said.

"Don't forget, we also have to deal with those giant octopuses swimming around," Wyatt added.

"Looked like a mother and her infant, to me. Perhaps they left in search of food in deeper waters. It has pretty much depleted the fish in the bay," Sheldon observed.

"No." Carter shook his head. "We saw it take down a great white yesterday, like it was a guppy. It's been pulling the seals that dare to sun themselves on the rocks."

Wyatt thought for a minute. "Right. I remember that there's a great white nursery just outside of the inlet. We learned about it when I lived here." His face paled. "Feedings are going to be too good for them to leave."

"Look at you, a regular scientist." Sheldon smiled. "You've been hanging around my brother too long."

Owens agreed. "Makes sense," he sighed. "I don't know what to do. It's not like there is a playbook for this kind of thing."

"There has to be a way to destroy those eggs," Melvin muttered. "What would they do in a movie?"

"This is real life, Saunders!" Colonel Drucker snapped.

"Easy, Colonel. These are trying times," Owens responded. "Does anybody know if they have sealed up the leaks in the underground aquarium yet?"

"Yes, sir," Colonel Drucker replied. "In fact, my son, Howard, and his friend, Keisha, are meeting there now to see if they can put together Vincent's phone." He walked over to the map.

The president studied the map and said absently, "Any ideas about where Vincent Konrad and my… and his associates have gone?"

Rosemary entered the tent, shaking off water. "It's starting to rain heavily out there." Grillos stood outside, his mighty body eased down so that he squeezed between a tree and the canvas wall. "Can you hear us?" Rosemary called up to him.

Grillos grumbled an answer and wiped the water from his face.

"I told you to wear a hat," she said.

"Don't nag me," he responded.

Rosemary opened her mouth to reply, but the president spoke instead.

"Well?" Nate Owens' gaze swept the room.

Wyatt cleared his throat. "Howard and *um*… I… *um*… "

"Spit it out, Baldwin!" Major Yerbol, the president's bodyguard, said. He was surrounded by his crew of three. They seemed attached to his hip. They never left his side.

Wyatt took a deep breath and blurted. "Well, sir, we… *um*… think he's aboard an alien ship."

Carter's head snapped up from where he was studying the map. "What!"

"We saw a weird kind of craft moving around at an unbelievable speed. It did some crazy things." Wyatt displayed the pattern with his hands. The room went still.

"Why didn't you mention that earlier?" Carter demanded.

Wyatt shrugged. "In between pirates, giants, and killer clowns, I should have remembered to tell you."

Carter smiled wryly. "I guess so." He turned to Nate Owens. "Do you have anything in the armed forces that can do that kind of maneuvering, Mr. President?"

Owens shook his head. "As Vice President, you'd think they'd let me in on everything, but no. In fact, sometimes I thought many of those politicians had a hidden agenda."

"Like what?" Carter asked.

"I don't know, like they didn't belong, they were different, that they weren't…" Owens searched for the right words.

"Normal?" Sheldon asked. "Maybe they were lizards from another planet masquerading as politicians—"

"Sheldon, not you too. Stop. We don't have time for you or your brother's fantasies," Colonel Drucker ordered.

"What about Area 51?" Melvin called out.

All eyes were on the President. "There are secret documents. I had just been given clearance before the coup happened, and never had a chance to review them." He paused, staring at the floor, and appeared to be speaking to himself. "Things were developing too quickly." Owens touched his forehead, his face troubled. "Look, if there are files with Top Secret clearance, you know there has to be something going on. There is a protocol when the president dies in office, you don't get to see everything until something like that occurs."

"McAdams is dead. Shouldn't you have been debriefed?" Carter's eyes narrowed with distrust.

"He told you. He didn't have time to review them." Yerbol moved defensively in front of the president. His crew is creating an additional circle.

Carter's jaw tightened. He looked from Colonel Drucker to Nate Owens. "I don't believe for one moment that you guys don't know what's going on."

"I understand, Carter. I don't make the rules. Fact is, I was not prepared enough, but then again, maybe McAdams, and for sure, Vincent Konrad never intended for me ever to be President." He looked troubled, his eyes heavy-lidded.

Colonel Drucker took a deep breath and said, "I knew about things." It was silent in the tent but for the patter of the rain and their breathing. Colonel Drucker added, "I was stationed there."

"I knew it!' Wyatt said, wishing Howard were here to witness this. Melvin smiled at him from the other side of the tent.

Carter nodded. "I suspected as much."

"So did I," John Raven said from the corner of the tent. "I worked there," he clarified.

Carter glanced at him with surprise. John Raven sat in a chair in the shadows.

John Raven stood and walked over. "There was a ship, a saucer."

"Thinking of leaving now?" Wyatt smirked at Melvin.

"Not in your life." Melvin laughed.

There was a lot of shuffling, and Grillos shouted to Rosemary, "What are they talking about?"

She shook her head. "I'm not really sure, but I want to know."

Carter waved impatiently for everyone to be quiet. He hadn't stopped his staring contest with Yerbol.

Owens moved between the two men. "Look, you can choose to believe me or not. McAdams kept me in the dark about lots of important information. Sometimes, I wasn't sure why he even had me on the ticket."

"You appealed to the young vote, you know, college kids," Sheldon offered. "Don't underestimate the electoral votes you brought him with California and your home state of Ohio. He wouldn't have won without them."

"This is not the time to rehash the election. You were saying?" Carter said with resolve.

"We all heard about it in Congress. Don't forget all those crazy budgets for two-hundred-thousand-dollar hammers or toilet seats. There was no way to explain things like that except that it was Top Secret. There is a *Need to Know* on all these things, and McAdams made sure I never got the clearance."

"He's telling the truth," Colonel Drucker said. "Very few are privy to the information."

"I can't believe you never said anything to me, John," Carter sounded hurt.

John Raven gave a sheepish shrug. "I was sworn to secrecy. They said they would do something terrible to everyone on the reservation if I said anything."

"I find that hard to believe." Owens looked incredulous.

"There must be other scientists and troops that know," Sheldon called out. "There has to be."

"There've been leaks," John Raven acknowledged, his voice low.

"Yeah, from kooks and conspiracists," Melvin said from his corner.

"That's what I'm talking about. The brass discredits anyone who spills secrets." Raven pushed his dark hair from his eyes. "They'll ruin your life… or worse."

"Yeah, like Otto Enoch," Melvin added. "They fired his ass the minute his accusations got weird."

A dozen voices began speaking at once, and the volume of babble grew in the tent.

Colonel Drucker cleared his throat and spoke over the din. "He's right. They have a way of making you lose credibility if you break with them."

"Well, does anyone want to fill us in?" Carter asked.

"There was a crash, two dead aliens, I never saw them," Colonel Drucker stated. "I

worked with the reverse gravitation people."

"*Whoa!*" Melvin said in awe. "You took their ship apart?"

Colonel Drucker nodded. "Yes, and then my team put it back together."

"What does this have to do with us and my father?" Rosemary asked.

"If Konrad is on an alien ship, it means he's communicating with them, or he could have formed an alliance," Wyatt answered grimly. "There's no way we're going to win against advanced technology like that."

"They'll crush us like bugs," Melvin's comment left them all speechless as they considered the ramifications. "Were they gray, like in the documentaries, with big heads?"

"Yes," Colonel Drucker said.

Grillos spoke from his corner, "We found reptiles."

"Alligators?" Yerbol asked. One of his crew of commandos visibly shivered.

"No, aliens. Reptile aliens," Grillos answered.

"Like lizards?" Wyatt asked.

"Big lizards." Grillos nodded.

"I told you!" Sheldon yelled. "I knew the reptiles were here." He looked at his father. "Did you always know there were more than one kind?"

Colonel Drucker gave his son a stern look and then directed his question to Grillos.

"What happened to them?"

"They were hostile, and so were we. We're bigger." Grillos snapped his fingers. "Also, I forgot. In my father's time, he told us of a ship that crashed. There was talk about a female. They said she was gray."

"What happened to her?" Sheldon asked.

"I don't know. She died, I guess." Grillos shrugged.

John Raven sucked in his breath. "On the reservation, we found gray ones, too. They had these big heads." He opened his palms to look as if he were holding a large object. "We buried them and never said a word."

"It's turning into a two-front war, one from the sky and the other from the sea." Sheldon broke the silence.

"And it sounds like we could be outnumbered." The president's voice was grim.

"As above, so below," Carter said. "As below, so above."

"*Huh?*" Wyatt said to his stepfather.

"It's from the Bible, Matthew 6, verse 10," Sheldon said. "It signifies the connection between the spiritual and physical realms, suggesting that whatever happens in the higher realms is reflected in our world."

"That sounds ominous," Wyatt said. "I think whatever is going on has nothing to do with the spiritual world."

"Yes," Owens said. "It makes a strange kind of sense."

"Anyway, we're in total darkness. We don't know which aliens are working with Konrad, and even if they are at odds with us," Wyatt responded. "They don't have to be."

"Whatever is going to happen, I'm leaving for Monsterland, unless you'd prefer me to stay and help in the fight?" Rosemary asked.

"No," the President said. "Go to Monsterland. You need to organize the giants. I understand they have a World Wide Web," he chuckled.

"Underground," Grillos added. "We will contact our cousins all over the world. This will be a bigger fight than we had with Konrad. We will help save the planet."

Colonel Drucker's face had so little color that Wyatt's stomach tightened into a small ball, and he recognized an acid taste in his mouth from when he was nervous about taking tests. He turned to Carter, searching for an answer, or perhaps for comfort. Carter reached out to rest a hand on his shoulder and squeezed it.

Grillos rose to his full height to leave. Rosemary yelled at him to wait.

"No, go," Owens told her. "Speaking of alliances, we will need one with the giants. All of the giants, even the ones we haven't met yet. It's clear that they trust you."

Rosemary followed the hulking figure as he made his way down the path in the direction of the Hollywood sign.

Owens came back to stare at the map as if it held the answers. "Stop them!"

Yerbol ran to the front of the tent. "They're too far."

"How can you tell?' Wyatt asked.

"The ground isn't shaking from Grillos's footsteps. Move out, catch them!" He shouted to his crew. They took off.

"Give me a piece of paper." Owens snapped his fingers. "We need an agreement, a treaty to bind them to us."

An aide handed the president a spiral notebook. Owens sat down and hastily scribbled a few sentences.

Yerbol stood menacingly in front of him, his expression ending all conversation. Slowly, the senior staff disbursed, orders rapped out by Colonel Drucker's aides.

"Wyatt," Owens called out, waving the paper. "Bring this to Captain Rosemary, stat. Tell them to wait, we need to speak." Wyatt grabbed the paper and raced down the dusty road. His mind drifted back to when he, Howard, Keisha, and Jade went door to door to mobilize Copper Valley after the Battle of Monsterland. There weren't enough for the Glob; would the giants, as allies, be sufficient for what was coming next?

CHAPTER 8

HIS NAME WAS...?

"WE HAVE TO attack before they do. We must be on the offensive," Otto mumbled as he moved around the lab. He was lecturing her again.

Jade grimaced when she touched the patch that covered her eye, wishing she could get a glimpse of what she looked like. A huge scar ran above and below, bisecting her face. It was puffy and sore. "What happened to me?"

Oblivious to her question or discomfort, Otto went on, "They've landed. We're alone in this, but I've been working on something for a long, long time. I need you to tell me everything you know about the aliens."

Again, with the aliens, Jade thought. This guy was nuts. Jade ignored his ramblings and stared sullenly at the stump at the end of her wrist. She was slumped in a hard plastic chair, her back too weak to sit straight. Much as she wanted to get up and pace the room, it was difficult to maneuver around. Her left leg still dragged heavily as if it weren't connected to her brain. With a sigh, she blew the tendrils of hair from her face that stubbornly clung to her sweaty forehead.

Otto piled equipment from one table to another, keeping up his one-sided conversation. "The giants would be a mistake, but the Sasquatch would be better, but they are so elusive." His voice trailed off, and he stopped what he was doing to stare at her. "You're not listening. I need you to remember and tell me where they are landing."

"I have no idea what you're talking about."

Otto leaned close. "Yes, you do. You communicate with the other beasts." He watched her and made a *tsking* sound. "It will be better if it comes to you naturally. If you'd only try to connect-" He held a remote-like device and clicked it rapidly at her chest. Nothing happened. He tossed it aside with a disgusted sound.

Otto wouldn't let her out of his sight, and she had no idea what she looked like. She thought it strange that anything with a reflective surface had been painted over with a dull gray film, preventing her from examining herself. Her face was still numb, and although the skin was smooth, it had the stiff feel of metal rather than flesh. She couldn't coordinate her right hand to rub the spots on her body that ached; what she wouldn't do for a full-body massage, or even a spa pedicure. *Lavender,* she'd order the lavender package even though it was double the price of a regular pedicure.

"Superior smell and hearing might work in locating their enclave, then it's on to the landing site. *Hmmmm.*"

"Stop!" she yelled. "My head hurts." She looked at him and demanded, "What happened to me!"

"You have to remember on your own." He shuffled over and patted her on the back. Jade shrugged him off. "You feel better than yesterday. You are healing at a remarkable rate."

She couldn't think straight. Everything was muddied. Vague memories teased her, pulled from the deepest recesses, only to vanish before she could identify them. She recognized older recollections, but they seemed hazy at best. Jade sighed with frustration. There must have been some brain damage from her time underwater, Otto explained. Only she couldn't recall any of it.

Otto informed her that he had dragged her long after she had stopped breathing. It still hurt to inhale deeply, and her mouth carried a brackish taste that left a slimy feeling on her tongue. She wasn't sure how she ended up in some pond in the middle of nowhere, and the former teacher was cryptic in his answers.

There were long blank periods, and as much as she scrunched her forehead, nothing came back. Her brain felt fuzzy; for that matter, nothing appeared to be functioning in sync with the rest of her. It hurt to think, still, she tried. Her last memory was of her working on a project with Wyatt Baldwin. A lopsided grin tugged at her lips. She knew he had a raging crush on her, and her cheeks tightened with shame.

Jade smiled with chagrin; she was using Wyatt to make a statement to Nolan Malloy, her boyfriend. It wasn't very nice of her, but she had to find a way to get rid of Nolan. The appeal of dating Copper Valley High's star quarterback had faded as their relationship changed. Nolan started charming enough with his fast pickup truck and the perks that came from dating the wealthiest boy in the valley.

She learned there was a price for this. Nolan shared nothing, including her. His possessiveness soon turned uncomfortable. She didn't like having to explain every move she made. Nolan resented it when she went out with her friends. After a girl's night out, he'd be sullen and angry, making their time together no fun at all. His tantrums led to mood swings. Being with him was like walking on eggshells half the time. She had to be careful of anything she said, lest he explode with anger.

Jade was a cherished member of her household and the cheerleading squad. Even her friendship with Keisha was a special one. When Nolan began threatening to beat up her younger brother if she didn't see him more frequently, Jade realized she needed to end the relationship. Being Nolan's girlfriend was not what she expected.

Much as she tried, she couldn't get any of the other kids to ask her out, so when Wyatt provided the opportunity, she grabbed it. He wasn't hard on the eyes and seemed nice enough. Over time, as they worked on their project together, she had grown fond of him. If only Nolan would take the hint and leave her alone.

On top of everything else, her dad was overprotective. She was afraid of telling him what was going on with Nolan. Her father actually liked the meathead and thought she was safe when she went out with him.

Daddy would go nuts if he knew about Nolan and did something that would land him back in prison. That would positively ruin everything. He had just started getting his life back together, and if violence sent him to jail, her mom would have a breakdown.

An overwhelming sadness filled Jade when she thought about her mother and brother. It hung like a dark cloud blotting out all the light. Images of waxy figures with a strange slash down their midsection flashed in her mind; she bit her lip, trying to break the train of thought. *Think about school*, she told herself, and the bright auburn head of Wyatt's friend, of all people, replaced the darker images.

In chemistry, she paired up with Marvin Saunders, *no*, his name was... *Melvin*, Wyatt's best friend. He helped her with the experiments she didn't understand. Most people thought Melvin was strange, but she found his quiet solitude restful. She enjoyed her time with him. He didn't just stare at her and wax on about her prettiness; he talked to her, asked her questions. Some of the kids said he had a weird fascination with werewolves, but when he spoke about them, it was reverential, his voice filled with wonder and awe.

Jade remembered she could be herself with him, and for the first time in her life, she realized that it was comforting. Everyone expected her to show up polished and perfect, not Melvin. He accepted her, even if she had a huge pimple on her face! She had fantasized about spending the evening with him, laughing that the idea would shock her friends. *Jade, the Copper Valley High Homecoming Queen, is dating the school freak.* Only, she never saw him as a freak. Whether it was with Wyatt or that kid, Melvin, she needed to make sure Nolan got the message she wasn't interested in him anymore.

Jade glanced over at Otto. The teacher was fiddling with the wall of computers that hummed and beeped. The constant whirring of their engines made her head pound. It was so loud.

"Mr. Enoch, I have to go home now. My dad is going to kill me," she whined.

Otto looked at her strangely.

"I need to go back to school."

Still no response but a look of pity.

"I have to pass science or I won't graduate."

Otto went about his business, ignoring her. She heard the microwave *ping*, and Otto

plunked a hot dog and beans on a paper plate before her. She hadn't eaten much for days. Her mouth watered from the smell of food. Finally, her stomach growled with interest.

"*Ah.*" Otto's face lit up. "See, your organs are beginning to work again. I told you you'll start feeling better soon."

"That's disgusting. They've never stopped working."

"Well, that's true. Let's agree that they took a break of sorts. A rest, if you will, while you recover."

Jade jumped to her feet, using her remaining hand to balance herself by gripping the back of the chair. Eying the doorway, she shook her head and turned her face away. "I don't eat meat."

"Peculiar," Otto said slyly.

"Why?" Jade demanded. "Why do you find that strange?" The last word came out in such a guttural snarl that surprised even Jade.

Otto snickered condescendingly. "Well, for one thing, your father *is* a butcher."

She shook her head, slightly dizzy. "I don't know what came over me."

Otto observed her keenly. "Your strength is returning. From the bone broth and meat I've put in your food."

Jade shuddered. "I told you, I don't eat meat." She paused and asked. "You said, for one thing. What's the other?"

Otto returned a secretive smile. Easing himself opposite her at the table, he pushed the plate to the other side of the surface. "Think about it."

A cloudy memory flitted through her mind. Taking a deep breath, she smelled blood and roasting meat. Saliva coated her mouth, her body recoiled, turned inward at an image of her sitting at a campfire gnawing on a bone of gristle.

"I think you do like this." Otto eased the plate even closer, his eyes never leaving hers. "Let the memories come."

Auburn hair again filled her brain. She heard the echo of a giggle, the memory of a freckled bare chest being pounded. She knew only two things: it wasn't Nolan's body, and she missed the strong arms attached to it.

Curling her hand into a fist, her knuckles whitening, she hit her temple. "Remember," she whispered.

"It will come back," Otto said, his voice all sympathetic. It felt fake, and Jade moved to stare at the wall. "You have to eat to get stronger. Yesterday, you didn't mind eating it."

"I don't remember yesterday. Why is it so messed up?" She dashed a tear from her remaining eye, her hand movements clumsy.

"Enough said for now. You'll understand once we get you feeling like your old self."

Jade wasn't quite sure what her old self was. Confused and disjointed, she shifted between the perception of being a perfectly dressed but uptight student, head cheerleader, vegan, and yet, there were other recollections, scenes of a dark beach in the shadow of ruins, a red-haired boy, a sensation of complete freedom, worry-free, and the lack of pressure to be perfect. "I want to go home." The words came out as a whimper, feeling unnatural. She knew she used to complain, but somehow she understood that had changed.

Otto leaned down. "Poor, dear, butterfly."

Cringing, she turned inward, creeped out by Otto. She wanted to go home, even if the idea of home was a hazy, mysterious concept. "Don't call me that!"

"Why, you're my butterfly. My little changeling."

"Stop that, you freak!"

Jade hid her face with her one barely working hand. She was trapped and knew there was more to her story. Otto's following words chilled her to the bone. "It's all gone, Butterfly. Remember what I taught you in school? I told you they would do it. Those damn politicians finally made a deal with the reptilians, the ones from space. They've gone and destroyed our world." Otto was sweating, his bald head looking like unbaked bread, his eyes wide and unblinking. "All the things I've warned you all about when you were in my class." His cheeks

turned as red as apples, and spit flew from his lips. He hit the table with his hand, emphasizing each word that came from his frothing mouth. "I warned you all. They're descendants of Charlemagne, each one of them!"

Jade had no idea what he was ranting about. She lowered her gaze, afraid of him.

"Progeny of the reptilians. They are conquering the world, one country at a time." He dropped to one knee and came close to her face. She backed away, uncomfortable with his invasion of her personal space. "They're taking over the government. Deals! They make deals with the aliens."

Jade's one eye opened wide. She shook her head and pleaded, "Please, please let me go home."

"I can't, little butterfly. I need you."

"You can't keep me here."

"That's true," he told her with maddening calm. "You have to find them. You will go outside and direct me where to go."

"I don't even know where I am!"

"You do. You do. You just have to clear your mind. I need to know where we should go, East or West, North or South."

"I'm confused. I want to go home."

"Think, Jade. Close your eyes and think about where the aliens will go."

Jade closed her working eye, trying to relax her body. Every muscle screamed with pain, but if she wanted to get away from this lunatic, she'd play his game.

"That's right," Otto urged. "Let the thoughts come. Which direction should we go?"

Her mind wandered. She was walking down a tunnel. It was dark, but she was not alone. Squeezing her eyes tight, she concentrated hard. It smelled in the tunnel, and it was filled with a waxy residue. A waxy, gray residue.

"A tunnel."

"Where, where is the tunnel?"

"I don't know!"

Otto was leaning over her. He shook her by her shoulders.

"Stop! You're hurting me."

"The tunnel! Tell me about the tunnel." His face was wild.

Her head rolled to the side. She was exhausted. "It's a secret place. Underground."

"There's a secret tunnel that runs to Area 51. Is that where they're telling you to go?"

Jade shook her head, feeling exhaustion pull at her. Otto held her chin captive, squeezing her bruised flesh. Jade reared up, adrenaline coursing through her veins. She grabbed his wrist in a vise-like grip. As soon as he mentioned Area 51, Jade's stomach tightened. She had a visceral need to run. Her muscles twitched, and she knew on some level Otto Enoch was right. She needed to go. "What are you talking about?" she demanded. Her body felt strange.

"Yes! Yes! You're better. You can do it," he screamed. "You're finally going to morph!"

Jade squeezed harder, watching Otto wince. She could hear the bones of his wrist grinding against each other. He was panting, but then so was she. Looking up, she let out a howl. It erupted from her throat like a volcano and felt so right, like a great release. It echoed in the soundproof room, bouncing off the walls. Tears were streaming down Otto's flushed cheeks. He was babbling about pyramids being interdimensional portals, giants living in underground cities, Mothmen, Wendigos, and dragons. For a minute, Jade wished she had paid more attention in school.

Teeth, sharp and pointed, filled her mouth, which extended to an elongated snout. It hurt. Her skin pulled, ripping as if it were being stretched over a tight drum top. Jade glanced at the hand imprisoning Otto's forearm. It had changed into a hairy, claw-shaped appendage. This was a fever dream, it had to be! Blinking twice, she hoped the image would disappear. Jade opened her mouth and screamed.

"It's happening! Can you control it, dear?" Otto's frantic words seemed far away.

"No! No. You've drugged me. It's a hallucination," Jade insisted. Otto laughed at her.

Jade squinted, her gaze glued to the reflection in Otto's wire-rimmed glasses. She realized she was looking at a werewolf. Turning her head to the right and then left, she searched the room, her mouth drying with the comprehension that there was no one else there.

"This is a dream, a nightmare," she panted. "You're giving me drugs. It's not real." She squeezed Otto's wrist and growled. "Make it stop!"

He grabbed the remote and aimed it at her. When nothing

happened, he threw it at her face. It clinked against the metal when it hit her.

"You're killing me, girl! Release!" Otto stopped laughing and shouted. "Release, I said!"

His command frightened her. She shivered.

Jade dropped his hand, feeling nauseous, fighting the need to rip out his throat and feast on his blood. What was she thinking? *She's a vegan!*

Otto was babbling again. "It's all come to pass, everything I warned them about. Did they listen? No, they branded me a nutjob, a maniac, a conspiracist." He looked her full in the face. Jade knew then he was insane. "No worries, my dear. I've prepared. I will save what's left of the world."

Jade lay her head on the table, her heart sinking. Everything was gone: her beauty, her confidence, her world. This couldn't be true. She was a prisoner of a madman who was making her think crazy things.

Her tongue lolled, and exhaustion pulled at her. All the tension fled, and she felt herself shrinking back into her body again. One pale hand lay on the table next to her face. It looked human. She was human. She was a human stuck in a nightmare.

Instinctively, Jade realized she had indeed changed in some terrible way. She knew without thinking that she was no longer vegan and didn't seem to care about it. She was not Jade of Copper Valley High; she was something else.

A tear slid from her eye to plop on the metal tabletop. Another followed it. Jade was trapped in a body she didn't recognize. If what Otto said was true, she didn't have a home anymore. Something tugged at her heart. Raising her head, she stared hard at Otto. He had scurried away from her to a workstation and was fiddling with a metal contraption.

"Don't be upset, I'll be attaching a prosthetic hand tomorrow, and I might be able to install your new eye the day after."

She stared forlornly at her stump. *I will not let you change me. I must go home,* she thought. A hole burned where her heart beat under her skin. She knew she had a home where she'd find out the truth. She just couldn't remember where it was.

CHAPTER 9

DON'T FORGET TO ADD ROSEMARY

VINCENT HAD BEEN deep in thought ever since they left the bridge of the spaceship.

"I think Spekator and his kind are up to something," he complained to Dreg. "You! You let them keep me asleep too long. I could have prepared for this...this—"

"Pickle," Dreg supplied. "Hardly, Vincent. They tried, they really did, but I made them stop when I saw steam coming from your ears! Besides, we're stuck on this ship."

"Exactly. We need to get down there and take control."

"B... but—" Dreg stuttered. "We can't tell them what to do."

"What does that mean?"

"That they care about our... I mean, your position. They've been very nice. Hospitable. Vincent, if you could see how tenderly they took care of you…"

Vincent slapped him, his plastic hand awkward. The door *whooshed* open, and Spekator drifted into the room.

"Is all well, Doctor?" Spekator's voice had a hint of menace.

"As well as can be expected," Vincent grumbled. "Since your enemies are now circling the planet, I believe timing is becoming critical."

"For once, we agree, Doctor. We are moving into action. We will deposit you on the planet's surface—"

"Put me in the mountains, near Copper Valley—"

"The giants are in those mountains. It's not safe. Aren't you their sworn enemy?"

Vincent fumed. "It's where I need to be."

Spekator narrowed his almond-shaped eyes. "You need to be where we set you down.

We will be the judge of that."

"The giants have joined forces with humanity," Vincent declared. "I have to regroup with my militia— and find my daughter. We need to capture her before she births the child."

Spekator's ghostly brow furrowed. "This is true, doctor. But we find we are not happy with how you left things on the planet." His voice became cold. "You were supposed to keep them all from forming pacts with each other. You promised to control them with your zombies! You said the humans were indolent and ripe for our takeover."

"You concern yourself with nonsense. I know the giants. They don't trust anybody. They'll be at each other's throats in no time. Giants have been underground for so long, they will never be able to get along with any species."

"Being isolated has resulted in them being unspoiled by technology," Spekator said. "They might make a good hybrid."

"Giants are unstable. They must be eradicated, just like the rest of the monsters. Most humans are weak, stupid, and easily influenced. While they might make better subjects, there are others to consider," Vincent told him.

"We want only the strongest, like your daughter. You indicated she is superior in most things when we first communicated."

Vincent smiled, a feeling of pride seeping into his chest. "Yes, yes, she is. Just do whatever you have to do to get me down there so I can begin preparing for your invasion. I'll regroup with my armed forces once I land and choose the species," Vincent ordered.

"You forget, Doctor, that you are *our* guest." Spekator's pale temple trembled and then pulsed angrily. "You don't give orders here."

The room was quiet, except for the sound of Dreg's breathing and a strange, thumping beat coming from Spekator. Vincent saw Spekator's soft, rounded shoulders tense. He glared at the alien, noticing the opalescence of the color had changed.

If Spekator had eyebrows, Vincent knew they'd be raised. He wondered how such a blank-looking face could appear contemptuous. Still, Vincent couldn't rein himself in. "If you would agree to blast the colony they've created in Los Angeles—"

"We've discussed this already, Doctor. It is forbidden to use our weapons on your planet, yet."

"They must be brought to heel if we are to regain control," Vincent demanded.

They moved so close that they appeared to be toe to toe.

"That will violate the Milky Way Intergalactic Treaty of 10954 and bring Va'Rok wrath down upon us." Spekator's voice was clipped, as if all his patience had run out.

"Don't patronize me," Vincent warned.

"I am not being patronizing," Spekator's voice had definitely changed. It had a commanding quality. "Time is running out. We have to claim Earth as our territory, starting with the birth of my child implanted in your daughter's womb."

"Perhaps other aliens have spread their spawn on Earth as well. There've been rumors about it for years." Vincent's voice turned speculative. "You know, I always thought McAdams had a reptilian quality about him." He paced the room. "That's why I had him eliminated.

"You expressed some concern about his Vice President as well while we were operating on you."

"Never," Dreg exploded. "Nate was a good boy. My boy. Flesh of my flesh, not some alien lizard!"

"Water under the bridge, Dreg. Nate's gone and—"

"And what?" Dreg demanded, his face filled with fury.

"And let's not forget his great sacrifice for our cause." Vincent neatly turned the conversation. "I will erect a statue in his honor when we gain control, once again."

Dreg retreated to a corner, biting the cuticles of his fingers, his eyes darting around the room.

Vincent turned to Spekator. "Let's not deviate from our mission. We have to destroy all invading species and keep the least intelligent to enslave with me as the Supreme Leader."

"The last thing the Intergalactics want is a bloodbath in space. No doctor, whoever gets to claim first rights, includes Earth and Earth's resources in the new Intergalactic Map." Spekator seemed to inflate and loomed closer so that the two holes that served as nostrils almost touched Vincent. "*We* colonize and choose which breed survives. If the child takes it, it looks good for *your* humanity."

Vincent made a sound of disgust. "Then you better make sure that the Thalens are victorious, and we both know that won't happen if I am left here to rot!"

"Are you threatening me, Doctor?" Spekator turned to leave the room but halted as Vincent continued, "I never agreed to choose humans as the surviving species."

"Come now, Doctor. It was a foregone conclusion. Vampires, werewolves, and zombies are too unstable. The giants appear too large to handle. Who does that leave?"

"Exactly *who* do you think you can trust on Earth?" Vincent laughed.

The room turned icy.

"The Sasquatch has its appeal," Vincent said quietly.

Spekator ignored the comment. "Unfortunately, the Va'Rok have always shown a peculiar interest in the Sasquatch."

"If you don't even know what Va'Rok looks like, how could you have this information?"

"We have our sources, Doctor." Spekator moved closer to Vincent, and his voice took on a menacing tone. "Believe me, Doctor. You don't want either the Scalis or the Va'Rok to win this contest."

Vincent paced the room. "I just want my planet back."

"As we promised, Doctor, along with the species we expect you to dominate."

Spekator turned to them both, the iridescent uniform glowing a rainbow of colors and emitting a sound that made both of them wince.

Dreg erupted from the corner and grabbed Vincent's arm, as if to rein him in. Vincent jerked away with a start, flinching.

"That's exactly why I created Monsterland!" he sneered, purple saliva flecking his lips. "Negotiation won't work with any of them. You need me."

Spekator nodded abruptly. "We are not naive; we know why you created Monsterland. However, we do agree it will be easier to negotiate a treaty with one type of being instead of multiple species."

"That's right," Vincent was smug. "Me. You have to work with me. I hold the ultimate power."

"No, *we* hold the ultimate power."

There was a tense minute where nobody spoke; Spekator stared at them without blinking his large, almond-shaped eyes.

Vincent grabbed his skull. Intense pressure was building inside his head as if it would explode.

A tendril of steam rose from Vincent's nose, his cheeks flushed. Vincent was sure of two things. Spekator was proving these aliens held the upper hand for the supposed treaty, and he could indeed blow both Dreg's and his mind. The temperature seemed to freeze the room, Spekator's dark eyes iced over.

"I spearheaded this project with your Dr. Frasier. I brought it to the Grand Council. If you fail, then I've failed," Spekator's voice was loud in their heads. "And *I* never fail."

There was an intense minute, and Spekator spoke again, his tone conciliatory. "You had to realize that once we impregnated your daughter, the choice would be humans, unless they proved them-selves to be completely inept. Speaking of your daughter, she must be entering the second semester of her pregnancy."

Vincent whipped his head around so fast that it almost fell off. "What do you mean by semester? Pregnancy contains three. It's called a trimester."

Spekator nodded. "Yes, with a human child, it takes nine months. Our offspring have a gestation period of four months. At this point, she should be halfway into her term and growing larger by the moment."

Vincent frowned. "What do you mean?"

"She needed to be watched and examined. We are not sure if she will be able to handle the gestational sac that surrounds our infants."

"She's normal, larger than most women on the planet," Vincent said.

"I would call her a raw-boned female," Dreg offered.

"Be that as it may, she might become incapacitated by all the fluids. It could tax her vital organs. She is smaller than our female counterparts."

"You didn't share that information with me."

"The nurse we provided had all the necessary medical details. Too bad, it may become too much of a burden for her. We had planned to remove the child before—"

"You never prepared us with this inform—." Vincent's pale face turned magenta.

"Careful, Doctor Konrad, it's your own fault. You should have secured her better."

Vincent gnashed his teeth and spun away to watch the earth rotating outside his porthole. "I'll find her. She's a wily one," Vincent said with pride. "But I'll find her once I get down there."

"You'd better. Have you ever heard of the term semelparity?"

Vincent went utterly still.

Spekator sighed. "I can see by your reaction that you understand."

The alien exited the room. Dreg turned to Vincent. "What game are you playing, Vincent? And, you can't believe that Nate was some sort of reptile!"

"Of course, not Dreg. He was an unfortunate casualty. Happens all the time. Look,

It's not a game. This is war. We need to head into the mountains above Monsterland."

"The mountains? Why?"

Vincent glanced at the closed portal to their room and leaned close to Dreg's ear. "Last year, I began negotiations with a community of Sasquatch hiding in the upper hills," he whispered.

"Sasquatch," Dreg spat. "Troublemakers. Always toying with us, showing a little fur, and then hiding like cowards. Why would you…" Dreg's eyes widened with shock. "You don't trust the Thalens." It was a statement, not a question.

"I always hedge my bets. Besides, these aliens use the same tactics," Vincent said firmly. "I've seen their bait-and-run tricks. Crafts with blue lights that play hide and seek with the air force. They have more in common with the hairy beasts than they know. Why not enlist them?"

"That was not in the original plan."

"Neither was the presence of the Scalis and Va'Rok! We don't know anything about them. Damn that Keisha for turning Dr. Frasier into stone."

Dreg smiled, remembering how much he hated the scientist.

Good riddance to him. He wasn't too thrilled with the idea of meeting a Sasquatch, those overgrown apes. "They may not be happy if we work with the…the Bigfoots," he spat. "Besides, how could you set up a meeting from way up here?" Dreg snorted.

"All I have to do is give a signal once we land. We communicate using a pattern of pine cones in a special spot in the forest. They always have a scout nearby. It's amazingly efficient. They'll be there."

"Boss, you think of everything," Dreg said with admiration and then remembered Spekator's last words. "What does semelparity mean?"

Vincent remained silent, his face contorted with anger.

"Vincent?" Dreg prodded.

"It means that, like some creatures on Earth, like deep-sea octopus, scorpions, and Pacific salmon, the females die after giving birth."

Dreg was speechless.

"We must get down there, make contact with the Sasquatch, and find Rosemary." Vincent paced the room.

"Bigfoot. I hate those guys."

"Don't be obtuse, Dreg. Your feelings on these things don't matter."

"That's a big planet. She could be anywhere." Dreg scratched his head.

Vincent turned to a porthole, his eyes glued to the surface of Earth. "She's going home to Monsterland." He put his hand on his chest, above the place where his heart used to be. "I can feel it right here."

CHAPTER 10

FEE FIE FOE FUM

ROSEMARY WALKED FROM the tent, doubling her pace to catch up to Grillos. "Hey, where are you headed?"

"It's time we returned to my people. Time is running out. We must mobilize the other clans."

"Wait." Rosemary tugged on the hem of his shirt. Grillos stopped and folded his arms across his broad chest. Breathless from running, she held her belly. She could swear it had grown in the last few hours. Rosemary gestured back at the encampment. "Don't you think we should wait for those shell things to hatch? Maybe we can help."

Grillos raised his eyebrows and then glanced at her stomach. "Don't you think we should protect her?" he asked.

Rosemary looked down and smiled. "It's too early to know the baby's gender."

Grillos pointed to the long spine of his nose. "*Fee, fie, foe, fum,* I smell the presence of a wee girly one."

"Now that's a superpower." Rosemary forced a laugh.

"*Harumph,*" Grillos grumbled. "You heard your president. He told you to return with me and open up negotiations between our clans, organize them. This way, we can protect the human flank."

Rosemary furrowed her brows. It was true. Still, she didn't like leaving in the middle of a fight. She had friends here and worried about the looming difficulties ahead. Despite their alliance, she sensed an element of distrust between them. Rosemary couldn't put her finger on it. Grillos was nice enough, but there was definitely a frosty air surrounding his brothers.

They were none too happy to leave the girls, especially their father. Rosemary sighed, wondering if she bit off more than she could chew. With the baby coming, did she want to take on the responsibility of making the giants feel safe? It was not her nature to be a diplomat.

Grillos turned to walk again, pausing when he noticed Rosemary was staring longingly at the ocean. "I will show you a new ocean, one that's underground. I promise it will take your breath away."

"An ocean underground? Well, that's something I want to see."

"The most beautiful place in the world."

"If it's so beautiful, why do you want to leave your home?"

"It's a long story."

"Jötnar always says that." Rosemary tossed her hair impatiently while speaking about her former first mate. "I think it's your way of avoiding things."

"Perhaps," Grillos said thoughtfully. "Jötnar had secrets. But now, he's fine, *eh*? He has found a home among the humans, just as you will find a home among the giants. You will learn that it is our custom to hold onto our worries. Giants accept the way of the world. What's the use of complaining?"

"I disagree. Your nieces aren't so accepting of their fate. Their willingness to discuss it has brought their plight out into a conversation. Don't you think an open dialogue is important? How else can you expect to be heard?"

"I assume you had this… *open dialog* on your boat, Captain?"

"That's different!" Rosemary snapped. "You need tight control when you are captaining a *ship*," she said, emphasizing the last word. "Otherwise there'll be chaos… possibly even a mutiny." Shading her eyes, she peered at him. "It is my job as the captain to keep everyone safe."

"And so it is mine as the leader of my clan to enforce our laws for our society. We need strict rules due to our limited resources." Grillos smiled, revealing a mouthful of huge teeth. "For the safety of everyone."

"That sounds a bit oppressive." Rosemary winced.

"If it makes sense for you on a ship, why shouldn't it make sense for us? Rosemary, don't judge until you see the entire picture. Our limited land and food resources necessitate the enforcement of these laws. It's the only way to ensure our survival. We've been held hostage underground for years by humanity. Our lairs are filled with all sorts of dangers, prohibiting the growth of our community."

"Now that you will be surface dwellers, maybe you can relax your legislation."

Grillos looked down his long nose at her. "Did you ease your rules when you weren't on the ship, Captain Rosemary?"

Rosemary firmed her lips, and she didn't answer. Glancing backwards, he saw the hostile glares of Grillos's brothers. She was unused to being questioned. She was the commander, and as such, she determined the law. Every sailor accepted these edicts; otherwise, there was the specter of an overthrow. "I told you, I do the things I need to keep everyone safe," she said more to herself than Grillos.

Grillos chuckled. "You think we don't. Our civilization is old. We created laws over time as problems cropped up. Come along." He reached down for her to hop onto his arm and perch herself on his shoulder. "Let's get you packed so we can leave, and while we travel, I'll tell you our story."

Rosemary studied the encampment. "It doesn't feel right to leave them."

Grillos shrugged, nearly dislodging her. Rosemary grabbed a handful of his shirt.

"I don't know. They've managed a couple of millennia without us before. If there is indeed a threat from invaders from the sky or the ocean, I will have to prepare my people. I have a responsibility to them first."

"It won't be more than a two-day journey, correct? Your base is behind the defunct theme park?"

"Yes, but there are dangers if we travel in the mountains."

"Why travel in the mountains, then?"

"We must return quickly. We may face dangers you are not prepared for. I must think of my brothers as well as your safety, especially in those hills." He looked at the mountains separating them from the desert.

Rosemary nodded with understanding. She protected her mates with the fierceness of a mama bear. The sailors were her tribe, just as the giants who lived underground were Grillos's responsibility. She started to ask about the various dangers, but a voice interrupted her.

"Rosemary!"

She heard her name being called. Twisting from her spot, she saw Wyatt running after her, waving a paper in his hand. "President Owens wants you to have this." Wyatt rolled it into a scroll and held it aloft.

Grillos bent so she could grab the scroll from Wyatt.

"It's the treaty," he called up to her.

"Let me see," she said, scanning the document. It was a hastily prepared statement that indicated the alliance between giant-kind and humanity. She frowned. Simply put, it said they would protect each other in the event of an attack. "President Owens is on the way. He asked you to wait for him."

Rosemary felt Grillos's chest shudder with an impatient sigh.

"I'm sure it won't take long." She tapped him to let her slide down his arm. She saw the president moving in her direction, followed by a trio of uniformed commandos.

"Glad we caught you before you left, Captain." The president was breathless.

"I would have waited..."

The president waved off her comment and looked up at Grillos. "I need you to mobilize your people."

Grillos nodded.

"We don't know how bad this is going to be when those eggs hatch." He pointed back to the ocean. "This is a time for us to unite our species." He paused for a minute and took a deep breath. "There's a chance Vincent is alive and on an alien ship."

Rosemary paled, her hand automatically moving over her belly to protect her unborn child.

"Are you sure?" Grillos glanced up at the sky.

"No." Owens shook his head. "It's a theory, but it does make sense about his sudden disappearance. In any case, we are going to need all the help we can get."

"Depending on which ship it belongs to," Grillos said grimly.

"Which ship?" Owens said. "Care to elaborate?"

Grillos shuddered. "Yes, as we said back in the command tent, there are many kinds that have come here. We found Grays and lizards. We've heard from some of my cousins that they have had run-ins with Blues and even human-looking ones that could fool you." Grillos's orange-flecked eyes scanned the faces of the humans surrounding them.

Nate Owens stared at the giant. "Go on." He shook his head. "I wish they had shared the information with me."

"Some are good, others-' He shrugged. "They have visited here before and disrupted all life on earth. It is in our book, written by the old ones."

"What book?" Wyatt asked before anyone could comment.

"A story of our people, from the beginning of time."

"Can we see this book?" the President inquired.

Grillos took a deep breath. "No one has seen it for ages. It is locked deep in one of our caves. It tells the history of our diaspora and what *others* did to us."

"Why would they hide that away?" Wyatt asked. "And just who are the others?"

"We don't like to speak of it. Our book is the Holiest of Holies and hidden from all eyes. We believe that if you read it, it will happen again."

"That makes no sense," Yerbol said from his spot behind the president. His commandos stood to the side, at ease.

"Indeed, it does. Sometimes, even if you think about something, you will make it happen. That's why it's forbidden for us to argue or curse somebody in our clan."

Wyatt screwed up his eyes in thought. "I've heard of that from Howard. It's called mani-something."

"Manifestation," the President offered. "It's a concept that if you read it and think about it, it will turn into reality."

"Like me," Melvin said. "I read and thought about becoming a werewolf; I made it happen." He came up from behind Wyatt, slightly breathless from running.

Yerbol made a face. "That's stupid. I want to manifest weapons to defeat the monsters, and it's clear that's not going to happen."

The president held up his hand, halting the conversation. "It begs investigation."

"Well, sounds to me like *someone's* been reading it," Melvin said.

"I must go now. If the Gray ones have returned, we have much to do." Grillos's voice echoed in the small clearing. "Now, can we get on with our journey?"

"I don't understand." Rosemary looked at Owens, her face stark against her dark, red hair. "I don't feel right about leaving."

"Excuse us for a minute." Owens took her arm and pulled Rosemary off to the side. "Grillos trusts you." He rubbed his forehead as if it pained him. Rosemary noticed ink smears on the edge of his palm. She knew he had created the hastily scribbled document. "You have to go with them and make sure you can convince them to help us. This is bigger than you can imagine. We've got enemies both above and below. We are going to need all the help they can provide."

Rosemary looked at him as if she couldn't comprehend.

"There have to be hundreds of thousands of giants underneath us. According to one of Grillos's brothers, they have honeycombed the entire earth with tunnels to connect the assorted clans. They have the means for us to defend the planet."

Rosemary nodded with understanding. "Without an air force or navy, we will be able to reach distant places without crossing an ocean or large land masses."

"Exactly! But we must earn their trust. I am afraid that humans have not treated them well. When I think about… well… I am ashamed of the things we've done to them." He reached out to grasp her arm. "You must go and assure them we will not do those things again."

"I understand, sir. We'll be back. Together, we will save the planet."

The president saluted her, and Rosemary returned the gesture.

CHAPTER 11

OLREC OF THE SIERRA MOUNTAINS

OLREC SNARLED INTO the mirror, revealing long, pointed canines. He noticed the tip of one tooth was missing. "So much for my fierce grin." Since Olrec of the Sierra Mountains passed his fiftieth year, he had to admit to himself that he wasn't feeling all that dangerous. Last month, he shamefully realized that his fearsome roar sounded more like a weak whimper, and the pack of *stupes* he stumbled into barely registered his presence. It probably didn't help that they were half-dead zombies. His face flushed with embarrassment at their total lack of reaction.

Olrec was equally anxious that *he* failed to see them, coupled with the fact that they apparently didn't care that he did. He wasn't called the Great Night Owl in his youth for nothing. His night vision was legendary, and lately, he had found himself squinting more in the dark than he would have liked.

Anytime Olrec lumbered into the forest, he knew the tall trees enveloped him like a cloak. He walked with deliberation, meticulous in the placement of his feet. It took a considerable amount of talent for his big body to sidestep the soft, mushy earth and not create a trail, no less evidence of his existence. He was the epitome of carefulness.

He was taught that his footprints were considered prized possessions for the *stupe* population. Ever watchful for pockets of mud, he'd balanced on mossy beds or dried piles of leaves. Keeping alert, he took extra precautions to avoid the odd pesky humans wandering around. If only the Watchers would return and take care of their enemies below ground. After all, it was promised in the misty legends of the past.

In all his years, he looked back with pride; he left no evidence, not a hide nor hair, or even a footprint. He was pretty sure he'd never been photographed.

This skill was considered a great value to the pack. Some of the younger members often brought danger, playing cat and mouse with souvenir hunters, getting too close for comfort to their hiding spots, or even the village where they and their clan lived. There was a general rule in their group: you could play hide and seek all you want, but never bring them near the settlement.

Olrec loved sharing his expertise with the next generation. He was adept at disguising tracks, secreting skat, or any other evidence of their existence. When Kokkus, his toxic brother-in-law, was elected as head of the tribal council, everything changed overnight. Kokkus thought Olrec had gotten sloppy and took every opportunity to minimize Olrec. He criticized everything Olrec did. He was also opposed to any form of fraternization with humans. His philosophy was to leave humans and their diseases below them on the flatlands.

Olrec understood that, but humans were slowly encroaching on their homeland. Rock climbers, nature freakin' lovers, and now the zombies were making encampments too close to home. Someone had to go and destroy their campsites, forcing them to go home.

He couldn't help but notice that Kokkus was much shorter than he was. He knew it pricked Kokkus's pride. It always had, from the first day he courted Zilli. Lately, though, his brother-in-law had been especially caustic.

It started in earnest a few months ago, when he tripped on a rope, alerting a *stupe* encampment of their presence. They were spying to count the humans. Anybody would have missed it. *And, who hangs pots and pans in the middle of the forest anyway?* Why were *stupes* up this far North?

Their scouting party followed, and for the first time, the *stupes* got too close. Fear ripped through the village. Some of the elders wanted to relocate again, but the younger generation dug in and refused to budge. They held a meeting in the town center.

"It's always something," Jofro the Younger complained. "We're bigger than the hairless ones, more powerful. Why should we tiptoe around them? Let's show them!" A group of younger cubs tittered.

"Don't be rude!" Zilli shouted. "Call them what they are, *stupes.*"

"What we call them, or what they call themselves, Zilli? They refer to their kind as humans," Olrec told her.

"Stupes is what they are and always will be!" Zilli answered. "They bring chaos and disease wherever they go," Zilli responded, her arms folded over her chest.

"I agree with my sister, and we must keep away from them. We were here first!" Kokkus reminded everyone. "And we'll be here long after they've destroyed their own homes. We don't have to do anything."

"Remember what happened when we shared the land with the giants! They ruined it, ate all the food until there was nothing left," Frendo called out. "We had to make them move, and I say we do the same to the *stupes!*"

The crowd cheered.

Kokkus raised his hands. "Everyone, quiet down. We live in relative peace. We don't want hairless…" He laughed. "I mean, *stupes* invading our space. As long as we stay out of their areas, we'll be fine."

"But they aren't staying in their locations. They are making camps closer and closer." Frendo stood. "And there is no reasoning with the dead-looking ones. Talk about no brainers!"

The argument sparked a significant rift within the tribe. The young ones in the village desired to reveal themselves and mark their territory. They wanted to scare the interlopers away.

Olrec found himself solidly in the middle. He understood the need for secrecy, but he thought the young cubs did have the right idea. His clan wouldn't have been harried this far up the mountain, fearful of their existence.

After all, look what *stupes* did to the giants. Forcing them several millennia ago to move to higher ground, they invaded and compromised their tribe's territory. It was discovered there was not enough room for both his kind and giant-kind. Those overgrown monsters destroyed everything, taking down trees and consuming the food sources. They simply could not share the space. After an epic battle, his species was able to push the giants underground, where they belonged. Let the giants fight it out with the poisonous slugs and see who wins.

Olrec looked at where the cobalt sky met the snow-covered peak of the hills he loved. He shook his head. If they were uprooted from their homes and had to resettle further north, their hair would turn as white as his cousins across the sea.

The argument raged on around him, young against old, warmonger against peace-seekers. He took Zilli's hand inside his own and patted it.

"We forced the giants from our land," Kokkus shouted. There were grunts of agreement. "Let's not disturb a sleeping enemy."

"That was ages ago, old one," Jofro the Younger shot back. "The giants are afraid of us now. They are without allies. The *stupes* are intrigued. I say we use this to our advantage. Why should we be relegated to the hills alone! When the Watchers first came—"

"Forbidden!" Kokkus screamed, drowning out the younger cubs.

"Why? It's our story and we should be able—"

Kokkus stood and brandished the staff of leadership at Jofro. "We must never speak of the Watchers, and so it has been said." He walked around the fire, his voice low and quiet. Many had to strain to hear him. "We leave no written record. We sing no songs of their journey here. We must not share the story of our ancestors who landed in ancient times." He shook his staff, and the acorns and pinecones attached rattled noisily. "We honor their memory, those who gave us life and a haven by keeping their story…*here*." He pressed his fist to his chest.

"That's all they are, fables, old stories, myths—" Jofro shouted. "We don't even know what we are looking for!"

Several of the crowd gasped. There were the sounds of grumbling, even a curse or two.

"It's true, if only the elders had drawn pictures or written it down, we'd know what to look for. All we know is that one will come and she will save us," Kokkus replied.

Jofro stood, and a group of the younger cubs gathered around him. "You are old, and it's time to change our ways. We are tired of waiting for the saviors who may never come!" They stormed off.

A movement sprang from that night. Junior members of the tribe wanted to change the policy and howl in their presence. They were tired of hiding. Everyone knew vampires existed, and no one gave a rat's ass about the werewolves. But *noooooo*, the Sasquatch had to remain a myth.

This argument made Kokkus and the older members of the pack angry. Olrec found himself drifting into the rebellious point of view.

"By the great goddess, Tala, why do we have to be a secret?"

A shocked silence fell over the table after Olrec's question. Kokkus joined them for dinner after the meeting.

"Don't swear!" Zilli hissed. "The cubs can hear you." She gave a meaningful glance at their two male cubs wrestling in the front room.

Laughing, Kokkus said, "Use your brain, Olrec. Even if we wanted them to see us, it should be to terrify *stupes,* not entertain them."

"You should meet with that doctor. The one who built Monsterland, Kon-something," Zilli announced. "Konroad? What does he go by?"

"Konrad, Vincent Konrad," Olrec supplied.

"Olrec, control your female. Don't encourage her," Kokkus hissed.

Olrec felt his face go red. "I may not agree with Zilli, but I always listen to what she has to say."

Kokkus laughed out loud, and Olrec resisted the urge to punch him in his grinning face. He held up one furry paw. "Indulge me, sister. Why do you want me to meet with that crazy man? He cheated the giants."

"Our natural enemies," Zilli said, raising her chin defiantly.

Olrec smiled. She was adorable when she wanted to prove a point. "The enemy of my enemy is my friend," he said gravely.

Kokkus laughed again. "You quote the Watchers, you're a brave idiot. The *stupes* borrowed that one from us."

"Maybe we should have written it down. Recorded it in a book, like they do," Olrec said, but as soon as the words left his lips, he knew Kokkus saw it as a challenge.

"You question our laws?" Kokkus's voice was soft, danger-ous. "Oh, Olrec, sometimes I really worry about you. It's like our argument—"

"Oh, not that again, brother!" Zilli called out.

"I don't care what you say, humans are more intelligent than giants, after all, they're the ones living above ground," Olrec knew this would irritate his brother-in-law. They constantly argued over which of the two monsters was smarter.

"Nonsense. You don't know what you're talking about. We harried the giants underground!" His tone was harsh, and his face was red with anger.

Olrec felt himself shrink. Zilli watched him, her eyes gentle and supportive. She changed the subject. "Someone has reported that the lizards have been nosing around."

The room cooled down.

"You have no proof," Kokkus accused. He looked nervously at the doorway. He sighed and added, "There was only one real sighting."

"We can't just sit here and wait to see who finds us first. You know what the lizards do when they track us down," Zilli whispered, her voice urgent. "You should go and meet with Konrad."

"Those are rumors, Zilli!" Kokkus's fisted hand struck the table, making the utensils rattle.

"You cannot deny the missing or the ones we did find. Konrad might be our safest choice, or maybe even the savior," Olrec defended her.

"If you and your wife think it's a good idea, you can both go and meet with that madman when and if he tries to contact us! I am the guardian of your cubs, and let's see how they like life with their uncle."

Olrec stood up to his full seven and a half feet. "No, I'll go. Alone."

Zilli cried out with dismay, "No, not you, Olrec."

"Why not, Zilli?" Kokkus challenged. "Lower your voice, sister. We don't want the others to hear our family squabble."

Olrec paused for a minute and then said, "Maybe the younger males have the right notion, and the doctor can help us move off this mountain and settle in the flatlands."

"You might have a good idea there, Olrec," Kokkus agreed. "We deserve the right to everything this planet has to offer. Many don't want to hide anymore, and we can't sit here waiting to see who attacks first."

"I forbid it!" Zilli twisted a dishcloth.

"I don't think you have that right. Olrec will go. I have declared it."

"Yes, it may be the right time. How will I find him?" Olrec lowered his brows and gave a warning glance to his wife.

"He'll find you." Kokkus was drawing a map of the lowlands on the dirt floor. "Right here." He stabbed his staff into the hard-packed earth. "I have someone watching the pine cones. I'll have them arrange for a sign."

Marem and Logu scrambled into the room as though they were racing. "I'm hungry," Marem yelled.

"Starved," Logu howled.

"Let me see your hands," Zilli demanded. "Are they clean?" She was still steaming that Olrec was wrangled into going.

Olrec whistled. "Wow, I never saw such scrubbed cubs." He leaned over, making a big deal of examining their paws.

Marem and Logu giggled at their father's antics.

Kokkus was frowning. He held up the front page of a magazine with a colorful picture for all to see. "Talking about the right time, I've been waiting for this moment to show you something." He pointed his hairy finger at a photo. "They caught sight of Marem."

"That's not Marem," Zilli said in that calm way of hers. "It could be Logu. Marem is always careful. Logu likes to spy on their encampments." She gave Logu a stern look, then turned to her brother. "They're kids," she laughed nervously. "Don't you remember what we used to do?" They stood beside her, and Olrec smiled. Zilli was a mama bear when she needed to be.

Olrec wondered when he saw Kokkus's face color up. Marem saved him from asking the question when he blurted, "What did you do, Uncle Kokkus?"

"Never mind." Zilli shooed the cubs from her corner and bade them to sit at the table, then finished addressing her brother. "You have to expect them to do things like this." She plunked a bowl on the table, none too gently, letting the twins know she disapproved of their actions despite her conciliatory tone.

Olrec looked at the photograph, bringing it close to his eyes.

He glanced up at his sons. Marem and Logu stared back, their faces innocent. Olrec's brows drew together in what he hoped was a fearsome frown.

"It's fuzzy and hard to tell exactly who it is." Olrec studied the picture. Logu, or perhaps Marem, was hidden behind a bushy conifer, the bulbous part of his head poking above a branch, his hairy limbs blending with the bark of the trees.

"You shouldn't have gone!" Kokkus barked, slapping the table in anger. "You'll bring back human diseases. They're filthy animals! What if you touched something bloody?" He smacked both teens in the head with his huge paw. "This is a grim reminder of how vulnerable we are. We've beaten back the giants, and now you invite *stupes* to find us. You may be right, Zilli. We need to contact Doctor Konrad, and Olrec is the one to do it."

"Don't hit my cubs!" Zilli pushed his hand out of the way. Their behavior is natural for their age. At least they aren't making deals with the devil!"

"Hey, that was *your* idea, sis," Kokkus laughed.

Zilli leaned close. "I didn't expect Olrec to be the one to travel down the mountain! Just because I mentioned it doesn't mean that I like Konrad."

Olrec interrupted her, "He has to be better than the lizards." They all shivered at the thought of it.

"They always make me feel like I'd make a tasty dinner," Zilli said softly.

"You'd cook for them?" Marem asked, his eyes innocent.

"No, dummy. They'd like to eat us," his brother, Logu, said.

Kokkus looked up and snarled. "It's settled then. It should be you, Olrec, who ventures down there. Your cubs put us at risk!"

Zilli blushed to the roots of her hair. "I don't like it."

"Zill, we don't have a choice," Olrec pleaded. "Better meet with Dr. Konrad and not have business with the liz—"

"Forget about the lizards!" Kokkus slammed the table, rattling their cups.

"Konrad is an unknown," Zilli said.

"We have an obligation to see what he can do for us," Olrec said reasonably. "And I'm—"

"It doesn't have to be you!" she blurted.

"You talk as if you have a choice, you foolish female!" Kokkus was furious; his jowls shook with anger. "Have you no shame! There is talk that the Great Night Owl has gone soft."

Olrec looked up, chagrined. "Zilli has a mind of her own, and I like that." He patted her hand. "I will be careful, dear." He went back to his meal, chuckling to himself. "Besides, she's probably right. How do you know if you can trust this… this… creature? He is a *stupe*, after all."

Kokkus waved at him in disgust. "He's not human anymore."

Olrec looked up. "He's not. What is he then?"

"We're not really sure. It doesn't matter. We need the alliance."

Olrec shook his head. "I don't trust him. He is still a *stupe* or something of the sort."

"He screwed the giants with his theme park," Marem piped, his voice cracking.

Olrec smiled and didn't admonish his son for speaking out.

"Yes, that is to our benefit," Kokkus informed him. "Little cubs should be seen but not heard."

Olrec cleared his throat and motioned for them to leave with a shake of his head. "Go." He smiled as they made their escape. "They are rash," he said in apology to Kokkus.

"They'll be the death of you, and that's your choice. I don't want our home endangered."

Olrec nodded in agreement. "I'll speak to them."

Kokkus stood.

Olrec walked him out. They stopped at the entrance. Kokkus grabbed his forearm. "Control your female, Olrec. I can't protect you." He leaned closer. "There is talk at the council to consider meeting with the lizards."

"You would never!" Olrec looked shocked. "They are dangerous. We are nothing more than a meal to them."

"In the past, they raided our villages. They claim they still have the abducted." He shrugged. "They promised Pojim the return of his wife."

"Oh no, oh no. I doubt she's alive. I found Lemar's body. I don't like them, Kokkus. No, not at all."

"It was never determined that the lizards killed him." Kokkus paused at the doorway.

"I said I found his body. Trust me, Kokkus. It was the lizards."

"Then make sure you make a deal with Konrad. Oh, for fur's sake, don't get caught again!"

Olrec nodded. He understood the need to remain hidden. Nothing good ever came from the *stupes* or the lizards, for that matter. He didn't have to be reminded of how the humans hunted for proof of their existence for years. *Stupe* curiosity would be the death of them.

CHAPTER 12

THE NEEDS OF MANY

KEISHA RUSHED DOWN the tunnel connecting the mainland to Vincent Konrad's compound on Prendick Island, her sandaled feet slapping against the rock walkway. Her thoughts circled her brain, the phrase curiosity killed the cat repeating *ad nauseam* in her head.

She glanced at her watch. She was late, but she'd never tell Howard why she was delayed. If she mentioned her experience in transforming into a dragon, he would drop everything and ask a million questions, hindering any progress with Vincent's phone. No, she had to keep this to herself. Biting her bottom lip, she frowned. She wanted to talk to him about it more than anything. He was her best friend, the only one who understood what was important to her. She knew instinctively this had to stay private. The one thing she hated more than being late was keeping secrets.

Clicking her tongue with impatience, she sighed heavily. Howard was waiting for her, and the thought of it made her cheeks tighten and blush. Howard Drucker never complained, especially now that she had remembered what they meant to each other.

Lowering her brows, Keisha wondered for a second if she should turn herself into a falcon to make better time. Frowning, she decided not to attempt it. This morning, she tried to change into a falcon and ended up a giant dragon. The memory made her tingle with excitement mixed with fear.

When she slid into her meditative state, Keisha wasn't sure if a hissing goddess, a bird of prey, or a flying serpent was showing up. She rubbed the area between her brows where it felt pinched. Swallowing, she realized she was parched, her tongue scorched where fire had raced through it this morning. This was too much to handle.

She could smell smoke faintly in her hair. No telling what might happen without John Raven's guidance. There was even a chance that she could make a mistake and shape-shift into Medusa again. Keisha was rocked, always confident in herself and her surroundings, but right now, she felt like she was swimming in quicksand.

The one thing she was sure of was that when she was angry, there was the possibility that snakes might involuntarily sprout from her head, her eyes would begin to glow, and she would develop some kick-ass special powers. The problem was that she had little control over who she turned into stone. It was like making a party and not knowing who was going to show up. Biting her lips with indecision, she worried whether this made her happy or sad. On one hand, she was learning to morph at will; on the other hand, the outcome was like a box of chocolates. She wasn't sure which one she would get. Keisha sighed deeply. Her eyes stung, but she willed them to stop. No tears. Howard might sense something and ask too many questions.

John was thrilled with her shape-shifting dragon, and while it was a splendid experience, Keisha couldn't show much enthusiasm. Everything felt out of control; her stomach ached with nerves. John Raven was supposed to teach her how to harness the energy to transform into a falcon. They decided this way, she would be able to pick her targets, and while she wouldn't do substantial damage, she'd be able to confuse and disarm the enemy.

The problem was that she wasn't able to control these new abilities. Today, she was confused by throwing a *freakin'* dragon into the mix.

Her teacher crowed with delight. John Raven was over the moon. Keisha, not so much.

She had begged John Raven and her classmates not to share this new transformation with the rest of the camp.

Picking up her pace, she reached the broken rubble that was pushed aside in Vincent Konrad's main dining area. A vast stone table had been overturned. Howard Drucker had his hand against the glass window, looking out on the seabed where schools of fish swam lazily past them.

"What took you so long?" he asked without turning around.

Keisha navigated seawater puddles that dotted the floor to join him at the window. She ran a finger along the jagged fractures that were injected with silicone to prevent the ocean from pouring into the chamber. "They did a good job sealing it up."

"*Hmmm*," Howard agreed. "This place was about to pull an Atlantis on us, and we'd lose the opportunity to study Vincent's work, if not for my dad's ingenuity." He sniffed and turned to her. "Keisha, you're not taking up smoking?"

"No, Howard. *Um…*John made *um..*John made a bonfire this morning." She averted her gaze. Keisha was not comfortable lying.

"Oh, interesting. Is that part of the ritual when learning to morph?"

Keisha faced Howard. He was so endearing when he was curious. "No. You don't need anything like that."

Howard cocked his head. "What then? Tell me."

"It's so easy, it's almost scary, Howard. You turn your thoughts inward and think like the beast you want to become."

"Sounds almost too simple."

"Breathe in and breathe out. That's all, and picture the animal." Keisha lowered her eyes.

"Did you fly again, my daring falcon?"

Keisha gave a half-hearted laugh. "I was definitely flying."

"Great. Breathe in and breathe out. I'll have to try it." He sighed. "These eyes are troublesome. I don't see a solution."

They both turned to study the hundreds of round eggs nestled in the coral and reef vegetation. Some of the spheres appeared discolored, their tops sunken in. Keisha bit her lower lip as she observed them. She touched the seam of silicone sealing them in the underground building. "Your dad certainly was prepared."

"Yeah, prepared for fixing broken glass, but not for the swarm of creatures that are about to be hatched."

"School." Keisha corrected him. "Look over there." She pointed to round-shaped objects lined up like scalloped carvings, the eggs filling the dips and valleys of the sloping hills. "It doesn't look naturally formed. Could that be machine-made?"

"The eggs?"

"I'm talking about the reef. It's not natural-looking. Too perfect."

Howard pursed his lips and shrugged. "Right now, I'm more concerned about what is inside those eggs."

"The roundness of the reef looks manufactured. The eggs appear too smooth, as well. We'll have to see when the fish come out."

"I'm not sure if I'd categorize them as fish, yet. I'm reserving judgment until I actually see one." Howard was stuck thinking about their category instead of the oddly shaped coral reef.

"Howard, don't you think the seabed shape is odd?" Keisha persisted.

Howard shrugged. "Nature imitates many contours." He thought for a minute. "Maybe it's the other way around. We copy nature."

Keisha tapped the glass impatiently. "I don't want to debate life imitating nature or whatnot. It looks weird. Unnatural," she clarified.

"Some of the eggs look…I don't know… *different*." Kiesha looked at him, her patience at an end, "Howard! Don't you ever use just your imagination? Does it always have to be about facts and numbers?"

"Really, Keisha. I don't know what's gotten into you. Science is always about hard facts. Look, the eggs are perfectly oval, perhaps they play a role in the formation of..." Howard's voice trailed off, leaving nothing but silence in the room. He turned his head sideways to study the rolling hill-like landscape. "The reef *could* be artificial."

"Yes! It resembles the shape of barrels, or containers of a sort," Keisha said absently, something niggling her memory.

The dark shadow of a great white passing over them momentarily distracted her. It moved slowly, its dead-looking eyes the size of her palm. Squinting, she gasped when she realized their color.

"I know, right?" Howard said without looking at her, diverted by the enormity of the shark.

"The eyes are an astonishing shade of blue, not black."

Keisha nodded dumbly, amazed once again that Howard knew what she was thinking without her saying anything. She got a whiff of her hair and coughed.

"You okay?"

Keisha gave a curt nod, her eyes watering.

"They say that each shark has a different personality," he continued, rapt with the creature's movements. "I could stay here all day and watch it."

"Her," Keisha said absently. By naming its gender, Keisha felt it gave the shark an identity, maybe even a soul. She nibbled on a cuticle, an old habit from years ago when she was worried. The intensity of Howard's observation alarmed her. His passion for learning about life around him suddenly ate at her gut. She stepped back to see Howard's intense gaze and shuddered. *What if she became the object of his passion, but not in a good way, a… a scientific way?* She gasped. She used to think it was charming, part of his allure, yet the thought of him observing her with those fascinated eyes filled her with dread.

Her face twisted with regret, and Howard turned to look at her, his expression just as alarmed. He reached out to grab her wrist gently but urgently, as if to reassure her. "I never heard of anyone morphing into a shark."

"What?" she asked. Keisha stared back at him blankly, and then her jaw dropped. *Oh my God, he thinks I'm afraid to change into a shark.* "But someone could," she responded, her voice nervous. "You study it like it's an oddity."

"Curiosity, maybe, not an oddity," Howard said dismissively.

"You do. Admit it. It's like you're obsessed with it." Keisha's voice was hollow. Closing her eyes, she pictured Howard's expression once he saw her leathery wings and fire shooting out of her snout. Memories flooded his mind of the awe he felt when she transformed into a mythical monster. If morphing into Medusa excited him, what would happen when he realized she could turn into a *dragon*? Could he ever look at her the same way again, or would their relationship turn cold and clinical? Would he see her as a woman or… She shivered with dread. … a… *monster?*

"Are you talking about Melvin?" he asked her. "I'll admit, he's different."

"Maybe…" she paused, then added, finishing the sentence, "maybe me." *Could love be sustained under the shock of realizing she was not the same person Howard had known in the past? Would his fascination turn into repulsion?* She looked him straight in the face. "Do you feel the same way about him?" Her voice was high.

"Keisha, you're not the same as that." He pointed to the shark.

"I asked you a question."

Howard took a shuddering breath. "I don't know. I'm still processing."

"Processing?" Keisha felt weak, her strength deserting her.

"Keish, it's not the same." Howard moved closer, taking her other hand. "Are you sorry that you've learned how to change?" He rubbed her knuckles, his gaze softening.

Keisha hesitated, then shook her head. "I'm not sure."

A soldier cleared his throat in the doorway. "*Um*…the Colonel is waiting for the phone."

They jumped apart guiltily.

Dragging in a ragged breath, she turned the subject. "Yes. We're running out of time. Where's the phone we have to work on?"

"Here," Howard said, his eyes searching hers. He held up the smashed phone in his hand.

To Keisha, it also represented a breakdown in their communication. Keisha sighed and said to the soldier. "We'll notify you when we're done." He nodded and took off toward the army encampment.

Howard and Keisha returned to the overturned stone table and began working on the phone. Keisha sorted through some parts on the floor.

The undulating sea painted their faces different shades of blue, from teal to pale violet. Their discussion hadn't been finished, and it hung heavy between them.

Howard cleared his throat noisily. "You're nothing like the others—" A disturbance in the ocean cut off his words. Thick, orange-striped arms slithered down the water, feeling along the glass. Huge suckers the size of truck tires plastered themselves along the surface.

"The octopus!" Howard said, his voice became breathless. "That's a big motherf-"

Keisha stifled a scream when the thick arm snapped around, grabbing the great white by the tail. She grabbed Howard's hands. The teens stood frozen, mutely watching, the shark twisting in a demented dance to escape.

Another arm shot forward, the giant head, like a deflated hot air balloon, floated into view, its slitted glassy eyes zeroing in on its prey.

The big body pressed up against the glass, almost obscuring the view. Howard rose onto his toes to see better. Keisha barely breathed. She pulled her hands from Howard's grip, clasping and unclasping them with nervous energy.

"*Oh* my stars!" she choked out.

The shark was enveloped by tentacles that wrapped around its struggling body. It made all movement impossible. It grappled against the punishing hold, surging her muscular body as if fighting a powerful current.

The tentacles loosened, and Keisha's heart filled with hope. "Swim away," she urged. "Swim!" she shouted, knowing her voice was lost against the impenetrable glass. She banged against the surface with both fists. "Get away!"

Howard joined her, his voice echoing her shouts. The shark wiggled furiously close to freedom, and the arms roped around so tightly that the great white's eyes bulged from their sockets.

"It's like it's toying with it." Howard sounded shocked.

Indeed, the octopus continued the game, releasing its hold, then grabbing the shark as it attempted to escape. The shark's sickle-shaped maw opened in a soundless scream, bubbles escaping as if it were being crushed. Food ejected, pilot fish skittered away, and the gray body was pulled backward in a relentless tug.

Keisha and Howard craned their necks, watching the shark being drawn toward the enormous body of the octopus.

"It looks like a sardine, compared to that thing." Howard's voice was small.

"Without a navy, that monster will deplete the oceans. With no natural predator, the whales are doomed."

"The *whales*," Howard said with dismay. Howard and Keisha looked at each other, all sound receding into silence.

"It's too horrible to even think about." Keisha shuddered. "If we fix Vincent's phone, we can control its impulses."

"Help me." Howard moved to the stone table, trying to lift it. Keisha went to the other end, and together they overturned it. It hobbled. Pulling two chairs upright, they sat down and studied the phone. Howard turned it over, the glass making a crackling sound where it spiderwebbed across the surface. "I'm not sure..." His voice trailed off when he looked up to see Keisha watching bits of the gray skin of the shark float around the water. Small fish nibbled on the leftovers. "It's the cycle of life." He touched the underside of her chin. "We'll figure something out, Keish. We always do."

Keisha wasn't listening.

"Keisha?" Howard twisted and looked in the direction of her gaze, realizing she was not staring at the pieces of flesh but the barrel-shaped coral, her brows lowered with concentration. "What is it?"

"Those shapes. I think I know what they are."

Howard raised his eyebrows. "Yes?"

"In the middle of the last century, they dumped toxic waste along the southern California coastline. I did a paper on it last year." She got up, moving closer to the window. "Howard, look where the surface appears broken or jagged; the eggs seem discolored. Some of them are completely dead-looking."

Howard joined her at the glass and studied the spheres. The darkened ones floated differently, as if they were—

"Empty," Keisha supplied.

"Wait." Howard pulled at a lock of his curly dark hair, a sure sign he was deep in thought. "I remember reading something about that. It was DDT, thousands of barrels of the deadly insecticide."

"Dumped—" Keisha interrupted.

"In the oceans—" Howard was facing the seabed, his eyes faraway.

"They didn't know what to do with it," Keisha said, rapidly. She started to pace in front of the window. She stopped and twisted to him, her eyes bright.

"So they buried it offshore—" Howard responded.

"In supposedly airtight containers so it would never leak," Keisha finished the sentence, then looked him full in the face. "Because if it degraded on land, it would be deadly for all life-forms. It might have leached into the soil, or gotten into the wrong hands." Keisha chewed her bottom lip, then continued. "In the ocean, it would slowly become part of the—"

"Landscape," Howard finished.

They stared at each other for a full minute, Keisha said, "But if we disturb it, the surrounding life—"

"A small price to pay—" Howard wrung his hands.

"Not if you're a fish—" she gestured to the watery vista.

"Keish." Howard grasped her by the shoulders. "The needs of many outweigh the needs of a few."

"Howard! This isn't a plot from a movie!"

"Still." He squeezed her hands, his gaze holding hers.

"We could—" she lowered her eyes.

"We could—"

They rushed to the table.

With determination and gritted teeth, they bent their heads together to tackle the phone, putting the next stage of their plan in motion.

CHAPTER 13

GIANTS, LIZARDS, AND HUMANS BE DAMNED

**Mount Whitney, Sierra Nevada
Central California**

"DO YOU REALLY have to go?" Zilli was anything but happy about his assignment. "Can't they send someone else?"

Olrec scratched the top of his sparsely covered head, his claws leaving three red marks, pretending he didn't hear her.

"Olrec!" she implored.

Frowning, he considered the precious few hairs and rearranged them over the expanse of his scalp. He was just beginning to go bald, and it bothered him to a considerable extent. He heard her foot tapping on the densely packed earthen floor. "Don't make a big deal about it, Zilli," he mumbled, still distracted by covering the top of his egg-shaped head. "The scout reported that he's made the pine formation. The Doctor will see it, respond in kind, and a meeting place will be arranged. We're halfway there."

"Easy for you to say!" she replied tartly. "They're not going to ostracize you at the knitting circle if you mess up."

"It was *your* idea." Olrec winced as soon as he said it. "You heard the elders. We have an obligation. We left the signal; now we have to follow through."

"I didn't mean for them to send *you*!" She drew out the last word into a whimper. Olrec hated when Zilli whined.

"He did get rid of the giants for us."

He tried to ignore the expression on his wife's face. It was true, he shrugged. She had pushed for this strange negotiation with a madman at the last council meeting. Zilli was known for her common sense and had helped them navigate through many crises affecting his tribe. It was one of the things he loved best about her.

He continued to study himself in the mirror as if he didn't have a care in the world. Truth was, he felt like a group of butterflies was wiggling in the pit of both of his stomachs. He had to leave the safety of the village, wait at the junction at the base of the mountains, and then find the crazy doctor. It was too much to think about. Olrec decided to stay in the present and concentrate on things that didn't make him nervous.

Moving backward, he angled his head and realized the mirror was crooked. Straightening it, he admired the polished metal finish on the frame. He had brought it back from a camping site for Zilli. It was a grand thing, a great prize stolen during the raid. If they had electricity, he'd hook up the lights lining the top of it.

Out of the corner of his eye, he watched Zilli busying herself with folding laundry. "I'm sorry. That was harsh of me." She moved over and abruptly kissed his cheek. "You are always well-intentioned.

It's just that… just that… you're so impulsive and never realize the danger until it's too late."

"Almost too late," he corrected her. "I've lost too much hair up here." He deliberately tried to refocus their conversation. He selected a pine cone to use as a comb, raking it over the hair covering his shiny scalp.

"Last time I *almost* lost you." Zilli's voice was sad. She buried her face in a towel. If she started to cry, he was done for, he thought with a sigh.

Olrec firmed his powerful jaw. "I have to do this, Zilli." He fought the urge to enclose her in his arms.

Olrec knew, despite their love, that both she and her younger brother had little faith in him. But this… this was bigger than faith. This was about proving he was not a wash-up. "They didn't catch me or my image. Kokkus always exaggerates." Olrec pushed the hair forward and tried spreading the strands from another direction. "Still not enough." He sighed.

"Oh, you mean your hair? You are as handsome as ever," Zilli gave him a watery smile that weakened his knees. She was beautiful when they married and remained just as pretty, twenty-nine years later.

Zilli kissed his cheek again. "It looks good." She rolled the towel and snapped it against his hairy leg. He was the tallest of the pack and had been judged the most handsome of all the males close to thirty years ago. Lifting his chin, he touched his sagging jowls.

Olrec rolled his brown eyes. "I don't know about that." Every time he caught a glimpse of himself in the lake, he saw the top of his head looming above his eyebrows like a giant moon. It made him feel old and decrepit. Zilli *pooh-poohed* his comments once again and responded that his near-naked pate gave him a distinguished air.

It did him no good for his reputation as the most fearsome representative of his pack. Still, there had to be a reason they agreed for him to volunteer. Olrec laughed. That's because everyone else was afraid to do it. That, and his troublesome cubs. This feat will certainly buy them some goodwill.

He walked from their moss-covered hut buried deep into the hillside, inhaling the pine-scented air. It was a glorious morning.

Baring his teeth, he growled, causing the birds behind him to fly away in terror. He smiled, his canines large, gleaming, and yellow. *Guess I still got it,* he smirked. He heard the patter of small animals that hid in the undergrowth scatter. Maybe Kokkus was wrong; his better days weren't behind him. He nodded and waved to his neighbors as he strolled from their village.

Lurren was busy hoeing a flower bed; Ehora was sweeping the ground in front of her home. Mingu straddled part of an airplane spread out before him, throwing useless pieces into a growing junk pile. One by one, they waved, a negligent hand here, a grunt there. His irritating brother-in-law didn't even show up for his departure.

They could have assembled as a group to wish him well. He glanced around, a little dismayed. Moving down the mountain was always dangerous; the least they could have done was appear to care.

"Time to go to work. See you in a few days," he announced loudly and watched for their reaction.

Smiling, he heard Zilli call from his doorstep, "Good luck, be careful, and don't touch any human blood!"

"Absolutely, General Zilli!" He saluted her smartly.

Kokkus had introduced the idea of Olrec meeting the Doctor at the next meeting.

The group was firmly divided about the entire enterprise, anyway. They couldn't agree that Olrec was the right choice to go. Jofro bellowed loudly that Olrec was old and clumsy. It was a dangerous mission, and they needed the bravest to go.

The lack of faith in Olrec rankled him somewhat. He admitted to himself that this represented a trend. It's just that they weren't including him lately, he thought sadly. Twice, he'd been asked to hang back when they ventured down the mountaintop, relegating him to stay with the old ones who didn't do much of anything. He thought about that a lot.

While it was true that he had bungled a raid two months ago, his brother-in-law, Kokkus, wouldn't let anyone forget about it. He took every opportunity to remind the tribe, and Jofro and his buddies beat their chests to demonstrate their strength.

Olrec sighed. Indeed, there were younger bucks that could have gone. He thought he made a convincing argument about his ability to communicate with other species.

He stood up to Zilli's horror-struck face and announced in a loud voice that, whether it was to petrify or tease, Olrec of Sierra Nevada had a reputation for getting the job done.

However, lately, as his delightful brother-in-law said, Olrec was to be blamed for everything that went wrong when they went on a foraging expedition.

Olrec argued back that it wasn't *his* footprints that were left in the mud, and certainly none of *his* coat was missing, so the strands of fur stuck in the trees couldn't belong to him. He gave Jofro a dark look.

Jofro turned his face away. "I am careful," he bellowed, shaking the acorns from their trees with his loud voice. "And, don't forget, it was his two cubs that sent the danger!"

Tall and imposing, in his younger days, Olrec reminded them that he sent loggers, rock climbers, and campers screaming back to the safety of civilization. He strolled over moss-covered rocks, stepping nimbly, lest his feet leave indelible proof of his existence.

Darn those cubs of his. If not for their exposure, he wouldn't have had to volunteer, yet he knew Kokkus would find some way to hang the job around his neck.

The scout reported he had set the pine cones in their special design. The meeting had been initiated. Olrec would travel from the safety of the hills, down the mountain to the edge of civilization, to the ruins of Monsterland. There, he will listen to Konrad, the doctor known for his lies and duplicity, and decide what is best for his family and tribe. Olrec knew one thing above all else: he would protect his home with every fiber of his being, giants, lizards, and humans be damned.

CHAPTER 14

THEY'LL ANNIHILATE US

"DO YOU THINK it will work? Controlling the octopus, not your other hair-brained idea." Keisha whispered, picking up a tiny screwdriver from a canvas bag Howard had near his feet. It was filled with an assortment of tools, still displaying the price stickers from the local big-box store. The table they had turned over was broken and unusable. Every time Howard placed his elbows on it, it tilted, causing Keisha to yelp. Anybody could tell she was distracted and edgy by the way her fingers plucked nervously at the tools.

She kept rearranging them in various configurations. Nuts and bolts in one pile, flat-head and hex screwdrivers in another, washers in a third. They had moved to the concrete floor, and parts of the phone were spread out around them. Howard handed her an Allen wrench.

"I don't see why not. Konrad's satellite is still up there. If Owens will let me, I can jerry-rig something up and we'll have communication with our troops again using his system." Howard snickered at the idea. "Kill two birds with one stone."

"*Jerry-rig…* Who are you? That sounds like something Mr. Enoch would say."

Howard stopped, and she caught him looking at her. "Otto Enoch? *Oh, jeez,* I love that guy. Watching him is like eating cotton candy… for the brain," He paused and added, "You may be right, but it seems appropriate." He fiddled with the phone for a bit, then said, "Tell you the truth, I wouldn't mind a few minutes with the old troll right now." Howard rose, brushing off his pants. "We should share this information with my dad."

Keisha shuddered. "*Ugh*, that guy creeped me out with all his boogie-man stories."

"My dad?" Howard squeaked. He pivoted so she saw he was looking at her, his head cocked in question.

"No, Howard, Otto Enoch," she replied with a roll of her eyes. "You need to tell your dad what you're planning to do with Konrad's communication system." She looked up at him. "Or did you do it already?"

"All my dad has to do is okay it. I'll flip the switch."

They each stared at the phone in Howard's palm, both deep in thought. "Howard Drucker, you did it already?"

"Prepared, not carried out." He sighed, deep in thought. "I dunno. Some of his theories don't seem as far-fetched—"

"We are talking about Otto Enoch, now. Right?" Keisha gave him a stern look, her lips pursed. "He was a crackpot." She crouched down and made her voice a sibilant whisper in a credible imitation of their former teacher. "The pyramids are a portal to another dimension, *woo woo*." She waved her hands around, her eyes wide and wild. "Bigfoot exists, fairies, trolls, and—"

"Giants?" Howard responded, one eyebrow raised to his hairline. "He had a lot to say about gremlins and dragons, too."

Keisha paled, her fingers shook for a minute. "It's all stupid. Okay, so giants are real. Once Captain Rosemary gets some intel on them, we'll probably discover they're throwbacks to Neanderthals or some missing link. Dragons, *sheesh*," she said under her breath. Keisha vibrated with tension. She paced back and forth across the room. "Gremlins, it's the stuff of fairy tales."

"I kind of like Gremlins. It would explain a lot, planes disappearing, or going down mysteriously."

"You… you don't believe in that sort of stuff?" Keisha's shoulders stiffened. "Gremlins…" She gulped. "Dragons?"

"It bears further investigation, is all I'm saying." Howard watched her, frowning at her expression. "Is something wrong, Keish?"

She shook her head quickly.

"You seem troubled. You sure—"

"It's this damn idea of yours. I don't like it," she said rapidly while wringing her hands. "If you activate all of our phones, Konrad will know what our plans are." She threw down the tiny screwdriver she'd been toying with. It clattered on the floor. Keisha turned to glare at the seabed.

"Keisha, it's going to be okay. We need to activate the phones. It's a big country out there. The only way this thing ends is with us crushing Konrad. If we can't find him—" Howard joined her at the window. "Look at that thing."

The water was crystal clear, the sun's rays penetrating the depth and lighting it up like a jewel box.

"But you're allowing *him* to find *us*."

"Yeah, but this time we'll be prepared," Howard told her firmly. He squeezed her shoulders.

The octopus was floating by, its enormous size taking up the entire length of the window. The legs were as thick as telephone poles, the suckers moving as if rimmed by thousands of muscles reacting to the stimuli around them. The animal's head was the size of a four-door sedan. It dragged behind the long reach of the arms, changing from blue to green and finally the color of the coral it trolled.

"She's looking for her baby," Keisha said.

The creature disappeared for a moment, blending into the landscape.

Keisha knew Howard was fascinated by his narrowed eyes that searched for it. His rapt expression of this giant of nature enthralled him, and he continued to comment on its fluid movement.

The baby shot across the top of the window like an arrow released from a bow. The mother thrashed, catching it with one of her powerful arms and hugging it tightly against her massive body. Keisha watched as Howard's throat moved convulsively as he swallowed, his eyes misting with emotion. He told her about the creature's three hearts and the wonder of how they worked.

Keisha tapped her foot with impatience. "I still can't figure out why you want to put us on Konrad's radar."

Howard was glancing at her sideways. She could tell he knew she was in a bad mood. She smiled half-heartedly, and he grinned back devilishly. Howard was up to something. "What is it, Howard Drucker?" She punched him on his upper arm, but not hard.

"Keisha, think." When she stared at him blankly, he added, "*Ultra-secret?*"

"Ultra—" Keisha's eyes met his, and Howard smiled broadly. He was waiting for her to put it all together. They had visited the Spy Museum on their junior trip to Washington a few years ago. They had nerded out looking at the primitive tools used to spy on the enemy during World War II.

Dragons and morphing forgotten, her jaw dropped, and Howard's face softened. She knew he was as weak in the knees as she was, and she felt a rush of tenderness for him. He reached out to take her hand and squeeze it. For a minute, Keisha was back in high school, and none of this had happened. She and Howard were meeting on the intellectual plane that brought them both joy. Her intense glow was back, lit by some inner fire.

She gasped, her voice excited. "OMG! The Allies used the Nazi's codes to send inaccurate information to the enemy, directing them from their real plans. You're a genius, Howard." She smiled and caressed his cheek with her free hand.

Howard gaped at her with a goofy grin on his face. His keen eyes were studying the worry line between her brows. He shook as if a chill had gone up his spine.

They both knew it had been a rough few months for Keisha. She had lost her parents to the alien purple material that fueled Vincent's heinous plans, morphed into Medusa, and turned people into stone with her eyes. She had learned to shapeshift into a peregrine falcon, and she got amnesia when she was kidnapped by giants, which caused her to forget everything they meant to each other. She finally remembered Howard, barely a few weeks ago.

Howard was biting the inside of his cheek.

Keisha saw his jaw working. He was watching her. He moved close, his head almost touching hers.

Sighing deeply, he whispered, "You know, Keisha, you can tell me anything."

Keisha gave him a pained look. She opened her mouth to respond when Howard's father strode into the room, followed by the president.

"Howard! You're supposed to be getting this phone working! We need to control that giant octopus."

They jumped apart, and Howard spun around guiltily. "We were just leaving to find you, Dad. We think it will work."

"It better," Colonel Drucker said softly, his worried eyes on the window.

President Owens said, "Show me what to do." He held out a hand. "We have to stimulate the baby to leave and hope mama octopus will follow."

"Before you do anything, Sir, Howard's come up with a great plan," Keisha announced.

"We don't have time," Colonel Drucker said harshly.

"This is important, Dad," Howard told him.

"Go on," Nate Owens ordered, lowering his palm.

Howard stepped forward. "I can configure our cell phones to operate using Konrad's satellite."

"What good will that do?" Yerbol, the president's bodyguard, interrupted. He pushed himself from the shadows, his imposing bulk visible. He was followed by his commando crew of three. "Konrad will know our every move."

"Not if we feed him bad information," Howard said with a smirk, holding up the phone.

The room went silent. The president smiled and nodded. "Not bad, but will it work?"

"I don't see why not. It worked in World War II between the British and the Germans," Howard replied.

"We don't have time for this nonsense," Yerbol ground out.

"You don't know that," Owens told his guard. He held up the phone in his hand. "If this doesn't work, nothing will matter. You worked in the Secret Service before we met. They must have done things like that."

"I worked with moles planted all over the world."

"Wait, was there a mole in Monsterland or in Vincent's organization?" The room went silent.

"Yes, of course, but the one we had working with us in Monsterland was made, well before the opening, and he disappeared."

"By made, you mean exposed," Howard said

"You have no idea where he is now?" Colonel Drucker interrupted before Yerbol could confirm that the agent was compromised.

"None, sir. I wouldn't even know how to find him. I mean, we lost him. It happens when people go too deep undercover; they break. I knew what he looked like, but he went by a code name."

"What do you mean by that, break?" the president asked.

"Deep cover agents need to forget about their former existence. The long-term effect can smudge the lines between their real and fake identities. This person was flipped initially; he went undercover to avoid prosecution. Truth be told, I wasn't surprised."

"What was his code name?" Colonel Drucker asked.

Yerbol looked at the president. "It is Top Secret."

"Doesn't matter now. Go ahead, I run a transparent administration." The president paced the room.

"Halo Eleven."

"Interesting. I'd like to speak with you further about it. Perhaps we can try to find some of these plants and use them to spread misinformation. Do you think you can track some of them down?"

"I'll try."

"Well, Howard, it's a good plan. Let's get started on it!" Colonel Drucker gazed with admiration.

Howard smirked. "Already done. I just have to flip a switch. I wouldn't do it without your permission."

"I don't like it," Yerbol's voice rang out. "Konrad will be able to hear all our plans."

"Already taken care of. I changed the frequency on a small group of phones, say, calls between you and five others. The rest will be on a channel he can't access." Howard held up his phone.

There were murmurs of appreciation in the room.

"You kept a separate frequency for us to communicate?" Owens asked.

Howard nodded. "We're good to go as soon as you give the command."

"Yerbol, start feeding them fake air reports. Bring up the Nellis, Elgin in Florida, and Edwards Air Force bases. Business as usual. Mock up some chatter, pilots to base, that sort of thing," He turned to Sheldon and Lieutenant Appel. "Create troop movements along the southern border, as if Mexico is coming to our aid. Set

up something similar in Canada. We can confuse him with—"
He leaned over a map and pointed toward Monsterland. "Three
imaginary forces and have them moving from here, here, and here.
Let's go!"

Sheldon looked longingly at his father, but the Colonel gestured
to the door. "Go. Get it done, and that's an order. Mr. President, the
octopus," Colonel Drucker implored, while he pointed to a large ten-
tacle floating in the window. It slithered into the entire vista, which
was taken up by a gray-blue mass.

Howard stepped in front of him. "Now, Mr. President, if you
touch this icon, we'll see if we can go fishing." He pointed to the eyes
of the octopus that were pressed up against the glass.

"That thing is disgusting," Yerbol said with a full-body shiver.
"Where's a Navy SEAL when you need one?" He moved out of the
door, cell phone and plans in hand. Lieutenant Appel followed him.

"That *thing* is enormous." The president stepped forward to take
in the panoramic view. He craned his neck, looking for the infant.
"Where's junior?"

Keisha moved next to him. "Right there in its mother's arms. See?"

Indeed, the baby rested against the bigger animal, its slitted
eyes watchful.

Howard held out his hand. "If you'll allow me?"

President Nate Owens nodded. A scuffle broke out at the doorway as more people poured into the room.

Howard heard Wyatt's voice yell, "Wait for us!"

He grinned as his friends entered and pushed their way to the
front. Carter brought up the rear with Wyatt and moved silently to
stand near the glass window.

Howard climbed onto the wobbly table, holding out both arms
to balance. He lifted the phone high into the air so they could see
him, but Carter's words made him freeze.

"Mr. President. I think you'd better take a look at this."

All eyes were drawn to the sea floor, where thousands of eggs were in motion. Some had cracked open; small, shell-like arms protruded from the jagged fissures, reaching upward and chipping furiously at the hard shells encasing them.

"It's started. They'll annihilate us," Melvin said softly.

"What are those things?" Wyatt asked.

"It's what killed my…" Melvin's voice was raspy. "It murdered Jade, one of those shell creatures." Melvin closed his eyes and said under his breath, "Jade, Jade… *Jaaaade.*"

"Let me at 'em," Jade's father, Mr. Zadowski, roared, plowing to the front of the room. "I'll kill the mother—" His voice died off as they took in the enormity of the mass of creatures emerging from the eggs.

"It's hopeless," Melvin said in the deathly silence. He looked upward and implored, "What more can you hit us with?"

CHAPTER 15

PLACES TO GO

"YOU'RE HOPELESS. WE'RE lost. Can't you read directions? We're too far south," Vincent grumbled, his face twisted. They were back on Earth, each with a magnificent steed. Vincent's was coal black, Dreg's mare was a dappled gray.

"Well, you didn't want them to know where we're going." They both looked at the small, round-shaped craft hovering above, keeping a watchful eye on them. "We should start heading toward the home base."

"Wait." Vincent halted him. "Not yet. We have to find Rosemary, but first we have to make contact with the Sasquatch."

"The Sasquatch are not reality accessible. They've been hiding out in these mountains since the beginning of time."

"A lot you know," Vincent scoffed. He squinted into the fading light, his narrowed eyes searching the hills. "You see that cleft in the rocks up there." He pointed to an outcropping surrounded by a

V-shaped formation of Pondarose Pines. "Head up there and place five pine cones in a circle. Put one in the center standing upright."

"You want me to go up there?" Dreg squeaked. "That's where the giants hang out."

Vincent ignored him and glanced up at the sky. "Are they still watching?"

Dreg peered up and observed the small white craft perform a lazy circle and then take off toward the coast, vanishing from view. "They're gone."

"Good riddance." He turned to Dreg and ordered, "Go on. We don't have all day. Place the message the way I told you."

Dreg opened his mouth to repeat his misgivings. Vincent held up a hand, halting him, and rotated impatiently in the saddle. Dreg watched enviously at the expert way Vincent held the reins. It was so easy for that man, no matter what happened to him, Vincent adapted. It was the seemingly indecisiveness that disturbed Dreg most of all. First, we loved the aliens; now, it appeared he hated them. *What next?*

He could never figure out where Vincent's interests were. His mercurial swings were growing more pronounced every day. He appeared to be dead set in one direction, then, in an instant, he changed. Dreg would have bet money that Vincent didn't care one bit about his daughter. After all, he hardly knew her, and now there was this urgency to find her. Was it about the pregnancy, her safety, or control? Dreg couldn't figure out his motives, and it frustrated him..

"Am I being short with you?" Vincent arched an eyebrow, his voice conciliatory. "It's Spekator. His plans have become tiresome."

Dreg pursed his lips. *Oh, so we're being nice now. Could it be because you need me?*

"You were happy to ally with them before."

"Who else did we have? We didn't know how to communicate with the lizards, and nobody knows what the Va'Rok are about," Vincent said, his eyes scanning the mountains.

"The Thalens met every demand. I don't know why you're having this change of heart."

Vincent looked at him and shook his head. "Terms and conditions have changed. I will use every means necessary to achieve my goals."

"You can't ignore that they've been supportive allies."

Vincent's mouth turned down with displeasure. "They've had a hidden agenda from the beginning."

"So have you!" Dreg exploded.

Vincent shrugged. "Perhaps one of the others will be more generous."

Dreg nodded, then frowned. Vincent managed to land on his feet no matter what happened. He always had an alternate plan. Dreg couldn't keep up with all these strategies. At this point, they were probably on Plan G. Inhaling a deep gulp of air, Dreg said, "Vincent, you can't think to change slides—"

"I can do anything I want. I hold all the cards."

"The Thalens put you back together. Believe me, it was no easy feat."

Vincent shrugged and hit his chest, which reverberated with a hollow sound. "We must consider very carefully who we choose above as well as below." Vincent sighed. "I agreed to splice Rosemary's DNA with theirs. They never told me about the consequences of her pregnancy."

Dreg swallowed a gasp. He bit his bottom lip, but couldn't stop the following sentence. It came out as a whine, rather than laced with the fury Dreg felt. "What about my son? What about Nate?"

Vincent turned his dead-eyed stare to Dreg's pale face. "You can't compare your offspring to mine."

Dreg fisted his hands. This was it; he was at the end of his rope. Grinding his teeth, he assessed his useless legs, then stared at the powerful mannequin thighs clamped tight to Vincent's mount. He fought the urge to push Vincent, punch the superior look off that violet-colored face. Leaning down, he saw Vincent pat the coal-black coat of the stallion. It gleamed in the fading sunlight like obsidian, the two of them looking fiercely awesome.

Dreg handled his mount awkwardly, and the horse skittishly danced a bit. Listing to one side in the saddle, anyone could plainly see the mare was as uncomfortable with its rider as the rider was with her.

A wicked thought must have worked its way into Vincent's brain. Dreg watched him rein his steed in a tight circle. Vincent slapped Dreg's mare firmly on her rump. "I said, go! We'll rendezvous by the river." He took off, galloping as fast as the horse could take him. Dreg saw him smiling evilly back at him.

Dreg shouted, "*Whoa!*" The horse began to canter. Bouncing like a five-year-old in an inflatable castle, he cursed when his chin hit his mount's neck. "That's gonna hurt," he muttered in the wind, his mouth full of hair from the horse's mane. He ascended the incline, alert and wary of any giants lurking among the tall trees and jagged rocks.

Dreg hightailed it out of the mountains as soon as he placed the pinecones in the agreed order. Oddly enough, he noticed they had a similar circle, and he needed to take that information back to Vincent. He caught up to Vincent an hour and a half later. They splashed through the river and paused on the other side. Mud splattered Dreg's face, churned by Vincent's steed.

Vincent pulled the stallion to a stop. "Here." Vincent nodded. "The Sasquatch will find us here."

Dreg noted his graceful halt was designed not to bruise the animal's tender mouth. It seemed Vincent didn't have the same consideration for him. He burned with resentment, his face flushed and windblown.

Dreg suppressed his anger, squeezing it back into a ball to tuck under his heart. He was accustomed to handling things this way. His whole life was a series of disappointments, starting with rejection from his parents, his wife, and finally, the world. A tidal wave of regret washed over him, and he whispered Nate's name. How he missed his son, the potential, the loss. *Don't think about it,* he told himself, concentrating on staying on his mount. Vincent's laugh tore him from grief back into self-preservation.

"Don't mean to be too rude, but you're a terrible rider. Did you manage to set up the message?"

Dreg pulled up next to him, clinging to the side of his horse. Too winded to talk, he nodded curtly. After a minute, he said. "I set it up, but Vincent, they had already had a circle of pine cones there in the same formation."

Vincent barked a laugh. "*Hmmm.* Better and better, it seems the Sasquatches want to meet with us. This is better than I could have hoped."

"Either that, or they're planning to negotiate with someone else," Dreg ground out.

"Don't be an idiot. Of course, the message is for me. This changes everything." Vincent went quiet, and Dreg could see his calculating mind working.

He turned to Dreg and said slyly. "*Ha!* Love it!"

"I don't understand." Dreg had trouble staying in the saddle. He leaned to the side.

Vincent inhaled deeply of the mountain air into his artificially manufactured lungs. "See, here, Dreg. The universe is already working in our favor. They contacted us first. They need us. Our bargaining power has improved. It's a good day to be back on Earth!"

Vincent's powerful grip caught him and pulled him back onto the saddle. "You're not done yet, my little friend. You're going to have to rustle up something for us to eat. I find I'm peckish."

"*Oww,*" Dreg whined from the inhumane clamp of the fingers on his upper arm.

Vincent smiled, flexing his gloved hand. "Sorry," he said in an insincere voice. "Getting used to the mechanics of the new appendages." Vincent inhaled again. "Can you smell that, Dreg? Less pollution." He pounded the pommel of his saddle for emphasis. "We are already making the world a purer place." Vincent took another deep and satisfying breath. "I love the smell of the planet in the evening!" He smiled. "My senses are finally returning."

The air was definitely cleaner, a result of the absence of planes and traffic. The world was renewing itself, cleaning up the litter from an uncaring populace.

Dreg looked sadly at his dusty pants and then at Vincent's gloating face. Sniffing tentatively, he shrugged. He didn't mind the aroma of civilization, the stench of humanity, the perfume of progress. In fact, he thought, it smelled a little boring right now.

The scents of flowers competed to overwhelm each other, blending their fragrances into a mishmash of odors. Still, the idea of starting over, fresh and new, stayed in his mind, and he kept returning to it. He thought about Nate and his chubby baby feet, so many years ago, those trusting infant hands.

When he was a newborn, it was the happiest time of Dreg's life. He was Andrew back then, Nate Owens' dad, his teacher, his protector. "I wonder if one can wash away the sins of the past and be reborn like nature," Dreg said, not realizing he spoke aloud.

Dreg shivered when he heard Vincent's response.

"And I quote from the bible, Hebrews 9:22, 'Indeed, under the law almost everything is purified with blood, and without the shedding of blood there is no forgiveness of sins.'"

Dreg's heart twisted. Yes, blood had been shed, his son's blood, and he could not find it in his shriveled heart to forgive. He threw his lot in with Vincent, caring neither for monsters nor humanity. *Only Vincent.* Once he lost his son, he gave everything he had left to Vincent.

He looked up at Vincent's face. Vincent was all that mattered. Dreg took care of him, much like he did Nate. He stared at the other man's eyes. The difference was that Nate never glared at him with contempt. *Why do I stay with him? What's in it for me?*

"Never met a human who gave a rat's ass about his surroundings, except what they could get from it. Sure, society is filled with do-gooders who talk a fine game, but do nothing unless it enriches themselves somehow," Vincent said.

Dreg jerked in the saddle. He hadn't been paying attention. *Was Vincent talking about him?* He smiled insincerely at Vincent in an attempt to hide his roiling thoughts.

Vincent slapped Dreg's back playfully as if sharing a joke and continued talking.

"They have their charity events, host dinners, give money, but do they really care? Protect a habitat? Save a monster's dignity? Do any of them actually take a monster under their wing? Make him feel needed, or even cherished? Do they give a thought about what life was like for someone like that, someone like you?" He poked a hard finger in Dreg's chest.

Dreg stiffened. Someone like me? *I'm not a monster.* He opened his mouth, then snapped it shut.

Vincent's voice was loud, talking about the indignities of being different, the struggles of not fitting in.

Dreg looked down at his club foot, the way it twisted to fit in the stirrup. He peered at Vincent, listened to his rant, and a bubble of resentment formed in his chest. I may be different, but I'm not a *monster.* I'm not like them. Narrowing his eyes, he looked at Vincent, taking in the magnificence of the mannequin's body.

Vincent had no idea. Up until he had his head transplant, he was perfect in every way. Handsome. He conformed, melted into a community. He couldn't understand the struggles that others faced trying to satisfy society's idea of normal. Dreg was perceived as weird and strange by others. He had a clear understanding of what he was and indeed what he was not. Dreg was not a *monster*, he screamed the word in his head. Sure, he performed with the vamps, stole the show in his opinion, but it was part of the act. When Vincent told him he wanted to control the monster population, he could not have possibly meant *him*.

"Humanity fiddled, Dreg. Just like Nero in Ancient Rome, as the world burned around them. Talk, talk, talk." Vincent made a face. "But when hard decisions had to be made, where were they? Nowhere!" He bent down, his voice lowered. "It was left to me to make the changes to protect everyone. Even if I have to hurt some of them to get the job done, we all have to make sacrifices."

Dreg stared at the other man, dumbfounded.

Dreg glanced up at the cloudless sky. He remembered the vacant homes and buildings they passed. He thought about all the losses the world had suffered. A sharp pain in his chest reminded him of that ultimate sacrifice. His son. *What did you sacrifice, Vincent?*

What did he care about the rest of the world? For that matter, did he even care about Vincent's greater plan anymore? The all-consuming mission seemed to have shrunk in importance. A worm of confusion wriggled in Dreg's brain, taking up a permanent spot. It lodged somewhere between resentment and doubt.

Vincent peered at the growing darkness. "I hope those beasts get the message soon. I have places to go and a daughter to find." His laughter echoed in the dusk. "Now, go find us something to eat!"

CHAPTER 16

ONE GIANT STEP

THE SIX GIANTS and Rosemary left barely an hour later, laden with sacks of supplies. Her meager belongings were stuffed in a knapsack Jötnar had thoughtfully prepared. She stood with her former first mate at the entrance of her tent. He had grown six inches taller since he had revealed that he, too, was a giant. It seems that he and the girls were having their annual growth spurt.

"Now that you've admitted who you are, you can come along," Rosemary told him hopefully. She wasn't talking about him revealing that he was a giant.

Jötnar blushed bright red to the roots of his orange hair. "They will have a hard time accepting me, now that I've emerged from the cupboard."

"You mean closet," she laughed. "No, I suppose not."

"No one in my clan has ever admitted such a thing before.

Besides," he added sheepishly. "I've made friends here and I don't want to leave."

"There will be a battle soon."

Jötnar nodded. "I know. I want to help."

Rosemary looked behind him to see a young man waiting patiently for him.

Jötnar turned his head to smile at him, and the man returned the wave shyly.

"He looks nice." Rosemary nodded.

"He is. So are his friends. I can be who I want to be around them." Jötnar handed her the bag. "Captain, a word of advice?"

She saw Jötnar's gaze watching the six giants, who would soon be her traveling companions.

"They will not be like your crew, and don't take kindly to mink-ins."

"Minkins?"

"Your kind, humans. They have little trust in humans and will look to make things difficult. They like to be admired and appreciated."

"I can handle that," Rosemary said, with a smile. "Looks like we're both taking giant steps in our lives."

Jötnar grinned ear-to-ear and then added, "It's been an honor to serve with you. Rosemary, don't be pushy, or…. you know…. bossy. If they close off, you will not be successful."

"I'll keep that in mind. Thanks for saving my life."

"Thanks for giving me mine," Jötnar said, his voice husky. "Remember, giants don't like to be ordered around." He rushed off, pausing to swing the man onto his shoulder. They loped off laughing, a trail of dust in their wake.

Rosemary sighed at the memory, lost in thought. Grillos had placed her inside his elbow as if he were cradling her. "I can walk," she told him. "It's not necessary for you to carry me."

A murmur went through the group, and she could tell her com-ment irritated them.

"Let her walk, Grillos," Zaf said sarcastically. "You don't *need* to carry her," he mimicked.

"Yea, maybe we'll get home in time for next year's spring celebrations," Brontes called out.

"I'll be able to keep up with you," Rosemary responded tartly.

"With your small bladder, I bet we'll have to stop twenty times," Brontes challenged.

Rosemary opened her mouth to reply, but Grillos interrupted her.

His calm words brought the conversation to a close. "You'll stay nice and safe right here, and we will stop as many times as you and your child need." His expression made it plain that he was in control.

Rosemary settled herself on Grillos's shoulder, puzzled that she was having trouble with this group. How was she supposed to influence them when it appeared they distrusted her?

She ruminated as the landscape went by in a whir of dusty browns, the giant's large feet making good time. They didn't speak much, and Rosemary had the distinct impression that aside from Grillos, nobody else was too happy about her presence. She attempted to engage in conversation using different tactics, but it was hard when they pretended they didn't hear her. "I don't think your brothers like me."

Grillos shrugged. "They don't especially trust other species. Our history is filled with minkin betrayal."

"I'd like to learn more about it," she said, loud enough for them all to hear. It was met with hostile silence. She sat back and closed her eyes. Soon, the gentle swaying allowed her to fall into a light doze.

Rosemary roused herself to see that they had entered the high desert. "You guys are fast!" she exclaimed.

"It has helped that you have not slowed us down," Grillos replied. "Besides, we must make haste."

"Yea," Brontes agreed. "The higher we go, the more unsafe."

"The lower we go, the more dangerous it is," Zaf added.

Rosemary perked up. "What are the dangers you speak of?"

"You tell her," Brontes sneered at Grillos. "Maybe it will scare her enough to run back to her people."

"Are you calling me a coward?" Rosemary challenged. She struggled to sit up. Grillos's swaying movement made it impossible.

He pushed her back with a gentle but firm finger. "Relax, Captain Rosemary. Everyone saw your bravery." He glanced back with a stern look at his brothers. "We have the dangers well in hand. We know these valleys and mountains like the back of our hands. We must avoid the creatures that perch above us, as well as the ones slinking below us."

"That's the second time you've spoken about monsters underground. Are you referring to those slugs Danai mentioned?"

"*Ha!* You told her about the giant slugs. Demons, I call them. Do they make your heart flutter with fear?" Brontes taunted.

"Hardly. What's so scary about a gastropod? They taste delicious with a little garlic and butter."

The giants laughed, their great shoulders shaking with mirth. "Well," Grillos said. "Let's see if you feel the same way when you're eye-to-eye with one so big it would feed a village for a month."

"Except we don't eat them," Brontes warned, his voice ominous.

"Oh, come on, is this one of your inventions to keep curious humans away from your home?"

"Regular guard slugs, they are," Grillos told her.

There were a few grunts of agreement, a smattering of chuckles, and even a loud guffaw. The group thawed a bit. She studied their faces, wondering what could have changed.

Rosemary began to ask why the brothers started humming robustly, the melody drowning out her voice. Eventually, she gave up trying to speak. Brontes burst into song, which she recognized from her youth. "Hey, that one belongs to a group of little people who work in an underground mine. I love that fairytale."

"*Ha!* Fairy tale, she calls it," Brontes said. "Who do you think taught it to them?"

"Wait, what?" Rosemary shouted.

"I told you it was a long story. If you're finished yapping, I think we might share our story." Grillos patted her leg that rested against his shoulder. "In the beginning…"

CHAPTER 17

CONICAL FOIL HATS

"IT ALL BEGAN when they zapped us with their Gamma rays," Otto explained as he fitted a conical aluminum foil hat on her sore head. He pulled it sharply against her tender scalp, and Jade moaned. "You'll have to learn how to protect yourself when you go back out there." He pointed to the doorway and shoved her out into the blinding sunlight. She fell, landing on all fours in the dirt. She wasn't used to her newly installed eye.

Otto had implanted it a few days ago, and she had spent most of that time piecing together the likeness it projected into some form of reality that made sense.

At first, all she saw were flashes of color, fragments of confusing images. Of course, her depth perception was off, and the shin on her good leg was black and blue from bumping into everything. It was as though she was seeing everything for the first time.

Yesterday, something had shifted, and she learned she could

zoom in on tiny details, pick up infrared, and, best of all, process multiple focal points simultaneously. She wished she could talk to Keisha about it, who would explain the mechanics of it. Her face brightened. *She remembered Keisha!*

Jade allowed her eyes to adjust to the bright light.

The sky was a soft apricot; the absence of sound was startling. It was so desolate that she felt like she was the last person on earth. The occasional screech from hawks circling overhead broke the heavy silence. The birds coasted in lazy figure eights, searching for prey. She turned her attention to her surroundings. He had sent her outside to get used to her new appendages. Jade straightened her back and looked around her. Otto was carrying on again, demanding she tell him where they should go. Taking a deep breath, she sniffed the wind and begged for an answer to appear. She had no idea where she was or where the nutjob wanted to go.

Otto's hideaway was constructed underground, its doorway camouflaged by rocks and sagebrush. It was an old metal shipping container, he had informed her, bought for pennies on the dollar. A tall pipe was planted in the dry soil next to the entrance. It looked for all the world like a movie set she'd seen in the desert outside of Copper Valley when they filmed some television show about the end of the world. *Where's a zombie when you need one,* she laughed.

The pipe rotated, and Jade knew Otto was using it like a periscope to watch her.

Jade growled deep in her throat, surprised at the guttural sound as well as how good it made her feel. Saliva pooled in her mouth, and she wiped it away with her non-robotic hand, leaving a trail of dirt on her cheek where it itched her sensitive skin. She wondered how she wasn't freaking out about her smeared face or the imperfection of her appearance. Not to mention the enormous claw-like appendage Otto had fastened to her wrist. She gaped at it with a mixture of revulsion and fright. *OMG,* her rattled brain thought if *her friends could see her now.*

Which friends? Who were her friends? The only thing Jade was sure of was that she wasn't sure of anything. There's Keisha, Wyatt, and… others. Who are the others? She tried to remember, but it hurt too much to think about it.

Shading her eyes, Jade attempted to search the horizon, but she didn't know what she was supposed to be looking for. Her new eye was having trouble identifying things, and the small print and numbers she was seeing confused her. She sniffed again, licking the breeze as if it would reveal something to her. She preferred using these senses. It was as if her tongue could taste the changes in the atmosphere. Definitely weird, but somehow, natural. *Hmmmm.*

Tumbleweeds rolled around the corral, and Otto's strange arrangement of glass bottles tinkled from where they hung on the bare branches around the perimeter of their encampment.

She pushed the conical aluminum foil hat from her damp forehead, feeling stupid. It fell to the ground, scoring the skin on the clean side of her face and leaving a red mark. It stung, but not enough to send her running to complain to someone. But really, she thought, looking around the encampment, who would listen to her?

Her heart gave a twist, and pursing her rosebud-shaped mouth, she winced when her flesh pulled the newly healed patch of skin next to it. She licked her lips to moisten them.

Did she miss her dad? Yes, but there was someone she missed more. It stood on the outer reaches of her fuzzy memory. Her cheeks tingled, reddening with the effort to think. Errant thoughts like little hummingbirds flitted through her brain, teasing and pulling at her, but dissolving like sugar in the rain. No matter how hard she tried, she couldn't grasp that memory.

A gust of wind lifted her conical helmet from the ground, twirling it like a mini-spaceship. It landed on the pointed spike of an aloe vera plant. Otto warned her not to lose it or remove it from her head. He claimed aliens could read her thoughts. Glancing up at the sky, she laughed. Her new eye spun like a gyroscope, and she staggered for a minute, dizzy and breathless. The world righted itself, and she made a fist to the heavens. *Bring it on!* She mouthed silently, not knowing where this newfound defiance was coming from.

Jade got up and walked over to the hat, attempting to kick it off the plant with her booted foot. She missed, wobbled as she tried to regain her balance. Closing her good eye, she did it again, laughing with triumph when her foot connected and sent the aluminum flying. She strolled over and crushed the foil under her toe with a satisfying crunch. Placing a rock on top of it, she murmured to Otto through the transistor he'd implanted under her ear. "I've secured it so it won't blow away."

She heard an exasperated sigh and then, "You should put it back on. Tell your eye to find branches one meter long," Otto commanded.

She tapped the mic with her finger, knowing the reverb would irritate him. "I don't know how big a meter is," she snapped back.

"*Ugh*, didn't you pay attention to anything I said in class?"

Jade pictured Otto cupping his forehead as he attempted to stifle his frustration. She smiled. "Well, I don't."

Otto responded with exaggerated patience. "Just do it the way I showed you."

Jade closed her eyes and said, "One meter branches."

Her new eye exploded with shapes, identifying everything around her in different colors and designs. "*Whoa!*"

Jade turned in a small circle, gasping as everything from plants to clouds was identified in colorful blips. She locked onto a pile of broken twigs and branches but was too excited to stop. She forgot Otto's command and lurched around, resting her hands on bushes and rocks. Sitting down on a boulder, she squinted at the bleak landscape. Where was this place? With her new eye, she could see for miles. A hot wind blew through her, leaving her feeling exposed. Her mood shifted, and Jade felt herself deflating. She shivered uncontrollably. Maybe Otto kidnapped her and took her in a spaceship to Mars. Melvin talked about a movie he saw… *wait a minute*, she paused. When did she ever exchange more than an order for hamburgers at Instaburger with...with... *Melvin*?

Otto's voice came through her receiver, making her jerk back into reality. "Stop wasting time. Collect the wood," he ordered.

Sighing deeply, she started to organize a small pile of twigs and branches, her right hand stiff and unyielding, the metal claw-like fingers crushing the wood into dust. Frustrated, she brushed her robotic hand against the blue overalls she wore and considered her new appendage.

It was like something out of a sci-fi book —a highly efficient machine, strong and capable, if she'd only gotten the hang of it. *Bet Melvin would like it,* she thought, wondering how and why the auburn-headed guy's opinion could matter.

Every time she spoke about Copper Valley, Otto said some strange crap that left her with more questions than answers.

She understood only one thing: she was Otto's prisoner, stuck in the middle of nowhere, with metal replacing bone and skin, and without a clue as to what happened to her. The back of her neck rippled, and her scalp tightened when she recalled the incident in the bunker— had she actually morphed like a *werewolf*? Maybe it was part of a fevered dream. It couldn't have really happened.

Now and then, the flashes overwhelmed her fragile mind. Rapid flickers of memories teased her. Painful and contorting, her skin stretched and pulled. Everything hurt like nothing she'd ever experienced. Then there was this impulsive desire to howl coupled with the need to sniff the breeze. She imagined kind green eyes watching her, not the soulless, black voids of Otto's avid gaze. That man was creepy as a teacher and equally scary now.

A pain lodged in her chest when she thought about her parents: they were lost to her, but she wasn't sure how her life had disintegrated. Otto seemed to believe that she should remember on her own, and the stingy morsels of information he revealed made her hate him all the more. She thought about running, but he had scared her with tales of roving murdering gangs, the result of a society gone crazy. Part of her doubted him, yet here she was, leaving her to believe something of what he claimed must have struck a chord within her.

Licking her pointer finger, she held it aloft, feeling the direction of the wind. She looked toward the setting sun. That was in the West, she was certain. Copper Valley was in that direction, but she wasn't sure how she knew that. She sniffed tentatively, yes, she was positive. That was where she needed to go.

She should be thinking about escaping. Her gaze followed the mountain ridge to the north, which resembled the backbone of a giant, sleeping dinosaur. *Her brother loved dinosaurs.* The thought of him made her heart contract painfully, and her good eye stung, which was odd. Generally, she couldn't stand the little monster. He was always into her things, and then there was the whole Nolan issue, where she was being held as a hostage; her bully of a boyfriend was using her younger brother to force her to stay with him.

Wait… she held her normal hand over her face, trying to blot out the stream of images. Nolan laughing maniacally, the handsome planes of his face turning soft and mushy, the color changing to puke green, dotted with open zombie sores. Cringing, Jade screamed, tears leaking from her eyes, she cupped her hands over her ears to drown the sound of an axe meeting flesh and bone, the splatter as someone… *Nolan* was split in half. And she knew that somehow, she was responsible.

Shivering, she fell to her knees, cold immobilizing her, the feeling of being encased by purple goo, her brother's muffled cries as he was … *smothered.*

Jade fell back on the hard-packed earth, exhausted. Her face burned where it met the sand, her skin still raw and tender. She lay there broken and defeated, knowing her life had changed in ways she failed to comprehend. Taking a shuddering breath, she searched for a memory, and once her bruised mind found it, she latched onto it like a lifeline. Her fingers sifted through the loose soil of the compound as if they were threading through curls, *the red hair of Melvin Saunders.*

Jade rose on a shaking elbow and looked just north of where Copper Valley existed, toward the gully behind the school where they were constructing the new theme park, Monsterland. Something was drawing her in that direction. She knew her parents' home was not the one she wished to return to.

She howled then, a long mournful cry, the longing in her heart making her eye water.

Touching her cheek, or what was left of it, she knew Otto had bolted a metal plate to half of her face. It had been smashed by a sea creature that left her shivering. She had awakened five times since finding herself here, choking, feeling rock-hard hands squeezing the life from her, the memory enough to give a bit of credence to Otto's wild explanation.

Nightly, he schooled her. Fantastical tales of traitorous, reptilian politicians in league with hostile aliens, monsters on the loose, and a New World Order wavering between fascism and the final apocalypse. He made her take notes, using her new claw to strengthen it. Resting her chin in her good palm, Jade barely listened, her mind drifting to laughter in a lagoon and a freckled chest, topped by a head of red frizz. *Melvin. It was Melvin.* Until today, she hadn't been sure of her identity, but now she knew. She wrote his name in the sand where she lay, her heart full of joy.

"Hurry!" Otto stumbled from the opening. He wore the triangular aluminum foil hat and looked for all the world like a demented clown. Eyeing Jade's discarded helmet, he cursed loudly, retrieved it, and smashed it on her head, none too gently. "What are you thinking?"

Jade snarled, saliva dripped from the corner of her mouth. She snapped at him, her teeth clicking against each other. It made her feel powerful, especially when he jerked away, his eyes wild.

"None of your werewolf shenanigans today! You must protect yourself. Do you want them to suck your brains out like they did to the rest of Copper Valley?"

While she thought she'd never hear the word 'werewolf' connected to herself, let alone picture the image of her brains being vacuumed out of her skull, the visions today convinced her that there was more truth to Otto's story. It gave her a lot to think about.

"Did you get anything? Any memories surface?"

Jade looked away and shook her head no. Otto gripped her by the shoulders. "Look at me. You did. I know you did."

The aluminum foil scratched her skin where metal met flesh. It dawned on Jade that he was looking to her for answers. This was her chance to escape, to go home.

"Yes. Yes. Whatever you are looking for, you'll find it in—,"

"Tell me!" Otto shook her so hard, her teeth rattled.

Jade felt a driving need to return to a special place where she could be authentic to herself. It didn't matter if she was perfect, beautiful, smart, or funny. She could be Jade. The real Jade. Strong arms beckoned her, a safe embrace, and a wolf's head necklace with emerald eyes flashed in her mind. She shouted, "Monsterland. They—." She pointed vaguely to the sky and then touched the triangular foil hat on her head. "They want you to go to Monsterland."

Otto nodded sagely. "Of course."

CHAPTER 18

BEAR FACTS

"I DON'T WANT TO end up being a freak in Vincent Konrad's Monsterland," Olrec thought glumly when he left the confines of his village. Even though he knew the theme park had been destroyed, he didn't trust the doctor or his intentions. Olrec traveled down the mountain, his large feet nimble and leaving no footprints. He hummed casually as he moved, his eyes alert, not wanting to give away how nervous he was. His superior hearing protected him, allowing him to duck and run for cover if he came upon *stupes,* but at this altitude, they'd never venture, so he didn't have to worry about them. He wasn't afraid to come this far south; he knew what he was doing. He just wished his brother-in-law had more faith in him.

He glanced up at the ice-blue sky. No planes roared overhead. Not the clunky, cumbersome ones that humans used to traverse the planet, and not the streamlined, fast ones that moved high above them.

It was quieter, even at this distance; he recognized that the usual buzz of humanity didn't fill his ears. Farther away on the super roads, there was no congestion. Both his nose and ears told him that. The ground didn't vibrate with the machinery *stupes* used to control nature. It was more peaceful.

Olrec wondered what had happened to the *stupes*. They'd heard rumors, ones that traveled through the forest grapevine, and while he didn't do more than scare humans, he was able to communicate with the critters who shared their home.

Once it was established that Sasquatches didn't eat meat, friendships began to develop. Speaking squirrel or bear helped. While he was fluent in one, he managed pretty well in the other. He rounded the bend toward a vee-shaped formation of trees. Bending down, he examined the pine cones arranged exactly the way he was told they would look.

Olrec stood, his back creaking as he straightened. The doctor had received their message. Now, he only had to travel to the designated spot by the river to make contact.

The steady *pat, pat, pat* above him drew his attention. He sauntered higher, parting trees and proceeding with caution. The roar of a cougar on his left made him pause. The message was indistinct. Olrec opened his mouth to ask him to repeat, but sensed the cougar's impatience. He waved, and the creature nodded back. It leaped from boulder to boulder, and its poise arrested Olrec. He wished his twins were here to share the moment. The large, padded paws landed lightly, the perfectly balanced touchdown as graceful as a dancer. He watched the tail curl like a snake, swaying as the cougar descended the incline one huge rock at a time.

Olrec sniffed. No *stupes,* but he bent to smear his forehead with mud as a precaution—no reason to get sloppy.

The sound of something being swatted pulled him back to his mission. This time, he eased behind trees, mindful of where he stepped. It was not inconceivable for a *stupe* to venture into this part of the mountain.

Listening, he followed the melodies of the birds, knowing they'd be silent if no one intruded on their enclave. They were the best alarm system in the world—no fluttering of wings, no shrieks from the treetops.

Still, he trod carefully as he proceeded. The dark surface of the trees provided excellent camouflage, and he blended in perfectly. He picked the widest trunks, allowing the fan of branches to hide his bulk.

He hugged the tree, and a large chunk of his hair ripped off. "*Owww.*" Olrec tried to pull the fur from the rough surface of the bark, but it was stuck fast.

The sound became louder, more insistent, followed by a frustrated whine. Olrec smiled broadly and stamped noisily from the brush, forgetting about the tuft of hair left behind.

Holding a hand high in greeting, he gave a warm hello to a large brown bear.

Far from home, he told her in perfect bear.

The bear gave a mournful salute, her eyes full of worry.

What's the problem, my furry friend? Olrec walked toward her. *Any humans about?*

The bear only looked upward. The steady hum of a swarm of bees filled the glade; a giant hive hung suspended from a branch high above the bear, who was swatting it with a broken tree limb. Bees flew around her head, landing on her thick coat, only to be brushed away with her impatient paws.

Oh, for fur's sake, let me help you, Olrec offered. He needed only to reach above her and pull the hive with his long fingers. Dozens of bees tried to sting him through his coarse hide, but he flicked them away easily.

The bear grinned as she took the proffered hive. Reaching inside, she pulled out a thick rectangle of wax dripping with honey.

Seen stupes…er… I mean, humans? Olrec asked again, taking the golden honeycomb.

A few. She shrugged. *Mainly the walking dead ones. Oh, a strange duo, an ugly walking doll, and a stunted gnome-like creature.*

Purple face?

Yes, but be careful. Purple-face is with a troll.

Sounds like the one I'm looking for. Olrec lifted the honeycomb high and allowed the

syrup to drip into his eager lips. *Delicious.*

They were a creepy pair, but watch out for the giants, friend, she cautioned him.

Olrec stopped and looked at her. *Seriously?*

She nodded. *Yes, sir. I've seen a pack of them, headed that way.* She pointed east, back toward his village.

You sure? How many?

The bear raised her eyebrows. *I know a giant when I see one. There were six,* she mumbled, her mouth filled with honey.

Olrec thought for a minute. *Strange, they'd venture this far north. They usually avoid this high up in the mountains.* He smiled toothily.

Odd group. Had a human with them.

Probably caught on a raid, Olrec said, sucking a honeycomb. *Looks like they found their dinner.*

I don't think so. She seemed to be part of the group. Sat on the largest one's shoulder like a princess riding an elephant.

What would you know about princesses and elephants?

Insulted, she sniffed and pulled the hive close to her chest. *I've seen a book or two in my time. Anyway, you don't have to believe me. But I'd watch my furry hide, if I were you.* She turned in a huff and rumbled off, a swarm of bees trailing after her.

Olrec laughed at the absurd image of a giant walking with a human on their shoulder. He sat down on a flat rock to finish off the honey. He sucked the comb clean, then lay back on the stone surface, enjoying the warm rays of the sun.

A shadow blotted the sunlight, casting him into darkness. Shading his eyes, he blinked. He had made good time and was early for the doctor. He'd better take a look and make sure the giants were nowhere near his village. Olrec heard a humming noise. He looked up and cursed.

A round ship with blue lights hovered in the sky. It did an impossible maneuver, then silently flew away as if ejected from a slingshot. Grays. He hated Grays.

He took off in the direction of the giants.

CHAPTER 19

WHICH WAY SHOULD THEY GO?

WYATT HUNG BACK as the president returned to the camp. Melvin turned to him and said, "Come on!"

Wyatt waved him off and said, "You go ahead. I'll be along in a minute."

"Anything wrong?" Carter asked him.

Wyatt turned, his face startled. "I didn't see you."

Carter shrugged. "I know. A lot was going on. It's not every day you get asked to help in negotiations."

"I… the president asked," Wyatt said, his eyes going wide. "You don't think I'm starstruck?"

"Not in the least. You're a good kid, always have been." Carter was quiet for a moment and then said, "I'm amazed by what you've been able to do."

This comment caused Wyatt to blush. A tightness gathered in his chest. "Did my mom feel that way, too?"

Carter looked him straight in the eyes. "You know, I didn't have much time with her." His voice sounded strange, like it was being squeezed from his throat. "One thing I learned real fast is that you and your brother made your mom the happiest person in the world. She was proud of her boys every day."

They stood stock still, lost in memories. Wyatt saw Carter wipe the corner of his eye. They deliberately looked off in opposite directions. Wyatt didn't respond; he couldn't get words past the lump in his throat.

"After the crap I went through with my parents, you know, the drinking, dementia, I never thought I'd want to—" Carter stopped, his face stricken.

Wyatt smiled, "You were sick of family?"

Carter relaxed and shrugged. "Not exactly. I never thought I'd want to take care of anybody else." He straightened, his jaw dropping. "I don't want you to think I feel like you or Sean are a burden."

"Stop, Carter. You've been more accommodating than we deserved. We didn't make it easy."

Carter shook his head. "No, you didn't. But your mom, she never gave up trying to make us a family."

Wyatt looked Carter full in the face and said softly, "Neither did you."

"Thanks for that. She is… I mean, was something, *huh*? A real special lady." Carter cleared his throat noisily, "I've been meaning to talk to you. We haven't had much time alone to touch base." Carter stopped as if gathering his thoughts. "What do you want to do now?"

"I think they're expecting us back at Prendick."

Carter shook his head. "I wasn't talking about right now. You left Copper Valley to see what's happening in Los Angeles." He looked down the road as if to emphasize its barrenness. "Did you find what you were looking for?"

Wyatt didn't answer. He locked his eyes on the Hollywood sign. There was nothing here, no friends, no family, no nothing. He said, finally, "I don't know why I wanted to come here, I just knew that I did."

"Sometimes we are driven by an inner need. I understood you had to go."

Wyatt sighed. "I'm not sure what I feel now." He looked up to Carter's face. "Man, I'm like one of those party balloons, after the party is over, all wrinkled and deflated."

Carter snorted. "I know that feeling. It's all the adrenaline. You're coming down from it."

"Okay, so where do I go from here?"

"That's what I'm asking. We were thinking of heading back to Copper Valley." Carter paused. "Sean, me… and we hoped you'd come too."

Wyatt shook his head. "There's nothing for any of us back there. Copper Valley is dead. It's a ghost town."

"I know, but it's our home. The one thing I'm sure of is that your mom would want you to be in the safest place."

"She's gone, Carter." He swallowed. "You… and Sean have no place to live."

"John Raven invited us back to the reservation. I think Howard will stay with his parents. Melvin?" Carter paused and raised his eyebrows in question. "Lily will be there, too."

"Howard hasn't said anything to me. Melvin either. I don't think Mel's ready to return because of what happened to Jade, and all," Wyatt replied. He didn't mention Lily, but he knew his cheeks were flushed.

"Of course. It's a shame." Carter observed him, a slight smile on his lips. "We can talk about it, if you'd like."

Wyatt ignored the comment. "Look. I don't think we should go back. Jade's gone, Keisha is in a strange place. Howard wants to be where he can do the most good, and Melvin." Wyatt looked at the tree line on the mountains behind them. "I know what he's feeling." He paced the road, his hands deep in his pockets. He looked at Carter. "Do you really have to go back? Do you *want* to go back?" he asked in a small voice.

"Are you asking us to stay? There's going to be a lot to do in Copper Valley."

Wyatt bit his bottom lip. "There's going to be a lot to do here." He pointed back toward the ocean. "We don't even know what's going to happen when those shell things hatch." He searched Carter's face. "Don't you want to be close to the action? Didn't you hate not knowing what was going on?"

Now it was Carter's turn to look troubled. "I can't think your mom would want you or your brother in harm's way."

"No, Carter, the only thing she'd want is for us to stay together."

"True, that." Carter nodded. "Look, I'll admit either choice is pretty crappy."

Wyatt nodded. "We can go to Copper Valley and wait for the world to come to us, or we can go out and meet it head-on. I can't sit and wait to die like… like…" Wyatt's voice cracked.

"I know. Like your mom. Okay. You're right. I can't protect you and your brother by hiding. We'll stay together."

"Yes, " Wyatt nodded. "As a family."

Carter squeezed his shoulder, and for some strange reason, it made Wyatt's eyes bright. He swallowed past the lump in his throat, and they turned around to walk toward the army encampment.

Wyatt looked down at their feet. They moved in perfect unison, as if they were soldiers marching into battle.

CHAPTER 20

HUNGRY HUMANS

"YOU DON'T BELIEVE me?" Grillos said without breaking his stride, Rosemary, ensconced comfortably on his shoulder. He looked hurt, the hard angles of his face softening. Rosemary felt it tug at her heart; she patted his face, her hand minuscule against the vast expanse of skin. She examined the hard planes of his face. He was anatomically different from a human. His face was broader, his nose small, and the orbital ridge jutting out like a shelf, but something was endearing about his kind eyes and winsome smile. She resisted the urge to caress his cheek.

"It's a little hard to…" She gulped and said, "Swallow. I mean, you're telling me you've been able to remain hidden for thousands of years, back to *biblical times*." She grew quiet for a minute, feeling the muscles of his shoulder bunch underneath her. She rested her head against his shoulder and sighed while he spoke. Grillos even smelled different than a human. She was surrounded by his scent, a blend of cedarwood, wildflowers, and a hint of rain. An earthy and somehow comforting scent. She would have enjoyed it more if not for the nagging pain in her midsection.

"Your anthropologists need only a bone from the thigh or an arm to measure true height," Grillos observed, her shifting uncomfortably.

Rosemary grimaced and said, "Okay, other than fairy tales, I've never seen anything about a race of giants."

"*Ha*! Your Bible tells stories of giants… What about David and Goliath? Og, King of Bashan, the Anakites, and let's not forget the Nephilim. Are you well?"

Rosemary stayed quiet for a minute, then answered. "I feel a bit off. I don't know much about my condition; I'm sure it's just my body adjusting. I'd rather take my mind off of it." She groaned and shifted around. "My biblical history is sketchy. Let's go over this again, please."

Grillos launched into his story, but Brontes shouted, drowning out his brother's words.

"We were here *first*."

"So you say—" Rosemary shot back.

"Are you going to let me tell the story or not?" Grillos gave his brother a dirty look.

"I'm sorry, go ahead." Brontes had the decency to look embarrassed.

"Our people led a simple life. As I told you, we hunted great beasts that covered the grassy plains. Bison that stood ten feet tall, woolly mammoth, and giant sloths that could feed a family for a month. Our women preserved the meat, made clothing, and repaired our homes. It was simple." He shrugged. "A nice life. We are wanderers by nature." He looked at her sideways to check if she was listening. Rosemary nodded with encouragement for him to continue. "My people followed the herds of beasts that fed and housed us."

"Hunters and gatherers, much like the early tribes that populated the planet," Rosemary added. "I'm a wanderer, myself," she said wistfully, wishing she could see the ocean. They had lost sight of it when they turned inland just over an hour ago. She already missed the rolling waves and salty air.

"Nothing like your people. Those monsters came later. They arrived with the fiery chariots that filled the sky." Brontes waved his beefy arms. "See, this is where I'm having trouble. Whether you follow the Bible or Darwin's theories, we come from here, and according to the ancient stories I've seen on TV, giants are said to be the offspring resulting from alien and human mating. It was on the show *Grim Myths*."

"Lies!" Zaf erupted, his face turning red. "Twisted history!"

"That's the name of another show I watched." Rosemary smiled.

"Easy, brother. Let me explain. They change the narrative by whitewashing their evil deeds," Grillos continued. "Our stories are recoded in our Book, the Holist of Holies."

"You can't believe everything you read." Rosemary smoldered with resentment.

"Don't mock our Book!" Brontes spat.

"I am not mocking. Who wrote it?"

"It's been handed down from many, many generations ago. The old ones recorded before our story could be forgotten."

"I understand, but Brontes, don't judge everyone by just a few encounters with us. You sound a bit extreme. Not all humans have bad intentions."

"That's just not true! In the annals of our Book, minkins... er, humans are responsible for the atrocities of my people," Brontes huffed.

Grillos looked backwards at his brother. "Brontes, your daughters decided to stay. Stop blaming minkins."

"*Atrocity* is a strong word, Brontes. Surely when species clash—" Rosemary argued.

"Just like a minkin to justify bad behavior..." Zaf grumbled.

Rosemary stiffened her back with resentment.

She could feel Grillos's jaw clench, and she heard a grating noise. Her senses went on high alert when she realized it was the sound of him grinding his teeth. Was he mad at her, humanity, or was he losing patience with his brother? She certainly couldn't tell.

Really, what did she know of either him or his kind? Her body prickled with alarm, and she could almost hear her good friend Shandy warning her not to go off willy-nilly with every Tom, Dick, or, in this case, hairy giant. Her old mate would give it to her for daydreaming about Grillos's scent and beautiful cheekbones instead of thinking about her safety! Taking a deep breath, she assessed her surroundings, looking for an escape route if she needed it. Three of Grillos's massive brothers walked before her, two others bringing up the rear.

They were climbing along the ridge of a mountain in the high desert landscape. Frowning, her lips thinned. She should have paid more attention. They were off the highways, the ground rocky and burned, the recent fires making short work of any foliage she could have used to hide. Large boulders offered little to no cover. Above her, the sun beat down mercilessly. Grillos took her lack of response as a sign of discomfort and asked if she needed to stop.

When she looked down, she realized Grillos's large, orange-flecked eyes were awash with concern. "I don't want to upset you, Rosemary, but I would never lie."

Rosemary bit her lip. There was a quiet moment between them, and Rosemary knew it was important how she answered. "I believe you," she said slowly. "But it's *your* truth. Did it ever occur that there may be another point of view? That whoever wrote your book had a certain perspective?"

Grillos thought for a moment. "So let me speak our truth and then we'll compare and decide which one rings correct."

Rosemary mulled it over. They had hours to go, and she wasn't thrilled about a bash fest of humanity, especially if she didn't feel responsible. After all, she had never hurt a giant. In fact, she helped one; she smiled, thinking of Jötnar. Still, the problem had many facets.

It made sense. Shandy had always told her that there were three sides to an argument: *yours, mine, and the truth.* "Yes, go on."

"In our stories, we tell of a time around 10,000 years before your people started recording history. There was a sudden shift from what you called hunting and gathering to farming and settlement in our civilization. Barley, oats, and corn were grown. Animals found their way to these farms, and our clans started keeping sheep and goats."

"Sheep and goats?" Rosemary eyed his assorted brothers' massive size and laughed.

"According to the drawings, they did not look like those today. They were big, *like, like,* the horses your people rode before machines."

"Cowboys?"

"Yes, yes, soon, we were using copper and iron." He pointed to one of his brother's crude belt buckles, which he displayed with pride. "Our women made baskets, wove cloth. No more animal skins for clothing, we wore wool and..." Grillos paused, as if to gather his thoughts. "Many have questioned how my kind could have made this jump so quickly. Some of our elders say we are the descendants of magical creatures, but our Book." He raised his eyebrows and amended. "Our scriptures indicate that strange beings called humans mated with those from far away, and their offspring brought the new ideas and technology to our settlements, enabling us to build architectural wonders like the pyramids located around the world, stone monuments, and even the crop circles that drive your people crazy."

"What do you mean, *strange beings*?" Rosemary asked.

"Just wot I said. Strange, new beings. They weren't here before, and then suddenly, *poof,* they were all over the place."

"Are you implying that humans don't come from here?" Rosemary looked horrified. "That *we* are the colonizers?"

Grillos shrugged. "I'm retelling our history. There's more. Are you ready to hear it?"

Rosemary took a deep breath. She wasn't sure if she really wanted to know. She had her perception of creation and the world, and one part of her wanted to keep her belief system

in place. Yet, she touched her belly where her child rested; maybe she needed to know.

Grillos glanced at the direction of her hand and chuckled. "Once minkins made their appearance, they multiplied, and *boy*, did they ever!"

Rosemary smiled when she heard all the giants laugh.

"They were all over the place. Getting underfoot," Brontes said, holding up his huge leg as if humanity was swirling underneath him.

"Not that our kind is minded," Zaf added. "They taught us great things, advanced our society, and made life easier."

"But there was a cost," Grillos interrupted. "Because of their agile size and advanced intelligence, they began telling *us* what to do. Food started to run low."

"If you haven't noticed, we need a lot to keep from being hungry," Brontes said.

Grillos nodded. "They began to limit our resources, took the best for themselves, and decided where *we* had to live."

"Why?" Rosemary shook her head in disbelief.

"To control us," Grillos said between his teeth.

A rumble of discontent went through the group.

"Soon they were telling us how many children we could have."

"But you did that too!" Rosemary said.

"Yes, but that was *our* choice, not *yours*."

Rosemary wanted to defend humanity, tell them that it couldn't be true, but the specter of history stood on the giant's side. She remembered the colonization of Africa, India, Asia, and the Americas. What of the subjugation of the animal kingdom? Slavery? Shame washed over her. As much as she wanted to argue this couldn't be accurate, doubt assailed her. *This is not who we are*, but then Vincent popped into her mind, along with the late President

McAdams, and all the other world leaders who put greed and convenience before compassion when dealing with the monster population. Could this be endemic to humanity? Have *we* justified every evil deed by rewriting history to account for *our own selfish needs?*

"They pushed us from our homes into the mountains," Fangi barked from his spot in the rear.

"Wait. You said they made you move underground."

Brontes looked guiltily from brother to brother. No one answered, but she felt an undercurrent of tension. "Yea, my mistake. I meant underground. Your kind took the best of the world and kept it for themselves."

Rosemary squirmed; her insides were feeling cramped, as if they were too tight. Her eyes stung, her face reddened, but not from the discomfort; it was the realization of what the giants were saying. She wanted to jump off Grillos's shoulder and run for the hills. This was too much to absorb. *Are we the invaders, the destroyers, the conquerors imposing our will on the rest of the population?* "I can't believe it's all been a lie."

"Your leaders have picked how they want history to be told. We studied your secret Book of Enoch. It's incorrect, of course." Grillos snorted. "The man, Enoch, had it backwards. I don't blame him. He wrote what his own kind told him."

Brontes cleared his throat and added. "The minkin religious leaders hid the Books of Enoch. Did you ever wonder why?"

Rosemary opened her mouth to retort, then snapped it shut. She wanted to say that maybe people told history the way they saw it; however, Brontes's comment plunged her back into uncertainty.

She sat back with surprise, her nostrils engulfed with the scent of pine and earth rather than the salty sea. She missed her former life, where she could close down an argument that made her uncomfortable or had no direction. She could find no justification.

Rosemary's mind whirled, stuck in the cycle of blame, with no real proof of where the answers were. She liked Grillos and his family.

They had a kindness, lived by a similar code of ethics that ruled a ship, but that didn't make their side of the story right, either.

A gruff laugh escaped her lips. She was stranded in a sea of uncertainty.

Rosemary remained thoughtful, and they plodded on in silence for a while. Grillos stopped by a cluster of trees. He lowered her to the earth gently, then tore a young tree that must have escaped the fires from the ground, shook it like a sapling, and then twisted the trunk over her head so that moisture pattered down like gentle rain. Using a rag that resembled

a piece of his old shirt, she wiped away the dust of the road. Rosemary watched Grillos's back ripple with strength as he continued to wrench out the saplings from the soil for what she assumed was a fire. "You want to tell me you couldn't take on the puny humans? You nearly crushed an entire army back there." She pointed in the direction of Los Angeles.

"We are no match for your arsenals of weapons."

"Weapons of destruction," Zaf added.

Rosemary made a face. "Your strength and cunning make for a formidable enemy."

Grillos nodded sagely. "Yet a young boy named Wyatt outwitted us, managing to subdue my small clan by simply drugging and tying us up." He grew thoughtful. "Well, if I remember my history, there was a leader… Gila… Glia…"

"Gilgamesh, brother," Roosti supplied. "How could you forget?"

"Yes, yes, Gilgamesh. He ruled over, who was it…?"

Roosti opened his mouth to answer, but Grillos remembered. "Oh yes, the Sumerians and he attacked and murdered Huwawa, Guardian of the Forest. He was one of our ancestors. You will find tales of giants and their destruction all over the globe."

Rosemary squinted, trying to remember the Epic of Gilgamesh. Shandy had brought it back from a shore leave and made her read it.

"Wot about the North Americans?" Brontes reminded them. "That was genocide."

"The indigenous tribes are not giants," Rosemary dismissed his claim.

"I'm talking about one of our homes, a place you call Lovelock Cave, in Nevada," Grillos responded.

"That's right," Brontes shot back, his face flushed. "The local tribes massacred an entire clan of giants."

Grillos nodded with gravity. "They claimed the red-haired ones…" He pointed to his carroty locks. "Raided their settlements and ate the people of the land."

"*Bah*," Zaf made a sound of distaste. "Too stringy for my taste."

The brothers shared a laugh.

Rosemary swallowed and opened her mouth to ask how Zaf knew what humans tasted like, but Grillos interrupted.

"There is an old legend in both giant and indigenous culture found in America about an entire clan that was wiped out by the local humans, claiming *we were cannibals*." He made a disgusted noise. "It's barbaric."

"Your cousin Hetty didn't think so," Rosemary responded tartly.

"Look at the company she was keeping," Fangi said with disgust. "She should have stayed with her clan and not run off to live with the minkins."

The sun had gone down, and Rosemary's teeth chattered from the cool air. Each of them was hunched over, caught up in their own thoughts. Rosemary rubbed her bare arms. "It's much colder up here," she commented.

Grillos grunted in agreement, then swung a massive cape from his shoulders and wrapped it around her. She felt the heat of his body trapped in the material and welcomed the warmth. "We make camp here." He leaned close. "We don't eat human meat," he whispered in her ear. "To even suggest it is against everything we believe."

"Then why…"

Grillos laughed a bit. "He's fooling with you. We did let the legend continue to scare minkins. After all, compared to them, what else do we have to defend ourselves except with fear? It worked just fine."

Rosemary thought about all the firepower humanity had at its disposal. Too much for her taste, she nodded silently. She took in the massive size of her companions. Other than clubs and perhaps a knife or axe, they had nothing to defend themselves with except their fearsome reputation. She couldn't blame them for sustaining the myth. It reminded her of her favorite pirate, Blackbeard, and his flaming beard. The old salt was said to twine hemp in his facial hair and light it up for a fearsome effect.

All six of the giants broke formation to gather more branches. Baloo created a bonfire; the embers flew up in the darkening sky, drawing Rosemary's gaze to the stars that began to twinkle against the cobalt blue above her. Baloo looked down from his lofty height at her.

"They took everything we had, then threw us away," Grillos said, his lips twisted in a sneer. He busily created a huge bed made from broken branches of the pine trees that rimmed the clearing. The tangy scent of their crushed needles tickled Rosemary's nose, causing her to sneeze.

An owl screeched, followed by the growl of a mountain lion. Rosemary shivered.

Grillos lifted her and plopped her down in the center; soon, she was surrounded by five lumpy bodies that bore the brunt of the chilly mountain weather. Zaf sat like a boulder near the fire, his large form facing outward, his eyes watchful.

Grillos lay down with a sigh and patted the area next to him, his voice soft. "Sit. I'll finish. You must eat, Rosemary."

"I've lost my appetite." It was true. The giant's story was disturbing, but she was not feeling all that well, either.

"He didn't tell you the end of our story. Brother, please complete your tale so we can get some sleep," Brontes said wearily.

"There's not much more to tell," Grillos said after a huge yawn. "Soon there were more of them than us." He moved his massive head from side to side, and the clearing filled with the sound of his big bones cracking.

"We call them hungry humans. They feed like locusts with no regard—" Fangi ranted.

"Enough," Grillos stopped him. "That's another discussion. Food became too scarce. They fought us and killed many. We pushed our clans north to hide, and there we have been for thousands of years."

"But how did you come to live underground?"

Grillos's body seemed to deflate. He sighed and whispered. "That's another story."

Fatigue washed over Rosemary; she put her head down and tried to block out all the areas of her body that hurt, but Fangi's last words echoed in her thoughts throughout the rest of the night, preventing her from finding sleep.

"Yea, it is, and it is terrifying," Fangi added. "But we want to share the sun, and we will not live below anymore."

CHAPTER 21

DIVIDE AND CONQUER

THE FIRE BURNED feebly. Dreg thought they should have gone without one, what with all the assorted creatures creeping around the area, but Vincent merely laughed and demanded one lit. "A pile of rabbit carcasses was at their feet. " Vincent commanded. "You'd think Spekator would have sent us with supplies."

"I can call them." Dreg held up Vincent's new cell phone.

"No, you idiot. I want them to go away." Vincent sat on a fallen log.

"They said they'd stick around in case we needed them." Dreg watched the branches catch and listened to the crackle and hiss of the wood.

"We don't. And we don't want them to know what our next move is." Vincent made a disgusted face. "You picked green wood. I thought you used to camp. We need dried out branches."

"It was the best I could find." Dreg looked up to the star-filled sky. It was serene in the woods, quiet but for the hooting of owls and the cry of coyotes. Above was dark as ink, and streaks of light shot out, making a dazzling display. One of those moving beams was where their former hosts waited and observed. The triangular pattern of blue lights was unmistakable. Dreg wondered who else saw it and what they thought it was. "Just how do you expect to find your daughter, Vincent? It's a big planet."

"I have a device implanted under her skin."

"She removed it." Dreg made a face. Vincent was acting more and more delusional as time went by.

"*Ha*! You think that's all. I knew she was smart, so I implanted two. One inside the child and one within her. All I have to do is download my newest app."

Vincent turned his back and fiddled with his device. "*Ah, ha.* Rosemary is up there." He pointed to a ridge above them on the mountain. "Once we rendezvous with the Sasquatch, we'll go find her."

Dreg shuddered at the thought of the different species hovering above them. Giants, aliens, Bigfoots, and whatever else were roaming around. A chill ran up his spine. At first, Vincent had colluded with the Thalens and treated them as allies, but now he sensed a shift in their attitude toward him.

The Thalens seemed mild-mannered enough when Dreg first met them. Textbook-like, with their large almond-shaped eyes and spindly, ghostly gray bodies. They came across as benign, interested in helping. They had natural enemies, the Scalis, a reptilian breed, and the Va'Rok, an unknown type of alien. Each civilization was very advanced, he had learned. The three were locked in a battle for domination of Earth's resources, which included the population. The Thalens explained that they'd tried negotiating with various governments, but it proved impossible to organize anything. Vincent contacted them through Dr. Frasier and laid out a brilliant plan. Divide and conquer! Just like Napoleon. While Dreg's knowledge of history was murky, he did remember reading somewhere that Napoleon was eventually overwhelmed and lost. Dreg shrugged. He hoped Vincent knew what he was doing.

So far, he wasn't impressed with Vincent's brilliant plans, especially when it cost him the life of his only son.

Dreg ground his teeth, hatred flaming in his chest. The well of bonhomie he felt for Vincent has dried. He narrowed his eyes distrustfully and glanced up. He wasn't feeling all that cozy with the aliens either. Dreg shifted his hips on the ground before the tepid fire and decided he was glad to be sitting on the hard-packed soil of his home rather than floating above it on an alien ship.

He thought back to the moment right before they were transported aboard and wondered what part of his imagination had made him think he saw his son.

Strange beings surrounded him, Vincent becoming the most bizarre of them all. Dreg stared at the dead rabbits. They looked harmless, and he felt bad about trapping them. He shrugged. *Well, a person has to eat.*

Something didn't feel right in the pit of his stomach, and for a minute, he wondered if he was as helpless as those poor rabbits. Glancing up at the circling spaceship, he gulped anxiously. Maybe someday he might become someone else's dinner.

The space creeps did make him uneasy. They were *too... too...* accommodating. Too kind, with an oily charm. It was as if there was some hidden agenda going on behind the emotionless masks they wore. He shivered. Didn't he pat the bunny he trapped on its unsuspecting head before he twisted its neck? He touched his own throat, nervously.

Dreg never heard them speak to each other, their telepathic communication keeping their thoughts as well as their conversations private. He knew they were communicating behind his back, even when they weren't speaking. It was the eyes, he nodded to himself.

When he complained on the ship, Vincent scoffed at his accusations and told him he was being stupid. "They're using us in the same way, we're using them. I only need them until we reestablish our base. Once we reunite with whatever's left of my army, we'll get rid of them."

Dreg wasn't positive they would be so easily dismissed. He shrugged. "Are you sure of their intentions?"

"I know exactly what they want," Vincent said with a satisfied smirk.

"They would not be happy if you aligned with the Sasquatch."

"Don't you worry about that."

He wondered if he and Vincent were just as trapped as the roasting critters. Fat and juice dripped into the flames, making a hissing sound, and Dreg's mouth watered.

The food on the craft annoyed him, too. Meals, if you could call them that, had a strange consistency. The aliens fed them soft pellets that tasted like cardboard.

"Sometimes you surprise me with your skillset, Dreg."

The comment rankled. Time and time again, he had pulled Vincent's chestnuts from the fire. He had found his decapitated head and reanimated it, keeping it alive for crazy Doctor Frasier to attach to the host body for a time. He had gotten Vincent's head out of Monsterland before the army leveled it..

He had also managed to keep him functioning with a steady supply of alien fuel and had assisted the aliens when they reattached him to a vacuum cleaner. Vincent had a lot to be grateful for. Dreg opened his mouth to reply, but the deadly gaze watching him made him stop.

Vincent was observing him as if he were an insect.

Instead, he said, "Trapping the rabbit was easy. I camped regularly with Nate."

Vincent growled an answer, but Dreg wasn't listening. Talking about camping brought back fond memories of his son. A strange new feeling erupted in his chest; his heart twisted with the pain of loss. *Man, he was maudlin tonight.* He swallowed past the lump in his throat. Dreg blinked, fighting the tears that threatened. Dreg couldn't stop a sob from a deep well of grief. It felt like it came from his gut and sounded loud in the quiet of the forest. He was pulled back to the present by Vincent's harsh voice.

"*Shhhh.*" Vincent hit Dreg hard on the shoulder.

The shadows hid Vincent's face, but his hand movements motioned for Dreg to lie low.

Dreg heard the rustling then. Sliding to the ground, he searched the dense foliage for the culprit.

"Quick. Douse the fire!" Vincent ordered.

"Do you think it's Bigfoot?" Dreg made short work of the fire by smothering it with dirt.

"Don't call them that, it's Sasquatch," Vincent growled. "No. He's coming alone. Get down, man!" They lay on their stomachs, side by side. Vincent continued, "There are too many of them. Besides," he whispered. "These are lighter footsteps. Listen, *drag*, step, *drag*, step. Reminds me of something I heard back in Monsterland."

"Zombies!" Dreg said in a rush. "How did they get up here?" His eyes darted nervously. "Maybe it's an escaped werewolf."

"Again, too light on the feet. There are no more werewolves. I saw to that! Except for that red-headed monster." He sniffed. "*Ah, here we are.*"

The stench of rot filled the glade. The steady *yum, yum* sound of a hungry zombie replaced the shuffle of their feet. They spied Vincent and Dreg, changing direction, their arms spread out before them.

It was a couple, both with remnants of a uniform that hung in tatters from their arms. "Monsterland," Vincent said, pointing to the round patch on one of their shoulders. "Former employees. Too bad." Vincent stood up and walked calmly toward them. He reached for the male and twisted off his head in a smooth movement. Turning swiftly, he kicked the female in the midsection, winding her, then bashed her skull with a swift chop. He turned to Dreg with a satisfied smile. "Guess they won't be collecting their 401k." He stamped on both their heads.

Dreg winced at the squish of their brains spilling, followed by the sound of bones being crushed. "You didn't have to kill them." It was pitch in the forest, but Dreg would see Vincent's dark outline as he stamped on the zombie remains.

"Are you going soft on me? I merely put them out of their misery. It is the most noble thing I could do. Besides, they were expendable. Proves one thing, though."

"What?"

"We were not too far from home."

Dreg stared at the creatures, wondering what made one of Vincent's minions expendable. *Is that how he saw the aliens, humanity, or even himself?*

He glanced from Vincent's broad back to the dead monsters on the ground. It was true, they had no future; their lives were essentially over. You could say that Vincent was merciful.

Only this time, the thoughts didn't stop there. Something happened that never occurred before. Another voice echoed in Dreg's brain and demanded, *Who made him the one to decide a being's worth?*

They walked back to the camp, Vincent whistling, Dreg wrestling with his new conscience.

"I'm finding that I'm famished!" Vincent rubbed his fake belly.

Dreg filled with revulsion while looking at him and the mosaic of gore on his cape..

They didn't speak again until another rabbit was cooking over the bright flames. Dreg kept silent as he turned the spit over a fire, thinking about the assorted roles of each person in Vincent's orbit.

Vincent was perched on a fallen log, and the crackling flames painted a dazzling display on his purple-tinted skin. He wiped his hands on his pants, splattered brains making a macabre pattern.

He looked more inhumane than anything else; his pallid skin appeared devoid of life. Dreg thought about all the blood they collected at Monsterland, taken from the now extinct vampires, and asked, "Vincent, what were you planning to do with all the vamp blood?"

"You speak as if I don't have it anymore." Vincent had a sly grin on his face.

"I assumed it was all destroyed at the park."

"You think so little of me? I prepared for every possible scenario. I didn't trust McAdams, no less than that tin-pot army, from the start. I have a stash hidden in Monsterland."

"But the army—"

"They'll never find it. It's buried beneath the tanks where I grew the shell creature."

Dreg shivered. "Freaks of nature."

Vincent shouted with laughter. "You're talking."

Dreg's face burned with resentment. "I never understood what you needed that perversion of nature for."

"It's the perfect organism. By mixing zombie and vampire blood with starfish DNA, I was able to create the ideal creature. It regenerates. I can create an invincible army with just one egg."

"When I left, there was only one egg there. That's mightily risky, depending on a single egg." Dreg smiled smugly and sat down. "And how did you expect to create eggs with just a single creature? Last time I looked, it took two to tango."

"*Ha!*" Vincent slapped his knee. "Sometimes I marvel at your stupidity. Ever hear of parthenogenesis? No, then let me explain. My creature is neither male nor female; it was developed from an unfertilized egg."

"How...?"

"It's not uncommon among invertebrates, but some vertebrates like fish, reptiles, and birds can produce offspring without a partner. I sprinkled some of their DNA, as well."

"But Dr. Frasier—"

Vincent shook his head, his eyes filled with humor. "He studied them. I gave him a few. Those morons at Area 51 thought they were aliens." His shoulders shook with mirth. "I had them fooled. Little did they know they were homegrown, made in the good old USA."

"You could have done that first instead of dragging us through space. You didn't even need the Thalens."

"It's true I was negotiating with them, but don't forget, I had little to say when they transported us aboard the ship. You agreed to all the surgeries. I was out of it."

"I…I…"

"I had to bide my time anyway. The creature was reproducing on its own. I simply let nature take its course. By now, there'll be thousands of eggs. I will have a formidable army of indestructible shell creatures. And there is nothing that little pest Wyatt Balwin can do about it."

Dreg thought for a minute and gasped, "You'll be, you'll be—"

Vincent smiled his Jack-O-Lantern grin. "Immortal with an ever-growing army."

"Why didn't you tell me sooner!" Dreg stood, pacing the small glade. "We didn't have to spend all that time with the Thalens." He quivered with disgust and plopped down beside Vincent, exhausted.

"The only one who has to know anything is me. You're just here for the heavy lifting."

Dreg grunted a response, disguising his anger.

Vincent picked up the end of the log Dreg was leaning against, dislodging him. He rolled onto the grass, Vincent's laughter filling the night. "Stop pouting! Maybe I don't need your help, either. I appear to be fit as a fiddle!"

Vincent ripped off a leg of the rabbit, his metal teeth splintering the delicate bones of the animal. His chin pinkened with blood as the juice ran down his chin.

Dreg sneered, his voice filled with loathing. "It's not fully cooked yet. You'll get worms eating raw rabbit."

"Not with this body! I don't have to worry about trichinosis or any other human setbacks." Vincent hit his midsection near his supposed belly, and Dreg heard the hollow thud of an empty body. "I need the sustenance for my brain. Someone has to keep their wits about them." Dreg automatically opened his mouth to say that Vincent could depend on him, but snapped it shut.

The implication was clear. Vincent felt he was the only person with strength or intelligence. The question was, would that make Dreg expendable?

CHAPTER 22

PLAIN SIGHT

JADE FELT NOTHING from the top of her head to the tip of her toes. She was numb inside and out. Still, Otto kept up his daily tirades and convoluted history tales.

"We have to get moving," Otto shouted to Jade. "They've surrounded us. They're watching us."

"You're delusional. No one's spying on us. We're in the middle of nowhere, you crazy kook."

"Don't be disrespectful! A lot you know. They've been watching us for years. Listening to our conversations, with all the devices we use. I'm on to them."

"The only thing you're on to is a nut house," Jade yelled at him, her good arm folded across her chest. "I hate you."

Otto slammed on a projector, and the wall lit up with a map of the United States. His face was an eerie shade of blue in the gloom. He went on as if she hadn't spoken. "The aliens landed here, here, and here." Otto Enoch was pointing at the images projected onto the wall. Jade drummed her fingers on the metal table, her gaze darting to the exit. "I saw proof that they've created bases underground and are working in collusion with… *Jade!* Are you even listening to me?" Otto demanded. He threw down the thin stick with disgust, shaking his head. "You were a poor student back in Copper Valley and—"

Jade looked up, alert, her expression stopping him mid-sentence.

"Yeah, yeah. I know all about your theories," she said, standing straight. While never a bright student at school, she couldn't understand how critical ideas seemed easier now. Her mind felt energized. It was as if she knew things, could articulate her opinions, and had more information readily available in her brain. "The forbidden Book of Enoch." She nodded to him and cut him off before he could say anything. "I understand it's a coincidence that you share the same name, the real Enoch being that guy from Bible times." Jade was thoughtful. "Hey, is your name really Enoch?"

Otto's face became reverential. "I took that name to finish the original Enoch's job."

"That's an impersonation. You can get in a lot of trouble for that."

"You and what police force!" Otto laughed. "Nobody's left!"

Jade picked up the stick and pressed it into Otto's chest. "Well, you and your so-called biblical namesake think that in the ancient days there were beings called… Watchers." Enoch nodded with encouragement. Jade went on, "The so-called Watchers were sent to… observe—"

"And protect, like we were children, or inferior."

"Okay, but instead they became obsessed with humanity and…" she swallowed. "They mated with them."

"Yes! Yes! It is mentioned in the Five Books of Enoch. The hidden stories. One hundred chapters of truth!" He stood and began pacing, his head lowered between his shoulders. He glanced up, his voice changing pitch barely above a whisper. "The church suppressed it, like the school suppressed me all these years, but Galileo knew. Da

Vinci, too. Newton, for sure." He spun and shouted. "All the great minds knew. They had secret knowledge, but they were suppressed."

"Yeah, yeah, secret X-files—" Jade placated him.

Otto brushed off her comment with a wave of her hand. "Television nonsense! They buried the evidence. They all hid it. Kept people in the dark because they thought it was safer for us. *As if we wouldn't understand,*" he added with a suitable amount of sarcasm.

"They! They! Who are they?" Jade wasn't sure what he was babbling about now.

"The government!"

"Right. It's been a secret for thousands of years." Jade rolled her good eye. "And the offspring of these events were called…" She snapped the fingers of her working hand, trying to recall the name.

The word escaped her memory, but Otto supplied it. "Nephilim."

She looked at him, refusing to say it. Otto's pudgy hands were flying across the keyboard attached to the antique projector. She wasn't sure what the contraption was. Otto had dozens of them, convoluted machines made up from junkyard body parts. Just like her, she thought glumly, touching the metal in her cheek.

On the wall, pictures rapidly flew by too quickly for Jade to identify them. Otto barked with triumph, stopping on an image of what looked to be the Middle East. The rolling green and brown hills were filled with two types of humanity attacking each other. The battlefield was strewn with body parts and corpses, the smaller humanoids triumphant over the larger victims. In the far corner of the picture, a group of larger beings was chomping down on fallen enemies.

"Nephilim," Otto repeated, gesturing to the images. "They were imprisoned underground."

Jade studied the illustration with her good eye. Otto had put a patch on the new eye. It hurt too much, she complained. She rubbed the empty socket.

After a minute, she laughed and added, "Man-eating giants who were forced to live underground or die." She paused and said. "Otto. You're nuts."

"No, no, don't you see. Our history's been altered by whoever is in power."

"You can't keep a secret like that." Jade played with the pointer, making it look like the wooden part of a bow. She considered the flexibility, wondering if she could find twine somewhere in this dump and make it function. She could use pencils as arrows, like Howard Drucker did when he took out the vampire leader, Raoul, at the Battle for Monsterland. Jade gasped at the memory, surprised at how easily it came to mind. *She wanted more!*

Otto was babbling again, and Jade turned inward, ignoring both his ramblings and the illustration on the wall, her brain attempting to slow the flashes and see what else she could recall.

Otto was oblivious and ranted, lost in his lesson. "Enoch became the middleman between the giants and the rest of the known world. But the Watchers were angry, and then there was the great flood, and they took Enoch away in a fiery chariot, *a spaceship*! *Jade?* Jade!" Otto smacked the desk with his hand. "Aren't you listening?"

She looked up; her expression was bland.

"You still don't believe me?" Otto demanded, spit flying from his mouth. He clicked a few keys, and the illustration disappeared. New images lit up on the wall. Modern ones, not hand-drawn. Black and white photos of people from the last century. Jade guessed that it was somewhere in the sixties to the eighties of the twentieth century, judging from the mullets and other hairstyles.

"Slow down!" she ordered, and strangely enough, Otto complied. Jade stood to get a better look. She moved to the wall, her hand lightly grazing the projected image. Men were standing next to a huge femur that appeared to be six feet long. Giant skulls held up by two people, ditches with normal-sized humans positioned beside skeletons that made them look like toy soldiers. Old-fashioned newspaper articles from another era, with sensational headlines splayed across the poorly printed image, reporting a race of massive humans that could easily crush modern man under their oversized feet. Jade read the words, her lips moving silently.

"This one is from the Amazon rainforest, and here, Jade, this one was discovered in China. There's Russia, and Africa, too." Otto wiped sweat from his bald head, exasperated with Jade's lack of reaction.

"Stop. Stop here. You're going too fast."

Otto craned his neck. "Yes, you see it's been around for years. Marco Polo wrote about finding giants in Zanzibar. He said—"

"I can read," Jade snapped. "'They were so strong they could carry as many as four ordinary men.' Impossible."

"Why? Why is it impossible? The people who live in Morocco claim that Tangier's founder was a giant named Antioth," Otto said defensively. "It's all in plain sight. All you have to do is open your eyes, well, your good eye. With your keen wolf vision, you should be able—"

"Don't!" Jade spun to him, her cheeks flushed. She was still wrapping the werewolf thing around her head. She wasn't ready to discuss it.

Otto backed away. "I didn't mean anything. It's just with your superior—"

"I told you to shut up," she growled. She felt the hairs rise on her arms, a sure sign that something strange was happening to her. She breathed deeply, trying to calm herself.

Otto held up two hands, his palms open wide. "Look, I'd much rather tell you about the Irish myths. I read about a causeway, you know, a highway along the northeast coast of Ireland. It has forty thousand interlocking columns of rock that were allegedly built by the Irish giant, Finn McCool."

Jade relaxed, sliding back into her seat. Her joints loosened, and she felt like herself again. "McCool, *ha*. I have a bridge, I can get a great price for you," she mocked him.

"He did it so he could walk across the sea to Scotland and fight with other giants." Otto went on as if he hadn't heard her.

Jade shook her head slowly. The pictures were probably fakes, and the stories were made-up lies. If giants were real, why didn't everybody see them? Vampires, werewolves, and zombies existed. Everybody knew that, had seen at least one of each kind somewhere or another, *but giants?*

"Sorry, Otto, they're too big to hide. These are all legends and stories. Made up stuff to amuse people, plain old folklore."

"I could go on and on," Otto persisted. He held up his hand and ticked off each point with his fingers. "There are Norse legends, Greek, Romanian, you name it. Giants did exist. It's too common in chronicles around the world for it not to be true!" His eyes were lit with an inner fire. "It wasn't just the book of Enoch; the Sumerian texts tell of a story of these beings called Anunnaki." He raised his eyebrows high and gestured toward the sky. "These Anunnaki were very much like the Watchers, and started to mate with people, creating an entirely new species of humanity. There's too much there for it not to be grounded in truth."

"Sounds like they just keep retelling the same old stories." Jade stood. "I don't know, it feels too far-fetched. Until I actually shake hands with a living, breathing giant, it's just going to be a fairy tale for me." Jade left Otto staring disconsolately at the flickering image on the white-washed wall. She walked out, shaking her head, wondering when this nightmare would end.

CHAPTER 23

100 BARRELS OF DDT ON THE FLOOR, 100 BOTTLES OF DDT...IF ONE OF THE BARRELS HAPPENS TO...

THE ENTIRE SEA floor was covered with eggs that rocked gently with the current. Some had cracked, others appeared off-color. Howard jumped off the table and moved closer to the window. He placed his palm on the cool surface of the glass as if he could examine each specimen. The president followed him, standing silently next to Howard.

Howard traced his finger on the glass, his eyes distant. There was a lot of grumbling in the packed room, but Howard appeared unaffected by the noise. He was deep in thought.

"What? What are you looking at?" Wyatt squeezed through and tapped his shoulder. "Howard," he persisted, "what do you see?"

"There," he said, pointing to a cluster of dull, oval-shaped objects. "Look. They're..."

"If you say *fascinating*, I'm gonna dead arm you," Melvin warned from right behind them.

Keisha's jaw dropped. "*Ohhh.*" She pointed to the grouping of eggs that were indeed different from the rest. Not only were they darker, but their tops were deflated as if they were deformed. "I'm not sure, but those look strange."

"Maybe they're dead," Howard's voice trailed off.

The word dead whispered through the chamber quicker than lightning, and the timber of multiple voices increased in volume.

"They are different. What do you think happened to them?" President Owens asked.

"*Hmmm...* it appears as though they are dormant... or diseased." Howard tapped the glass. "Like they didn't hatch."

Murmuring in the chamber became louder. People repeated what Howard was saying.

"How do you know?" The president demanded, his voice rising over the din.

"I've been observing them," Howard said absently, still absorbed with the seascape. He leaned forward, his eyes narrowing. "Watch."

The noise level rose, and people shuffled to get a better view.

"Quiet!" Yerbol shouted.

The room hushed. Everyone's eyes were glued to the window, searching for clues.

As if on cue, one of the eggs collapsed completely, and a dingy, rusty fluid was expelled.

Wyatt moved closer to the window. Melvin was next to him, and

Howard was on the other side. The mob pressed forward, squeezing them against the window.

A collective gasp went through the room. The crowd moved restlessly. It was hot, as if all the oxygen was being sucked up.

Wyatt felt lightheaded. Sweat beaded his forehead and he felt slightly nauseous. Fear prickled the skin on the back of his neck, and his scalp tightened. He craned his neck to search the back of the room, spotted Carter, and made eye contact. Carter nodded, and for a reason he couldn't understand, his anxiety diminished.

President Nate Owens leaned forward. "I see it. What just happened?"

"It collapsed. It didn't crack open—nothing but a dark fluid expelled into the ocean. I think something went wrong with them," Howard said.

"You can't stand here, jawing about it like it's some science experiment! Do something, already!" Melvin's voice rose an octave. "Move back! You're crushing us." He was panting, his face flushed. Wyatt wasn't sure whether it was due to the heat or frustration. "Those things are about to hatch!"

Wyatt rested his hand on his friend's shoulder. "Relax, Mel," he whispered. "You don't want to… You know… *change* in here." He felt the supersized muscles in Melvin's shoulders ease from their tense state. He sighed with relief.

"No. See, the ones resting on the curved coral appear discolored, like they're gone, empty," Howard said.

The crowd in the room buzzed with comments, and the people in the back stood on their toes to see over those in front of them. Wyatt felt himself being pushed so closely to the glass that his chest met the cool surface. One shove from behind, and he was afraid it might shatter.

The mama octopus moved to the center of the window, blocking their view. Her beady eyes calmly watched them.

There were a few gasps and many comments about the size and color of the behemoth floating in front of them.

"Look at that thing!" This from a person at the back of the room.

"Her eyes. She's staring right at us. It's making me sick." A man staggered through the crowd to leave the chamber.

"It's a monster!" Another declared.

"Enough!" Yerbol ordered. "Or I'll clear the room."

President Nate Owens was mesmerized by the creature. He stood behind the teens, barely able to catch his breath.

The long, thick arms of the mother octopus undulated in the water, the baby resting in her giant embrace. Her movements had a hypnotic effect, and Wyatt swore that she was aware of it. She was the size of a freight train; the infant was as big as a Mack truck. The suckers were as big as airplane tires. They rippled as if they had a mind of their own.

"*Ah-hem.*" Keisha cleared her throat. "I don't think that's coral," Keisha said, pointing to the rolling landscape behind the octopus. The symmetrical hills were covered with plant life that was mostly brown and dying. She spoke up so her voice could be heard above the noise in the chamber. "It's too perfect. It looks manufactured."

"What?" the president asked.

"Don't listen to the kids. We need real scientists!" someone yelled from the back.

"Mr. President! Mr. President. I have a theory!"

"No, I have an idea!" A scuffle broke out.

"I object." Two people were fighting to get toward the president.

"Shut up." Factions in the throng fought to be heard. Voices rose to a fever pitch.

"Stand down," Yerbol shouted. The room had a mixture of troops and civilians that was beginning to have a mob-like quality.

Wyatt's face was beet-red, and he was having trouble breathing. He twisted to look for Carter and closed his eyes with relief when he heard him shouting.

"Back off!' Wyatt heard his stepfather's voice. Carter continued to yell. "Give the kids some room."

"We don't have time to stare at the octopus, Mr. President," Keisha said grimly. "We can't debate what will work best either. Howard and I have spent the most time down here. You have to trust us."

President Owens looked back at the group, then at Howard and Keisha. "Keep 'em quiet, Carter. In fact, clear the room. That's an order."

Wyatt shook his head and turned to Owens. "I want to stay."

The president nodded curtly.

The sounds of Carter and Yerbol moving the crowd out slowly receded as it emptied. The president turned to Howard. "Thoughts? I'll take anything at this point."

"I do have a theory." Howard took a deep breath.

"Explain, Howard… Keisha?" Owens persisted.

"I think the darkened eggs are resting on top of barrels of DDT that were dumped here in the last century," Howard answered. "It's poisoning them."

"How can we be sure?" Owens eyed him keenly.

"I'll put on a wetsuit and see," Yerbol volunteered. He had moved back to his spot next to the president. He looked at his crew as if to give them new orders.

"Stand down," the President ordered.

Wyatt wiped the sweat from his forehead. He noticed Howard's and the president's faces were dotted with perspiration as well. He turned to see Carter closing the door and then standing in front of it like a barricade.

President Owens shook his head, oblivious to the tension around him. "No time, Melvin's right. We have to do something now."

"May I, sir? I have an idea." Wyatt held out his hand, palm up. "Give me the phone."

"You know what to do?" Carter called from his spot near the door.

"We can't sit here and do nothing." Wyatt turned to Howard. "Can this thing trigger the Octomom?"

Howard shook his head. "No, Konrad attached the transistor only to Junior. I'm not quite sure how the mother octopus will react—"

"How much are you not sure?" Wyatt asked quickly.

"I'd say the odds—"

"Oh, enough, Howard Drucker, hand Wyatt the phone. This has got to work." Keisha was breathless.

The President stood motionless, indecision written all over his face.

Carter cleared his throat. "I would, Mr. President. Give Wyatt the phone. Kids are better at this."

Nate Owens paused for a minute, then handed the phone to Wyatt.

"Password?" Wyatt asked.

"Keisha put a new one in," Howard said.

"Asshat," Keisha answered, then added. "Well, you know who owned it."

Wyatt was already typing. The screen opened up; Wyatt touched the octopus icon, revealing a toggle and assorted buttons.

"The goal is to thrash as many of the barrel things as you can, cracking them open so the poison will kill the shell creatures." Howard leaned over Wyatt's shoulder, watching him work.

"What if some of them escape?" President Owens asked.

"Nothing will escape Wyatt. He is the top dog on all our gaming sites," Howard responded without looking up, his eyes on the screen.

"That may be true, but just in case, Yerbol." Owens turned to the bodyguard. "Get a detail down to the beach and blow up anything that comes out of the water."

Yerbol nodded once. He turned to Carter. "You got this?" He gestured to the room. He paused and handed Carter his gun.

"Affirmative."

Yerbol rapidly left the chamber, followed by his crew. Carter closed the door and stood in front of it again, this time brandishing a weapon.

Wyatt glanced at the teaming sea floor, feeling a heaviness in his chest. Fish flitted in and out of fronds that grew out of the barrels. "There's going to be casualties."

President Owens rested his hand on his shoulder and said, "Nothing we can do about it. Let's get it going."

Wyatt's pointer and thumb flew over the screen. He moved the toggle. All eyes were on the large arm of the octopus that floated before them.

"Do it!" Melvin yelled. "Now." His face was pressed against the glass at the vista before them.

As if they knew they were in imminent danger, thousands of shell creatures, no bigger than a seahorse, emerged from the eggs.

All eyes were on the baby octopus waiting to see if it reacted to the stimuli from the phone.

The animal lay serenely in its mother's multiple arms, not moving.

"What's holding it up?" Owens demanded.

"I don't know, sir." Wyatt was fiddling with the icons on the screen. "It seems frozen."

"We're running out of time." Carter's voice was anxious. The crowd was getting restless. They heard them on the other side of the door, clogging up the passageways. The Colonel shouted over the din to subdue the crowd, echoing in the tunnel.

"Give it to me." Howard snatched the phone, pressed a button, and wiped the sweat from his temple with his shoulder. "I don't know why-"

"Reset the phone!" Keisha urged.

Melvin shouted as the shell creatures shimmered in front of them. They were the size of a forefinger, orange and spiky, with a fish head and gills on either side. They rammed their minuscule bodies against the glass, their egg-shaped eyes dark and soulless.

"This would be a good time—" President Owens began.

"I think we should get you out of here, Mr. President." Colonel Drucker had pushed his way into the room and touched the president's elbow as if to escort him away.

"Do it, Howard!" Melvin wailed, his face red, fur erupting on his knuckles.

"I told you now is not a good time to morph," Wyatt whispered hoarsely to Melvin.

"You think I want to do this?" Melvin's eyes bulged from his head.

"Here we go!" Howard's voice cut through the noise at the same time the baby octopus jerked from its mother's arms and spun a frantic jig in the center of the ocean. The arms flung outward, the slitted eyes opening wide as if shocked.

The mother sank, the bulbous head floating into view, her worried eyes locked on her infant. She circled the smaller animal, her arms reaching out to lock onto the swirling octopus. It pulled out of her embrace, the beak open and shutting furiously.

Thick tentacles banged against the glass window, the tire-size suckers attaching as the mother's fury mounted. The balloon-shaped head moved downward, its color changing from blue to purple and finally to an angry red.

"That thing is pissed!" Wyatt said.

"Move away from the glass!' Carter yelled.

She looked at them then, and Wyatt felt a shiver run from the top of his head to the end of his toes. Her weird-shaped eyes locked onto his face.

"She knows!" Melvin moaned. "She knows we're making that thing move. She's gonna smash the glass."

The chamber was filled with the sound of the mother octopus's other arm banging against the window. The underground building shook from the force of it. Howard handed the phone to Wyatt. "Get the barrels."

Wyatt's gaze was intense. He pressed the toggle, directing the baby to thrash the curved coral, releasing grayish fluid to seep from the cracked surface.

The room exploded with cheers.

"Keep going, Wyatt. Just like at home!" Carter urged.

Wyatt moved the octopus, spinning it for maximum damage. Its powerful arms sliced through the corrosive metal like paper. As the substance escaped, its murkiness reduced visibility.

Melvin's face was plastered against the glass, his hand making a tunnel over his eyes. "It's killing them," he howled. "Faster, more, before the mother takes her kid and leaves!"

As if she heard him, the mother octopus pushed against the window, her enormous head filling the entire view. She pummeled the glass tank, the water cushioning its impact, the room echoing from the sound.

She reached out two of her arms, trying to subdue her infant, and in the chaotic dance, she caused the eggs to be shoved to the ocean floor, their toxic resting place crushed to release more poison. A muffled but high-pitched whistling noise filled the room. It was emitting from the gaping mouths of the shell creatures, their eyes becoming hazy as they drifted, gasping, to the seafloor.

Wyatt pushed the device to the limits, his fingers guiding the octopus to the farthest reaches of the area, where it continued to damage the reef. Soon, the water outside turned opaque with debris, and Wyatt wasn't sure of his success with the baby octopus.

The building trembled as if hit by a giant hand, followed by a tearing sound. There were cries of dismay around him, but Wyatt ignored them. He heard the colonel shouting for the president to leave and then Owens' calm refusal. "I'll stay here with Wyatt."

The lights flickered and went out, plunging them into darkness.

There was another smack, this one so loud, Wyatt was sure it cracked the glass. He fought the urge to look up; he was intent on moving the toggle. He heard Melvin assuring him they were safe.

Looking down, his face wild, he turned to Howard. "It's not working. It's frozen again."

"Give it to me!" Howard grabbed it.

Wyatt refused and rubbed a spot clear on the glass in front of him. "I can't see anything!" he shouted. The entire window was a clouded mess; the room behind him was tense, filled with silence. He continued moving the toggle, but couldn't tell if he was having success.

Melvin jumped up on the ledge, cupping his hands around his eyes. "The octopus is gone."

"The baby?" Wyatt asked.

"I can't tell," Melvin stated. "Wait," the room was quiet, but for their labored breathing. Wyatt glanced up to see Melvin's red and sweaty face. "… They're both gone."

"What do you mean?" President Nate Owens demanded.

Brownish-gray particles swirled before them. Slowly, as if the current calmed down, it settled, falling like dust coating everything on the ocean floor. Dead fish floated upward, but there was no sign of the shell creatures.

"There they are," Keisha said, pointing to thousands of tiny corpses blanketing the seabed. She bent down and searched the whole expanse of the window. "The octopus and her baby are definitely gone."

Melvin jumped down. "The shell things look dead."

The lights flickered and came on again, along with the air conditioning.

"How can we be sure? They came back to life when Melvin thought they were dead," Wyatt asked.

"The poison was very toxic. Nothing could survive that. It was an effective tool," Howard said, his voice a tone of sadness. "Unfortunately, it hurt a lot of the other sea life, but those shell things are finished."

Keisha studied his ravaged face. "It's not our fault. We didn't put the barrels of poison there."

"Yeah, but we used them and look at the devastation," Howard said.

Nate Owens rested his hand on Howard's shoulder. "Don't take on that guilt. They were bound to break open someday."

"Yeah, blame it on the jerks who put it there in the first place," Melvin added.

"Maybe you should thank them instead," Colonel Drucker said. "There was no way we'd win against them."

Indeed, the ocean floor was covered with dead creatures, their eyes open and staring, their color changing from orange to a dull pewter.

The President finally agreed to leave the room.

Carter patted Wyatt's back. "Nice work. I'm proud of you."

"Thanks, Carter," Wyatt said, his face sad.

Carter examined his stepson, his eyes intense. "What now?" He turned to leave. "You coming?"

Wyatt shook his head and felt the presence of his friends surrounding him. "I think I'm going to explore this place a little bit. We didn't have a chance after the army rushed us out of here."

"What are you looking for?" his stepfather asked.

"I'm not sure, but I'll know when I find it." Wyatt's face looked resolute. "Wanna join me?" he asked Howard and Keisha.

Howard shook his head. "I'll catch up. I have to find a frequency that will work with the phone."

"I'll stay with Howard." Keisha moved toward the stone table.

Carter filed out of the space into the crowded tunnels.

"Let's go," Wyatt said and ran from the room without checking if anyone followed him.

Melvin looked bitterly at the exit and called after him, "I want to get some air. I'll be there soon."

CHAPTER 24

SWEET DREAMS

BY THE GREAT goddess, Tala, the giants finally stopped late last night to sleep, Olrec thought with relief. *Now what was he going to do?* He recalled an earlier part of the day when he came upon the strangest sight he had ever seen. The bear had been telling the truth. He was immediately contrite for not believing her.

Olrec had stopped short when he had seen the group of giants plodding along the road a couple of yards away. It was almost dusk, yet here they were, unafraid of discovery and with a female! *A female stupe.*

Olrec had squinted hard, his skin tightening across the broad orbital ridge on his forehead. Scrubbing his eyes hard, he tried to clear his vision. He still couldn't believe what he was witnessing. Could they be a raiding party? They hadn't clashed in his lifetime, but he had heard stories about the fearsome giants. *What were they doing in Olrec's territory!*

The *stupe* was perched on the shoulder of the tallest giant, not as a prisoner or prospective meal. She was laughing! *Hysterically! Olrec* knew he had to investigate the site. He might be late for Konrad, but this was urgent.

Staying hidden by an overgrown bush, sweat beaded his brow while his two hearts drummed wildly in his chest. Kokkus would tell him he deserved whatever befell him. Olrec worried his bottom lip. They were within a day's walking distance from his home. *Should he run back and warn them?* He would shame his family for failing to connect with Vincent Konrad! They'll call him a coward, that he shirked his duty. He leaned heavily against the trunk of a tree.

Olrec knew better than to venture this far down the mountain range, but once he had spotted this worrisome sight, he knew he had to trail after them. If only to see where they were headed.

Zilli might call him a fool, but this simply could not be ignored. Olrec made his decision. Konrad would have to wait. This was too important not to investigate. Once he had an idea of their direction, he would rush back to the designated meeting spot and finish his mission.

This was an impossible situation and had to take precedence. Giants and *stupes* together. The two species hadn't interacted for, at least, he glanced down at his long, hairy fingers and counted the centuries. *He didn't have enough fingers!* It had to be over two and a half millennia. This was bad, very, very bad. If these two enemies allied, nobody was safe.

Olrec clicked his tongue in disgust. The two species despised each other. Belligerent *stupes* couldn't get along with man or beast, and those self-righteous overgrown giants thought they were too good for everybody else. If only he could move close enough to hear what they were saying.

While Sasquatches had played an elaborate game of hide and seek with humanity, the giants were a whole other story. His kind had warred with the giant community for eons. They were forced to; the giants had a gruesome reputation for eating what they captured.

Olrec watched the long-haired woman rest her head on the great beast's shoulder. Searching her face, he looked for signs of terror, but all he observed was the two of them sharing an animated conversation. He blinked his eyes and rubbed them with his knuckles. *She was smiling at the orange-haired monster, fondly!*

Olrec glanced at the disappearing sun in the western sky. This detour had cost him valuable time in his journey to meet the infamous doctor. Yet, he felt compelled to track them, at least for a bit longer.

He estimated how much time he had left. Biting the inside of his cheek, he figured he'd make up the difference by doubling back during daylight. Hopefully, there would be no *stupes* wandering about. He heard a rustling behind him, and he ducked behind a wide tree, knowing he was blending in. He sniffed the air, recognizing the smell. Someone from his pack was following him. Much as he wanted to expose the spy, he had to worry about the giants lest they find him and overpower him and his unwanted guest.

Crouching, he darted from tree to tree, keeping a safe distance; his ears had pricked upward to hear their discussion. Scattered parts of the beast's conversation reached him; their words punctuated with laughter.

It was a history lesson! The discovery made him jerk to a halt. The giant was telling the woman tales of their past, like a bedtime story he shared with his own cubs. Olrec had smiled at the thought of his brood, their sleeping faces when he kissed them goodbye early this morning. Zilli had her hands full with those rascals. He shook his head to clear his mind of distractions. He had a job to do, and to do it, he must!

Olrec skirted trees, ducking between heavy branches and keeping downwind so his scent would not be detected, all while hoping the pursuer following him wouldn't keep up. *What were those oversized block-heads up to?*

Maybe the giants were planning to lull her into complacency

with their dull stories and eat her for dinner. He was certainly bored to death with their mythical tale.

By the time the group bedded down, he watched incredulously as the giant tenderly tucked in his human like a pet. Soon, snoring erupted in the clearing, and Olrec was left with nothing but questions.

He drummed his fingers on his knee, wishing Zilli were here to tell him what to do. She had a way of seeing things a bit more clearly. Olrec was known as a dreamer, going off chasing butterflies or following a line of bees to their hive. While the honey he discovered was considered a delicacy, he was often berated for putting himself at risk. It's not like he had ever been photographed to his knowledge, but he would admit he did skirt danger a bit too closely. Kokkus constantly reminded him of the threat of being identified. He looked around the clearing, then sniffed the air again. It seems whoever was following him had left.

He parked himself on a cradle of two branches, their astringent smell making his nose itch. He remained quiet and observant, like the Great Night Owl, his nickname. Leaning forward, he strained to hear the conversation; all he heard was the steady hum of their snoring and the occasional passing of gas.

Frustrated, he could feel anxiety building in his chest. *What if he made a mistake?* He should never have left the original plan. On the other hand, what if they were scouting to prepare an attack on his home? He'd be a hero then, *wouldn't he?*

Olrec huffed. The noise, though quiet enough, startled a bird nearby. Sucking in his breath, he went as motionless as possible. One of the giants coughed loudly, then rose, his slow lumbering body prowling around the campfire. Olrec barely breathed. He watched the giant's reddish eyes scan the area like a fiery searchlight. The giant gave a penetrating look in his direction, then resettled himself for the night.

Olrec debated leaving. Kokkus would undoubtedly agree with that. Closing his eyes, he imagined his brother-in-law yelling that he was easily distracted, that he had lost sight of the real mission and gone off on a wild *stupe* chase, much like his twin sons.

Olrec blew out a silent breath of relief. This was madness. He slapped the top of his bald head. *What was he thinking?* Even if he resented being sent, he was entrusted with a job. If he failed, it would prove to the pack that everything Kokkus said about him was true. Olrec would surely be labeled a laughingstock.

Suppose he could only bring back something, information, or a …a trophy to distinguish himself, restoring his glory days. He studied the sleeping giants, counting six big lumps and one tiny one. Everyone knew giants meant danger. He made his decision. Konrad would have to wait; after all, he was the one seeking contact with them. He almost shouted when a hand came out and covered his mouth.

"Quiet!" the voice ordered.

Olrec opened his eyes.

"I'm going to take my hand off your mouth. You won't shout?" Jofro the younger asked.

"Jofro! What are you doing here? I thought you left," Olrec whispered hoarsely.

Jofro smiled, revealing his perfect teeth. "Following you, in case you need some help."

"Well, I don't."

Jofro looked over his shoulder at the group of giants settling in. "Are you sure?"

"Well, maybe."

Jofro hefted himself onto the branch. "What do you need, Oh, Great Night Owl?"

Olrec wracked his brain for some pithy remark chastising Jofro for following him and then felt the spark of a great idea.

"Can you make it back tonight and let our village know that there are giants on the loose?"

Jofro nodded eagerly.

"I'm going to watch them tonight and see where they go in the morning."

"I can stay and watch." Jofro looked hopeful.

"You'll be more helpful if you warn our village against a possible attack."

"There hasn't been an attack in years. You think they will start a war?" Jofro asked a bit too eagerly for Olrec's taste.

Olrec shook his head. "Pray to the goddess Tala, they will not." Olrec bit his lips. "Looks like a scouting part. I didn't see weapons. I think they're curious."

Jofro glanced back at the giant's camp and nodded.

"We'll know tomorrow. If the giants head toward the village, you'll be ready. If they enter one of the caves up there, we're safe, and I can continue my mission."

"I'll deliver the message and head back to help you!"

"No, no—"

Jofor the younger looked at Olrec firmly, "I insist! See you in the morning."

Jofro turned to leave, and Olrec grabbed his forearm. "Will you tell them the Great Night Owl discovered it?"

"But of course. Then I'll return as soon as the message is delivered to help you in case the giants attack."

Olrec tapped him on the shoulder. "I'll be waiting for you." He glanced over to the sleeping giants. "Now go. Warn them to be ready and don't forget to tell them I sent you."

Olrec watched with a smile of satisfaction as Jofro bounded out of the forest.

The snores of the giants grew in volume, and Olrec's eyes drifted shut. He dreamt of a triumphant return, Kokkus hailing him a hero, and Zilli beaming with pride. Olrec's softer snores soon matched the giants.

I STILL HAVEN'T FOUND WHAT I'M LOOKING FOR…

WYATT HEARD HIS name being called. Carter was running after him.

"Where are you headed?" Carter caught up to him. "Hey, are you okay?"

"Fine," Wyatt said flatly.

"You sure?"

Wyatt stiffened at the question.

"Okay, okay, you just look…upset." Carter watched his face intently. "I don't know if you should go exploring this place alone."

"Stop. Please, Carter. Don't baby me. I won't be alone. Howard and Keisha will come, and Melvin won't be long. He just needs a bit of space."

"Wyatt, you're going on little to no sleep." Carter looked concerned.

"Who isn't? Everything keeps changing."

"I never wanted you to live like this. Your mom just wanted your life to be uneventful."

Wyatt's voice was bitter. "Yeah, we don't always get what we want."

Carter looked around. "Lily? I haven't seen her all day."

"She's… we're…"

Carter eyed him sympathetically. "Never mind. I'll go with you." Carter fell into step alongside him.

Wyatt took a deep breath and spoke slowly as if he was considering every word. "I appreciate it." Wyatt stopped and looked at Carter. "But, I need to do this alone." He took in the hurt on Carter's face. "I mean, it's not about you. Sometimes you—"

Carter halted him with a wave of his hand. "I understand." He sighed gustily. "I think I know what you are looking for. Are you sure you really want to find it?"

"I have to know. I want to try to make some sense of my life, of my father, and his motivations. I have to do this for Sean, too. He's bound to have questions later."

Carter looked him full in the face. "You're nothing like him."

Wyatt shrugged, his face forlorn.

Carter nodded. "I get it. I just don't want you hurt anymore."

"I think it's a little late for that," Wyatt laughed without humor. "My entire world's been turned upside down—my identity. I thought I knew everything. I have missing puzzle pieces. I need to have it all make sense."

"The offer still stands. You don't have to do it alone. Sometimes we have to let sleeping dogs lie."

"Would you?" Wyatt waited to see how Carter answered.

"No, I don't think I could. I'll be waiting for you back at the camp. Just know that I'll be anywhere you need me to be." Carter touched his shoulder. "And, Wyatt?"

"Yeah?"

"If you want to talk about Lily—."

"I know that." Silence hung between them, and Wyatt added, "Dad."

Carter smiled and said, "Go."

Wyatt headed down the darkened corridor; the lights, like those at Monsterland, turned on automatically as he traveled down the hallways. While it was becoming easier to call Carter 'Dad,' there was still an awkwardness about it. Not only did Wyatt completely trust and admire his stepfather, he also liked him.

All the resentment he felt toward him had gone away when he realized how much Carter would sacrifice for him and his brother. Referring to him as their father had been a struggle they fought with their mom about. It was unnatural to call her new husband 'Dad,' and they took every opportunity to let both her and Carter know. It was only after Carter placed himself in grave danger for him and Sean that their feelings changed. With the death of their mother, they had nothing left. The three of them became a family, and the need to gather around to feel each other's presence became a lifeline. In the new wild world, knowing there was someone to lean into not only made them feel safe but also helped them deal with the giant losses that left gaping holes in their life.

Carter showed Wyatt what a dad was supposed to be, and he understood that his father, Frank, had dropped the ball on that. Frank was a narcissist, a selfish, self-absorbed lawyer who placed everything before his family. Yet, Wyatt missed him, felt a loyalty to his memory, especially after his dad helped him escape a horde of zombies in Zombieville at Monsterland.

Wyatt wanted to know what motivated his father to do the things he did, including alienating his family and mistreating his mother. Carter made him feel loved, cherished, and valuable. His opinions and feelings held weight. Why did he have this perception that his dad thought the family didn't matter, that only his job was important? It didn't match with many of his core memories. It took up space in his head and heart. Did his dad see Wyatt as unlikable, expendable, a product of a loveless marriage?

His mom never said much about it. He knew the divorce was bitter. They were abandoned, his father's vast wealth withheld, leaving them to struggle in a backwater town with no future. *What kind of man would do that to his wife and kids?*

Wyatt took a shuddering breath, a sharp pain in the middle of his ribcage making him gasp. He paused, sucking in air, fighting back the tears that were collecting behind his eyes. Maybe Carter was right; he should let sleeping dogs lie. He shook his head. This was more about him than his dad; this was a voyage of self-discovery.

Wyatt had to know.

Otherwise, he felt like an empty vessel.

CHAPTER 25

WOO WOO

"THAT WAS SCARY," Keisha said with a heartfelt sigh.

"Well, I hope that's the last surprise that Konrad left us," Howard said to the room. They watched the crowd file out and onto their assignments.

"Get cracking on that phone. Hurry, son, we don't have much time," Colonel Drucker ordered.

"I'll do the best I can, Dad." Howard was already involved in working on the phone. "This is interesting." Howard was deep in thought.

"What?" Keisha looked up, realizing Howard wouldn't answer until he had more information.

Finally alone, Keisha and Howard's bowed heads almost touched as they worked in Vincent's former dining area. Keisha glanced up, her gaze arrested by what she was witnessing in the windows that surrounded the room. The dust had settled in the water, and rays of light pierced the shadowy depths in the panoramic view. "You can catch up to Wyatt and Melvin. I'm going to be a bit longer."

"No, I like the view," Keisha said, watching Howard work. "Besides, Melvin went in one direction, Wyatt in another."

"Where did they go?"

Keisha shrugged. "Dunno, I think Melvin's gone back outside, Wyatt went further into the building."

"It's going to be a while before the ocean clears. It can't be fun staring at all the dead creatures."

Keisha smiled at Howard's denseness. It was what she loved most about him. "I'm not here for the view." She was quiet for a minute. She looked at Howard and asked, her voice dreamy, "Have you ever thought about learning how to morph?"

Howard didn't answer.

"Howard Drucker! I asked you something. Have you ever thought about learning how to do what I'm doing?"

"What? Do you mean change into some creature?" he asked without looking up.

"Creature? Is that what you see?"

He looked up, his glasses askew. "You're offended, I can tell by your voice. By what?"

"Nothing."

"Now you're not telling the truth. What word, Keisha?" He thought for a minute. "Creature. That's a harmless word. The simple definition means an *animal, as distinct from a human being*. I don't know why you're acting offended."

Keisha thawed. "It's simple. You have to deepen your breathing. Measure each breath and think like the thing...*creature* you'd like to become."

He wasn't listening. Keisha sighed and turned her attention back to the window. Movement in the ocean caught her eye, her face breaking into a bright smile, their argument forgotten. "Look, Howard. They're back."

Howard barely heard her; he was intent on the mass of circuit boards spread all over the table top. He mumbled about people having too much sensitivity and creatures while he worked.

A group of stingrays, their willowy shapes drifted by like a group of stealth aircraft reconnoitering the area.

"Howard!" She shoved his arm, dislodging it from under his chin, and pointed toward the sprawling seabed outside the chamber. Howard's teeth clicked audibly as they connected, his glasses sliding down his narrow nose.

Howard adjusted his spectacles and turned to observe the window. Rising like a sleepwalker, he moved spellbound toward the glass barrier. Dead sea creatures lay still as a carpet on the ocean floor, and new shimmery schools of fish swept by like a curtain on opening night at a theater. "Beautiful," he said, awestruck by the display. "Tuna." He nodded to six feisty fish racing before them.

"I don't know if I'd eat that in a sandwich right now," Keisha replied sourly as she followed him.

"The water's diluting the poison." The spotted body of a fat calico bass swam past her, its tail waving like a fan. A school of bright orange and blue iridescent fish flurried into view in a V shape that resembled a flock of tropical parrots. "Amazing." Howard was rapt. "Look, Lingcod. That's another good eating fish."

Keisha sighed with relief. "I was afraid they'd never return and the area would be inhospitable. *Oh!*" The sand exploded on the ocean floor, and a flat halibut sprang from its resting place.

"*Aw*, Keish. You're so sweet. The sea is in constant renewal. Look at that fellow. He seems frisky enough. If you measure the poison parts per liter—"

"No. I don't need to. This is enough for me. Howard."

"I wonder if we collected a few specimens in a controlled setting, if we—" He continued speaking as he returned to the table to work on the cell phone.

Keisha winced behind him. "I don't like it when you call them specimens. It's so… *so*… sciency."

"Sciency? That's rather unprofessional of you, Keisha. They're just fish."

"Just fish!" she shouted, throwing her hands up. "Just fish! They're living, breathing creatures that have feelings."

"Feelings?" Howard laughed. "Are you talking about your vast experience with the trout reproduction project we did last year in the science club? You weren't concerned about your subject's feelings back then."

"Well, that was pretty callous of me." She pivoted in the other direction so he wouldn't see the distress in her face. Hunching her shoulders, she felt chilled to the bone. "Is everything a science project for you?"

"Well." He thought about it for a minute. "Yeah."

"Don't you ever see a flower as a riot of color or stars in the night sky as a display of nature's fireworks?"

"I'm not a poet, Keisha. I see cell structure and atoms as a thing of beauty."

"It's not the same. You're objectifying nature."

"I am not. You're making an argument out of nothing."

Keisha noted that his voice changed, and she folded her arms across her chest. "Don't mock me."

Howard sat down and began assembling the phone. "I'm not making fun of you, Keisha. I don't know where your logical side went. Science isn't messy."

"Messy!" Keisha screeched. "It doesn't always have to be clinical."

"We have an obligation to examine everything."

"Says who?" she snapped. "Why do we have to study every damn thing we see under a microscope? Can we leave some of it as mysteries or… or miracles, even?"

Howard twisted in his seat, then stood to observe her. "What's wrong with you? What's gotten into you?" He moved closer. "I am curious, that's all," Howard added under his breath. "It's never bothered you before. In fact," he said in a loud voice that carried through the whole room. "I thought it turned you on, you know, a bit."

"Maybe that was before I saw another side of it."

"I don't know what you're talking about."

Keisha was silent for a while, collecting her thoughts. "It started with the octopus. I kind of realized it was someone's offspring. That the mother- I mean… Its mom came looking for it because Vincent captured her baby."

"That's ridiculous!" Howard said. "Stop assigning it human characteristics. Next thing you know, you'll want to name it."

"What if I… we did."

Howard shook his head. "We have an obligation to study and understand the world around us. It's our duty."

Keisha raised one elegant eyebrow. "But what if we're harming creatures?"

Howard shrugged. "I'm not harming any creatures, Keisha," Howard said hotly. "I go out of my way to be gentle and considerate when I study them."

"But you still have no problem removing them from their environment to do that."

"I don't have a lab filled with test lab subjects, if that's what you're inferring. I wouldn't harm another life form intentionally, Keisha."

Keisha rubbed his arm. Howard looked dejected. "I know that, Howard. I know you're kind, but what if… what if… we're the ones being studied?"

"But we're not," Howard said. "This is a silly argument."

"You don't know that. What if Vincent is truly with aliens and they are studying us? How do you think you might feel?" Keisha rushed on, even though Howard looked unconvinced. "They might be examining our every move, making hypotheses. Right now." She moved close, and her pointer finger darted out to poke him in his scrawny chest. "How would you like to be the case study? The control subject, *huh, huh*. How would you like that?"

"*Ow*, Keish. That hurt."

She moved to be eye to eye, their breaths intermingling. "Once in a while, don't you just want to forget about science?"

He walked back to the dismantled phone on the table, speaking as if he expected her to be right behind him. "Science is the most important aspect of life, especially now. If we don't know how things work, then how can we expect to survive this catastrophe?" Howard's eyes opened wide with shock. "Forget about science? I could never do that!"

"Never is a long time, Howard Drucker."

Howard went on as if he hadn't heard her. "While I think John Raven is doing some amazing things, don't go all *woo-woo* on me." Howard wiggled his fingers in the air, his eyebrows lifting to his hairline. "Besides, I think I've found the answer to all our problems." He looked around. "*Keish*. Keisha?"

Howard threw down the tiny screwdriver. He handed the phone and a hastily scribbled note to the soldier waiting outside the door. "Bring this to headquarters. They'll know what to do." He went back to the stone counter and drummed his fingers on it. With an exasperated growl, he shoved himself away from the table and went in search of Keisha and the others.

CHAPTER 26

PEANUT BUTTER AND JELLY

MEVIN SAT ON a smooth boulder outside Vincent's facility, the dying rays in the west making his eyes water. He brushed them away.

It was beautiful outside. The sun glimmered as it sank, its rays gilding the water. It looked like a seascape Monet would have painted, with a soft glow and an orange ball shimmering on the horizon. A stiff breeze caressed his cheek, helping his tears vanish. Heat from the rocks seeped into his tired body, easing the stiffness that had been brought on by his morphing back and forth. It was exhausting, but he'd never admit that to anyone.

He marveled at the way the world continued despite his life collapsing around him. Birds cried out with joy, their songs creating a musical score to match the rolling waves that washed the beach. Melvin sighed heartily. He wished Jade were here to share the sunset with him. A feeling of forlornness washed over him, stealing whatever strength he had left.

The cloudless sky changed from a soft peach to a deep blue that seemed to go on forever.

Forever, the word sat heavy on his chest, and resentment burned through him. He and Jade were starting their lives together. They were supposed to have more time. He was building a future for the two of them —a home, cubs, and a peaceful world he'd create for them. Life had just begun, and Jade was stolen, yanked away viciously by the killer creature.

"Dear, sweet Jade." Thoughtful, kind, generous, and brave. She didn't serve to die. She was his peanut butter because her love turned him into jelly. His heart ached with the loss.

He peered down at the choppy waves, looking at the detritus floating like soap scum on the water. Oily and mauve colored, it was industrial waste. Pollution that ruined his life, his world.

It was hard to believe that the creature cradled within those innocent-looking eggs could be so deadly. He slammed his fist onto the rock surface. She thought they were decorations, colorful stones!

Those eggs were nothing now, fish food, useless bits of waste that would dissolve and end up on the ocean floor to be lost and forgotten.

He should feel avenged; those awful creatures were dead, but he felt no justice.

Jade was gone. Beautiful Jade. *"Jaaaade, I love you."*

The warm breeze stung his eyes, making them water. He sobbed then. Gut-wrenching wails that were snatched on the wind and carried across to the shore. He blubbered, his face drenched, the wetness running down his ruddy cheeks, his chest heaving with emotion.

He leaned forward, his tears making pockmarks on the surface of the water, his face red with fury, and screamed, *"Jade. Jaaaaade, I'll never forget you."* The sound of his voice was carried away by the roar of the surf and the wind, drifting inland. Melvin stood and yelled again, his hands fisted, *"Jade, I love you, Jade!"*

He sighed, feeling empty. Melvin held out his arms, imagining Jade walking into them. She fit perfectly, her head just under his chin. He missed her body next to his, the feeling of completeness, of home. There was a whisper, so faint he thought he imagined it.

He looked up at the heavens, but the sound drifted from inland. Quieting his raging thoughts, he went as still as possible, even holding his breath.

He heard it then, *"Mel?"*

Mel? He heard it. It was her. He'd know that voice anywhere. Chills ran up and down his spine, and for a minute, he almost collapsed from the shock of it. His knees shook, and he was overcome with weakness. They would say it was grief. It can do funny things to a person, but *no*, he was sure. It was Jade. His teeth chattered, and his chest heaved with a sigh that seemed to come from his toes. He was breathing so hard his lungs burned. He inclined his head and shouted her name. "Jade. I love you!"

Mel, I love you, too.

Was it his imagination? No, no, he was sure of it.

Home. A heartbeat later. *Home.*

Melvin sobbed. It was her. Jade is alive. He knew it.

Jade is alive. Jade is alive, he repeated it like a prayer.

"I'll find you," he shouted, jumping off the rocks. *"I'll find you!"*

Ah-wooooh! He called to the hills.

Ah-wooooh! The cry was for his mate. She was alive, and he would find her. He sent out a message to all his friends roaming the hills. *Look for my mate. Look for Jade and let me know when you see her. Pass the message along. Ah-whooooh!*

He dashed back into the building to let Wyatt, Keisha, and Howard know of his discovery. Melvin would leave forthwith. He knew he had one destination. Home. He must go to Monsterland.

The pale-yellow dot he knew as Saturn brightened the southeastern horizon. One by one, more stars and planets made their appearance, popping out like diamonds on a velvet backdrop. Melvin's heart leaped with joy, and for the first time in days, he felt a glimmer of hope.

CHAPTER 27

AN APOCALYPSE NOW

JADE HEFTED THE military knapsack on her back. Rocking on her heels from the weight, she turned to Otto. "What the heck do you have in here?"

"Never you mind. We'll need it in case we come up against aliens." Otto answered without looking up. He was stuffing maps into another bag.

Jade gave an exasperated sigh. *Who used paper maps?* "You're nuts, Otto." Formalities had fallen by the wayside, and Jade had stopped calling him Mr. Enoch. Plus, the fact that she had a sneaking suspicion that if she tried, she could rip out his throat.

Jade wasn't sure why she didn't give in to the urges tugging at the edges of her consciousness. She shrugged slightly; she was afraid something would indeed happen. She stared down at the knuckles of her good hand, wondering if she had dreamt she sprouted hair and long claws the other day. Sucking in her breath, she pondered if she had imagined the whole incident.

Everything was hazy, as if she had just awoken. She glanced at the harsh landscape surrounding her, feeling as if she were behind some glass panel, separated from home and everything familiar, leaving her an observer to life.

Otto unrolled a map, his dirty finger tracing a line as he mumbled to himself.

"Where are we going?"

"None of your concern," Otto sneered. He watched her through the gathering darkness and added, "Supplies. We need supplies."

"I told you, we need to go to Monsterland."

"Not yet."

Jade watched him slyly. She was still getting used to her new eye. "The aliens want you to go there."

"It may be a trap."

Jade raised her eyebrows. *The man was crazier than a loon.*

She shook her head. She wanted to throw down the bag and leave Otto in the dust, only she had no idea where they were. Shading her eyes, the new one was sensitive to light; she again searched the backdrop of deep rust and orange cliffs. Clicking her tongue, she turned her gaze to the maps spilling out of his bag. Her fingers itched to grab one to see the tiny names printed along the squiggly lines. Squinting, she tried to focus on the letters that she assumed represented towns, but she couldn't make them out.

Otto peered up suspiciously and rolled the paper into a tight scroll.

It didn't matter; she was never good at understanding charts or graphs, let alone a map. That kind of thing just wasn't her strength.

She missed the female robotic voice on her phone, which told her everything in a frustratingly calm voice. It recited the time of day so that she wouldn't be late, or the weather, allowing her to coordinate the proper clothing. Taking a deep breath, she longed for the smells of home, her mother's cooking, and her collection of cheap colognes that made her feel elegant and pretty. Wandering around Otto's metal cube of a residence, she checked every surface for that small, round speaker connected to an imaginary cloud that apparently no longer existed. She longed to ask the questions to fill in the gaping hole of her memory.

Life had turned into a nightmare, *no,* she amended, an apocalypse. *Not even a zombie apocalypse!* She remembered the virus outbreaks, and other than some crazy idea of a theme park with monsters, the world had managed fine. Sure, people lost jobs, the supply chain was interrupted, and homelessness became a problem, but it wasn't like it was anything *new.*

She remembered scrolling through all the social media on her phone, catching plenty of historical reenactments that proved things like this had happened throughout the ages, and humanity had always found a way out of it. Besides, the government was in charge. She lived in the best country in the world, her dad always said. She had complete faith that the grown-ups would figure it out.

Her dad told her not to worry, so she didn't. Chewing the nail of her non-mechanical hand, she pursed her lips in thought, eyeing Otto disdainfully. He was scrabbling around on the hard-packed earth, having a rather involved conversation with himself. Jade needed to get information from a reliable source, not the crackpot next to her. She scanned the horizon, but the wonder eye he'd put in only told her the shapes of rocks and trees. It wasn't some miracle thing, she wanted to say to him. What did she need *that* information for?

Swallowing her dry throat, she returned to search the desert landscape, looking for anything resembling a ribbon of a road or the sparkle of a stream. They could be anywhere from Arizona to Utah; nothing looked familiar, and her eyes showed a mishmash of colorful lines.

As soon as she recognized a major roadway, Jade planned to

escape and let Otto and his crazy mission be damned. She supposed they were headed to someplace where Otto could prove his nutty theories, but truthfully, she had no sense of direction and refused to ask the maniac walking behind her.

It didn't matter that he saved her life; she felt nothing but mild contempt for him. His constant harping about aliens, giants, and other boogeyman conspiracy theories confirmed what she always thought about him. Jade sighed gustily with exasperation. She couldn't wait to tell Melvin.

Wait, what? Jade gasped, her thoughts coming to an abrupt halt. *Why Melvin?* Yet, the mere thought of the auburn-haired klutz filled her with eagerness and an intoxicating sense of peace. Jade turned west, sensing the answers to that question lay there.

A slight rustling coming from a clump of bushes drew her attention. Jade spun, slightly off balance, the metal hand making her clumsy. Her new eye identified an animal hiding under the brush. Crouched in the shade of a cactus, a coyote stared at her, its head tilted in question, the brown, watchful eyes concerned. *Could a coyote even express that?* She cocked her head in a fair imitation of the coyote.

Jade? she heard her name called as clearly as the wind chimes dancing on the breeze. *Jade?* She moved closer to the animal, but it backed away.

Jade. The sound came from another direction.

Jade pursed her lips. Glancing over her shoulder, she confirmed that Otto was busy with his maps again, talking to himself.

Jade… Jaaaaade. She heard the call again, soft as a feather, and barely a whisper. The coyote continued to observe her with steely eyes.

"Did you call me?" she asked Otto from over her shoulder.

"No, stop interrupting me," he grumbled.

"*Humpf,*" she said breathlessly, hopeful and excited all at once.

Jaaaaade. I love you. I'll never forget you. The call was long and drawn out, almost musical in tone. It danced above her, as if caught on a breeze. Her heart did a little lurch, and she placed her hands over her chest to still the rapid tattoo.

"Mel," she said tentatively, her voice soft. Then, without thinking, the following sentence came out in a rush of rightness. "Mel? I love you, too."

She repeated it, in a whisper more urgent than before, longing crashing through her. She swayed, lost in a sea of tender sensations, leaning into an embrace that was not there. "Home." It was a simple word, yet it said everything. She repeated it. "Home." Taking a deep breath, she imagined walking into Melvin's arms, feeling them caress her back, giving her the security she needed. She knew he'd be resting his chin on the top of her head, where they fit together like one puzzle piece complete and whole. Her heart leaped with joy. *I'll find you.*

Opening her mouth to return a response, she snapped it shut almost as quickly when she felt the earth move with the vibrations of Otto's impatient stride.

Jade smelled Otto before she saw him. She didn't move fast enough. He was aiming that stupid remote at her again.

"It doesn't work, you idiot!" she yelled.

The older man grabbed her in a punishing grip by the wrist, holding her captive. "Who are you talking to?" He had a gun in his other hand, and the whites of his eyes surrounded his irises. Jade was not afraid for herself; she worried about the animal in the bushes.

"No one," Jade stammered, trying to chase the cobwebs holding her brain hostage. She averted her gaze so Otto couldn't see in that direction, but her keen ears picked up a menacing growl from the low scrub. *No, no, no,* she warned the coyote.

She spun in the opposite direction, her steps still a bit awkward, and walked a slight distance. "I thought I heard something, that's all. It's your stupid chimes back at the camp. They hurt my ears," she complained loudly, trying to distract him from spying the coyote. Hands behind her back, she waved away the animal, knowing instinctively that Otto would kill it if he saw it.

"That's because of your superior hearing. Superior werewolf hearing. Maybe you're going to remember how to morph?"

"I don't know what you're talking about."

Otto released her hand with disgust. "Come along before it gets dark."

Jade glanced back at the wall of bushes; the coyote was gone, leaving her bereft. *Melvin*, she sighed, missing him with every cell of her body. Even if she couldn't recall her life, she knew all she needed was Melvin. Nothing else mattered.

She looked up at the setting sun, a memory niggling at the furthest reaches of her brain, then, without looking at Otto, asked him, "You're not afraid to go out with me here… I mean… *if… if* I really am a werewolf."

Otto laughed. It was condescending without humor. The sound of his harsh chuckles repelled Jade.

"*Oh*, you're one of them, all right." He shook his head. "I'm not afraid. It's not a full moon tonight. Now, if it were next week, that would be a different story."

Jade nodded absently. Werewolves only changed with a full moon. Everybody knew that. Uneasiness assailed her. But that wasn't the whole truth; she couldn't understand where the knowledge was born. Melvin could change, she thought with shock. Melvin could change at any time he wanted to. *How could she know that? Melvin, Melvin, where are you?*

Taking a deep breath, her lids slid shut.

In the purple-shrouded mountains toward the west, a wolf howled.

She focused her eyes, trying to see the animal in the gathering dusk. The desert shimmered in a haze of orange and magenta. Straining, she sought out the creator of the mournful sound. It was followed by another and then another, soon becoming a symphony of cries that caressed her heart in a way she never imagined.

Her throat tightened, and she looked at Otto with contempt.

She couldn't possibly be a werewolf. Yet she knew with certainty that Melvin was a werewolf, and she wasn't scared. She felt nothing but deep love for him. She glanced at her hand again, wishing to see the claws just to prove it really happened. The skin on her ears tingled, and she fought the urge to open her mouth and join the wolf's song.

They set off just as lights should have winked on, and the sun sank over the hills. They skirted towns, which appeared dark and desolate. Jade shivered, not from cold. Her mind was in overdrive; images spun like a demented Ferris wheel, blurred and indistinguishable from one another. Sadness pulled at her, forcing Jade to turn her attention outward. She carried a light stick Otto had given her.

They walked in the gloom, her eye adjusting as the sky changed to inky blackness, the neon stripe of bright light turning the landscape a dusty blue.

Jade held the rod before her, then hid it away, marveling when she realized she could see things despite the darkness. Her mouth opened in a perfect circle of awe. She didn't need the illumination. Her breath caught with a strange sense of excitement. She was not having the same trouble as Otto. Her steps were light and nimble.

Glancing ahead, she saw Otto stumbling, his breathing harsh and labored; the feeble light he carried did nothing to improve his weakened vision.

"Hurry!" Otto ordered.

Jade placed one foot in front of the other, unsure of herself and the journey she was about to take. Her ears twitched again at a sound behind her; she paused, listening for the scrabble of paws. She wanted to go back. *But back to where?* She knew wherever it was, it involved Monsterland.

Otto pushed on, oblivious to her movements. Iridescent eyes peered at her from behind the low scrub. Her hand automatically went to her throat, feeling for a pendant that wasn't there. Her fingers traced the imaginary dips and contours of the silver wolf's head that was seared into her brain, the emerald eyes a beacon of comfort. *Melvin's pendant*, she knew without thinking. It was hers. *He was hers.*

Jade gasped as memories flooded back into her fevered brain. Flashes of their idyllic home in the ruins of the theme park, raiding the stores, eating at a campfire, the sound of them splashing in the lagoon they called home. Auburn fur on a hand that pointed to the clouds that revealed a bone-faced moon contrasted with her father's horrified features. Her breath felt frozen in her chest. She was sad and happy all at once, at the recollection of her mother and brother's deaths, and her marriage to Melvin. Now, she understood why she felt driven to go there.

The realization hit her like a tornado. Gut-punched, the air escaped her body in a rush so fast she sank to her knees. Stifling a sob, she raised her face to the silent stars above her, tears trickling from the corner of her one eye, the rivulets plopping onto the dry soil. The sound of each one became a small dagger to her heart.

As if her world hadn't changed enough, as if she hadn't grieved sufficiently, her heart cracked knowing Melvin must be worried sick. *The lagoon. The creature. The pain.*

Her skull felt the pressure of water as it closed over her lacerated face, punches from the shell-like creature as it dragged her from her bed. It came in a mosaic of agony, not a complete picture, but enough to know her world had been shattered. "How did this happen?" she whispered.

Jade's jaw dropped open with horror. They must all think she was dead. *Daddy,* she moaned—*Melvin, my poor Melvin.* Holding the sides of her face, she bit back a sob. "How long?" Her voice croaked with despair. "How long have I been gone?"

"What?" Otto's voice was far away. She heard his clumsy footsteps as he stomped back to her.

"Get up!" he ordered. He pulled at her arm. She refused to rise.

Touching her cheek, metal meeting metal, she realized everything was different now. She wasn't the pretty cheerleader Melvin adored.

She was different, as different as she was when she saw her father's revulsion when he realized she was not his little girl anymore. Jade could barely breathe. Staring at the moonlight gleaming on the metal of her palm, she knew she was not entirely human either. No more soft skin, she was all rivets and hard edges. Turning it over, her heart sank as reality set in.

Otto stopped. "Move, Jade. We don't have all night!" he snapped, yanking her arm. Otto dragged her a foot or two.

Jade blubbered a bit, her face down, as if the weight of her world was compressing her into a small ball. Snot ran from one side of her nose, and she brushed it away with her non-mechanical arm. This was too much to take in.

Jade was a werewolf. She glanced down at the clunky articulated metal of her fingertips. She was a robot, too. Otto's harsh breathing was above her, his looming presence and impatience like a radioactive wave making her skin crawl. He plucked at her jacket, and she wrestled her arm away. Jade's mouth opened with a silent sob, but she realized there was nothing left. She had hit rock bottom.

Then she remembered Nolan.

Taking a shuddering breath, she felt her jaw firm, flesh against metal. Nolan pushed her around, made her do things she didn't want to, and yet, Jade was able to protect both herself and Wyatt when Nolan attacked them. She was no wilting flower in Monsterland. She was brave enough to stand up to her father and make the right choices for her life.

She was not some high school girl to be bullied. Jade dug her feet into the softly packed earth.

"Leave me alone!" She tore her arm away, pushing Otto off-balance. Wiggling out of the backpack, she threw it to the ground, where it landed in a puff of dust.

Otto sank next to her. "You've remembered," he said plainly.

Jade stared mulishly ahead, refusing to make eye contact. She could hear his labored breaths next to her own. It was as if they had both run a marathon. "I'm not moving."

Otto studied her for a long moment. "You want to go home to Copper Valley?"

Jade remained silent.

Home, she thought. "Monsterland," she responded stubbornly, knowing by the tempo of her rapidly beating heart that she needed to go there. She knew Otto didn't understand they were the same.

"Soon. Once we get supplies—" The word hit her like a splash of cold water.

"Now!" Jade's head snapped up.

Otto rose to leave without answering her, his light stick a beacon.

"I'm not following you." Jade leaned back, resting her elbow on the knapsack.

Otto stopped dead, his shoulders stiffening. Jade watched his bald head fall backwards in exasperation. He stamped back, hovering over her like a black cloud.

Hackles rose along her spine, saliva pooled in the front of her mouth, and without blinking, Jade felt her teeth protrude from a mouth that no longer felt like her own.

She stood, her shoulders broad, her muscles pulsing. "I am not your lapdog." She swiped her new robotic claw, amazed at its dexterity, grabbing Otto by the front of his shirt. Lifting him high, she saw her face gleaming in the reflection of his glasses. "Give me one good reason I should be going with you," she ground out, her voice husky and strong.

Otto didn't respond; she was choking the life from him, Jade observed dispassionately. Loosening her hold, she allowed him to clear his abused throat. Otto kicked his feet uselessly. Jade was holding him almost two feet off the ground.

He whispered, "We'll go home tomorrow, Jade… we must be prepared before—"

"We are going to Monsterland…now!"

"Okay…okay," he choked out.

Jade's forehead furrowed. She knew all the answers were in Monsterland. She looked at her good hand, the velvet fur covering it, and then at the other, which was still bandaged. She needed to fill in the blank spaces in her brain. She glanced toward the dark horizon, where Monsterland lay in ruins, Copper Valley in devastation, and her love was waiting for her. She dropped Otto onto the ground, smiling when he landed with a painful grunt.

"You carry the bags," she said without looking at him. Jade strode off into the night, heading west and to her destiny.

CHAPTER 28

SHATTERED FRAMES

"**W**HAT ARE YOU looking for?" Howard asked when he caught up with Wyatt and Keisha. "Where's Mel?"

Wyatt watched as Howard tried to make eye contact with Keisha, who appeared to ignore him. "I saw him head outdoors. He said he needed some air."

Howard nodded. "Where's Lily? Wasn't she with you before?"

Wyatt's face closed in; he shrugged. "I dunno."

"But—"

"You heard him, Howard," Keisha's voice was equally terse. "He doesn't know."

"Oh." Howard's eyebrows went to his hairline. "Want to talk—"

"Forget it, Howard." Wyatt walked ahead.

They were at an intersection of four corridors. Wyatt had wandered into several offices that yielded nothing, slamming drawers and doors with loud whacks.

Glancing from Keisha's sullen face to Howard's inquisitive one, he wondered what was going on between them. Keisha seemed as edgy as he was. Sometimes, Howard could be thick about things and not understand social cues.

Howard turned around, examining all the hallways. "So innocuous looking. We could be anywhere from an office building to a school."

"It's funny how everything can be camouflaged to look ordinary," Wyatt said. "It's amazing when you think about how much we missed on our road trip here. Like, how did we not recognize Nate, I mean, President Owens?" Wyatt spoke absently while poking around. He had trouble thinking of the president as his former road trip buddy. Truth be told, he was more of Howard's buddy. Wyatt had a firm resentment toward him. It was hard to believe Nate Owens had hypnotized both him and Howard into thinking he was a rogue soldier returning to active duty. He considered all the Easter eggs he missed, just because he hadn't been paying attention.

"You are talking about President Owens," Keisha stated, her voice as hollow as the empty corridor.

"Yes, I mean, I think of him as Nate. He'll always be Nate to me. I can't believe how much I didn't trust him," Wyatt said.

"Well, I liked him right away, if you remember." Howard adjusted his glasses.

"You must have sensed something about him," Keisha said, her brows raised. She hung back a bit, biting her cheek inside her mouth. She glanced at her hand, knowing the skin was brown and smooth, yet worried that red scales could erupt at any moment. She looked up to find Wyatt's watchful eyes on her.

He held her gaze for a long while, his face sympathetic. Keisha felt her scalp tighten; she looked away, but knew Wyatt was still studying her.

"Where are we going?" Melvin called, running down the corridor. "What are we looking for?"

No one answered him, but he fell in with the rest of the group. He tapped Keisha playfully on the shoulder, but she acted as if she didn't feel it. He hung back and whispered to Howard, "What's eating her?"

Howard shrugged and picked up his pace without answering.

"Have you guys slept at all?"

Howard nodded absently. "Catnaps. Too much going on!"

They came to a row of doors, and he entered the first one. "Looks like a sick bay on a Starship," Howard said, taking in the single bed with machinery attachments. "*Whoops…* hello."

"What?" Wyatt asked quickly.

"We've got an android in here." Howard was on his knees examining the human-looking body. "I thought it was a corpse, but then I saw the charring. This place keeps getting better and better."

"Speak for yourself, Howard. This stinks," Melvin said with a scowl.

"It couldn't be a person, it would stink," Keisha observed from the shadows.

She watched Howard's busy hand examine the robot. Turning abruptly, Keisha began opening cabinets lining the walls and pulling out pill bottles, syringes, tubes, suction bulbs, scissors, and other assorted medical paraphernalia. "What do you make of these instruments?" She held up a strange V-shaped object. "It looks like a cigar cutter."

"It's an umbilical cord clip." Melvin took it from her and squeezed it together in a demonstration.

"And how would you know that?" Keisha asked, her eyes wide.

"I looked into this kind of stuff in case, well, you know…. It's not like there are many doctors around anymore."

Keisha's mouth dropped. "Was Jade pregnant?"

"No." Melvin looked away, his face grim. He picked up a stethoscope, placed the earpieces in his ears, and pressed the round disc against her back, whispering, "What are you afraid of?"

"Excuse me?" Keisha's voice was high and tight as she spun away from him.

"Come on, Keisha, I have known you for a million years. Something's bothering you." Melvin's tone was low, so only she could hear him.

Keisha's eyes darted to Howard's head, which was bowed over the robot's body.

"What… is it, Howard? Are you two fighting?"

Keisha gave a slight shake of her head, her fingers shredding a box of gauze.

Melvin's shoulders were large and comforting. Keisha longed to rest her head and not worry for a minute. Since Monsterland, everything had changed, including herself. When she began dabbling in shape-shifting, she had just lost her parents; her entire well-planned life had imploded. Lately, she was afraid she was losing something bigger.

She looked up to see Melvin's kind eyes. He was different. A bite from a werewolf changed the gawky teen into a buff-looking adult. Gone was his clumsiness, and his freckles reminded her more of a highland warrior than a timid nerd. Tilting her head, she wondered if he was suffering in the same way she was. "Are you happy?" she whispered.

He paused and sucked in a deep breath. His eyes were shiny with tears. "I miss Jade."

They held hands for a minute, each lost in thought.

Keisha shook her head. "We all miss Jade. I'm not talking about that. Are you sorry you… you…"

"Took the bite?" He laughed without humor. "Do I look sorry?" He gave a slight grin, revealing strong white teeth. "Is this about your—"

"*Shhhh,*" she warned, glancing at Wyatt and Howard.

"No." Melvin shook his head. "And unlike you, I'll never go back."

Keisha's head snapped up.

"John Raven is training you, teaching you to morph at will, but you'll always be you. If you decide you don't want to morph, all you have to do is stop. It's not permanent."

Keisha's lips thinned, and she shrugged her shoulders. "I'm not so sure about that. I may have changed… in here. " She pointed to the middle of her chest.

Melvin smiled. "You've got to expect some change, but heck, we're all changed. Some are just more obvious." He looked back at Wyatt and Howard. "Do you think they are the same people they were a year ago?"

Keisha nodded in agreement, her face forlorn.

Melvin went on. "It's still different for you, though. You are not governed by nature like I am. For me, there is no way back." Melvin's expression hardened. "Not that there's anything for me to return to there, either." His gaze lowered, and he seemed to be talking to himself. "It's like I don't belong anywhere." He swallowed, his Adam's apple bobbing with unspoken emotion. *Jade, Jade, Jade,* he repeated silently her name like a mantra, hoping what he heard before was not his imagination..

Keisha touched his forearm gently. "You belong with us." The words felt hollow. She wasn't even sure if *she* belonged anymore. "You know, I wish I had never learned," she said bitterly. "If I never morph again, it will be too soon."

"Keisha, you don't really mean that."

"Maybe I do."

They were quiet again, both sets of eyes returned to Howard and Wyatt, their hands deep in the robot's chest. Keisha wondered if she, along with Melvin, had changed too much for their group.

The room was filled with a buzzing sound, followed by a pop. Howard exclaimed, "*Aha!*" and an electronic voice began to whine, "Help me. Please. *Help meeee.*"

Wyatt and Howard lifted the android to its feet. It leaned to the side and began to walk in tight circles. "Dr. Konrad, help! Must save the baby. Dr. Konrad, help!"

"An android nurse," Wyatt said. "This must be where they impregnated Rosemary."

"I'd love to spend more time seeing what it can do," Howard said to the group. "I can access the information through Mythdot."

"I'm sure you would, " Keisha snapped. "What the heck is Mythdot?"

"That's what I was investigating back there." He gestured to the central part of the building. "I managed to hack Vincent Konrad's satellite and, through that, his programming. It's called Mythdot."

"There are more pressing things to worry about right now." She turned to a bank of cabinets, hitting them with the heel of her hand with a little too much force. "Sometimes we have to consider other people's issues," she grumbled. "For instance, Rosemary still doesn't know who the father is. Maybe we can find something." A door swung open, revealing an operating room, the walls lined with images of a fetus lit up from behind.

"*Wow!* Nice work, Keisha." Howard ran into the room, Mythdot forgotten. "Look!" The others followed him, the android rolling behind them like a lost puppy.

Melvin approached a white screen, an X-ray film shining brightly. "Guys," he called. "Take a look. Do you think Rosemary knows about this?"

They all stared at the strange image of an oversized head, with three small holes where the nose should have been. Its almond-shaped eyes appeared too big in the fish-shaped face. The white dots of the spinal cord continued down long after the infant's butt, ending in a curling tail reminiscent of the one Keisha had attached to her back early this morning when she morphed into a dragon.

"Do you think it's a mutant?" Howard asked.

"No," a tinny voice said from behind them. "It's Commander Spekator's child, from the Thalen ship."

"What?" All four teens spun around.

"Rosemary's baby is a human-alien hybrid," the android stated.

"What in the world was that man thinking?" Wyatt asked the room, but nobody answered.

"There are human-aliens all over the place," the android told them. "This is a new variety. New variety, yes, yes. New variety coming."

"What is he talking about?" Howard approached the robot, but it babbled nonsense and made weird electronic noises.

"Shut that thing up, I can't hear myself think," Melvin said, loudly roaring over the droid's grating voice.

"What do you think it means about a new variety?" Wyatt asked.

"Many, many hybrids. Must outnumber. Start with one. The square root of…"

"I said shut that thing up!" Melvin shouted.

"Clearly, the implication is that there are other alien-human hybrids roaming around," Howard yelled over the sound. "*Hmmmm,* this is disturbing." He pressed a few buttons and mumbled. "I transferred her records. I'll read them later."

The robot interrupted him. "Thalen's superior. Commander Spekator's DNA, superior child. Superhuman child…"

"Thalens…. Betcha that nutcase, Otto Enoch, would know," Melvin said. "He disappeared after…"

"After my mom took his job. I'm sure Carter knows where he is," Wyatt said quietly.

"Let's take as much as we can from here." Keisha was loading a folder with papers from the drawers.

Howard fiddled with a keypad on the android's back, and its voice deepened and slowed until it slumped forward and remained silent. "I'd like a few hours to see what else it can tell us."

"I'm sure you would," Melvin said, snatching the films.

"Let's get out of here," Howard stated.

"Not yet. I'm not finished." Wyatt's face was flushed.

"It's getting late, and we have to return Nurse Rachet here to my dad." Howard gestured to the robot with longing.

"You go. I have something else I need to see," Wyatt said.

"What else can top this, Wy? Let's get out of here. Who knows what else we're missing? Besides, Keisha and I have to finish configuring the phones so we can set up communications using Konrad's satellite." He was tying a cable around the robot's waist so they could drag it back.

"I told you, I can't," Wyatt snapped.

Howard hesitated. Melvin came up behind Wyatt. "I'll stay with him," he told the others.

Howard shrugged, his mouth compressed into a thin line. "I don't like leaving you both."

Wyatt's eyes softened when he looked up at him. "It's not like I'm leaving town. I have… I want to explore more."

"It's better when we're all together," Howard grumbled.

"Well, I'm still with you." Keisha looked angry.

Howard swallowed hard. He looked from Keisha's closed face to Wyatt's impatient one. Howard patted Keisha's shoulder. "Of course, you are. Let's go." She pulled away from his touch.

They left, tugging the android behind them.

"Where are you so eager to go?" Melvin asked Wyatt, who was already out the door.

"I have a hunch."

"I love hunches," Melvin said, his eyebrows raised.

"Where'd you go before?" Wyatt asked as they walked. "You look…I dunno, better."

Melvin did look different. His steps were lighter, his face more at ease. "Just wanted to watch the sunset."

Wyatt arched an eyebrow. "I know you and something's up."

"I think Jade is alive."

Wyatt stopped walking. "Mel. I know you miss her, but—"

Melvin waved a hand to interrupt him. "This is why I didn't want to say anything. I was watching the sunset, and I called her name."

"And… is that it?"

"Well, no. Not exactly. She answered me. Here." He pointed to his temple.

"That doesn't mean—"

"I know what I felt, Wy. I'm leaving. I came to tell you that I'm heading to Monsterland to find her."

Wyatt shook his head. "I'll go with you. As soon as I find what I'm looking for, we'll go and find what you're looking for. Deal?"

"You don't have to come." Melvin colored up.

"But I will, and so will Howard and Keisha. We're part of your pack. *Ah-whooo!*"

Melvin grinned. "You call that a howl. I'll show you how to do it!" He took off running down the corridor, wolfish cries filling the space and echoing down the passageway.

Wyatt followed him, his feet slapping against the tiled hallways. It was eerily empty, and a dank, musty smell let him know they were heading deeper into the building's bowels.

"What are you looking for?" Melvin called, jogging ahead of Wyatt.

Wyatt didn't answer. He stopped at each door, read the small plaque indicating the department, and with a grim expression went deeper into the building. Melvin paused, his hands on his knees, while he observed Wyatt checking each of the doorways.

At the end of a long corridor that seemed to be endless, Wyatt's face went white. He sprinted past Melvin, who yelled, "*Hey!*" and took off after him.

"It's here," he said, his voice cracking. "I knew it," Wyatt said, disappearing through a darkened doorway.

Melvin paused by the sign. "Legal," he read the word out loud. "What, are you gonna sue Konrad?" he shouted, but no one answered him.

Melvin entered the doorway at the sound of drawers being pulled open. "Dude, Colonel Drucker is not going to like this." He rounded a corner to find Wyatt on his knees, holding something against his chest. The shadows hid his face, but Melvin was sure he heard a sob.

"I think I finally found what I was looking for." Wyatt sat on the floor holding something he pulled from under a desk.

"What are you talking about?" Melvin sank to the floor next to him and pried a rectangular object from Wyatt's hands. He held the broken picture frame in his hands. "Wow, is that…?"

"Yes, it's me… and Sean. This is my dad's desk." He looked up at Melvin. "This was underneath it." They stared at the picture of Frank Baldwin and his two sons. "He cared about us, Mel. He cared about us, after all." He took it out of the frame and tucked it inside his shirt above his heart.

He thought for a second that Lily would love to hear about it, then his smile faded, knowing she probably didn't care anymore.

CHAPTER 29

PRETTY AS A PIRANHA

"SLOW DOWN, I need to take a break." Jade heard Otto's breathless voice behind her and paused impatiently. Nodding discreetly toward the bushes, she saw four coyotes stop as well. They backed into the low brush, their eyes glowing in the darkness. Jade had noticed them shadowing her and Otto sometime during the night.

Otto sat on the ground with a groan and opened a canteen. He held it up. Jade sneered in distaste.

"I'm your friend, Jade. Your only friend," Otto told her. "You owe me a lot. You were dead as a doornail when I pulled you from the lagoon; your eyeball and jaw were hanging loose."

Jade made a disgusted sound and turned away. "You should have taken me to a hospital. Maybe they could have saved my hand and eye."

Otto laughed. "Silly girl, all the hospitals are closed. The only thing I could have taken you to is the morgue. According to my ham radio, Washington was destroyed weeks ago. New York is a zoo; every major city has been disrupted by the purple foam that came up through the sewers."

"This is America!"

Otto nodded. "True and filled with small individual potentates now."

Jade furrowed her brow.

"Thinking about the rest of the world? Every country is just as chaotic as ours. I saved your life! If I had brought you to any kind of medical station, they would have let you die by the wayside. You wouldn't be considered worth saving. You should kiss my—"

"I don't believe you. People care. I know there are others out there who really do give a damn and are working together to save our country."

"Poor delusional butterfly." Otto made a *tsking* noise and shook his head.

"Stop calling me that!" Jade bit her lip.

"You've undergone a metamorphosis. Think of this as your chrysalis stage. You're morphing. Enjoy the process."

She slipped her fingers over the hard line of her cheek and jaw and took a deep breath. Placing her hand on top of her new eye, she felt gingerly along the wound. It still ached. It was bolted in and a part of her now. It jutted out of her socket, and she knew she must resemble something from a nightmare. Otto reconstructed her. "You should have let nature take its course, and let me die," she seethed. Jade sighed deeply. She was glad no one from Copper Valley could see her now, especially Melvin.

"Don't worry. You're still pretty, in a steampunk kind of way. I'm sure your boyfriend will be fine with you."

"Shut up, Otto." She sat cross-legged. "Why *did* you save me?"

Otto leaned on the pile of knapsacks he was carrying. The morning sun was peeking over the mountain ridge, painting a soft glow over everything, and somewhere nearby, a stream gurgled. Water made her nervous. Jade shivered from the sound of it.

"Because I could."

"What were you doing in… there," she paused, took a deep breath, and continued, "in Monsterland, that particular day?"

"What everybody else does. Scavenge, and lucky for you, I was in the park. I had been waiting for weeks to get a glimpse of the shell creature—"

Her memory hazy at best, Jade asked. "Tell me about it."

Otto bent closer, his voice gravelly. "Konrad created them, of course, although they could be alien—"

"Everything is an *alien* to you, the purple foam, the Grays, the—"

There was the sound of scrabbling paws in the bush.

"*Shhhh,*" Otto interrupted. He fell onto his stomach and hissed, "Get down."

Jade slammed herself onto the ground. Her ears picked up feral growls of the surrounding coyotes. "That's just a pack of—"

"Coyowolves," he cut her off. "I've seen them. They're a hybrid wolf and coyote. Many coyotes have appeared to have mated with wolves."

Jade visibly flinched.

"You don't like to hear about wolves mating, do you?" he wheedled. He reached into his bag and drew out the remote.

"You never give up. Everything is a lost cause, but you don't know it. Like your dumb inventions." She gestured at the remote in his hands.

"Not everything." He smiled slyly. "I remade you."

"I've had enough of you and your nonsense."

Jade jumped to her feet, but Otto's words stopped her in her tracks. "Give me a few more minutes and I'll finish the story."

Jade bit her lip with indecision, but the need to know outweighed her hatred for Otto. She sank onto the ground. "Go ahead."

"The shell creature had been in a tank in the belly of the theme park. I believe it was created there. Somehow, in the destruction, it made it into your lagoon. The one you shared with Melvin Saunders."

Jade perked up. "Melvin," She mouthed his name like a prayer. She missed him.

"Yes, I saw you there many times, frolicking like a pair of dolphins."

Jade ignored his last statement. "The shell thing could be some sort of hybrid."

Otto took another drink and shrugged. "Could be. The DNA samples were like nothing I've ever seen. Some Lycan and Vampire genes mixed, but there were strands I just didn't recognize. They multiply like mad, you should know. I saw you harvesting the eggs."

A memory flared in her brain. Jade playing in the water, picking up pretty rocks, decorating her new *home*. She sat back with a huff, feeling weak. "I was living there, in Monsterland."

"Yes, with Melvin."

"Melvin." She felt her heart flutter. "I was collecting them, the eggs. I didn't mean any harm. I thought they were pretty."

"Pretty as a piranha. They're deadly. No discernible brain." He appeared as though he was looking inward. "The eyes are connected to pure shell. Made no sense."

"What made no sense?"

"The shell creature, you idiot. The one who took off half your face. Well, no matter." He paused. "Did you hear that?"

"It's the coyothings,"

"No, not the howling, the thumping." He went completely flat on his stomach. "Oh my… Look, over there." He pulled out binoculars from the bag and aimed them straight ahead. He handed the binoculars to her impatiently. "To the left and slightly above the space in the boulder."

Jade peered over the tall grass and rocks. They were on the lower elevation of a mountain, her eyes going wide. Six giants were milling around what looked to be a campfire. They were stamping on the flames, extinguishing them. Each stood at least thirty feet tall; one was slightly smaller. All of them had bright orange hair and were wearing rustic, homespun outfits. A red-haired female of normal height climbed onto the shoulder of the largest of the beasts.

"Giants," Otto hissed. "I knew they were real."

"Holy cow," Jade said. "What do we do now?"

"Shush! They'll tear us apart if they find us. We've got to lay low!" He was breathing heavily as if he'd run a race.

"Look." She pointed at them. "They're moving upwards. Away from us."

Otto leaned up against the bark of a tree. He didn't answer her. Something in the back caught his attention. He dug furiously, chipping away the tree's surface. His fingers found a tuft of black hair. He pulled it from where it was wedged. Sniffing it, he gagged.

"What is it?" Jade asked.

"Skunk ape."

"There are no apes in any of the western states, unless they've escaped from captivity, or are you going to tell me all the animals are running loose, right now?" She became thoughtful. "I think we're too far from any major zoo."

"It's not an ape. You'd know this if you actually did my assignments. Skunk ape, one of the names for Bigfoot, the Sasquatch. I'd give my right arm to see one for real."

Jade was lost in her own thoughts and ignored him, but Otto's request went on. "I've hunted them for years, always just missing them. I've found footsteps, even their shit, but I never saw one in the flesh. He laughed manically, smelling the tuft of hair again. "Imagine if I get a glimpse of one today. Giants and Bigfoot, maybe even an alien. Oh boy, that will make my day!"

Werewolves, shell creatures, coyotewolves, giants, Bigfoot, Jade mumbled. She watched the giants disappear over the next outcropping of rocks.

"They've climbed to the other side of the mountain. Let's get out of here! Move fast before they spot us." Otto scrambled down the hill and was soon out of the giant's view.

"This is too much. I feel like I'm stuck in a bad video game. I want to go home." Jade followed him reluctantly. She covered her ravaged face with her hands. "I just want it to go back to the way it was."

CHAPTER 30

RED FLAGS

THE SUN ROSE, gilding the dew coating the rocky surface of the mountain behind them. A cool breeze blew in from the north, making Rosemary shiver.

"Winter is coming," Grillos said ominously.

Rosemary saw Brontes exchange a smoldering look with his brother. "What's going on between you two?" she asked quietly.

Grillos cleared his throat. "He's angry none of the girls chose to return home."

"No, I think there's more," Rosemary insisted. "I don't think he likes me."

Grillos paused, his eyebrow reaching the orange hairline on his forehead. Shaking his head, he pointed to a steep rock above them. The cliff was striped with layers of compressed soil in colors ranging from rust to peach. With a grunt, he said, "He doesn't like the idea of mixing with minkins."

"I don't know why. Food isn't a problem now," she offered, standing and shaking out the kinks in her back. She patted her midsection, which appeared distorted. Rosemary fought the sudden nausea; her skin felt tight, as if it were being stretched. Oddly enough, even her face felt swollen. She shook off the discomfort and firmly pushed it to the back of her mind. She was probably focusing too much on her changing body and making a mountain out of a molehill. She wished there was another person she could confide in about it. Rosemary sighed. Shandy would talk her through this.

Grillos ran his massive fingers through his bright locks. "After Monsterland, people will need ways to get things. Your supply chain has been disrupted. The cities are a mess. In case you haven't noticed, it's chaos out there."

"Maybe the timing isn't right," Rosemary said softly, arching her back as if to relieve the tightness.

Grillos paused. "Wot do you mean by that?" he asked quietly.

"I spent my life avoiding society. I don't know why you're so insistent on joining ours. I'd give anything to be back on the ocean."

Rosemary could feel Grillos bristle. "Really? I thought you wanted to come along with us."

She patted his knee, trying to soothe the tension. "I did. I mean, I wanted to stay with you. The sea makes me feel safe." His back went rigid again, and he stood up to a fearsome height. She had to look up to talk to him. She was afraid he'd hurt his feelings. If only she could smooth his furrowed brows, but she'd need to climb a mainmast to reach them. "Grillos, you make me feel safe, too. Safe and… cherished." She glanced up from under lowered lashes to see a hint of a smile. "It's just that the sea has always been my home. It's difficult now. There are so many changes going on." She rubbed her belly.

"Do you even know why you came?" Brontes yelled from his spot near the front of the clearing.

"Damn giant hearing," she muttered. She had a lot to learn about her new companions. "Yes. It was mutually beneficial. I need a secure place to stay for the next few months, and your clans need to learn that not all humans are bad."

The six giants bellowed with laughter that bounced off the rock wall and ricocheted around the canyon.

"Quiet," Grillos ordered. "You don't know who is nearby."

The group turned somber and quickly broke up their camp.

Rosemary frowned. She was not used to being the butt of anyone's joke. As captain, she was revered and respected. Her cheeks grew hot. "And, a person was needed to help your group adjust to living above ground."

"So you say, Madam Ambassador," Brontes mocked her, his voice a low growl once again.

"Like it or not, I seemed to be the one person the president felt could do the job," she responded, her words clipped.

"Perhaps this is why our partnership may work." Grillos sounded conciliatory. "We are all going through many changes. If the humans only see that we could make life better for them—"

"If they allow us to help," Brontes interrupted hotly from behind them. "An afraid minkin is a dangerous minkin."

"You have taken on a big challenge," Grillos said for her ears only.

Rosemary couldn't argue with him there. She had her work cut out for her. Not only did she have to gain the giant community's trust, but she also had to introduce and prove to the human general public that giants were not a threat.

Rosemary helped kick dirt on the remnants of the dying fire. It was an enormous pile of branches, and twice she inquired about the prudence of creating a bonfire of that size. She wasn't sure which was hotter, Brontes' gaze or the tart response from one of the other brothers.

"Fire keeps us safe."

Safe from what, she wondered. Elk and deer, not to mention mountain lions and coyotes, would be no match for the giants, yet she was sure she sensed fear from all of them except Grillos. Spending time perched on Grillo's capable shoulders was more comforting than her old bunk on board the first ship she sailed with Shandy. Hearing the warm resonance of his voice vibrate through his big chest almost lulled her to sleep. He was invincible, and Rosemary found that when she rubbed her nose and cheek against the soft material of his shirt, her insides relaxed. The anxiety that had plagued her entire life dissipated. With his massive shoulders, Grillos could knock down an opponent; his granite muscles were no match for any living thing she could think of on earth. Having spent her life in a constant state of readiness to protect, she had to admit it felt good to… *relax*. It was novel, this feeling of security. It gave her time to look inward and think about her own background, her mother, and even the monster who spawned her.

"You'd make short work of most anything, I think," she said with a smile, trying to ingratiate herself.

Brontes's lips firmed with resentment. "A minkin would think that," he spat.

Red flags of color flamed on Rosemary's cheeks. They matched the warning signals going off in her gut. She was tired of the animosity and their secrets. Detente worked two ways. *What were the giants hiding?* She stood, her hand going to her dagger. Grillos quickly came between them, his bulk darkening the sun.

"Stop, brother. She doesn't know."

Rosemary heard his gravelly voice. "I don't know what?" She eyed each of their tense faces, studied their expressions with the growing realization that she saw something she'd never seen before. Bronte's huge pupils were dilated with fear. Sucking in a breath, she glanced at the bright, cloudless sky. "Aliens? Are you telling me you're afraid of the aliens? Is that why we are rushing?"

The canyon filled with the booming sound of their combined laughter. Again, he warned them to be quiet.

"The little Gray ones," Roosti chuckled. "We crush them like lice." He pressed two fingers together and made a noise.

Rosemary winced, but a quick look at Brontes chilled her. He was the only brother not laughing. He spun angrily on one of his brothers and poked him in the chest. "You think it's funny? It's not your daughters you've left in this awful place." He turned to Grillos. "And you, all you want to do when you're not mooning over this puny minkin is thinking about living on the surface." He said the last part of the sentence in a challenging way, and Rosemary could feel the clearing vibrate with anger.

"We are starving underground, Brontes! We are out of space and resources."

"If we conquer the slugs and retake our caves, we won't have to contend with the hairy—"

"That's enough!" Grillos bellowed.

"Slugs," Rosemary repeated, thinking back to where she'd heard something else about slugs.

Grillos looked down at her. "The slugs are a growing danger," he explained. "They have multiplied—"

"Because of the elders' stupid laws," Brontes interrupted. "Back a hundred years ago, they decided not to kill slugs. It was not the giant way."

"They were endangered, and they do help eat our waste," Zaf interjected. "But the side effects…" He shook his massive head.

"Yes, yes," Brontes said impatiently. "They had a purpose, and it was against the law to kill them. Now, they've been allowed to overpopulate, and they've turned deadly."

Rosemary snapped her head toward Grillos. "Deadly? How?"

Grillos stood silent. "You do not have to worry. I will not let anything hurt you."

She looked at each brother, studying their faces. She saw differences now. Fangi had a chipped tooth, Brontes was shorter, and Zaf walked with a lilt. Baloo and Roosti were almost identical, except for the freckles that scattered in different patterns on their cheeks. All six had a subtle variance that, once she realized it, she couldn't understand how she had missed it before. She smiled at the largest, Grillos, certainly the most handsome. "I have never seen a braver group of people, so eliminate them now," Rosemary stated.

Grillos looked at his feet. "We can't. They have mutated, and our weapons are useless."

"Poison?"

"You think we haven't tried?" Fangi yelled. "Nothing works. They are monsters, eating our food, devouring our people. We have nothing, and Grillos believes that by giving up our home to them and coming above ground, we'll be safe." He looked at the horizon. "But winter is coming and with winter comes—"

"That's enough!" Grillos shouted.

"No, it's not!" Rosemary went toe to toe with one of his massive feet. "I want to know what Fangi is talking about. Come here, you big galoot and tell me." Rosemary pulled at his pant leg.

Grillos looked at his brothers. "I'll check ahead," one of them offered.

"I'll scout the perimeter." One by one, they left Rosemary and Grillos. He sat down on a fallen tree, and she leaned against the reassuring weight of his calf.

"You want to come clean?" she asked once they were alone.

"We don't like to look weak, especially to a—"

"If you say woman, I'll have to gouge out your eye," she said without looking up.

"Minkin," he finished.

"Okay, I'll give you that," she agreed.

"See," he started. "It's no good if you know our weaknesses."

Rosemary turned and touched his knee. "Grillos, if we are to grow together, there has to be trust between us."

"It's tough, Rose." He said her name like an endearment, and Rosemary felt herself flush. Her heart contracted in her chest as she watched him struggle with the following sentence. "Despite our size, there is a fragility to us. Brontes," he swallowed. "Brontes begs me not to have faith in humanity. He says I won't get disappointed that way."

Rosemary hesitated, thinking of a way to respond. She wanted to clap her hands in front of his sad face and order him to shake off his manner, but she wasn't a captain anymore; she was a diplomat. Aside from that, his demeanor tugged at her heart. At first, she realized she wanted him to have faith in humanity and in her. "Brontes has a right to feel the way he does. He's been hurt, his daughters have chosen, well, the enemy in his eyes. He's angry."

Grillos nodded in agreement.

"Don't you think it's time for us all to coexist?" She stared into the large, orange-flecked eyes. "If we don't find a way, then certainly humanity is doomed, and by the sound of whatever you fear, giants are not in too good a shape either."

"They walk on two feet." Grillos's voice was low. "They roam these mountains, preying on us."

Rosemary leaned in. "Who? Who walks on two feet?"

"The hairy ones."

"Hairy ones? What are you talking about?"

"They have been here for a millennium. Watching us from the trees. They blend with the bark." Grillos shook himself with a whole-body shiver.

"Do you mean apes? There are no apes here," Rosemary said.

"They are not apes. They are the stuff of nightmares."

"We're clear!" Brontes said breathlessly. "But I saw scat. We've been watched. We have to move quickly."

"Scat? Do you shit? Ape shit?" Rosemary was incredulous.

Grillos didn't answer; he quickly placed her on his shoulder, securing her with a length of rope to his waist.

"What's that for?" she asked, her breath catching, diverted from the earlier conversation. She didn't like being attached to anything.

There was a sense of urgency among the giants that left her feeling a knot in her stomach.

"We will have to travel fast," Grillos responded, placing one foot on a ledge. "We must climb to higher ground. Now." He moved upward, his speed increasing. Rosemary looked down, the ground growing smaller as they scaled the bare face of the rock wall.

"How much further?" Two days of travel had taken their toll. She was tired, and despite resting on the giant's shoulder, exhaustion pulled at her.

Grillos didn't answer; he heaved them onto another ledge. Looking down, Rosemary could see snake-like lines, and she realized they were the spaces between the rocky canyon below them. Water sparkled in the distance, the years of drought leaving a limescale rim around the basin. Not a car or person in sight, she shivered from the desolation. Peering under the brutal rays of the sun, her breath caught at the stillness of the vista—a boundless blue sky above them, and an unyielding landscape below. Trees, like an advancing army, stood like a sentinel blocking her view. Just as she had searched for ships on the sea, she peered out into the distance. Her skin crawled with the knowledge that Brontes was correct. They were being watched.

At sea, the waves entertained with their constant churning, the sky a kaleidoscope of ever-changing shapes and colors. Clouds became castles or, within moments, changed into dragons or galleons scudding across an endless sky. Grays turned purple or pink and orange; the swirling mass of moisture could light up with hope or turn angry and foreboding. It was a feast for all the senses, with a promise of more to come. Here, on land, despite the abundance of nature, all she felt was the endless appearance of emptiness.

Rosemary looked to the right and left, feeling nothing.

CHAPTER 31

CRACKS BEGINNING TO APPEAR

"I SAID, LEAVE IT to me," Dreg said impatiently. "I'll talk to the creature. You…" Dreg thought for a minute. "*You* can be imposing."

"*Moi*?" Vincent said with a fake French accent. "I'm never imposing. I'm the soul of kindness and inclusivity."

"Still, Vincent. Let me talk to them. It will be better this way."

Dreg stamped out the embers of last night's fire, mindful of the splatter of zombie brains that had sprayed everywhere. He wiped his black cloak, rolling his eyes. Vincent had been a tad too gleeful when he did the *cha-cha* on their attackers the night before.

Vincent's clothes had a layer of crusted body fluid. Some of it had landed on Dreg's coat.

Dreg brushed his hands together and stopped abruptly, holding his arms away from his body. "You can't still catch the plague from touching fluids, right? That was just an old rumor."

"Don't be an idiot, Dreg. It's dried up. The virus is dead. Dead and gone, like our two friends there." Vincent laughed, gesturing to the corpses splayed in the tall grasses nearby. "Now, if it were still wet, that might be a problem."

Dreg grimaced and pointed down a ravine. "I heard a stream gurgling before. I'm going to wash."

Vincent shrugged. "Suit yourself. Unless the fluids are damp or you ingest them, you don't have to worry."

Dreg didn't answer. Frankly, he wasn't sure what was true. The CDC and WHO could never provide an exact answer to the origins of the plague, let alone how it was spread. The story changed with every press release. Furthermore, various governments and agencies hold differing opinions, resulting in a lack of clarity on any issue. Vincent's waffling on every subject was making him nervous, too.

Everyone said something else. It came from animals, *no*, it came from an asteroid. He looked up at the sky, searching for the circular-shaped spacecraft that had dropped them off the day before. They said they'd be hanging out until they returned to the ship. He had a nagging suspicion that they might somehow be involved, and then, he glanced resentfully back at Vincent, as well.

Dreg groaned a bit. He wasn't keen on returning to the stratosphere. It was unnerving being so far from home. If man were meant to go into outer space, he'd have been born with rockets up his butt.

He took a deep breath of the pine-scented air. The damp earth squished under his feet. Solid ground, no matter if it was wet and muddy, still felt better than being up there.

He shivered, not from cold, but from the thought of returning to the colorless, sterile environment of the aliens. They had these big, glassy eyes, he learned, because their planet held very little light. The result of limited light was muted colors. Everything was in shades of grays, down to their skin.

I could do with not seeing those guys again. They gave me the willies, he thought to himself. They act all curious and polite, but he had the strange sensation that they could read his mind.

"If man were meant to fly, then he'd have wings", he grumbled to no one in particular. For all he knew, the darn virus might have come from that happy crew.

He missed his old life, the one he shared with Nate, the one that held hope before the plague brought the planet to a halt.

After this virus struck, everyone kept separate. It stalled the economy, of course, but it wasn't the world's first rodeo. This had happened before: the plagues of the Middle Ages, the Spanish Flu, Ebola, and the Pandemic. Everyone knew what they had to do. The entire globe was affected. Travel stopped. He shook his head as he walked down toward a bubbling stream. You'd think they'd have it down straight, already. He wished Nate hadn't been cut down so soon. His son held such promise. He would have saved the planet. Dreg wiped a tear from the corner of his eye.

The water was icy. Dreg stared at the colorful pebbles laid out like an ancient mosaic on the streambed. It reminded him of the floor of a villa he'd seen with Nate on a trip to England. They explored the ruins of an ancient Roman villa in the Cotswolds. It was an important home, lost to time, a civilization that became extinct. Sorrow washed over him. He scrubbed his hands, thinking of his son, Nate. Missing him was painful. It tugged at his heart, twisting his guts with misery. If only he could have one more minute. He glanced back up the hill where he heard Vincent stomping around on his artificial legs.

If only I could go back in time, he thought, his insides heavy with guilt and regret. If only Nate had never met Vincent Konrad. He trudged up the hill to meet Vincent, pacing impatiently.

"What took you so long? Let's get out of here. We have to find Rosemary and get back to the lab."

"Lab?"

"At Monsterland, my lab, you fool," Vincent sneered. "Hurry and mount up. The Sasquatch will be waiting."

Dreg sighed. "I'm tired, Vincent. I have to get some sleep."

Rosemary, his daughter, his theme park. It was always about Vincent's needs. Bitterness coated Dregs' mouth; resentment unfurled where his heart used to reside. It was gone now. Shriveled and decayed with the loss of his son, his life's work, like those ancient mosaics, was a remnant of a past that had disappeared within the shrouds of time.

Dreg's eyes hardened, his lips thinned, and he wished he were anywhere but next to Vincent. He shuddered, wondering about the consequences if he dared to ride in the opposite direction.

Vincent snapped his fingers for Dreg to hand him the reins. Dreg's nails dug into his fisted palms, and he resisted the urge to slap the stallion and watch Vincent hang on for dear life. Instead, he saddled his horse.

Vincent galloped away, his response trailing after him, chilling Dreg's heart. "You'll sleep when you're dead."

Dreg reluctantly followed him, hating not only Vincent Konrad but himself all the more.

CHAPTER 32

THE STUFF OF NIGHTMARES

OLREC AWOKE WITH a start. His dreams were filled with Zilli, and the hero's welcome he expected when he returned to the village.

Booming laughter echoed in the distance, feeling strangely out of place. Olrec shifted on his branch, but remained firmly in his slumber.

Sasquatches huffed and chuckled when they found something amusing. This sound was not of his world. It did not belong. *What were strangers doing in his homecoming?*

Olrec struggled to wake, but was kept firmly in the grip of his dreams. The laughter was cut off, and Olrec sighed. His head was filled with birdsong and wind, the sounds he associated with home.

Smiling, he bowed and accepted a wreath of flowers that they wrapped around his neck. Puffing out his chest proudly, he showed off the blooms, but slowly, it was tightening around his neck like a noose.

Soon, he was choking, his breath cut off. He was drowning or being smothered. He couldn't tell. He could not breathe.

No air, stop, can't breathe, wake up!

Wake up, you're dreaming, Olrec!

Olrec's eyes popped open. A great horned owl was perched on the tree next to him, curious eyes observing his distress.

It's just a dream. They're gone.

Who's gone? He choked out. Olrec heaved once as he tried to catch his breath, then rubbed his eyes vigorously.

He was splayed in the branches of a tree, memories of falling asleep in this spot rushing back.

Overhead, an explosion of birds took off into the sky.

The owl rotated its head, and they watched as they swarmed in an organized fashion, their gray bodies darkening the horizon.

The owl turned its gaze back to Olrec, its great, unblinking eyes sympathetic, and said, *They scared them—the birds. The giants are so loud and clumsy.*

Olrec pricked up his ears, but they could hear nothing. The giant encampment was silent.

But they left, that's why the birds left too.

Olrec watched as the birds formed an arrow and headed south. It was eerily quiet for a minute, then slowly the music of the forest started coming back.

The sun burned off the fog and blazed in the sky. He nearly fell from his spot in the tree. Birdsong surrounded him, the treetops filled with chirps and squeaks, trills and cries from hawks.

Olrec rubbed his face again to wipe off the resistant vestiges of sleep. He peered at the encampment. The giants and the *stupe* were gone; only a smoldering pile of ashes was left in their place.

You're safe, the great horned owl hooted. *They went up the moun-tain. Scrambled, I should say,* he chuckled. *Your scent must have driven them off.*

Up, you say? Not down toward my village? Olrec knuckled his eyes; he couldn't get them to focus. *Then my home is safe, too.*

Just to be sure, he jumped onto the rocks and mounted the cliff rapidly, all while sniffing for their distinctive odor. *Did you see Jofro? Has he returned?*

No, not a hide nor hair of him. I told you they've left. Early this morning, they went up and inside that cleft in the rocks. The owl settled on an outcropping, his large eyes unblinking. *See, the dust is disturbed from their trek.* He pointed to the trampled ground, huge imprints moving up and then disappearing as if they'd never existed. Olrec sighed; he had worried for nothing. It was a false alarm; his village was safe.

Thanks. He saluted the owl.

Be safe, the owl advised. *The crazy Doctor Konrad is waiting beyond the creek. Be careful of that one.*

Why?

He manipulates nature. He hasn't learned yet; it's best to leave things as they are.

Stupid stupe, Olrec agreed.

The owl opened its impressive wingspan and took off.

Olrec waved a farewell. By the time he met with Konrad, the giant menace to his society would be long gone, underground. His family and village were not in danger. He glanced for any signs of the Jofro, but saw nothing. Shrugging, he continued on his way.

Olrec smiled as he melted into the trees behind him, the way his ancestors had for thousands of years, and disappeared down the mountains to their meeting spot outside of Los Angeles. He wondered what plague Konrad had visited upon humanity and what his species' role was in it.

CHAPTER 33

HUMAN-LIKE BUT NOT HUMAN

"THERE." BRONTES POINTED to a small clearing below them. "There they are! Animals!"

They had rounded the cliff, and Rosemary gasped in awe. The mountain overlooked a sprawling forest. A river zigzagged across the jagged landscape. Chir Pines and Cedar of Lebanon hid the forest floor. "It's beautiful. I've never seen this side of the hills."

"The altitude hides a plague," Baloo said.

"Zombies?" she asked.

"No." Grillos pointed to an area camouflaged by a canopy of trees. "There they are."

Rosemary squinted to make out a handful of huts. They were tall and conical. Smoke drifted from pipes built into the slanted roofs.

There were people, and she held a hand over her eyes. Her jaw dropped. No, not people. They were apes. Tall, hairy apes. "Are those…apes?"

"I told you," Grillos's voice was grim. "They are not apes. They are our enemy."

Rosemary craned her neck to see better. They walked tall, human-like but not human. "What are they?"

"Some of your kind call them Bigfoot. We call them *barbarians.*"

"I've heard stories about them. People are always looking for evidence of their existence."

"Oh, they exist!" Brontes declared. "They're the reason we were harried into the mountains."

"You are smarter, bigger, stronger, surely they had no chance against you!" Rosemary scoffed.

"A lot you know. They had the help of creatures in the sky. We were here first. They came from up North, and with the help of their allies and their superior firepower, they squeezed us from our homes. Ran us into the caves, where we've been prisoners—" A strident horn interrupted Brontes's comment. "They see us, brothers! We must run!"

They'd been spotted. Below her, the crowd milled. The bipedal apes gathered at the base of the cliff and started yelling at the giants. She watched the group swell, becoming an agitated, screaming mob. They swarmed, growing in number, shaking their fists at the giants.

Smaller ones, many of them carrying infants, ran to the safety of their huts. Rosemary observed their faces. They were more frightened than threatening. "They are terrified of us," Rosemary stated with shock.

"That's crazy!" Fangi spat. "They're the aggressors."

The sound of the horn pierced the glade below again. Rosemary saw hundreds more ape-like creatures pour out of the dwellings and point in their direction. Rocks were thrown, but they fell short. It was clear that neither side was in danger.

"We are far from them. We couldn't possibly do them any harm from here," Grillos said. "I don't understand their fear."

Rosemary looked at the panicked faces of the creatures in the thronging crowd below. "They seem more afraid of you than you are of them."

Grillos laughed, but it held no mirth. "Looks can be deceiving. They are amoral."

"They attack without any provocation!" Zaf added.

"When was the last time you clashed?" Rosemary asked.

"Not long enough for the memories to fade," Grillos said grimly. "Brothers, quickly!"

Grillos vaulted up the side of the cliff. Rosemary could feel his back tremble as his muscles pulled from the effort.

She peered down. While the ape-like creatures jumped and screamed, she saw no real weapons aimed at her group. "Wait, why are you afraid? They seem harmless enough. Surely you could over-power them?"

"Drop her, Grillos," Zaf yelled, his eyes fierce. "She doesn't trust our words."

Grillos turned his head to look deeply into Rosemary's eyes. She stared down at the steep incline and the roiling crowd below. She brought her gaze back to Grillos, her eyes shadowed by fear. It was a long way down. Every muscle in her body tensed. Her fingers gripped Grillos's shirt convulsively.

"I would never drop you, dear heart." Grillos looked wounded. "Don't you know me by now?"

"I...I..." Words clogged her throat. She had never felt such love emanating from another being. "It never entered my mind," she lied.

The big body heaved upwards, the massive muscles bunching as they made their way up the cliff. Rosemary buried her face in the back of Grillos's neck, ashamed she ever doubted him.

Pulling themselves up onto an outcropping, Rosemary lifted her head and watched Brontes shove a car-sized boulder away from the rock wall, revealing an entrance. One by one, the brothers entered the cave. Grillos paused in the bright sunlight and said, "Welcome to my world. I will keep you safe, never fear, Rosemary mine."

"Rosemary, *mine,*" Brontes said in a high-pitched voice, mocking his brother.

Zaf made a gagging sound.

Grillos yelled, "Shut up, before I ram my fist down your throats."

He turned his massive head toward Rosemary, "Beware, my sweet. Don't touch any slime left by the giant slugs."

"Why?"

"Let her take a bath in it and see what happens," Zaf snarled.

Grillos stepped inside the cavern, where darkness enveloped them completely.

CHAPTER 34

THE ODD COUPLE

OLREC TRAVELED FOR what felt like hours, his mind whirring with what he'd witnessed. He skirted the main roads, his head down, his brain replaying the scene over and over again. He hoped Jofro made it back to the village, and he hadn't made a mistake by sending him.

If I tell them I saw this, they may not believe me, especially if Jofro was playing a prank. You couldn't trust these young bucks nowadays. No moral compass. *Where's the proof?* They'll taunt, and I'll lose whatever headway I made by volunteering to meet Konrad.

If I went home myself and missed meeting Vincent Konrad, they'll be furious that I risked the rendezvous. Olrec scratched his head over the dilemma. It was like choosing a path, each one shrouded in darkness and with no easy solution. If Konrad were this savior they'd been waiting for, Olrec would be hailed a hero.

Humans, or *stupes*, were his sworn enemy. Everybody hated the giants, banishing those creatures from the surface of the planet thousands of years ago and relegating them to fanciful stories of make-believe. At least his kind got the television specials where the *stupes* wondered if they really existed.

He passed several encampments, smelling the humans a mile away. He hoped Jofro wasn't distracted by them. Their rancid, cheese-like body odor filled the air like the stench of a ten-day-old dead animal. He kept to the higher altitudes where the trees grew thicker. His feet dragged, heavy with fatigue, but he didn't stop. His reputation was on the line, and he was determined to bring back information to his tribe.

Early morning brought birds chirping, the sun drying the dew, and Olrec squeezed himself into the crevice of two rocks high up on a ridge. Climbing up, he settled on a warm boulder. They would be coming soon, he reckoned tiredly. He closed his eyes for a minute, and soon he was snoring and knew no more.

The sound of hoofbeats yanked him from a peaceful dream. Olrec stretched his cramped muscles, then rose upward to observe two men on horses. A beautiful black stallion and a clumsy gray mare raced along the ridge of the mountain top.

They arrived in the clearing, pulling their horses to a stop. Their clothes were dusty from travel. Olrec didn't budge. He had never met Vincent Konrad or his associate, so he held himself back, watching and waiting for a sign. They were not impressive, and Olrec began to have doubts about Konrad. A strange pale color, dirty-looking clothes that had to be two centuries old, and awkward movements didn't give Olrec any sense of importance. Surely, he did not appear remotely powerful.

Olrec's sharp eyes scanned for accomplices. Counting forty breaths, his ears turned upward listening for the telltale sign they weren't alone. He heard a curt command issued by the taller man. The order was repeated, loud enough that Olrec could hear him.

"Listen, I don't know how to summon them. Think of something to get their attention!"

The little gnome of a man was almost bent in half, his curved spine making his torso appear tiny and frail. Listing sideways in the saddle, it looked like he couldn't sit for much longer. Olrec saw him put his hands in a cup shape around his nose and mouth and started making strange sounds. "*Caw-Cawww.*"

"Do you see them?" the larger figure demanded. His imperious demeanor confirmed this was the one in charge.

The little man shook his head.

"Try again!" Vincent ordered, pulling off a hat and hitting his dusty clothes with it.

Olrec considered his lilac-colored face and tried to remember if humans came in that variety.

"*Caw-Cawww, Caw-Cawww.*"

"Where do you think the big hairy beast is hiding?" Konrad asked.

Olrec jerked in his spot. *Big hairy beast?* Did they mean him? Curling his upper lip with resentment, Olrec knew he was reddening under his fur. *Are they bird-calling to contact me?*

"*Caw-Cawwwwwwww. Caw-Cawwwwwwwww.*"

That's irritating as well as a bit insensitive, Olrec bristled. *Do they think we can't communicate?*

"*Caw-Cawwwwwwww. Caw-Cawwwwwwwwwwwwwwwww.*"

Cawing? Really?

He crossed his arms and slid down the side of the boulder. The crooked little man on the horse kept up his incessant cawing, which began to hurt Olrec's ears.

Olrec stewed for a minute or two, letting them wait. He debated turning around and disappearing back into the woods, but he knew Kokkus would be angry if he didn't find out what Konrad could do for his tribe. *Don't they know who we are?*

Olrec jumped down from the top of the ridge, landing as lightly as a cat. This stunned the two men as well as the horses, who reared.

It seemed that the little man was having trouble controlling his animal. Olrec straightened his eight-plus-foot body, wanting to look as impressive as possible.

"You are Vincent Konrad?" Olrec pointed to the bigger man.

"You can call me Dr. Konrad." The purple man inclined his head. "And you are?"

"Olrec, Olrec of the Sierra Nevada Mountains."

"I see you received our message as we have gotten yours, Olrec of the Sierra Nevada Mountains."

Olrec nodded. One of Zilli's patient admonishments echoed in his head. *We have two ears and one mouth. We must listen twice as much as we speak.* He wished she were here to place her gentle hand on his if he spoke in haste.

The spooked horses did a little dance. The smaller of the two men looked as if he'd be unseated in a minute. Olrec discovered he did not pity him. Konrad seemed to have a better hold on his horse. He looked imposing, clad in his dark outfit and with a sturdy appearance. His head did not match either the proportions or the condition of the body. Olrec wondered if Konrad was a hybrid of some kind.

"As arranged." Konrad smiled, his eyes gleaming.

Olrec enjoyed observing the naked terror on the smaller man, but his gaze settled on a ragged cut around the older man's neck. As he drew closer, he realized the body was stiff, with exaggeratedly movable joints, like a mannequin he had once seen in a store window in a small town. The skull was attached to a body in a ragtag kind of way. The lilac head smiled, its teeth gleaming with a weird metallic light. *Not completely human*, he thought.

Olrec was so close he knew he could tip them both, as well as their horses, like he used to do when he was a young cub. We'll see what this savior is made of, he chuckled under his breath. His sons would certainly enjoy watching that.

He wondered for the first time if this was a big joke played on him by the pack. He glanced around the clearing; the babbling brook beside them was the only sound. No, if the pack were here, they'd be rolling around and laughing at his expense.

Olrec and the odd couple stared at each other silently for some time.

Finally, Olrec spoke. "So here I am, as my tribe arranged. What is it you want, Dr. Konrad?"

Konrad laughed, "So you call me Doctor Konrad, true? I am actually The Konrad, a Watcher, the slayer of monsters, destroyer of governments, and the person to save our world."

"A Watcher?" Olrec raised both eyebrows. "You are a Watcher?"

Konrad inclined his head regally. "As you can see."

"You don't look like a Watcher." As soon as the words left his mouth, Olrec regretted it. He added hurriedly, "If you are a monster slayer, then why are giants roaming above ground?"

"The world is not black or white. Sometimes the perception of a monster belongs to the beholder."

"Vincent!" the little man gasped. "What are you insinuating?"

Olrec shivered. He was no match for Dr. Konrad. The man scared him with his evil stare and implications. "Are you calling me a monster?"

"Do you consider yourself one?" Konrad asked quietly as if he was digesting the entire conversation.

This felt like a fighting match. *He's testing me and everything I say!*

A Watcher wouldn't do that. Olrec furrowed his brow. Watchers were good and kind. Non-judgmental. At least, that's what had been passed down through the ages. The Watchers were coming back to deliver us from evil.

Olrec wanted to bite his tongue. He was afraid he had spoken out of turn. Kokkus would say he was in over his head. Sweat beaded his brow. Kokkus or one of the tribal elders should have been the ones to come; even Jofro would do a better job. *I do not like this man, Doctor Konrad.* I don't believe he is our savior, thoughts whirled in his brain. They shouldn't have sent him. He was a hack, not a diplomat.

He didn't belong here, but he had to say something. "No, *erm*, no." He beat his chest for effect. "We are the first, the originators. We are not monsters! Put here by the Watchers to populate this planet." He eyed Konrad suspiciously. "If you are a Watcher, you would know."

"Indeed." Konrad looked around dramatically. "I see how successful you've been. Designated to hide in these hills." Konrad leaned forward, his dark eyes holding Olrec.

Olrec's cheeks reddened. "If not for the annoying *stupes,* we'd populate fine. First it was the giants, then *stupes*, humans," he said it with disgust. "They confine us to the mountains where we must keep the population from expanding, until—" Olrec stopped. He couldn't prevent the flow of words even if he wanted to. It was as if there was a strange hold on his mind. Konrad had a hypnotic way of making him talk, causing him to say too much. Maybe he was a magician, or perhaps he *was* a *Watcher.*

Konrad looked at him, his eyes sharp and piercing. "Until."

Olrec paused, reluctant to speak, but the gaze continued to hold him, and the words poured out of him. "There is a legend with my people that one day a flaming chariot in the sky will come and we will not have to stay confined anymore."

"Yes, and I have arrived in a flaming chariot. Surely, you saw it."

Olrec bit his lip, doubt creeping in. It was as if he had an argument going on inside his head. "It was neither a chariot nor flaming."

"But you saw I came from the sky. You see, our technology has improved. I am one of the Watchers, and I am here to save you."

Olrec stared at them for a long time. "Is he a Watcher too?"

"Him, oh no, no, no," Vincent laughed. "He's just a servant."

Dreg stiffened his spine as much as he could and narrowed his eyes with anger.

"You didn't come from the sky; you created the theme park that destroyed the world."

"Correct! I was preparing the world for you. It is part of the great Watcher plan. I am here to liberate you."

Olrec rubbed his nose. Something didn't seem right about these, too. While he had never seen a Watcher, all the legends pointed to something more impressive. Something he could relate to.

They stood assessing each other for a few minutes. Olrec refused to be the one to break the silence. He knew instinctively that patience was necessary here. Konrad was inscrutable, and the little man by his side oozed with tension.

"Vincent. It grows late," Dreg implored from his skittish horse. "We must get this done." He gave a meaningful glance at the sky. "We must find Rosemary."

"What do you want from us?"

"You have been left on the sidelines for too long. The Watchers have different plans for you. I will control this planet. Tell me." He leaned forward in the saddle. "Have you allied with the Scalis?"

"Never! Flesh-eating lizards."

Konrad pointed to the Eastern horizon. "They have a ship somewhere over there."

Olrec shivered.

"They were located over there." Konrad pointed to the sky over his village.

Olrec's brows lowered with worry for Zilli and the boys.

"There is a war coming. A war of the worlds. They will allow only one species to survive. It is as it has been told in your lore."

"Go on."

"They are pitting everyone against each other for an epic battle."

"I'm not sure you represent the Watchers." Olrec buzzed with indecision. This was too much. He wanted to go home. He needed to tell Zilli about the conversation; she would know what to do. "We will stay in our mountains as we have done since the beginning and let them kill each other." Olrec turned to leave, but Konrad's following sentence stopped him.

Vincent shook his head. "It is to be a total extinction."

"Does that include you?" Olrec shot back.

"This will become a prison planet with the surviving species being used as guards. There are only two species capable of doing that, Sasquatch or giants."

Olrec's eye twitched. He hated giants.

Vincent Konrad watched the Sasquatch with interest. A night owl hooted in the gathering gloom.

"You can't work with giants. They take up too much room," Olrec responded.

"There'll be plenty of room once my plan goes into effect."

"Humanity is doomed."

Vincent nodded. "Not quite. The strongest will survive if they learn to adapt to change. However, I will need an army to keep them in line."

Olrec sighed. *He doesn't understand us.* We are peace-loving, non-confrontational. He cannot be a Watcher. *They would know.* "Get to the point, Doctor."

"I need brute strength. You will corral the humans so I can control them."

Kokkus and the others will not like this. "You said one species will survive. What happens to us? We will not be tamed."

"As my army, you will be at the apex, the apex predator," Konrad guffawed at his humor.

"What if we choose to decline? We don't care what happens to *stupes*."

"I thought you were smarter than that. Look, I'm allowing you a lifeline to take your rightful place on the planet."

Olrec digested the information. There was a long minute of silence between them.

"I have to bring this message back to my village." Olrec couldn't help his eyes moving to the spot where the Scalis ship was stationed.

"Don't wait too long. We will meet up at Monsterland. There, we will show them who will rule the planet. Choose wisely, Olrec. The Scalis may become your new Watchers, and I know you wouldn't like that. The Scalis see you as a tasty meal for their banquets." Vincent shook his head. "I think you have no choice but to team up with me."

"That does nothing to comfort me, Doctor," he sneered. "We heard you used the giants to build your theme park and then, you betrayed them."

"Lies, all lies. I merely allowed the giants to come out of their caves and return to the surface."

"No, you didn't," Olrec spat. "You had them do your dirty work and then you sealed them underground."

"Have you seen giants roaming around?"

Olrec's jaw dropped. "As a matter of fact, I have."

"See, if they were locked underground, how could they be running rampant up here?"

"Strange, and they had a *stupe* with them. A female, a roly-poly female. I thought they were going to eat her, but she wasn't afraid."

"A female, you say? Where?" Konrad demanded.

Olrec pointed toward the west. "They entered the hills, over there. See the cave?"

"*Hmmm.* Visit your tribe and check if we have a deal in place. We will meet at Monsterland to repel the invaders. If you don't come, I will take it that you've chosen to disregard your Watchers, and I'll leave you to the Scalis."

A loud humming filled the air, and a cigar-shaped ship floated to land neatly in a clearing on the other side of the river.

"Quick, hide!" Olrec urged.

Konrad and his servant jumped from their horses and led them quickly behind a cluster of bushes.

"*Shhhh,*" Olrec told the horses and clicked a message in broken pony. They seemed to understand with a nod and backed into the darkness of the forest.

Konrad was crouched behind the most enormous rock, and the little man was on his knees, peering to the other side.

A door opened, and music filled the air. Olrec cursed softly and whispered, "Scalis." He'd recognize their music anywhere.

Four giant lizards descended a ramp, one of which had a huge pole.

"It's a hunting party," Olrec informed them.

"How long will they stay?" Vincent whispered back.

He clicked an answer to the horses to stay silent and turned to Konrad. "Not long. They'll be looking for something close by, an elk or bear." He closed his eyes, saying a silent prayer that the mama bear he helped with the hive would be safe.

They sat still for what felt like hours. Twice, the little man opened his mouth, and Olrec shook his head, warning him to be quiet.

"I don't know if they've tasted human flesh, but once they do, they'll be insatiable," Olrec warned.

"A rare delicacy. So, there's no negotiating with them?"

"Are you crazy, Doctor? No."

"I've heard that several political leaders are lizards in disguise," Vincent told him.

"If that's true, there was no negotiation," Olrec said grimly. He sighed; his backside was starting to feel numb.

A short time later, they heard the strange sound that passed as laughter and the stomping of footsteps. Olrec leaned over and contained a gasp. A Sasquatch was hanging on a pole, its eyes closed."

Olrec's insides froze. He took a deep breath and expelled slowly, then cursed.

"One of yours?" Konrad grunted.

"Jofro, a young buck," Olrec said softly. "I'll have to tell his mother."

They watched the lizards climb up the ramp, the doors closed, and it took off with a high whine that hurt his ears.

"Well, that eliminates the Scalis," Konrad stated.

"Doctor?"

"What about the Va'Rok?"

Olrec looked at him incredulously. He whistled for the horses to return. "I don't know what you're talking about."

The horses whickered, and Konrad vaulted into the saddle. The little man attempted to climb, but Olrec pushed him onto the top of the mare. He patted her neck, and she eyed him sadly. He heard Konrad's menacing voice. "Don't make me wait too long."

He slapped Dreg's mare on the rump.

Konrad did a neat circle with the horse and took off in the direction of the cave, the twisted little man following.

Olrec turned around, his heart heavy with all the news to share with his clan. There was a strange flash of metal on the other side of the river. Olrec ducked behind the boulder and watched a woman stand. She was half metal and walked with an awkward gait. A small, heavy-set man followed her. They both wore triangular aluminum foil hats on their heads.

Olrec narrowed his eyes. He knew that man and had evaded him for years. They all did. It became a game, and they nicknamed him Nosy Ned. Even his sons had played hide-and-seek with him.

Olrec rubbed his face with his hands. He couldn't wait to get him to Zilli and the cubs. He had so much to tell them.

CHAPTER 35

TRIFECTA!

"GET DOWN!" OTTO whispered harshly as Jade dropped to the ground. "Keep your head down. I don't have anything with me to repair you."

They were on their bellies behind a dune. They had been walking for hours. Jade was still not healed; her legs hurt, her face was sore, and she resented the inhumane pace Otto had set. Fisting her hand, she resisted the urge to smash his face and rip out his heart. She felt the presence of eyes on her back and turned, but saw nothing. *I know you're out there.*

Yes. She heard the answer in her head. *We're watching out for you. It's not safe, but know we are here.*

Who are you?

Part of the pack, Melvin's pack.

Jade buried her face in her hands. She wasn't sure she wanted anyone to see her, most of all Melvin. She was ugly and would repulse him.

"Did you hear anything I've said?" Otto's demand brought her into the present.

"I heard you," she lied.

"Then why aren't you looking where I'm pointing?"

She turned her attention to the direction of his finger. A cigar-shaped object was hidden behind a clump of trees. A cloud of steam shrouded it, but Jade could see a shade of green she'd never seen before flash through the gloom. "What is it?"

"Not sure, but it's alien," Otto's voice was an awed whisper. "Today is a trifecta!"

Jade rolled her eyes and sighed. "Really, Otto! Do you have to make everything out of this world?"

"Bigfoot and the Giants are from here. I don't make—" Otto gasped. "Holy, sh—,"

Jade placed her hand over his mouth. "Shut up." Four seven-foot-tall lizards in shining uniforms walked toward the craft. Strung on a heavy pole, a hairy ape, its head hanging slack, was carried by two of them. She could hear them talking in a language she couldn't understand. Blood trailed behind them. One of the lizards hissed, his long forked tongue slithered out, and he bent over to lap the blood dripping from the apish beast. The three others made a *rat-a-tat-tat* sound like nothing she had ever heard.

"They're laughing," Otto said in wonder.

"Oh, so now you're translating? We'd better get out of here."

Don't move. They have a keen sense of hearing.

Jade heard the coyote say to her.

The four lizards stopped, and the slits used for nostrils twitched. One spoke quietly to the other. Jade could see their vertical-shaped pupils dilate as they scanned the underbrush. Otto grabbed her arm, his fingers digging into her tender flesh. Biting her lip, she held her gasp in.

The lizards stood for a bit. The ship made a sound like an exploding exhaust pipe. A doorway appeared along the chassis. Jade heard soft melodies coming from within. One lizard turned, his voice curt and abrupt, as if he were ordering them inside. The others followed, the last lizard grumbling but ignored by the others. The ship emitted a loud squeal and lifted off, disappearing from the ground instantaneously.

They watched it hover above them and zip away.

"Oh my stars!" Otto could barely contain himself. He pulled out a pencil and a pad, sketching hurriedly all the strange sights they'd seen today. "If only… if only—"

"If only, what?"

"If only I could tell the rest of the world about this. On my podcast."

"That's what you are excited about? Look at me! Look at this place!"

"I don't know what you mean."

"It means if all these creatures are roaming freely, we don't stand a chance. This can't be real."

Otto stood up, brushed off his khaki pants, and shook his head. "Oh no, Jade. This is real, and you all did it to yourselves. It's just a matter of time until you all take responsibility. "

Jade sprang to her feet, her good hand fisted. "This isn't our fault. None of this!"

Otto laughed and walked away from her, shaking his head. "Really? I've been warning you all for years. You labeled me, what? A crackpot. Nutcase? You all had your fun. Complained to your parents until they fired me."

"We didn't get you fired. You did that to yourself."

"Sounds like gaslighting. Go ahead, if you want. Blame me. I wasn't the only one. I warned you that the monster problem was going to explode."

"Monsters were fine living in the shadows."

"Think so, my little numbskull?" Otto taunted. "It was a

tinderbox, and Vincent lit the match. It was bound to happen, stripping them of their rights, giving them no recourse to have any dignity."

"Since when was anything you did for monster dignity?" Jade sneered. "All you warned was that they'd be a menace."

Otto held up the fingers of one hand. "And, so they are. Look, Podcast 236 was all about the way politicians were going to use monsters to take our rights." He put down one finger. "Mission accomplished. I told everyone that cryptids existed, and it was a matter of time before our cultures clashed," He put down another finger. "That was in show number 403, but then you never watched. Don't get me started on the aliens, the proof of their visits here has been around for years, that purple stuff, animal mutations, crop circles, and let's not forget the abductions."

Jade took off her conical hat.

"Not safe, missy." Otto looked upward. "You don't want them to come back for dessert, do you?"

She placed it back on her head with a grimace. "I don't believe this does anything."

"They didn't see us." Otto rambled for a minute, and Jade couldn't understand a word he said. "I bet we've got some lizards disguised as humans. I've always said it's either lizards or insects, come to crush us the way we've subjugated them here all these years."

"Maybe it's space dogs," Jade shot back. "They'll love humanity from the way we've treated our pets."

"Don't be a smart aleck. We are in trouble, from what I just saw. We have to stamp them out, the giants, and any bigfoots found. Keep walking." He prodded her in the back, and they trudged on. "We're almost there."

CHAPTER 36

IT ALL BEGAN IN MONSTERLAND

"YOU'RE SURE THIS will work?" Colonel Drucker was watching Howard, his eyes sharp.

The room buzzed with key personnel, all working together on Vincent's enormous stone table. Carter and Wyatt created a map, and Yerbol was deep in discussion with them as they argued the best place to meet Vincent head-on.

"Dad, I told you. All we have to do is give some false information and watch for Konrad's response. Then we'll surprise him," Howard said.

"I still don't understand," Yerbol commented.

"I'm using Konrad's satellite and programming to send him false information about our plans."

"But you're using his technology!" Yerbol's face was red.

"Don't make it obvious," Carter said.

"*Duh*, of course we have to act like, like…"

"We're using code!" Wyatt said. "He'll think that we are communicating between ourselves, but we'll actually be sending him fake plans so we can propel him to take certain actions."

"It's not a bad idea," Nate Owens replied. "At the very least, we'll be able to anticipate his next move."

"Yes." Carter looked up. "We'll set a trap. Lure him in and then overpower him."

"All well and good, but how do we know he'll go where we want him to?" Yerbol asked.

"We need bait," Wyatt said.

The room grew silent. Everyone's eyes turned to Wyatt.

"No!" Carter said firmly.

"It's okay, Carter. I'll be fine."

"I don't like it. You're a kid."

"In a year, I'd be old enough to join the Marines. Just like you. Besides, everybody has to do their part."

Carter nodded. "I still don't like it. We don't know if he'll go after you."

"Are you kidding? Konrad hates Wyatt," Howard said, his voice trailing off when he saw Carter's thunderous face. "I mean, I'll go with him."

"That doesn't give me the confidence you were intending," Carter said flatly.

"Me too." Melvin was added, followed by Keisha and Yerbol. Carter brooded quietly.

Keisha broke the heavy silence, "Besides, someone has to find Rosemary and tell her about her baby. She doesn't know that it's half alien."

"Yeah, "Howard added. "She may need help with the delivery. Who knows what that will involve?" He shook his head. "I found some files on the computer, and I wasn't thrilled about what they said."

"More files? Please share the information," Owens commanded.

"Well," Howard paused.

"Spit it out, son," Colonel Drucker told him. "It can't be that bad."

"Actually, it's worse. The alien gestation period appears to be approximately two months, and it is unclear how that will affect a human. After giving birth, it indicates that, like many of our species here on earth, the mother dies."

"That's crazy. What species? I've never heard of that?" Yerbol responded.

"Sure, you have. Everybody knows that salmon migrate upstream to spawn and then die after laying their eggs."

"She's not a fish." Yerbol looked horrified.

"True, but we don't exactly know what kind of DNA the aliens have. Female octopuses expend so much energy taking care of their eggs that they die of exhaustion, and queen bees expire after giving birth to their successor, the new queen. It can affect males too, and antechinus dies right after mating."

"*Eww.*" Yerbol made a face. "I don't know what the heck that is, and I feel bad for it."

"A type of Australian mouse. Yeah, the high levels of stress hormones do them in. There are others—"

"That's enough, Howard." Carter stopped him. "Do we have any idea how far along she is?"

"As far as I know, she's about halfway, maybe a little less, but according to the files, the child was created outside of her body, in a lab with her DNA. Then it was implanted inside her. For all we know, she could be weeks away from delivery."

"Were there instructions on how to deliver this child?" Nate Owens asked.

"I haven't finished reading." He pointed to the robot, which was leaning against the wall. "I can try and reactivate Nurse Ratched over there and see if he knows what to do."

"You think you'll be able to deliver the child?" the President asked

"He's never birthed a human child," Keisha squeaked.

"I'm sure we'll figure it out. John Raven must have a midwife on the reservation." Howard stroked his chin. "That will help too."

"The combined effort must save Rosemary and her child." Owens was pacing.

"Not if we don't get to her in time," Carter added.

"We also have to figure out how to manipulate Vincent into thinking he'll be getting Wyatt," Colonel Drucker said. "Any ideas?"

Owens studied the map, his fingers tracing the area marked "Monsterland," his face distant. "We need to move out. Colonel, how much longer until all the zombies are contained?"

"Three hours."

Wyatt had been staring at a makeshift map. "We have to go back to Monsterland. He's going to go there."

"You can't know that," Carter said.

"I do. He's going there. Home. His home." Wyatt looked wistfully in that direction.

"How do you know?" Keisha asked.

"I'm not sure," he paused. "No, I am. I can feel it."

"Wyatt, you're making me nervous. Tell me you can't feel Vincent Konrad's emotions." Carter watched him, his face a picture of concern.

"No, stop. I can't really feel him. It's just that I know him. He loved it. He's going to make that his home base. It all began in Monsterland—"

"And that's where it will end," Melvin said.

"*Annnnd,* I've got it. I told you I had to wait for the information to load," Howard announced.

Owens rubbed the stubble on his chin. "Where do we start?"

"We've got to make it believable," Carter said.

"From what I remember from my mole, he has an underground lair, a laboratory," Yerbol told them.

Wyatt and Carter exchanged smiles. "We leveled that place."

"I saw." Yerbol grinned back. "But he has a deeper laboratory. One he created for that crazy doctor… What was his name?"

"Dr. Benedict Frasier," Howard supplied. "We didn't know about another lab. We would have destroyed that, too."

"Yes, Frasier split his time between Area 51 and Monsterland via underground tunnels." Nate Owens nodded.

"The same tunnels he moved The Glob through to erase the populations of the surrounding towns," Melvin said grimly. "Some of my pack explored those tunnels. As I remember, they were deserted."

"Correct," Owens interjected. "We had maps of those passageways. He claimed he dug them to absorb the rainwater because the soil in the area was too dry."

"Another Vincent Konrad lie," Carter added. "The only structure that's still up is Manny's Instaburger. It would be believable if we said the kids are heading back there to meet."

"Yeah, Instaburger! We torched those mummies! We could torch Vincent Konrad, too." Howard lit up with excitement.

"No, Howard. If we say we're going to be there, we actually can't be there," Keisha explained. "We have to be watching for him from the outside."

"How will we fool him? He'll see the place is empty," Wyatt asked.

To Wyatt's dismay, Carter answered, "No, it won't. I'll be inside waiting for him."

Wyatt looked at Carter and said, "No, Carter, I won't let you."

Carter wrapped his arm around his neck as they filed out of the tent. "What, do you have a monopoly on courage? I have to be able to do my part, too."

"But, Carter—"

Carter raised one eyebrow. "Everybody has to do their part, including me. "

Yerbol nodded curtly. "Let's move out." He was followed by his ever-present crew, nicknamed Moe, Larry, and Curley, by Melvin.

CHAPTER 37

MORNING, AFTERNOON, AND EVENING SICKNESS

THE STENCH WAS so pungent it gagged Rosemary as soon as they entered the cave. She choked and coughed, and Fangi, the brother in the lead, ordered her to be quiet. She threw him a dirty look and gagged again.

"If this is morning sickness, I don't know why women do this." Saliva pooled in her mouth, and she wiped it away with the back of her hand. Rosemary retched again, dry heaves wracking her body.

"It can't be morning sickness, it's late in the day." Grillos's voice was a hushed whisper.

"Idiot." She slapped the back of his head playfully. "You think I'm in control of this feeling? *Ugh.*"

"*Shhh,*" Grillos said gently. "Slugs. We have to be careful we don't step in any of their slime."

"Why?" Rosemary asked.

It was a pitch-black cave, but Grillos knew his way. He was sure-footed with confidence, Rosemary was impressed. She couldn't see a thing. Rosemary remembered that giants have superior eyesight and reasoned it must come from living underground. Their eyes had adjusted over the centuries. She glanced back at the brothers; all of their eyes had a bright orange glow. Just from the way they looked at her, she could identify each one. Fangi's eyes were narrowed, Brontes's eyes wide with fear. Zaf was careful; his eyes darted everywhere. Baloo and Roosti averted their gaze. That didn't surprise her; they barely said a word to her.

"Why don't you give her a biology lesson, brother?" Zaf sneered. "You bored us to death with the history lecture."

"Shut up, Zaf." Grillos turned his massive head and muttered, "He means no harm, he's just afraid."

Rosemary wanted to ask what scared them about an insect when her insides twisted. She moaned, dots filling her vision. Her head rolled back, strong arms catching her. When she opened her eyes, Grillos held her in his arms.

"Baloo saved you from falling. Surprised?" Laughter rumbled in Grillos's chest, the vibrations soothing her sore body. "See, we are not the murderous horde you minkins think."

A torch had been lit, painting their faces shades of orange and yellow.

Rosemary's smile turned into a grimace. She clutched her midsection. It felt like a vice was tearing her apart.

"What's wrong?"

"I don't know," Rosemary groaned. "I have no experience with this kind of stuff. I spent my entire life in the company of men and never anticipated having to deal with this."

She could feel Grillos's careful steps. Twice, Zaf or maybe it was Roosti, steadied him.

Water dripped all around them, and the brothers' voices were hushed. They whispered warnings to avoid touching a wall or a puddle they weren't sure of. Fangi held up a hand, halting them at a tunnel that bisected into two parts.

"Do you hear that?" he asked, his harsh voice now soft.

They were silent. Rosemary could see fear in their faces morph into horror. A roar like an incoming tsunami barreled from the tunnel on the left. The torch was extinguished, plunging them into darkness, and Fangi shouted, "Run!" They took off down the second cave-like passageway.

Icy water splashed onto her face as they dashed down the corridor. There were no lights, and Rosemary blinked in the darkness to see. They must have known these tunnels like the back of their hands, because they ran at a breakneck speed. They slammed into each other, becoming a jumble of arms and legs, the strong muscles on Grillos's arms encasing her and keeping her from harm.

Rosemary had hidden her face in Grillos's broad chest, the dizzying pace making her sicker than before. There was a strange echoing as if they were near a body of water. It was eerie and delicate at the same time, bouncing off the nooks and hollows surrounding them. A waterfall rushed in the distance. Rosemary arched up, desperate to see it, her legs and arms going rigid with the want of being closer to the source. Her body hummed as if she were in tune with water, which was where she was happiest.

There was the flare of a match, and the cavern lit up. Brontes held a rush torch, the acrid smell making her nose twitch. Rosemary's eyes opened wide with awe.

The cave lit up in a rainbow of colors; nickel and copper, buried in the rock wall, gave the interior a deep green patina. It sparkled with flecks of blue and purple.

"Brother, there is a problem," Zaf said.

"What?" Grillos moved closer.

"Someone has been tampering with the rock wall."

Grillos's eyes scanned the area where the rock had been chipped away. "Minkins. Probably mining. We don't have time to explore."

Rosemary's eyes widened as she took in her surroundings. The air rushed out of her lungs, and she gasped for breath.

"Are you well?" Grillos's worried eyes searched hers.

"Aye. This is beautiful." She pointed to the walls. "Are we near Copper Valley?"

"Underneath."

"Of course," she said in wonder. "The blues?"

"Copper and manganese. The greens are copper too. See that lighter-colored vein." He pointed to a thread of dark yellow that ran around the cave's ceiling. "Your miners seem to have taken an interest in it."

"Gold?"

The brothers laughed. "Silver. There are millions of lines like those, but it's too expensive for your minkins to mine it."

"If they were nice to us, we could help them," Zaf offered. "There's a lot we could do."

"I've never seen—" The words clogged in her throat when Grillos turned to face an ocean of water. It glowed aquamarine, a shimmering sea, calm and serene, a sandy beach on each shore filled with glittering stones that winked back at her. Rosemary was speechless.

"Over time, rain causes the rocks to release minerals," Grillos explained.

"Phosphorus," she said with wonder, taking in the vast array of colors. "Who knew rocks could be so beautiful?"

"That's the minkin name for it." Grillos showed her the landscape proudly. "We call it glowstone."

"How very beautiful. More appropriate." Rosemary craned her neck around him. She heard the sound of something being dragged from the other tunnel.

Behind them, a roar reverberated down the passageway. The brothers jumped into action. She heard Brontes's urge, "Be careful with it. You don't want to poke a hole in the bottom."

There was the sound of something being scraped against the rock wall, and Grillos groaned. "Gently. The raork is old."

"What's a raork?" Rosemary asked.

"Our ride," Grillos smiled and turned so she could see a huge flat-bottomed raft made from gigantic logs lashed together with hides.

"Where did you find trees that big?"

"The forest up north. You call them Sequoias. We call them Mother Trees."

"How…how?"

"How did we build the pyramids, Stonehenge…the Great Wall of China?" Grillos chuckled. "You think humans did those things? You have a lot to learn, Rosemary, mine."

"It comes!" Brontes yelled. "Hurry. Leave her behind! It will distract it."

Grillos roared then. "I will knock you out and leave you before I leave Rosemary." He turned in a circle and added. "One more word against her, and I will consider it a word against me."

Rosemary peeked from her spot to see five giants stare with astonishment at their older brother.

"I heard you! Now let's get out of here." Brontes's voice shook.

The sheer terror in Brontes's voice made Rosemary's skin crawl, and the reassuring hold of Grillos kept her fear at bay. Cramps gripped Rosemary again, and she thought she would faint from the pain. She was lifted high and recognized the calm feeling of being rocked on a ship. They shoved off, the raft dipping under the collective group's massive weight.

Lifting her head, she looked over Grillos's shoulder to see a snail as big as a house barrel into the cavern. It opened a giant maw, screaming in anger, the blast of its breath taking hers away. It had a horrible stench, worse than zombies, and her head swam for a minute from the force of it. Rosemary's eyes glazed with pain, and she allowed the current to ease her into the darkness.

CHAPTER 38

WAS IT ALL LIES?

"I DON'T LIKE *STUPES,*" Olrec grumbled to himself as he watched the doctor and his companion become smaller in the distance. He heard a whine overhead and saw a white, round object emerge from the treetops and take off after them. "*Ugh,* the Grays, if the Grays are involved, I wonder if he is telling the truth about being a Watcher?" he said speculatively and added, "I'd better report this to Kokkus and see what he says now. You can't trust a *stupe;* those Gray ones are even worse."

He brushed the dust off his fur, revealing a gray patch of skin underneath. Ironic, he thought, looking at the spaceship, so alike, yet so different. Interesting how much you can hate something even while finding similarities.

He glanced around the clearing, noticing the burnt vegetation and blackened rocks. Radiation from the ship. *How did I miss that? Your eyes are in your backside,* he could hear his brother-in-law's response.

Olrec hiked back to his village. He had so much to tell. Konrad indicated he was one of the Watchers, yet how could he be if he were in league with the Gray visitors?

Everybody knew the Watchers came on fiery chariots from the sky, not sleek, white circles that sported blue lights. Watcher crafts resembled their huts, with glowing lights and flames emanating from them. There was nothing special about Konrad's ship. Olrec frowned. There was nothing special about Konrad, beyond the menacing attitude. The more he replayed their interaction, the more he thought that Konrad and the little man were actually… *disappointing*.

Not that he had much information about the Watchers. With no written language, they had to depend on stories handed down from Mophat to Mophat to remind them of their history.

The problem was that their clan, Mophat, had been killed and eaten by a wild pack of zombies a few years back. No new Mophat had been trained. He reckoned that tales of the past were changing each time someone else told them.

In fact, he had forgotten how the *stupes* got their name. Most of their history was lost, like mists that evaporate every morning. He laughed, asked two Sasquatch to describe that morning mist, and you'll get five different answers. His tribe, as well as many of his cousins, could no longer agree on much. The only thing they all recalled the same way was that they were brought here by a fire chariot, left to populate, and one day the fire chariot would return, perhaps to take them home.

Olrec sighed. He wasn't sure what he had gotten out of this meeting. For a Watcher, Konrad understood precious little about his species. His contempt was palpable.

So the world was going to war, and it was going to be every species for itself. With no great love for the *stupes* or the giants, where did that leave the Sasquatch? Which side should they ally with? What if he interpreted something wrong? His brother-in-law would ridicule him.

Something rankled him about Konrad, but ultimately, he had to report to the elders. It would be up to them. It bothered him the way the ugly little man stared at him. He saw the revulsion in his eyes. He had made up his mind about my kind long before he met with us.

How can people think that of us that way? We have done nothing to them. We've never spoken to them, interacted with them, or looked for them!

"Somebody should tell them that we aren't monsters," Olrec said aloud. "We were here *waaaaaay* before humans," he scoffed.

A group of birds took off from their perches in the trees, his words disturbing their peace.

"Maybe we should unite with the giants and kick them all out of here." He imagined the gasps from the council when he would suggest this.

"Stay away from the giants!" the old ones would respond.

Olrec sighed. He was unsure which direction his tribe should take. Something deep in his gut told him that staying away, alone in the hills, had done a disservice to his kind.

He knew that Kokkus would challenge everything he would say. They had this discussion many times before. "Stupid! There has always been a cold war between us and the giants. They spread vicious lies and tell the *stupes* that we are monsters. They say that we eat their young."

"*Eeeew.*" Olrec winced. *That's not true!* He stopped short where he was walking, blinking with sudden clarity. *Maybe it was all lies. Perhaps the giants weren't their enemies… could it be the humans weren't so bad either?*

"We can crush their skulls with our big feet." Kokkus would brag later as he held up his oversized foot. "Bigfoot always wins! We should get all the clans together and attack!"

"*Noooo,*" Olrec said. "Don't say Bigfoot." Olrec shook his head, gravely. Nothing good would come of this.

CHAPTER 39

WHAT'S COOKING?

"**W**ELL, MY WORD. Would you take a look at this?" Vincent was absorbed in his cell phone.

"It works?" Dreg leaned over to see the face of his mobile. "Can I see?"

Vincent pulled the phone close to his chest. "It was a rhetorical question. Our boy, Wyatt Baldwin, and his nasty friends are on the move."

"How do you know?"

Vincent laughed. "Their pathological need to be connected."

"What?"

"They are communicating with their phones," he scoffed. "Using *my* satellite."

"They can't be that dumb."

"Can and are. I knew we'd get them."

"Vincent, maybe it's a trap?" Dreg raised one eyebrow.

"Don't be stupid. Look, look." He held the phone up. "They're trying to use Mythdot."

"You own Mythdot!"

"I told you they are morons. Now all we have to do is bait a trap and wait for them. Let me think."

Dreg leaned over his shoulder. "Well, what are they saying?"

Vincent watched the dots indicating someone was typing. "It's the smart one, Howard, he's typing."

"And—"

"They're moving out. Apparently, Wyatt has left already."

"Where are they headed?"

"*Huh.* They are speaking in some kind of code. They're talking about getting the shakes."

"*Getting the shakes,* getting the shakes. I'm stumped." Dreg shrugged. "What else?"

"The last stand."

"Crazy talk."

"Adolescents…wait, sometimes on the highway, they call the last place to get gas or recharge, the last stand? Vincent, can we go? If you want to find Rosemary, we'd better start looking before the Thalens decide to transport us back."

Vincent ignored him. He was deep in thought. He bit his lower lip. "*Hmmm.* Be quiet and let me think."

"Can't you think while we actually travel?"

"Why would they want *shakes*? Shakes, last stand…they're not talking about shaking, they're talking about shakes." Vincent did a credible imitation of someone vibrating uncontrollably. "They're heading to that vile hamburger shack."

"You mean Instaburger? It's where they had the last stand with the mummies…Oh, I see, Vincent. They're going to Instaburger."

"We'll just have to cook up a surprise for them when they get there."

"What about your daughter?"

"I'm thinking, Dreg. Don't interrupt me while I'm thinking."

"Me too," Dreg offered, his eyebrows scrunched together.

"You can't be serious," Vincent laughed.

Dreg straightened as best as he could. "Sometimes, I don't think you appreciate me."

"Would counseling help?"

"You would go to a therapist with me?" Dreg looked hopeful, his eyes shiny.

Vincent laughed so hard his horse stopped moving and neighed. "As if I'd waste a minute on that. No, and stop your pouting, Dreg. It's time you accepted your place in my universe."

"And what is that?" Dreg's voice was low.

"It doesn't matter. In your useless way, you've given me an idea. I will kill two birds with one stone. Let's go."

"How?" Dreg demanded.

"Back at the lab, I will locate Rosemary and bring her and my grandchild home."

Dreg watched him with confusion.

"I will flood their tunnels and push them into the open."

"Flood them with what?"

"Oh ye of little faith. I planted explosives near the dam that holds back the underwater river. Once detonated, it will flood the tunnels. Onward! We have a lot of work to do, Dreg. To Monsterland!" He galloped at full speed.

Dreg watched him go, his face twisted, reflecting the thoughts and feelings coursing through his skin. *Smug bastard.*

He looked to the other side of the empty road and shook his head. The Sasquatch gathered there. The mountains hemming the landscape were filled with giants that Vincent intended to drown.

Glancing up, saw the spaceship following Vincent and made his decision.

One of them was going to kill two birds with one stone, and maybe it wouldn't be Vincent Konrad.

CHAPTER 40

ARE YOU SURE ABOUT THIS?

THE HELICOPTER BANKED overhead as the sun was rising, and Keisha watched as the troops surrounded the derelict Instaburger building. Its bright yellow and red trim was faded, burned by the mummies as they flared into walking torches when their surface was ignited by Whisp.

Two mounds marked the left side of the building where they buried comrades who were murdered in the battle. She searched the ragtag group on the ground, recognizing Howard by the plain shirt he wore. She smiled, knowing his pockets were armed with pencils in case they came across any errant vampires. He proved he knew his way around a wooden stake, and she smiled, thinking of his bravery. Three dots showed up on her phone. It was a frequency programmed just for them. "Not now, Howard," she wrote him. "Stay radio silent. The chopper has to hide. Vincent may be nearby. We don't want him knowing he's surrounded, above or below." She touched the front of the phone, wishing it were Howard's face.

Worrying her bottom lip, she wondered how he would react if she turned into a dragon. She agreed to stay and report what she saw from the air. While she preferred to stand next to him in the fight, a small part of her was relieved to handle reconnaissance from the air and readily volunteered for the duty. This way, Howard's prying eyes would be far less jumpy in case she had some uncontrollable urge to morph into something *fascinating*. She knew these issues would have to be addressed at some point, but if they managed to subdue Konrad and she wouldn't be forced into a defensive mode, perhaps she'd never have to change again, and Keisha was okay with that.

Melvin scanned the bushes for any signs of life. His ears prickled at a distant sound, once unrecognizable, now familiar. He sniffed the air and caught one of Yerbol's guards giving him a dirty look, but he couldn't stop his nose from twitching. There was a sound behind him, and the commando raised his gun. Melvin jumped up and walked between the line of fire, holding up his hand.

"Hold on. It's just a coyote."

"That thing ain't no coyote," the soldier ground out. He took a bead on the animal, but Yerbol walked over.

"What's going on here, soldier?" He rested his hand on his shoulder.

"He's going to shoot. They are friendlies, these coyotes." Melvin stood defiantly.

A tense minute passed between Melvin and Yerbol. The older man nodded curtly. "Go ahead. Not everyone or everything is our enemy."

The coyote bared its teeth at the soldier, and both Yerbol and his commando raised their guns.

"No. Wait," Melvin shouted. He turned his back on the others and communicated.

"Go on, ask your question," Yerbol ordered.

Did you see them?

Her?

Melvin's breath caught.

They are hiding in the tunnels below Monsterland.

Melvin searched the area where the tunnels could be entered. He narrowed his eyes.

You can't see them from here. She's with the little man. She's changed.

Mevin shrugged.

Be wary of the uniformed ones.

Why?

They are not what they seem.

Melvin looked back at Yerbol and the soldiers..

All of them?

No, just the soldiers. The coyote turned to leave.

Melvin gave a slight nod. *Wait, do I know you, friend?*

The coyote hung its head. *Yes, we met a long time ago. You asked me to watch out for your woman. I failed.*

It wasn't your fault, Melvin told him. The coyote's ears pricked up, and it growled threateningly.

Melvin glanced back, and his nose twitched. He eyed the two commandos. He recognized the one they called Moe, but wasn't sure if the other was Larry or Curley. *Which one or both?* He asked, but when he looked back, the coyote was gone.

"Ask if they've seen anything. Konrad or the one he travels with," Owens called. He was heading in their direction. This question earned him a stark look from Yerbol.

Melvin didn't have to ask. The coyote responded from a safe distance within a cluster of trees. *They're hiding in the hills back there. They can't see you on this side of the building. Melvin, be caref—*

A gunshot rent the air. Yerbol turned and cuffed the commando. "What did you do that for?"

"It just went off, sir. I'm sorry."

Melvin took off for the trees. He signed with relief. There was no sign of the coyote.

He called the coyote by name, but it didn't answer. It was gone. Then he sighed her name, *Jaaaade.*

His skin prickled knowing she was close by. His hands itched to hug her.

"Is your contact alright?" Yerbol called.

"Who?" Melvin asked.

Yerbol sighed, "The coyote, man. What's wrong with you? You look like you've seen a ghost."

"I'm fine, no thanks to you or your troops." He eyed them distrustfully. He realized they refused to meet his gaze. He wondered if Wyatt or Howard ever noticed that before.

"It was a mistake, Saunders. Everyone is wound up. You know, walking on eggshells." He gave a dirty look to his soldier and told him to patrol the perimeter. "He's really not one of my troops." Yerbol seemed consolatory. "I never trained them. By now, you and your friends have to realize I'm commanding a bunch of ragtag strangers."

"Well," Melvin said. "He just gave up our position to Konrad, who is concealed in the trees on the ridge on the other side of the building. Don't look, but they are hiding in the hill behind us, Sir." Melvin addressed this to President Owens, who was approaching them.

"Who released that shot?" Owens demanded.

Yerbol shrugged. "Green troops."

"Get the troops in position," Owens ordered. "Saunders, can you—"

The ground shook. "What was that?" Yerbol crouched.

"Earthquake?" Owens asked.

"No," Melvin cocked his head. "Whatever it was, came from that tunnel. I'll check it out."

"Do you want Yerbol—"

"I'll go alone. We can't spare the troops."

"He's right. We're stretched as far as we can go, especially with these inexperienced troops."

"Understood." The president nodded and said, "Good luck, Saunders. See you on the other side of this." He turned to Yerbol. "Tell Carter to get ready."

Melvin started to sprint away.

Yerbol called out to Melvin, "Hey, kid."

Melvin paused and looked back.

"Good luck."

Melvin smiled. "You too, Yerbol."

Howard typed furiously using two separate phones. He glanced up at the black helicopter, banking in the sky and disappearing behind a ridge of the mountain. "Keisha," he whispered. He was worried about her. She'd been distant, strange. He had wanted her to stay near him. He felt she'd be protected better that way, but she insisted on being with the single helicopter they had in use. "I can help better from there." She pointed to the chopper.

They barely had a minute before orders were given out. Howard opened and closed his hands, making a fist. He hated rushing their goodbyes. *What if something happened to either of them?*

Regret washed over him and landed in his gut. He never told Keisha what she meant to him. His mind raced back to their conversation when she asked if he had ever looked at a flower and considered its beauty rather than studied its complex structure. He searched his mind for when her mood had changed. They were talking about creatures. He couldn't figure out why she was so sensitive about the subject. He didn't want her to get mad at him and change into— *OMG*, he thought feverishly. *She thinks I see her as a creature! Oh no, never. Keisha, you are the love of my life!*

Howard winced and smacked his forehead. She was beautiful, smart, kind, and good. *Keisha, Keisha, Kiesha! What was I thinking every time I addressed your questions?*

He looked where the sun was fast rising and brightening the sky. Stars wink their farewell as they disappeared in the fading darkness. The dawn limned the outline of the mountains in pink and gold.

The air flew out of his mouth in a rush. *How did he never compare to this kind of beauty?* When was the last time he spoke of anything but equations and hypotheses? *Keisha,* her name came out in a rush from his gut, and for a minute, he couldn't breathe. Anxiety bloomed, and he panicked. *What if he lost the chance to tell her that she was his first thought in the morning when he awoke and the last when he went to sleep?* Her name repeated in his head like a prayer, and for the vastly scientific and total non-believer, he realized that the thought of her alone brought him immeasurable peace.

Keisha, he thought again. *I have to tell you. I have to tell you what you mean to me.*

"Are you done?" His father's impatient voice was like a dental drill.

Howard looked at the chopper and started typing on his phone.

"Who are you writing?" his father demanded.

"*Umm.*"

"*Umm's* not an answer." He looked over Howard's shoulder. "Keisha! This is no time for declaring your love, Howard. Lives are at stake."

"I'm not—"

"Just finished the messages that must be sent. There'll be enough time afterwards for your love life! Now, and that's an order."

"Yes, sir."

Wyatt watched Carter recheck his guns. Piles of ammo lay at their feet.

He stood and made eye contact with Wyatt.

"Well, I'm ready."

"You don't have to do this alone." Wyatt's voice cracked.

"They'll need everyone out here."

"Still—"

"No, Wyatt. He won't hesitate to kill you. I can't let that happen. He sees you as the one responsible for everything that has gone wrong."

"You're just as much at risk!"

Carter nodded his head, "But eminently more expendable."

"Don't say that!"

Carter sighed. "You are the future. You and your friends. Your destiny—"

"What about *your* destiny?" Wyatt interrupted.

Carter considered the early morning sky. "That remains to be seen. Wyatt, the president, needs you. Go. Go and make yourself useful." Carter took a deep breath and called softly, "Wy."

Wyatt stopped. "Take care of Sean."

Wyatt grabbed Carter and felt the older man hug him back. "I'm sorry I never—"

"Don't say it. You have nothing to be sorry for. Being your dad has been the highlight of my life. You and your brother gave me the purpose I needed when I returned from the Marines."

Wyatt met his gaze.

"You are the best part of my life. Be careful, son."

"I will." Words clogged Wyatt's throat.

"Remember, we're not heroes, we're survivors. I'll see you soon!" Carter tore himself away and raced into the abandoned building. Wyatt heard the tinkle of glass and knew that Carter was now a world away from him.

CHAPTER 41

HAVING MY BABY

ROSEMARY'S HEAD ROLLED feverishly against Grillos's chest. She heard them talking about her as if from a vast distance.

"She's in a bad way, brother." It was Zaf, or maybe Brontes. She couldn't tell.

"Look, look how her stomach changes. It's growing fast. Did she touch the slime, Grillos?" Fangi asked.

"No. I was careful. I don't understand."

"Maybe we should dump… okay… forget it. I just thought it would put her out of her misery."

"No," Grillos bellowed. She felt herself being shifted and held closer.

"It hurts." Was that feeble voice hers? "Grillos." She reached up. "I want to tell you something."

"Yes, dear heart." Kind, orange-flecked eyes filled her field of vision. Grillos's massive hands held her carefully. Rosemary opened her mouth. She wanted to tell him something, something important. A pain tore through her abdomen. She gripped herself, feeling a baby move within. "Grillos, save my baby. Whatever—" Another lightning strike of agony silenced her, her voice trailing off.

The boat dipped and swayed in the current. She drifted in and out of consciousness. Every so often, she would open her eyes and see Grillos's worried expression. She wanted to tell him not to be scared. She wasn't, but the words escaped her with each wave of pain.

She heard Grillos bellow, "Noooo," the sound of his cry mingling with her own.

Rosemary knew she was being lifted. The cavern spun dizzily, and she watched the rocks above change into a sculpted ceiling of a home. It was painted a bright color and brought a smile to her lips.

"She's bleeding!" Grillos was shouting.

All around her, there was a flurry of lighter footsteps. A woman touched her forehead. Her hand engulfed Rosemary's skull, and it felt comforting. Rosemary opened her eyes and stared at Grillos. The lined face of an older woman, her hair faded and touched with silver, bent over her. She was smaller than Grillos, but she still filled Rosemary's vision. "Make a bed for her in this crate."

"Ma, it's where you store the onions."

"It's the only thing small enough for her to fit. Grillos, quickly, son. Get some blankets and cut them into smaller pieces. Now!" She paused and directed someone else to get towels. "Grillos, once you're done, leave. This is no place for you."

"Drink this," the woman urged.

"I can't. I'm being split apart." Rosemary's voice was a mere thread. She gasped, her breathing more difficult.

Gentle hands prodded her belly expertly, and through a spangled haze of pain, she heard Grillos bellowing her name.

"I don't understand. She's filling up with a strange fluid." The woman turned her head. "Grillos, is she a mutant?"

"No. What's happening to her, Ma? I'll die if—" Grillos held his head in his hands, giant tears coursing down his cheeks.

The woman turned and yelled, "I told you to leave. This is no place for you."

Rosemary saw Grillos towering above the woman. "I can't, Ma. I love her."

"Is this baby yours?" she demanded. "You know humans can't birth a giant's baby. That hasn't been done for thousands of years."

"Ma!"

"Well, is it?"

"No, of course not." Grillos's face was beet red.

"This is not normal for them. Who did this abomination!" she demanded.

"It wasn't my choice," Rosemary said weakly. "But she's mine now." She attempted to lift herself off the cushions. "Please, please save my baby."

"Ma, please, you have to help her," Grillos implored. "And you have to save Rosemary's baby."

Grillos's mother paced the room. "I don't know if it will work." Women rushed in and out carrying huge bowls filled with steaming water and stacks of towels. Rosemary's cries echoed throughout the cavern.

"There will be no way back for her," the woman said after a while.

"I don't care as long as she lives," Grillos said, his eyes full of tears. "You must."

"Did you see any slug slime?"

Grillos went silent.

Grillos's mother moved away, but Rosemary strained her ears to hear.

"In ancient times, I've heard stories. It's been a while, but… go quickly, son, and bring me a bucket. Make sure you are well protected."

"A bucket of slime?" Rosemary muttered before her eyes rolled back in her head, and she was lost to everything.

CHAPTER 42

THANKFULNESS

"I ASK YOU, WHY should we help him?" Olrec questioned the group.

"Well, Olrec. You were the one who met him. What did you think?" Kokkus observed Olrec closely, as if waiting to jump on anything he said.

Olrec was silent for a minute. He wanted to choose his words carefully and not give Kokkus ammunition to make fun of him. "He's sly." Olrec shook his head. "I don't trust him."

He did not get the hero's welcome he expected. The clan was too distraught about Jofro's death. His brother-in-law had been distant, as if he didn't want to declare in favor of anything Olrec reported. *Politicians,* Olrec thought ruefully. Always filled with promises they never keep. He watched Kokkus take his place next to him in front of the council; his brother-in-law's chest was puffed out with pride.

"But he did scare you?" One of the elders shouted. The old one shook his long ceremonial stick. He was the acting Mophat and had inherited the position before his predecessor could give him details about the Savior and the Watchers. "Watchers are supposed to awe, not scare," he declared.

"And you know this, how?" Kokkus demanded.

"It's not my fault the lizards took my uncle." He shook a long rattle and sang a melody. The group bowed their heads.

"These are perilous times." Kokkus paced in front of the crowd.

He stopped beside his sister and pointed his Council Staff. "You were the one who brought up the idea of meeting *this*… this Dr. Konrad. Do you still think it is a good idea?"

"I hate them all, *stupes*, giants, aliens. Why don't they just leave us alone?" She fell to her knees and cupped her hands. "Watchers, tell us what to do," she pleaded.

"Without a knowledgeable Mophat, we don't know if they even hear us." Kokkus's voice was harsh.

"Please, Watchers, hear us!" Zilli called out. Several others fell to their knees alongside her.

"Stop your pity party, Zilli. It's time to act." Kokkus looked out at the crowd. "Those in favor of joining Dr. Konrad, say it now."

There was a tepid response—more "nays" than "yays."

"Who would rather support the *stupes*?" Kokkus's voice boomed.

About an equal number of people voted for the human population.

"A stalemate. Olrec, what are your thoughts?" His narrow face had a smirk.

Olrec looked at his wife's worried eyes and then back to the hut where his cubs slept. He was torn. He didn't like Konrad, but he was terrified of the lizards. He had seen what they did to Jofro. What would it take for Kokkus to treat him with a minimal amount of the respect he sought? His answer was vital, crucial to his home, his heart, and his family. "It is a tricky question. Whatever we decide to do may impact our tribe's entire future."

At first, Kokkus didn't answer. Olrec was surprised. His brother-in-law looked overwhelmed. His large shoulders sagged under the weight of the tribe's safety. "Yes, yes. For once, we agree. Olrec. You met with him, took his measure. Our tribe is equally split. You ventured further south than any of us has dared. You must tell us what you think will serve us best." Kokkus's tone had changed. It was no longer sharp.

He's scared, Olrec thought, looking at Kokkus. White hairs had sprung up overnight at his brother-in-law's temples. Olrec felt the top of his own bald head, where he knew more skin was showing. Zilli was gazing at him, her eyes filled with respect and love.

"I think we should march and wait. Yes, wait to see which side is winning. We stay in the hills and observe. When we determine a winner, we support them. We will be the victors."

"How…how will we be the victors?" Kokkus asked.

"In their gratitude, they will see us in a new light. They will realize they couldn't have won without our support. The bigger our presence, the more important we will be."

"Indeed," the old Mophat nodded sagely. "We should call in the cousins."

"Call in the cousins! Call in the cousins, call in the cousins!" the crowd chanted.

"Yes." Zilli rose next to him. "You are smart, husband. They will be thankful. Thankfulness unlocks gratitude. They will be in our debt."

Kokkus sighed and spoke softly, so that only Olrec could hear him. "I hope for your sake you are right." His mood changed. He smiled broadly and slapped Olrec on the back. He shouted, "I like it!"

There was the sound of agreement around the fire.

Kokkus nodded sagely. "Those in favor of Olrec's plan say, yes."

The air was filled with a chorus of assents.

"It's time to contact all the clans and have them join us. We will meet and converge in Copper Valley!" Kokkus looked at Olrec and said, "I hope you are the right choice to do this." He walked away to talk to the Mophat.

Zilli wrapped her arms around Olrec, her dark eyes sparkled in the moonlight. "I am so proud of you."

The tribe danced around, shaking rattles and beating a drum.

"We leave at daybreak," Kokkus declared, and added, his eyes meeting Olrec's. "With Olrec leading the way."

CHAPTER 43

SECRET ROOMS

"ROSEMARY, ROSEMARY, WHERE are you?" Vincent crooned. He walked from console to console, turning on machinery. Soon, the underground lair was filled with the sound of beeps and blips—each one of the screens on the counters displaying moving dots.

"*Ah Ha*! I've got you!" Vincent said in a satisfied voice. "*Hmmm*, she's deep, deep underground. Much lower than us." He was pulling at his lip, his dark eyes watching the blip on one screen. He tapped the glass surface. "Why are you not moving?" he murmured.

"Where is she?" Dreg was poking around Dr. Frasier's lab equipment. He dropped a glass beaker, and Vincent scowled at him.

"In the giant's sanctuary."

"Are you sure about your plan? You said you didn't want anything to happen to her. If she's that far down, she may not make it out." Dreg dumped the contents of a plastic tray, wincing when everything clattered onto the countertop.

"It will take time before the water reaches their level, but the giants will hear and feel the explosion. They will race out, and we'll get the Thalens to neutralize them." Vincent turned his beady gaze toward Dreg. "What are you doing?"

Dreg dropped the forceps he was holding. *"Umm*, nothing."

"Then stop it. You're too noisy. You're making it hard to think."

Dreg's eyes widened when he found a blood-stained scalpel resting in the bottom of the tray. "She could get killed." He tested it on the edge of his thumb. It was sharp and drew blood. Gasping, he stuck his finger in his mouth.

"Cut yourself on the glass, you clumsy oaf?" Vincent laughed.

Dreg nodded and slid the scalpel into his pocket. "Yes, how silly of me. Are you done yet?"

"Almost," Vincent said absently. He continued to walk from screen to screen, pressing a button here, moving a dial there. He paused and drummed his fingers on the surface.

"This doesn't make sense."

"What?" Dreg was filling a bag with supplies. "Why is everything working down here?"

"Generators," Vincent answered absently. "*Hmmm*. The sensors indicate more people roaming the outskirts of the park." Vincent pressed a series of buttons.

"Could be zombies."

Vincent nodded. "Yes. Didn't think many of them were left."

"All it takes is a bite from one to make another."

"True, but statistically—"

"Vincent, we are running out of time." Dreg stood in front of the workstation as if he were hiding something.

Vincent walked over to a bank of computers. He punched a series of switches and walked to a large lever. "Well, here goes nothing." He pulled the handle, and nothing happened. He returned the bar to its former position.

He redid the switches, added a new one, and pulled it again. Sparks flew, landing on his cloak and leaving a smattering of smoldering dots. The entire lab was filled with the sounds of whistles and beeps.

There was a groan, followed by an explosion that shook the ground. Vincent smiled and clapped his hands.

"What was that?" Dreg asked.

"The machinery is unclogging. Ah, here we go!" The beeps turned into a strident alarm. "It will explode again in thirty-five minutes. The entire tunnel system will flood."

"What about your daughter?"

"The initial explosion will alert the giants. They will race to the exits. We'll intercept her there."

"We'll be no match for the giants."

"I told you, we will use the Thalens and their firepower to overwhelm them."

Vincent walked purposefully to a cabinet. A small tube protruded from the surface. Leaning over, Vincent took a deep breath and blew into the brass tube. There was a soft hiss of released air followed by the whisper of machinery clicking. A door appeared from the seamless wall and popped open. Vincent gave a satisfied grunt and said, "It worked!"

"What? How?"

"My secret arsenal. It can only be opened with my breath."

"Your breath unlocked that?"

"Yes, Dr. Frasier invented it. I do miss that man," he said wistfully. "Remind me to place his statue in the center of Monsterland. It will be a fitting memorial."

"Vincent, please," Dreg pleaded.

"Well, yes, the mechanism validates my breath profile. It's my signature, you see. We were afraid my eyes wouldn't be enough, especially after my head transplant. The timbre of my exhalation, combined with the rhythm of my breathing, is distinctively my own. Also, there are the humidity and chemical markers. When the live sample matches the stored template, *viola!*, the lock releases.

Vincent chuckled and walked through a narrow opening. He returned holding a giant hand-held gun that resembled a rocket launcher. The metal surface of the weapon gleamed under the flashing lights. It had a ribbed, brass tube almost twenty inches long. Tiny darkened levers held a series of gears in bright copper. Vincent held it by its massive wooden stock. Using his cloak, he rubbed a brass plate that was attached, Dreg presumed to hold against the shoulder. The muzzle flared like a miniature cannon. "We might not even need the Thalens, or the Sasquatch, for that matter. This little beauty might do the trick."

"What is that?"

"Oh, just something I was working on with Dr. Frasier. Grab that bag." He pointed inside the secret room to a duffel filled with a pile of pointed missiles, each about the size of Dreg's palm.

"It looks like an anti-tank gun. Why didn't we use it in the battle when they attacked us months ago?"

"It was under lock and key, and if you remember, I was barely conscious when Wyatt and his army of friends attacked. Which reminds me–" Vincent walked over to another console.

"What are you doing now?"

Vincent's face glowed from the multicolored dials he looked at. He turned a few dials and pressed a code. "This ought to do it."

"What?" Dreg demanded.

Vincent headed toward the underground exit. "My satellite just jammed their communications." He sighed with satisfaction. "I feel whole again. Watch them panic when they realize they can't talk to each other anymore. Now, let's head over to Instaburger and take care of my nemesis, Wyatt Baldwin. Finally, it's all coming together!"

Vincent started to snicker, the echoes of his guffaws turning into an evil shout of laughter.

Dreg joined him, wondering if Vincent knew the joke was going to be on him.

CHAPTER 44

NOTHING BUT EMPTY HUSKS

THEY ENTERED THROUGH an underground tunnel filled with the empty husks of people annihilated by the purple foam. Jade was surprised there was no odor. A wave of sadness filled her as the flood of memories rushed in, her mother and brother killed by the foam that fed Vincent Konrad's operation.

Their feet echoed in tandem in the tunnel; the only jarring sound was the scrape of metal from her artificial leg.

"Faster," Otto urged. His skin was pasty under the lighting. Sweat beaded his brow. He paused beside one corpse, drew the small rectangular control from his bag, and scooped up foam with his hands to place in the interior of the device.

"I wouldn't touch that if I were you," Jade told him.

"It's been lying here for weeks; it's got to be dormant."

"I remember it all now. That's the stuff that killed my mother and brother. Something weird happens when it touches your skin."

Otto held up his hand. "It has to have a shelf life. Alien jet fuel. It powered Vincent Konrad's head."

"How do you know that?"

"Remote cameras, Jade. There's not much I don't know about."

"I still wouldn't handle it."

Otto scoffed. "A lot you know. I should make you handle it, but I don't want it powering anything I've added to you. It's safe, see." He held up his hands stained with violet foam.

"Where are we going?" Jade demanded.

"Into the bowels of hell to see what this madman has cooked up!" He stood and, with a maniacal laugh, began rushing down the tunnel.

"You're no better than Vincent Konrad!"

"What did you say?" He stopped and stared at her, the whites of his eyes surrounding his irises like a painted doll.

Jade shivered. "You heard me. You think you're better than him, but you're not. You're keeping me prisoner. Changed me without my permission. You're the monster!"

"*Ha*! Look who's talking. You should be thanking me. I saved you."

"Forced me to live a life I don't want."

"Ungrateful child!" Otto ran ahead. "I made you, and only I can destroy you."

A single tear rolled down Jade's face from her good eye. She felt locked inside this mechanical body. She couldn't believe this was how she'd have to live the rest of her life, alone, isolated, and with Otto as her only companionship. She missed Melvin, and the thought of him never being part of her life filled her with despair.

Her skin chafed under the aluminum foil hat he insisted she wear. Jade's skin prickled, and she slowed. She watched Otto run ahead, but the whisper of her name pulled her back. She tore off the conical hat and cocked her head to one side.

Jaaaade.

There was no mistake. It was Melvin, and he was calling her. He found her. She looked down at her hands, scarred where flesh met metal, and her breath came in short, quick gasps. *Oh, Melvin, I miss you.* She sobbed, a raw guttural sound that came from the deepest part of her soul. She was torn in two by the need to be with Melvin and the shame of what she'd become.

He couldn't see her when she was like this. Jade began to run in the opposite direction until her body stalled, a force field seemingly around her. She glanced around, her new eye electronically detecting a barrier surrounding her.

She fought the imprisonment, but the nuts and bolts holding her together were screaming from the effort.

"It finally works!" Otto crowed in delight. "Where do you think you're going?" He walked toward her, holding the rectangular box in his hand.

"What are you doing to me?"

"Magnetic forcefield."

"Where did that come from?"

"I've had it all along. It wasn't working, but I've used some of the leftover alien fuel and now it seems that's done the trick."

Jade looked at him, her gaze landing on his hands. "What's happening to your hands?"

Otto shrugged indifferently and then glanced down at his fingers. They looked frostbitten. He brought his hand close to his face and stared in wonder as the dusty color traveled up his arms.

CHAPTER 45

BEAM US IN

THE GUNSHOT ECHOED in the air.

"Give me the binoculars." Vincent snatched them away from Dreg. "They know we are here."

"How do you know? "Dreg asked.

"The gunfire. That was a semi-automatic. It's not just Wyatt. They're all here."

"I looked. I only see one person in the building. In Instaburger." Dreg looked puzzled.

"That's why I'm in charge. I don't accept things at face value."

Dreg sighed with frustration. "Well, are you going to attack?" There was a long silence. He was growing tired of Vincent's snide remarks. "If not for me—"

"Yes?" Vincent looked at him with a raised eyebrow, as if daring him to finish. Dreg lost his nerve. He rubbed the handle of the scalpel he'd placed inside his pocket, which he'd stolen from Vincent's lab. Just waiting for the right time, he convinced himself.

Lost in thought, he wondered where he'd go if he killed Vincent. Humanity would blame him for Monsterland; the giants would eat him. He didn't trust the Sasquatch, and he was scared of the aliens. Vincent Konrad might be the only safe spot for him; he thinned his lips with indecision.

"I can feel it. They are all here, but on the other side of the building. I can smell them." Vincent kept his eyes on Instaburger.

Dreg sniffed. "I don't smell anything." He took back the binoculars. "We should really wait for backup. What if the Sasquatches don't come?"

"Oh, they'll be here," Vincent said with confidence.

"If there is an army out there, how do we get into Instaburger without getting killed?"

Vincent looked up at the cloudless sky. The morning sun baked the landscape. Dreg wiped the sweat from his forehead.

"Contact Spekator. Have him transport us inside. We will end our war with Wyatt and subjugate the rest of the world."

Vincent pushed himself up and shouted with joy. "We are saved. Look, look over there." He pointed to the top of the ridge overlooking Copper Valley. Rows and rows of Sasquatches lined the top of the cliff. There were hundreds of them. Armed with pikes, they raised them and erupted with a mighty roar.

"It's time to call in the artillery! Contact Spekator and tell him to stand by for instructions."

Dreg fiddled with the communication device the Thalens had provided.

"Hurry!"

"I'm trying."

"What's wrong?" Vincent demanded.

"I can't get it to work. I think when you jammed everybody's phones, you did something to ours."

"Forget about it. We'll do this on our own."

CHAPTER 46

REUNITED AND IT FEELS SO GOOD

MELVIN RACED INTO the cave, barely breathing. Leaping over the dried-out husks of humanity, he stopped suddenly when the coyote leaped from the shadows.

Slow down. You don't want to scare her.

Melvin ignored them and continued his dash, knowing they followed.

He rounded a corner, running at full speed, and slammed into what he thought was a brick wall. He bounced off, hitting the side of the tunnel, the impact leaving him senseless for a long minute. Getting up, he crouched over, holding his knees, while he shook his head to clear it.

There in the center of the tunnel, where Jade hung suspended, locked in a glowing force field. She was frozen, her face horrified.

Melvin moved forward. "Jade!"

She was encased in a shimmering cloud, faint hints of purple and gold colors that danced in the air like oil on water. Melvin could barely breathe. Jade was here, in the flesh. He didn't imagine it. He kept repeating her name like a litany. All he saw was her familiar face, her hair, the shape of her body; the changes in her didn't register. "Jade, Jade, Jade, I knew you were alive."

"No, Mel, look away." She tried to hide her damaged face, but her hands moved slowly, if at all. She saw Melvin's eyes lock onto her new appendages. "No, Melvin, don't look at me. Leave. Let me die."

"Noooo," he replied. He moved around the forcefield, trying to find a way to rescue her.

The ground shook again. This time closer, it rumbled, and with his sensitive hearing, he could make out the sound of water rushing.

The coyote howled. *You have to leave, a great river is coming.*

Melvin ignored him. He reached out, touching the rippling surface, and was jolted back. He fell on his rear, winded, his ears ringing. "Who put you in here?"

"It's a long story."

The noisy rush of water was louder in his ears. "Vincent Konrad?"

"No." She shook her head. "Otto Enoch. He found me in the lagoon—" She glanced at the darkened end of the tunnel. "Is that water? Melvin, run. It sounds close—"

"Not without you." He rose and came nearer, his hands hovering over the spot where her arms were.

She moved slightly, raising her hands so they matched his. Their palms mirrored each other, and Melvin groaned. "I've missed you."

"I'm not me anymore. Look." She moved her robotic hand. It squealed against the pressure of the forcefield. "You thought I was dead. Remember me the way I was."

"Jade. You think that all I care about is how you look?"

"I'm a freak."

"So am I, and you loved me, like no one else—" Melvin was

distracted by the growl of the nearby coyote. He spun and ran toward a darkened corner of the passageway. Otto Enoch lay on the floor, his eyes gleaming in the darkness, holding a rectangular box close to his chest.

"We were so close, so close." Otto's body was covered with frost. It steadily crept up his neck. He blinked, his lashes coated with white flakes. "Saunders, is that you? Help me."

Melvin shook his head.

A line started to travel down Otto's midsection. He screamed. "Make it stop!"

"Too late." Melvin spied the box in his frozen hands and bolted toward it, but the coyote slammed into him, throwing him to the ground.

Let me go! Melvin screamed.

You'll die like him. The coyote answered.

I need the box.

You can't touch it. It's covered with foam. The coyote growled.

I don't care. Melvin rose.

From behind him, he heard Jade scream, "Don't you do it, Mel! I love you."

"That's it." He surged forward, grabbing the remote. His fingers burned. The coyote leaped up and grabbed the box in its mouth. It yelped, the frost beginning to spread from its mouth to his face. Saliva coated the remote, and the coyote fell, dropping the box.

It's safe now, Melvin. Its voice was feeble. *You and your woman are safe.*

Why? Melvin asked in a tight voice.

Protect Jade… as you asked. Mission accomplis— it said before the gray color spread over its body and its breath stilled.

Melvin sobbed, *Thanks, friend.* He rubbed his hands together briskly, allowing the circulation to warm them. His fingertips still tingled. He snatched up the dripping remote and asked,

"Do you know what to press?"

Jade shook her head ever so slightly, but her eyes opened wide. "Melvin!" she wailed. "Run!"

Melvin twisted to see a raging torrent of water racing down the tunnel.

He aimed the remote and pressed every button on it.

Jade spun in a circle toward the right, and water pooled around his feet. Melvin shook the remote and pressed another sequence. Jade flipped upside down.

"Leave before you die."

"Then we'll die together."

He hit the remote against his thigh, pressed all the buttons at once, and a high-pitched squeal ensued. Jade dropped to the floor. Melvin grabbed her, kissing her full on the lips. His nose poked the metal plate on her face, and they stared, drinking in the sight of each other.

He grabbed her by the hand and started running. Melvin laughed out loud. "Seems like old times, run Jade and morph with me!"

They raced together, their snouts elongating, their hands and legs stretching out to allow them to run as fast as their wolf bodies would take them.

They exited the tunnel, and Melvin churned up the earth as they mounted a hill. Morphing back at the same time, Melvin grabbed her in his arms and kissed her full on the lips. "I will never let you go. Not ever, Jade." They were both breathing hard.

Jade buried her face in his shoulder. "I'm not the same."

"You are to me. You're the Jade I loved in science class, the one who changed her life for me, and the one I would die for."

He kissed her robotic hand and whispered, "I love every part of you, every cell, and every nut and bolt. They are the same, and that will never change."

They stared at each other for a long minute, and Melvin said, "Let's go prove that werewolves, even robotic ones, are the best monsters alive."

CHAPTER 47

WHAT I'D DO FOR LOVE

KEISHA WATCHED HUNDREDS of Sasquatches amassed on the ridge surrounding Instaburger. "Oh no," She called Howard on the phone, but the call dropped. She tried again, but the phone didn't respond. "Something's interfering with the phones." Frustrated, she grabbed another phone and punched in Howard's number. "We have to help them. They're going to be overrun."

"I can't leave without an order, miss," the pilot told her.

Below them, troops were spread around the building. The lights were on in the restaurant, and Keisha knew Carter was alone inside. She spied Howard near the command center. She'd never mistake his slouchy posture and glasses that were alternately on his head or placed crookedly on his nose.

In the distance, she saw Melvin in werewolf form exiting the tunnel located under Monsterland. He was not alone. A smaller wolf limped along beside him. At one point, she watched him stop and lift the petite animal onto his back. She tried contacting him, but the phone wouldn't connect with him either. They were running from the tunnel and racing up the ridge behind the restaurant.

She heard a gurgle, followed by a roar, and the tunnel exploded with water. It flooded the roadway and was streaming toward Howard and the command tent.

"Take us down!" she ordered. "Now. They're going to be crushed by the oncoming flood!"

"I…"

"I said now," Keisha's eyes blazed.

The rotors began to spin, and the chopper lifted, rising above the ridge of the cliff where they hid.

The pilot made a downward movement, and a round, white craft zoomed in to block them from flying. It shot a penetrating light beam at the body of the chopper.

"What the hell is that?" the pilot shouted. He held up a hand to block the bright light.

"No idea." Keisha searched the ground for Howard, desperate to find him.

The pilot made an evasive maneuver, dipping and trying to go around the small ship.

The round craft darted in front of them. "That thing is fast. I can't move around it."

"You have to. We're the only air support they have."

The pilot reacted by twisting the joystick to avoid a collision. The round ship swung around and blocked them again. The helicopter veered in the opposite direction, but the UAP anticipated their every move.

"We have to tell them they're surrounded." Keisha's panicked face searched for Howard among the milling crowd. "Try again!"

This time, their eyes were pierced by a blinding light. It engulfed the helicopter, and it began a downward spiral. "Brace for impact!"

The chopper was abruptly turned sideways, and Keisha felt herself being pulled from her seat.

"Do something," she shouted.

She twisted to see the pilot struggling with the controls, his eyes bugging out of his head.

The ground spun before her eyes, and she knew with certainty they were going to crash. The chopper shook as if possessed. The door fell open, chilling her with a blast of air. She felt the harness holding her stretched to an impossible length, and she was lifted from the seat to hang sideways out the side of the chopper.

The ground looked like a blurred watercolor, she thought inanely. Keisha heard a groan, and she felt herself dropping, her long legs dangling.

She glanced down and saw the nylon of her harness shredding. There was a snap, and she felt herself fall forward. She grabbed for the side of the helicopter cabin, but her slippery fingers couldn't gain purchase. The world tilted, and she was falling. Closing her eyes, her stomach vaulted into her throat, and she fought the nausea that assailed her. Splaying her arms, she found the cushion of the rushing air a comfort. *Morph,* she told herself. *Anything?* But it was as if she had a mind block and couldn't concentrate. Wind tore at her face, and she knew she couldn't hear, but a weird sense of peace overcame her. She attempted to take deep breaths, but the wind wouldn't allow her. The world took on a dreamy quality, and she felt detached from the girl in free fall. It was as if it were happening to someone else.

The ground rushed up at her in a dizzying pace, but she felt no sense of urgency. There was simply nothing she could do. Time slowed, and her heartbeat pounded like a drum in her head. Inhaling sharply, she tried to find her inner strength, but all she saw was blankness.

Everything unfolded for Howard in real time. Keisha and her helicopter rose from the ridge like an avenging angel. "No, no, no. Not yet."

He looked to the left and saw the opposing ridge fill with

hundreds of Sasquatch. "They do exist!" he said to no one in particular, and finally, the rush of the water behind him made him realize they were in huge trouble. He reached for the phone and found that every signal was jammed. Communication was impossible.

A white circular object appeared out of nowhere and began to duel with the helicopter. His stomach churned when he realized the UAP had no plans of letting the aircraft go. Fascination was replaced by red, hot anger. It burned in his chest until he thought he would explode.

Howard had never felt such rage. His brain fizzled with it. They were going to hurt Keisha. He saw the copter duck, but the craft followed its every move. When a tractor beam shot out and turned the helicopter on its side, shaking it like a salt shaker, the veins in Howard's temple pulsed with a life of its own. The door opened, and he watched in horror as Keisha hung suspended and then was ejected into freefall.

She was going to die, smash into the ground, and break every bone in her body. "Morph, Keisha," he shouted, but the wind snatched his words away.

Howard's legs trembled; his entire body shook. He had to save her. *But how?*

He never learned how to morph. Keisha told him anybody could do it. It was easy. What had she said? *Breathe.* Keisha told him to breathe. What else? What else? His mind raced back to the day she explained. He wasn't interested. He didn't listen. *He should have listened!* Why didn't he think it was important? *Calm down,* he told himself. Think. Think. *Think. Think* like the animal he wanted to become. An eagle, no, too showy, too majestic. What else, a hawk? What did he know about hawks? Howard studied mythical creatures and cryptids; he needed something to outthink a hostile spacecraft.

He knew of only one creature who could save them now!

Closing his eyes, his hands fisted, he concentrated as never before. He allowed his imagination to soar, gave it wings, yes, *small bat-like wings.* Gritting his teeth, he put his brain into overdrive, imagining what they thought, felt, and smelled. He looked up. Keisha was falling, and he concentrated on her and the love he felt for her. He closed his mind to all the tumult around him and allowed himself to think like the creature that could save her.

Fur erupted all over his body. Wings sprouted from his back. Howard shouted with joy and took off as if he had been shot out of a cannon.

He sliced the air, holding out small but powerful arms.

Holy moly, he thought, science and everything he treasured took a back seat to the powerful feeling of flying through the air. He stopped to analyze it and felt himself jerking to a stop. *No,* he thought, concentrate on the beauty, rather than the science.

It didn't matter how it works; it just does. He zipped higher, intersecting with Keisha's body. They slammed together and continued to drop. Using his wings as a parachute, he slowed their descent. Kiesha opened her eyes and sighed, "Howard Drucker, a gremlin?"

"You were right, Keisha. Sometimes you can't analyze things; you just have to try and enjoy them."

They slowed as they landed. The helicopter spun out of sight, exploding on the other side of the ridge.

"We have to help," Keisha told him.

"I can't do this alone."

"Then let's do it together." Her skin reddened, turning scaly. A tail sprouted from her back, and as her neck elongated and her leather wings opened up,

Howard looked at her. And shouted, "Yeah, baby! Let's take down that alien motherf—"

With a roar, they took off for the round circular craft.

CHAPTER 48

SIZE MATTERS

ROSEMARY CAME TO her senses with a dizzying perspective. The room was not cavernous. She was no longer in a crate like a pet cat. She felt different, but she couldn't understand the how and why of it. The gigantic woman she remembered taking care of her hummed and bustled around the room. She appeared smaller now.

"My baby?" She attempted to rise, but the room spun around her.

"Snug and sleeping in the crate." The older woman pointed to a bundle that was swaddled near a roaring fire. "I'll get her for you." She picked up the baby, and Rosemary felt a rush of longing.

Rosemary held out her hands, and tears smarted her eyes when the bundle was placed in the cradle of her arms. "She's beautiful," she said, her voice filled with awe.

Parting the blanket, she marveled at the large, almond-shaped green eyes staring back at her. There was a dusting of light red hair on the pale skin. Long, slender fingers, six on each hand, reached out to clasp Rosemary. And then the baby cooed. Rosemary felt her heart melt.

"She's one of us now," The older woman said. "As you are. There's no going back."

"I don't understand."

She turned, and Rosemary noted they were eye-to-eye. "She's sleeping, the little one. You gave us quite the scare."

Rosemary shifted. She was sore all over, particularly in her lower stomach. She peeked under the blanket and saw a bandage covering her midsection. Her body felt weighted with a sticky residue. She reached down, and the woman stopped her. "Don't touch it, dear. We need to get the rest off of you."

The woman took the baby and placed her back in the crate. Grillos entered carrying a tub. He was followed by a trio of women, each with a jug filled with water.

"Where do you want this, Ma?"

Rosemary looked up, her eyes opening wide with surprise. The first shock was when she realized she was of a similar size to the other giants in the room. The second was the realization that this was Grillos's mother.

"Ma?" she asked.

"Yes, Rose, this is my mother. She saved your life?"

"How?"

There was a rumble of something underground. They all stopped and exchanged concerned looks.

"An earthquake?" Grillos's mother asked.

Grillos shook his head. "I don't think so. I'll send Zaf to investigate."

The women busied themselves emptying water into the basin. Grillos's mother shooed them from the room.

Grillos paused by the crate and touched the baby; his gaze

softened. Watching him look at her baby caused Rosemary's heart to flip just then.

"Grillos! I thought you said you were going to tell Zaf to check out that explosion. Rosemary must bathe the slime off of her before she grows too big for even us." She waved Grillos from the room.

"Call me, Maude." She placed her hands on her ample hips. "Lucky for you, I am used to difficult deliveries. The baby was about to burst from your abdomen."

Rosemary placed her hands over a bandage on her lower stomach. "Burst?"

"Yes, I've seen it happen once before," she said, her face grim. "Many years ago, we rescued a Gray alien when her ship had crashed in the desert. We tried to help her, but once the baby exploded from her stomach, we couldn't save either of them."

"Oh my." Rosemary covered her mouth.

"Indeed." Maude shook her head in agreement. "You're too small, your belly was expanding at an astonishing rate. The only way to save you was to roll you in the snail slime."

"Grillos told me not to touch it when we were running through the tunnels."

"Yea. We discovered that exposure to the slime signals the gland up here—" she pointed to the center of her head just above her eyebrows.

"You mean the pituitary gland?"

"Yea, that's what minkins call it. The slime triggers rapid cell expansion and overproduces growth hormones. It is forbidden to go anywhere near the snails or their slime."

"How do you know—"

"Our ancestors didn't know, and our clan kept growing until we figured it out. We've dedicated all of our resources to making each generation smaller. Grillos told me you met my granddaughters."

"Yes, lovely girls."

Maude sighed. "Yea. I had hoped one of them would take an

interest—" she paused. "You see, I am the midwife here. I wanted one of the girls to follow in my footsteps."

"Danai is learning nursing—"

"Is that so?" Maude said with a smile. "I don't care if they learn it here or there." She pointed to the ceiling. "As long as they find a calling."

Rosemary opened and closed her hands. "If I wash it off—"

"You'll remain this size."

"My baby?"

"I covered her with the slime as soon as she was born. She will be like us. Big, I mean. She is mostly you, but I do see a bit of the Grays in her." Maude sat on the edge of the bed. "I'm sorry, it was the only way to keep you from dying."

"I understand. But—"

"There'll be plenty of time for questions later. We must wash the slime off. Be careful of the stitches. I don't want them to break."

Rosemary peeked under the bandage. "What kind of stitches are these?"

"Fungai strands. Tough but flexible. They will dry out in hours and adhere to the skin. You'll be back to your pirate ways in no time." Maude smiled. "Only I'm afraid you won't find a ship to fit your size anymore."

Rosemary frowned, and Maude continued. "No worries. I think my Grillos would build you a new one to see your pretty smile."

Maude helped Rosemary wash off the slime. She then provided her with new clothes, as her old ones appeared to be doll-sized. Next, Maude placed a tray on Rosemary's lap, and the aroma of soup made her stomach growl. "You must eat. You have a lot of empty spaces to fill," she said with a laugh. She turned to look at the doorway. "I see you there, Grillos. Let her rest."

Rosemary looked up shyly. "Grillos is nearby?"

"He hasn't left that doorway since he brought you there." She smiled. "I have never seen him this way about anybody before."

Rosemary finished the soup and lay down, exhausted. "Can I see him?"

"Grillos," Maude called. "She wants to see you."

Maude left Rosemary and the sleeping infant. Grillos came in and sat on the chair next to her bed.

"I—"

"Stop," Grillos said. "Rosemary, I'm sorry if we changed you without permission, but I couldn't lose you." He wiped a tear from his eye.

"No, I wanted to thank you. I… I can't explain it, but I was afraid that I'd never be able—"

Grillos interrupted her, "Rosemary, I love you and want you and the baby to be my family."

"Grillos, she's not of your world."

"She is now. I accept her as mine, and so will the clan. Say you'll stay with me, Rosemary mine."

"I thought you'd never ask."

Grillos bent over to kiss her, and the floor rumbled with another explosion. Grillos ran to the doorway and heard shouts from his clan. Maude rushed in and yelled, "We have to get out of here. Zaf has reported that the tunnels are filling with water! We must get above and out!"

"Water? From where?" Grillos asked.

"Zaf said from under Monsterland. That madman is trying to drown us."

Grillos wrapped Rosemary in a quilt while Maude grabbed the baby, and they ran from the room.

"Hold her, too." Maude shoved the baby into Grillos's arms.

"Ma!" Grillos roared. "Where are you going?"

"Our Holiest of Holies. I must save the book." She disappeared behind a doorway and a minute later emerged with a crossbody bag hung over her shoulder. Grillos watched it flap against his mother's hip as they ran from the caves.

CHAPTER 49

DEAD MAN'S TALES

WYATT TRIED TO contact Howard on the phone they were using for communication. *Nothing.* He pressed Melvin's number. He failed to answer. Looking up toward the ravine, he whispered, "Melvin?" Running up the side of the hill were an auburn werewolf, followed by a smaller, lighter-haired one.

There was no sign of Howard anywhere. Even the helicopter with Keisha had disappeared over the other side of the ridge.

"What the h——." Glancing to the other side of the valley, he saw an army of beasts lining the ridge. Tall, brown, and furry, they looked like overweight bears. Only he knew they weren't bears. Wyatt squinted; each had to be over seven feet tall. Howard would have called them bipedal, Wyatt thought inanely. *Freaking Bigfoot took this minute to make themselves known!*

Swallowing hard, he searched for Yerbol, but he couldn't find anyone. Carter was in the restaurant and completely isolated.

Wyatt sucked in a breath. Two figures separated from the cluster of trees to scoot down the hill. Wyatt recognized Dreg immediately. He blinked. The tall, loping dude had a violet face. He'd know that mug anywhere. Vincent Konrad had taken the bait. He attempted to call Carter. The phone was completely useless.

Carter, he thought. *He won't know they're coming!*

Wyatt was near the building, crouched low behind a trash bin. He heard the rotors of the helicopter and glanced up.

The chopper crested the mountain top, and out of nowhere, a circular craft appeared and blocked its movement. A blue beam shot from the alien craft, seizing the helicopter, causing it to twist and flip over. Wyatt watched as a door snapped open and Keisha dangled from the cockpit.

He glanced around, calling quietly for Yerbol, but received no answering reply. The air filled with the sound of roaring rapids, and Wyatt searched for the source. *What now?* The road from Monsterland was flooding with a river of water, and Wyatt watched as it knocked over their meager defense troops.

"Yerbol, where are you? Yerbol?" He looked back at the restaurant and couldn't see Vincent or Dreg. He had to do something, or the rushing water would sweep away Carter.

Running to the building, he slipped through a broken window.

"Wyatt?" He heard Carter whisper urgently. "Get down!"

When his eyes adjusted to the dim lighting, he saw Carter hidden behind a barrier of tables, his rifle poking through an opening. He darted across the room and slipped behind the barrier.

"What are you doing here? I told you to stay away."

"Something happened to our network. Nobody's communicating. A flood is coming this way. You have to get out."

"Wyatt, leave. It's not safe!"

They were on their knees in the darkened room. Wyatt's eyes shone in the dark. "I'm not leaving without you."

"It's not safe. Vincent is—"

A gunshot rent the air.

Wyatt's eye went wide. He pitched forward into Carter's arms, blood seeping from a wound in his back.

"No!" Carter shouted, holding Wyatt's body. "Wyatt!" He held Wyatt's face and couldn't tell if he was breathing. Blood stained Carter's shirt. "I'll kill you for this!"

"I don't think so." Vincent fired a round, Carter ducked instinctively, covering Wyatt's body with his own. "Let's end this farce," Vincent stepped through the doorway, a strange-looking gun in his arms.

Yerbol slammed into the room, followed by his ever-present trio of troops. Vincent turned and opened fire, hitting Yerbol in the shoulder. One of his troops sank to the floor.

The commando had collapsed near Yerbol's feet. Yerbol fell to his knees, his arm held out.

Everyone's attention went to the fallen soldier. His body shook, his skin turned a mottled green. The face morphed, the eyes narrowed, the nose became a duo of reptilian slits, and with a last shudder, green blood pooled around him as he died.

"Well, well, well, what have we got here?" Vincent walked over and kicked the reptilian with his foot.

The room and everyone in it slowed, and from above them Wyatt watched in astonishment. *The commandos were aliens.* He shook his head. He and Howard always thought there was something odd about those three. You couldn't warm up to them.

Wyatt peered at Yerbol, wondering if he was one, too. He moved closer, but the people below him didn't flinch. In fact, they barely moved.

Carter's face was wet with tears that trickled oh, so slowly. Vincent Konrad seemed to move in slow motion. Their voices were off, too. Wyatt knew that he understood them, but they spoke as if underwater. *Maybe the flood had arrived.* He checked the floor, but it was dry. For that matter, how come he was floating so high above them all?

The back of his neck tingled, and he felt a presence. Wyatt spun so fast he did a three-sixty. The room dipped and swayed, and when his vision returned to normal, he saw two hazy figures watching him. He moved closer. Their faces were glowing in a light so beautiful that it was almost painful to look at.

Wyatt raised a hand to deflect the illumination, but the female reached out and gently took his hand. His heart jumped; He knew her.

"Mom?" Wyatt closed his eyes, feeling weak, overcome by an emotion he couldn't explain. When he opened them, his father came into view, whole and healthy. "Dad," he cried. "What are you doing here?"

"We could ask the same question of you." His mom's voice was a gentle caress.

Wyatt stared at her lips. He heard every word, but they didn't come from her mouth.

"You didn't listen to Carter. He told you to stay back." She was smiling. "You came to save him. I guess you could say I can die happy, now."

Wyatt gasped.

"Sorry, son. That's a bit of graveyard humor. It was unfair, but I have to say your actions speak loudly about your feelings." She took his hand, and Wyatt stepped forward.

"Not funny! Not at all!" Wyatt yelled. He studied his parents. "You're together?"

"Of course, we're a family."

"You have to go back. You must save them," Frank told him.

Wyatt looked back at his parents. "I want to stay. We'd be whole again."

His mother laughed. "A pleasant thought, but how can we do it without Sean… and Carter. He's a part of us now."

"True, but, but, but—" Wyatt searched for words.

"No buts. You have more to do."

Frank placed his hand on Wyatt's chest. "Not your time, you have to go back."

"I don't want to." He looked at his father, who was young and healthy. "Why? Why did you leave us?"

His father ignored the question. "You still have a purpose. Besides, Sean and Carter— they need you."

He felt the gentle caress of a kiss on his cheek, and they were gone. Wyatt looked down. Carter had buried his face in Wyatt's chest. Carter's weapon was missing.

Yerbol stared at his troops, his face a mask of horror. The other commandos' guns were pointed at the Yerbol.

Ever so slowly, Vincent was inching toward Carter. His back was completely exposed. Vincent's gun moved into position to fire.

"Go back, son." He heard his father's voice.

Wyatt paused. "But I have so many questions."

"Everything will be answered." His father appeared once more. He looked over his shoulder at Vincent and Carter. "It's now or never."

Wyatt's eyes met his dad's. He glanced back at Carter. He knew what he had to do. He let himself fall. The air rushed around him, and it was as if he was being sucked backward into a vacuum.

Wyatt opened his eyes and screamed, "Watch out!" Pulling Carter's handgun from his holster, Wyatt fired at Vincent and missed. Vincent laughed, took aim, and fell to his knees, a startled expression on his face.

The door burst open. A group of four soldiers fired rounds, taking down the reptilian troops and Dreg before they could shoot back.

Colonel Drucker entered, followed by Nate Owens.

Vincent's eyes glazed, a scalpel protruding from his back.

"I knew it was you." Dreg's voice was thready. "I've killed him, Nate. I did it for you."

Nate rushed over to cradle his dying father. "Why?"

"You're a sight for sore eyes." Dreg reached up to touch his son's cheek.

"What were you thinking?" Nate whispered.

"For you. It was all for you." Dreg gurgled once, and his eyes closed forever.

Vincent staggered to his feet, laughing evilly. Picking up his weapon, he fired a round, taking out the unsuspecting troops. "You can't kill me." He loped around the room, the scalpel sticking out of his back. "Thinking of shooting me? I'm immortal. You can't kill me." His hands slapped the polyethene body. "This stuff is indestructible!" He reached behind and pulled the scalpel from his shoulder blade. "Now, I will finish the job I started for once and for all.

CHAPTER 50

TURNCOATS

OLREC WATCHED THE action from his spot on the mountain ridge. They hid in the bushes, their numbers increasing as clans from all over the region joined them. He saw his cousins from Tennessee, New Jersey, and even the Canadian Rockies, their hair whiter than his.

"Well, which way should we go?" Kokkus asked.

"I'm not sure," he murmured. Shots were being fired in the building that served terrible food. It was located in the center of a valley, surrounded by hills on either side.

Looking up, Olrec recognized the round craft of the Grays. Water was flooding the valley, washing away the *stupe* troops. Olrec waffled between staying and packing his tribe to head for the mountains. The responsibility of all the different tribes weighed heavily on him. *What if he misread the situation?* Maybe they should have picked a side, but which side? He wasn't sure whom to trust. "This place is a mess, both above and below." He gnashed his teeth. "Let them all kill each other and—"

"Look, giants!" Zilli shouted.

Giants poured from the tunnel entrance, followed by gushing torrents of water. They raced up the sides of the valley, holding their belongings. The largest giant held a wrapped bundle in his arms.

Olrec's mouth opened when he saw large but delicate female feet dangling from the quilt engulfing her. The male directed his people to safety on the opposite side of the valley. Olrec cursed. He hated giants.

The giant's voice carried far; he shouted four names, ordering them to break off a piece of the rock outcropping on the outside of the tunnel.

A group of identical red-haired giants chipped away, one with another stone, the other three with their bare fists. A chunk of rock separated, and the four pushed it toward the opening of the tunnel. The sun beat down, turning their faces the same bright red as their hair. They heaved the boulder, their muscles straining until they were able to plug the entrance of the tunnel. The water stopped gushing from the passageway, and they could hear the giants cheer.

His cub, Marem, came up next to him and said, "They've stopped the flooding. Do you think they'll eat the *stupes* now?"

"Probably," Kokkus answered.

"Zilli, take the cubs away. I don't want them to see—-"

To his astonishment, the giants began to pull the dazed troops from the water, helping them to safer ground. Cradling six to ten *stupes,* they carried them into the hills. Some of the female giants created fires for the *stupes* to dry. There was laughter and a camaraderie that puzzled and surprised Olrec.

"Why aren't they eating the *stupes?*" Logu slid between the legs of the crowd surrounding Olrec to stand next to his father.

"Why aren't you with your mom in the rear?" He ruffled the hair on his cub's head.

"This is history," Zilli was back, beside him, along with Marem. "When you said they were joking and talking to a human female, I didn't believe you. Look at them! Who knew they were capable of this kind of behavior?"

A roar from the crowd drew Olrec's attention to the sky. A fierce, red dragon, followed by a furry beast Olrec didn't recognize, flew into view. They were pursued by the Gray's circular, round ship.

"Look!" The Mophat pointed at the creatures in the sky. "What is that thing?"

"I believe it's a gremlin," Kokkus said.

"A gremlin!" the Mophat shouted. "I've heard about them, but nobody has ever been able to get a picture of one. They are known to bedevil the *stupes* by eluding them."

The Sasquatch all looked at each other and started to laugh. "Dumb *stupes!* They're surrounded by creatures they can't seem to see, even though they're right in front of their faces," Logu said.

"The *stupes* are going to have a field day with this one!" Olrec choked out.

The round, white ship followed the dragon and furry creature circling in front of them. There was a collective sound of awe when a blue laser shot out and singed the dragon's tail.

The dragon screamed in pain, and the gremlin started to spin, its face a mask of rage. The little creature blew on the burnt part of the dragon's tail, while its little bat-like wings fanned furiously. Teeth bared, the gremlin took off after the ship and landed on the very top of the craft. They could hear high-pitched growling mixed with cackles that made Logu move closer to his father. "What's a gremlin, Pa?" he asked.

"Watch. Watch. You'll find out in a minute," Olrec answered.

The gremlin scuttled up, hugging the side of the ship.

"It's crawling like a rat!" Logu's nervousness disappeared, and he grinned, enjoying the show.

"It's looking for an opening," Kokkus observed.

They watched as its sharp little eyes hunted for a way into the ship. The dragon lifted its rectangular snout, nudging it higher.

"The dragon is its friend," Marem shouted. "Whose side are we on, Pa? Do we want

the dragon and the grem, grem—"

"Gremlin," his brother supplied.

"Gremlin to win, or do we want what's inside that ship to be the victor?"

Olrec watched the action in the sky. He glanced down at the giants helping the *stupes*. Scratching his chin, he saw that Kokkus was waiting for his reply. "I'm not sure yet, son. We... I haven't decided yet."

The dragon blew a controlled flame on the wall of the craft. Soon, a crater appeared.

"Look! The dragon is helping the gremlin inside the Gray's ship," the Mophat called.

With a salute, the gremlin crawled inside. Groups of Sasquatches on the ground cheered mightily. They jumped and hooted with appreciation. The gremlin poked its head out and winked saucily at them.

The dragon moved away to create some distance for the craft.

Within minutes, pieces of the ship flew out from the hole made by the dragon. The spaceship spun wildly. There was a *crank*, followed by a *clunk*. An oblong-shaped object emerged from the crater held by four furry fingers. The gremlin lifted itself out with a snicker. Its tiny wings worked overtime, and the dragon passed by so it could jump on its back.

The two took off toward the hills, the snickers of the gremlin following them. They paused and, to the delight of the crowd below, did a graceful aerial move.

"They're showing off," Zilli said with a smirk.

The spaceship zigged and zagged across the clearing, smoke coming from multiple spots along its sleek sides. It gyrated until it dropped several feet to land in a heap on the wet ground. There were several pops and whines until the blue lights faded and went out.

The creatures continued their aerial antics, the gremlin's laughter filling the skies until the dragon stopped abruptly, as if it had run into a solid object. The dragon's head wobbled, its eyes rolled, and a puff of smoke exited its nostrils. The two beasts plummeted to the ground, disappearing on the other side of the valley.

The crowd gasped, and Logu asked, "What happened?"

"Not sure." Olrec scanned the sky for an answer.

"Do we go yet?" Kokkus asked him.

"Not yet. Not until I know what's going on—" Olrec's voice trailed off.

"When then, Olrec. If you make a mistake—"

"You doubt me now?" Olrec demanded. His demeanor had changed. For the first time,

Olrec answered his brother-in-law.

Kokkus's jaw dropped. "I… I..,"

"Be quiet, brother. Can you see Olrec is thinking?"

Olrec considered the giants on the other side of the valley. He watched the empty parking lot, knowing *stupes* were in the restaurant and allied with the giants. With sudden clarity, he knew which side to take. He made his decision.

Olrec began to descend the hill when a metal, cigar-shaped vehicle dropped out of the sky and landed in a cloud of dust. Pneumatic door opened, and reptiles poured out of the craft.

"Lizards!" Olrec yelled. He placed his hands in front of his cubs to stop them from going further.

The door to the restaurant creaked open. A male appeared in the doorway holding a younger *stupe*. Blood stained the younger *stupe's* shirt and dripped down his arm, leaving a red trail in the dirt. Three others walked out, followed by a magenta-hued male.

"Dr. Vincent Konrad," Olrec murmured.

"Should we go down now?" the Mophat whispered. "That is Dr. Konrad, the Watcher?"

Olrec shook his head. "I am not quite sure I believe he is a Watcher. We must bide our time—"

"Bide our time! We must declare or die!" Kokkus's face reddened.

Konrad waved a greeting to the lizards. He lined up his prisoners near the cigar-shaped alien ship. "Welcome, Scalis." He bowed his head. "I am Dr. Vincent Konrad, and I present you with these humans as a goodwill gift."

A lizard wearing a shiny jacket stepped forward. He pointed to the circular ship, and everyone watched as the door slid open.

"Thalens!" Vincent looked flustered.

The lizard commander roared an order, and the other reptiles raced to the Thalen ship, surrounding it and pointing long-barreled weapons at it.

Eight Gray beings descended from the entrance. Dazed, they shielded their large, almond-shaped eyes from the bright sunlight. The lizards towered over them, dragging them roughly from the steps into the craft.

One of the Grays passed Vincent Konrad and paused. He gave him a disgusted look. "I see we shouldn't have trusted you, Doctor Konrad."

"Trust builds solid relationships. Surely you didn't believe we had a strong alliance. I didn't betray you, I just never committed to you."

Kokkus whispered, "We could have walked right into this. You were right to tell us to wait."

Olrec took a deep breath. He looked at Kokkus. "Do you value my judgement now?"

"Yes, Olrec. I am truly sorry I doubted you in the past. What should we do?"

"I cannot put our lives in that…that *creature's* hands. He is diabolical." He pointed to Vincent Konrad. "See how he has deceived the Grays?"

"Then who should we align with? If we had gone with Konrad, he'd have given us to the lizards. The Grays are useless. Should we go back and hide in our villages?"

"It will be a matter of time before they find us. We must pick the winner… and then make them win."

There was a long silence, and a strange humming filled the valley. The lizards doubled over, covering the holes they called ears. The air shimmered between the two spacecraft, and a rainbow of colors appeared. It solidified into a golden bucket shape with beautiful, painted flames adorning its sides. The door opened, and horns blared. A procession of aliens descended, leading the way for a statuesque female wearing a purple robe and a crown of shining stones, who stepped down.

There was a collective gasp from the Sasquatches that echoed throughout the valley.

Olrec snorted with laughter and pointed at the new strangers. "Them. We side with them!"

His tribe murmured prayers of thanks; many, including the Mophat, fell to their knees. "We are saved, just as the legend says! The queen has arrived. Our savior!" the Mophat cried.

The crowd echoed his words. "We are saved. They have come. Finally!"

Several of the lizards attempted to aim their weapons at the newcomers. The new aliens aimed small rectangular boxes at the lizards. The lizard's guns melted in their hands, scalding and disarming them simultaneously.

The leader of the Grays pointed his long, spindly finger and yelled, "Va'Rok!"

CHAPTER 51

THE END OF THE ROAD

"I'LL KILL YOU!" Rosemary's face was twisted with anger. She raced from the brush where she'd been hiding, ignoring the trio of aliens in the parking lot.

The Va'Rok raised their weapons, and the queen halted them. "Allow," she said imperiously.

Rosemary went straight for her father, screaming a war cry. Barefoot and dressed in homespun, she towered over the group gathering in front of the spacecrafts. She reached down to grab Vincent by the neck. His head spun in a circle and unscrewed. He snatched his head from her grasp and ran away.

"No, no, listen to me," he shouted. "I had such plans for you and the child!"

"I don't want you anywhere near my baby! She's Rosemary's baby and don't you forget it!"

The ground trembled. Six identical red-haired giants scattered to capture Vincent, who was nimby evading them.

"She's Grillos's baby, too!" Grillos bellowed.

Rosemary glanced at Maude, who held the newborn in her arms, and nodded with appreciation. She straightened to her new height of just under twenty feet. "You'll never exploit me again!"

"I never meant to take advantage. I was saving the world for you and—" Vincent was adjusting his head back onto his neck.

The lizards turned their attention to Rosemary. The leader spoke excitedly, his mouth drooling in anticipation of a great catch, regardless of the new aliens who had appeared in control. They reached into their tunics to aim new weapons directly at her chest. Vincent Konrad ran in front of them, screaming, "No!"

Vincent Konrad took a consolidated hit from all their guns, making him fly backward to land in a heap at her feet.

The Va'Rok queen held her own troops from firing.

"Why did she allow that?" Logu asked, aghast.

"Perhaps she wants to see the true measure of the giants," Olrec whispered.

"True measure, oh Pa, you made a joke!" Loug laughed.

"*Shhh*, watch." They turned their attention to the giants and aliens.

Rosemary reached over and tore a Joshua Tree up by its roots and swung it like a baseball bat, knocking down half the lizards in one fell swoop. Zaf hefted two more lizards in each hand, spun around, and tossed them like footballs. They landed with a dull thud on the other side of the parking lot.

Five other giants skidded to a halt, the shortest one pointed to hundreds of creatures lining the top of the hill. He yelled, "Sasquatches! Run for your lives!"

"Pa!" Marem exclaimed. "They're afraid of us!"

Olrec's eyes widened. They *were* afraid of them. *Perhaps they did get it wrong!* It was time to make themselves known.

Olrec took this moment to descend from the ridge, his tribe and the combined groups from all over the region tailed after him. They bowed before the new aliens.

The old Mophat came forward on trembling legs. He shook his staff, the pinecones rattling, creating a hush over the valley. He fell to his knees, his hairy arms spread wide. "Are you the Watchers come to save us from the scourges surrounding us?" He peeked out, his eyes wary of the giants. He shook his staff again, smirking with surprise when the giants cowered.

Olrec observed the new aliens. He recognized them and found comfort in their familiar faces. He could see that there were slight differences between them. They were taller and had less hair covering their bodies. Their orbital ridges were smaller, more defined. He studied them, a gasp escaping his lips; there was a slight hint of *stupe* about them. He wondered if everyone else saw it as well.

"Well done, Rosemary." Vincent Konrad's shaky voice broke the silence. "You knocked them down like a champion. What happened?" He shook his purple head.

He began to rise, but Rosemary put her bare foot upon his chest, holding him down. "Why would you care?"

"The child?"

"None of your business." She folded her arms and stared down at the Va'Rok. "We seem to have some sort of impasse here. If you attempt any violence, we will crush your ship, and you will be stranded here."

The queen eyed Rosemary, a smile on her lips. "You act as though we are enemies. You speak for everyone?" She gestured to the various species scattered throughout the restaurant's parking lot. She peered at Rosemary and said. "You are not a giant by nature, I think?"

"I am a giant by choice!" she declared.

The giants hooted in agreement.

"I ask you again. Do you speak for everyone?" the queen asked graciously.

Rosemary looked to Grillos, who nodded. Each of the brothers placed their hands on the alien ships dwarfing them. President Nate Owens walked over. "Go ahead, Madam Ambassador."

"I speak for the giants and humans. Who do you speak for?" Rosemary looked at the

swarms of Sasquatches surrounding the queen's ship.

"Brothers and sisters. It's so good to see you again." The queen's bell-like voice rang out across the valley.

Grillos moved protectively in front of Rosemary. Howard Drucker, a tuft of gremlin hair still on his neck, arrived with Keisha. One of her pants legs was scorched. They sat on the ground next to Wyatt, who was barely conscious.

Melvin and Jade trotted down from the mountainside. As they walked, Jade morphed back to her human robotic form. She boldly approached the Va'Rok and blurted. "You call yourselves the Watchers? I know about you. Otto Enoch told me."

The Sasquatches murmured. Some yelled, and one or two fainted. "We've been waiting for you," Olrec shouted.

"Indeed." The Va'Rok queen bowed her head and responded to Jade, "Enoch, yes. He wrote many books about us."

Jade laughed. "Not that Enoch. He lived thousands of years ago. Are you angels?" Jade asked suspiciously as she walked around the queen, who allowed it.

The Va'Rok tittered, but the queen responded, "Hardly, my dear. Although some of your kind called us thus."

"Why?"

"Because they couldn't explain us any other way. We are not of your world."

"No kidding," Melvin said.

The queen gestured to her ship. "And you once defined our craft as a fiery chariot." She smiled benignly.

"Otto said that the Watchers were angels sent to watch over humanity." Jade stood in front of the queen, meeting her eyes.

"We were invited here originally to protect you from your

savage ways and wild imagination. You humans are the original species on this planet." Some of the Sasquatches cried out in response to this information, but the queen ignored them and went on. "Unfortunately, humans affected us in many ways we were not prepared for." She smiled devilishly.

"How?" Jade asked.

"We took on your customs. Forgot about loyalty, devotion, and discipline. We broke universal laws." She stared at the Thalens, her brows lowered in anger. "Rules we were *all* honor-bound to respect. We mated with humans and then turned on our poor offspring." She looked at the giants with pity and remorse.

"Oh, no!" Olrec shouted. "You're not telling me—"

"Yes, sad to say," The queen looked disconsolate. "You are our direct descendants, and the giants are the Nephilim. They are offspring of our forbidden union with humanity."

Shocked murmurs filled the valley. The giants moved closer to hear.

"It was dark days, we taught our children, the giants forbidden things. Gave them weapons, sorcery, magic—"

Grillos's mother pushed through the crowd. She wore a cloth bag as a crossbody. Reaching in, she pulled out an old, tattered book. "You are saying that you are the authors of our book?"

All the giants except for Rosemary fell to the ground, trembling.

"Ma! You hold the Holist of Holies!" Grillos held his hand in front of his face. "It's forbidden!"

"Get up. Protect your woman!" she ordered. "Someone had to save it from the floods."

The queen reached out and asked, "The book you will learn is the same for everybody. It holds all the truths in the entire universe."

Maude held the book close to her chest. "It is ours and ours alone! The Holiest of Holies!"

The queen bowed her head. "You are right to protect it, but it does belong to us all. Whether the tradition is oral—" She looked at the Sasquatches. "Or written, however it's been recorded, the words belong to the stars."

"And we are made of stars!" Howard Drucker yelled.

"Indeed. We are all made of starlight, bound by the same energy that gave us life. These words, this book is a gift from the cosmos and belongs to every heart, every being, from every world." She gave a stern look to the Thalens. "The book set down the laws of the land from thousands of years ago, before the first flood on your planet. It tells our story. All of the truths of our combined history." She moved toward the Sasquatch. "You understand that you are our descendants. Transplanted from our home many years ago to help nurture humans, show them the way. The Intergalactic Council invited us to help develop this planet to join the Federation. We came here to educate, help you understand the universe." She pointed to the giants. "Nephilim, children of our children. You are the product of the relationships. The Intergalactic Council saw that we had broken the laws. They sent a mighty flood, forcing us to leave, but we held on to hope for you. As time passed, each subsequent generation of Nephilim grew increasingly larger. You lived together, but—" Her eyes grew fierce, and the Sasquatch shrank from their heat. "Sasquatch, you forgot our beliefs, the tenets of our society. You refused to share the great bounty of this land. You gave names to what you didn't understand or tolerate. Monsters!" she spat the word with venom. "Soon, you began to fight among yourselves. You, mighty Sasquatch, were forced to the hills; you abandoned your cousins, the werewolves, and you, my children, were sent underground, and like the vampires, were forced to live in the dark. And you," she pointed to the humans, "Never knew the truth of your world. You held yourselves above all others. You forgot that everything is interconnected. Whatever happens to the earth happens to all of you! You, a human, did not create and weave the tapestry of life; here, you are merely a part of it. Whatever you do to the tapestry, you do to yourselves."

"Are you saying that we all spring from each other? We are acorns from the same tree." Olrec asked, his voice shocked.

"Yes, Olrec. We have watched you. You are an acorn directly from my tree. You are my son of sons, my prince."

Kokkus stood up next to Olrec, hoping to be acknowledged, but the queen ignored him.

Vincent got to his feet shakily. "Then what is all this nonsense about dividing up this end of the universe. Why are you competing with the Thalens and Scalis?"

"There is no Intergalactic Treaty dividing this planet. It has always belonged to Va'Rok. It holds our descendants. Like thieves in the night, the Thalens and Scali have raided our resources. They snuck in under our noses, stealing and corrupting. We had been banished and not permitted to retaliate until now. The ban has finally been lifted."

"How do we know you're telling the truth?" Vincent demanded.

"You don't. But it doesn't matter. Your days are numbered on this planet."

"Why? I only sought to save it." Vincent pointed to Rosemary. "My daughter will rule."

"With my child!" Spekator announced with a smirk. "She bore my daughter, a new hybrid."

"I am your daughter by genetic mistake, and so is my daughter. I owe you both nothing," Rosemary stated. "You invited the Grays for your own warped perceptions, and they came to enrich themselves. Who made you both judge and jury of all the species here?"

"The Thalens promised to help. They understood me. This planet is stretched beyond its capacity."

"They lie, just like you, to achieve their means." Rosemary looked at Vincent and Spekator with contempt.

"Your daughter speaks the truth. This planet is a planet of renewal. It is constantly changing and growing. It doesn't need you, Vincent Konrad. You are the exploiter, not the savior. It's time for you to leave Vincent Konrad." The queen raised her hand. The valley was filled with a strange humming. Vincent was pulled forward. He whooped and screamed, but the force yanked him to the center of the space. A gelatinous cloud formed around him, like a giant soap bubble. Vincent balled his fists against the rainbow-colored walls, but he couldn't break through. It began a slow ascent into the sky. "Rosemary, Rosemary, save me," he called, but soon his voice started to fade.

Rosemary moved next to Grillos. He placed his arm around her shoulders, and she watched as her father drifted higher and higher. "What will happen to him?" she asked.

"He will circle the Earth's orbit forever."

"What happens to us?" Rosemary called out.

The queen directed her soldiers to round up the Thalens and Scalis that still breathed and prodded them onto their ship. "You must make peace with each other."

"How can we all be so different?" Olrec asked.

"The best way to make peace with each other is not to expect them to be like you. You must all learn to live together in harmony or perish standing on your differences." She smiled and inclined her head regally.

"Queen! Queen! What shall we call you?" Howard Drucker called out.

"Serafera, my name is Queen Serafera." She moved through the crowd that parted. Serafera stood before Olrec, towering above him. Placing her hand on his head, she said, "Olrec, son of my sons, Olrec of the Sierre Mountains, you will lead the way." She threw a dirty look at Kokkus and continued, "You're kindness and patience will serve as a beacon to promote peace with your brothers, the giants and humans."

She walked toward Grillos and held out her hands. He crouched low, gently touching her. "Fruit of our unions, it is up to you to unite the species. Your combined love and experience will give people the confidence to follow your leadership."

She then approached the cluster of humans. A falcon and a crow flew from the trees to land on her shoulders. "Hello, my friends!" she cooed. Minutes later, Lily and her uncle John Raven transformed to bow before her.

"Sky Mother, we have waited for your return for a long time," John Raven said reverently.

"Yes, you have kept my story alive, with some variations," she laughed.

"Thank you for giving us life," Lily whispered.

"It is your story that I gave you life, but we made life together. Protect our children, the giants."

"Indeed, Mother." John Raven stood, Lily by his side.

Queen Serafera stood before Wyatt, his feverish eyes looking up at her. His face was pale, his hair matted to his sweaty head. She bent low, and her cool hand brushed the strands from his face.

"It is said in our book that, 'The wolf lives with the lamb, the leopard will lie down with the goat, the calf and the lion and the yearling together, and a little child will lead them.' Do you understand what that means?"

"Your highness," Carter interrupted her. He was on the ground, holding Wyatt in his arms. "We must get him to a doctor."

"Forgive me." She snapped her fingers. Another Va'Rok came forward and stopped in front of the queen. He made a face and muttered, "I'm a healer, not a mechanic. He has primitive metal projectiles in him!" He was carrying an iridescent satchel.

"And a healer can heal all." The queen inclined her head. "Make him better."

"You should lay him flat," the healer told Carter.

"I'll hold him." Carter's face was set.

"I don't have time to argue with you." He looked at the queen and said, "Their stubbornness—"

"Is what saved this planet. Get on with it."

The healer examined Wyatt. Searching his bag, he pulled a clear cloth and shook it vigorously. It sparkled as if lit by fire. Opening Wyatt's shirt, he placed it on the wound. It started to crackle, and soon smoke came from its folds. Carter was thrown backward to land flat. The healer raised his eyebrows and, with a universal smirk, indicated, *Told you so!*

Wyatt flopped on the ground with a *thump* and a groan. There was a popping sound, and a buzzing field surrounded Wyatt's entire being. Carter attempted to touch him, but the force field shocked his fingertips. He drew back with a gasp and a worried look on his face. All eyes were on Wyatt.

"Fascinating," Howard whispered, and then looked sheepishly at Keisha's glare.

Wyatt shivered. His eyes rolled back, and he went very still. Carter fell to his knees and yelled, "Wyatt! What have you done?"

"Give him a minute," the Va'Rok healer said.

A huge crowd surrounded Wyatt, the light blocked by towering giants watching. Carter stood and shouted, "Give him space. Move out of the way!" Yerbol, Melvin, Keisha, Jade, Howard, and Lily formed a protective circle around him.

It was silent in the valley until the sound of an infant wailing broke the quiet.

Rosemary rushed over to her child, and Wyatt opened his eyes. He took a deep, shuddering breath that came from his toes. Carter helped him into a sitting position. He moved the cloth and gasped. "It's healed." He looked at the queen. "Thank you."

Carter set the clear cloth aside; something was stuck to it. He picked it up. Yerbol was standing over them both and looked down. "Let me see that," he demanded.

"It's just an old photo." Carter tucked it into his shirt pocket.

"Where'd you get that?" Yerbol held out his hands. "Please."

"I took it from my dad's desk back at the Shark Park. He worked for Konrad," Wyatt said weakly.

"May I?" Yerbol insisted.

Carter looked at Wyatt, who shrugged.

Yerbol studied the picture, his back stiffening. "This is you?"

"Yes. My brother and my dad. It was a long time ago."

"This man is Halo Eleven."

"Wait, what?" Wyatt attempted to rise. Carter helped him.

"That's your dad? Really. He was an undercover agent. We flipped him. He was working

for us. Konrad must've found out and killed him."

Wyatt took a deep breath. "He made him a zombie."

Yerbol handed back the picture. Wyatt studied his dad's face and then looked up. "I'm

going to kill—"

Queen Serafera smiled. "The time for retribution is over. Vincent Konrad has been dealt with. He wanted immortality, and he will get it. He will circle this globe for the rest of time, neither touching its soil nor affecting any of the inhabitants ever again. Do you remember what I said to you?" Queen Serafera asked Wyatt.

"Some verse from the bible, I think. It's all pretty hazy."

"Isaiah 11:6," Carter supplied. "The Old Testament."

"It's part of our prophecy," Grillos called out. "It's in our book."

"It's part of our oral legend," Olrec said. "Carried down from Mophat to Mophat."

"Remember, it is born from the stars. It belongs to us all."

Carter nodded, "It seems we have more in common than we realized. It is interpreted to mean a descendant of King David will bring a time of peace and justice on our planet."

"It symbolizes that even natural predators and their prey can live together in harmony," Howard Drucker said softly.

"And the children will lead the way," Keisha added.

"They always do," Nate Owens said. He looked back at the restaurant where the body of his father rested.

Queen Serafera smiled sadly, making each one feel that she

understood their pain and loss. "Now is the time to heal the wounds that you've all suffered."

"And what about you?" Wyatt asked. He brushed off his shirt and pants, feeling whole again.

"We will do what we've always done. We are the Watchers. We will protect and guide you." She began walking toward her ship. "From a distance. But peace and harmony are now in your hands."

She ascended the ladder to her ship and turned. Raising one hand, she waved. It was as though her farewell was personal to each one of them.

Carter placed his arm around Wyatt's shoulder. "Let's go home."

Nate Owens stepped forward and turned to Wyatt. "I will need your help to rebuild. All of you."

Wyatt took in the diverse population surrounding them as the alien ship lifted off and disappeared into the sky.

The Sasquatches clustered together, their arms protectively around their children; their natural inquisitiveness matched Keisha and Howard Drucker's drive to understand life around them.

Rosemary held her child, Grillos, and the giants' bravery reminded him of Jade and Melvin's loyalty to everyone they loved.

Carter's unwavering support, reminiscent of the Va'Rok, caused Wyatt to gasp with understanding.

"We are all the same. Not monsters."

"Yes, there are no monsters," Lily said, moving next to Wyatt and holding out her hand. He took it. "We're good?" she asked.

"Yes. I missed you." Wyatt squeezed her hand.

Lily took the gray feather and placed it in his pocket over his heart and patted it.

Jade and Melvin joined them, and Melvin added, "Monsters aren't born. Never were."

Keisha and Howard lined up next, and Howard said, "Absolutely, they're forged from their experiences. They don't arise from the darkness on their own."

"Yes," Wyatt said with wonder as he watched the disappearing spaceship, "The circumstances and the scars of the world around them mold them. We and our imagination alone create them."

Wyatt walked toward the setting sun and said, "In the end, we gave them their power out of fear. They don't control us. It's not monsters that decide our fate; it was us. Always us."

EPILOGUE

CONDEMNED BY THE Watchers to circle the earth forever, Vincent Konrad discovered a fate that was neither above nor below, but a relentless punishment that would never end.

Here, he learned the true price of immortality.

AUTHOR'S NOTES

While writing the *Monsterland series,* I watched the world burn, literally and metaphorically. There were seasons of chaos: the passing of loved ones, pain and turmoil within my family's business, and moments where it felt like every certainty I'd built my life on, had turned to ash.

But through it all, the Monsterland saga, a story about facing fear, conquering the darkness, and embracing what hides in the shadows, endured.

Monsterland has always been more than a book to me. It's a mirror of the human experience, how we all face the monsters within and without, how we fall apart, and how we rise again.

In writing it, I've had to confront my own fears and meet the parts of myself I once tried to bury. And in that confrontation, I found something beautiful: that the only way to slay your monsters is to understand them, to embrace your shadow and become the truest version of yourself.

I've grown up alongside these characters. They lived in my imagination long before I ever wrote their names on paper, and they've taught me more about courage, loss, and love than I ever expected to learn. Wyatt, Melvin, Howard Drucker, Jade, Keisha, Lily, Carter, Dreg, and Vincent, will live forever. These characters are as real to me as my own family.

Speaking of family…

To my mother, Phyllis, this entire series belongs to you. We read it together, night after night, until our eyes couldn't bear another word. Those late hours, trading ideas, chasing meaning, arguing over commas and characters, were among the most exciting moments a mother and son could ever share.

You didn't just edit these books; you *lived* them with me. You made every sentence stronger, every arc deeper, every monster more human. You shaped not just the story, but the storyteller.

None of this exists without your heart, your patience, your faith, and your love. I will never forget what we created, together.

To Sharon, Alex and Cayla, thank you for seeing the world through these characters with me, for your insights, your laughter, and your patience through every sleepless rewrite. You've given my imagination its purpose.

To Eric, Jennifer, Hallie, and Zachary, your love, humor, and support have kept me grounded through it all.

To Jon Levin, thank you for believing in monsters, and for reminding me that story and heart always win. Your guidance has been my compass.

And to my readers, every single one of you who's ever written a review, sent a message, or shared your love for *Monsterland*…from the bottom of my heart, thank you.

Lastly to my dad, I can't see you, but I feel you in every win and every moment of grace. I feel unstoppable having you as an angel on my shoulder. Thanks for always balancing me out, Pop.

Michael
Long Island, New York

OTHER BOOKS BY MICHAEL OKON

Michael Okon
Monsterland (Book 1)
Monsterland Reanimated (Book 2)
Monsterland Below (Book 3)
Monsterland Above (Books 4)
Witches Protection Program
Dragged Down Deep

Michael Phillip Cash
Pokergeist
Stillwell: A Haunting on Long Island
The Flip
The After House
The Hanging Tree: A Novella
Brood X: A Firsthand Account of the Great Cicada Invasion
The Battle for Darracia – Schism (Book 1)
The Battle for Darracia – Collision (Book 2)
The Battle for Darracia – Risen (Book 3)

Michael Samuels
Just Ask the Universe
The Universe-ity
Keep Calm and Ask On